FUGITIVE MAGE

BOOK TWO OF THE MAGE AND THE BIRD CALLER

KAAREN SUTCLIFFE

Publisher: Inspiring Publishers,
P.O. Box 159, Calwell, ACT Australia 2905
Email: publishaspg@gmail.com
http://www.inspiringpublishers.com

 A catalogue record for this book is available from the National Library of Australia

National Library of Australia The Prepublication Data Service

Author: Kaaren Sutcliffe
Title: Fugitive Mage
Genre: Fiction

Paperback ISBN: 978-1-922792-60-0
Hardcover ISBN: 978-1-922792-61-7
eBook ISBN: 978-1-922792-62-4

Acknowledgements

I extend my heartfelt gratitude to all those who so kindly and professionally helped me, Everand and Lamiya on the journey. A huge thank you to my trusted readers who waded through early drafts, providing encouragement and constructive suggestions.

To AJ Collins, AE, and her gun assessor Liz, thank you for another insightful assessment that helped me to lift the story to another level. I remain eternally grateful to Gail Tagarro, AE, for another meticulous edit and for her further encouragement and support. I loved her comment about not wanting book two to end.

For the initiating inspiration, my thanks go to Nature Coast Dragon Boat Club, who took me training on the Moruya River and taught me to paddle. Nature Coast warrants a special cheer for hosting the wonderful launch of *Undercover Mage* with racing dragon boats and paddlers dressed in the Riverfall and Riverplain costumes! Thank you, paddlers from Narooma Blue Water Dragons and Sussex Inlet River Dragons for joining us to celebrate the launch. I encourage readers to take five minutes to watch the awesome video on my website, crafted by my talented brother-in-law and sister, Antonio and Phillipa Saraceno.

A huge hug for my husband Andrew for all his support, for cooking dinner, putting up with my spiritual absences and for sponsoring the matching bookmarks.

Once again, I thank the expert and tireless team at the Australian Self-Publishing Group for turning the story into another quality book that I am proud of.

Dear readers, I hope you enjoy the continuation of Mage Everand's twisted and not-so-simple mission, and the evolution of Lamiya into so much more than a caller of birds.

Finally, I hope the story does the sport of dragon boating justice and inspires some readers to give paddling a go.

Kaaren Sutcliffe, AE
www.kaarensutcliffe.com.au

CAST OF CHARACTERS

Axis

Everand	Mage, spy, member of the Mages' Guild
Mantiss	Mage, Head of the Mages' Guild
Agamid	Senior Mage, assistant to Mantiss
Beetal	Deceased, Mage and former mentor to Everand
Tiliqua	Mage, daughter of Mantiss
Pelamis	Mage, member of the Inner Council
Simoselaps	Mage, member of the Inner Council
Saiphos	Mage, member of the Inner Council
Elemar	Warrior woman who Everand loved previously

Riverfall

Dragon boat team (glide, paddlers 1 to 10, drummer)*

Tengar, Melanite, Mookaite, Selenite, Kunzite, Zeol, Persaj, Zink, Acim, Ybur, Beram, Micate

Atage	Town leader
Ejad	Reserve paddler — cloth maker
Lyber	Town second-in-charge
Thulite	Atage's wife
Vogel	Old man, historian
Mizuchi	River dragon
Mizukaze	River dragon

---

* In modern-day paddling, the steersperson is called the 'sweep' or the 'steer'. I found a reference to a 'glide', and felt it suited the fantasy terminology. The two lead paddlers are called 'strokes' as well as 'pacers'.

Riverplain

Dragon boat team (glide, paddlers 1 to 10, drummer)

Lamiya, Lazuli, Larimar, Laza, Lopa, Levog, Lattic, Lapsi, Lepid, Luvu, Ejad, Lulite

Riversea

Dragon boat team (glide, paddlers 1 to 10, drummer)

Cowrie, Conch, Chiton, Limpel, Clommus, Summel, Pippel, Spirula, Charonia, Clama, Nawpra, Chella

Riverwood

Dragon boat team (glide, paddlers 1 to 10, drummer)

Malach, Torrap, Magle, Mahog, Kwah, Tiek, Perid, Melan, Meralb, Kerish, Folnak, Yosper

GUILD LAW — AS ESTABLISHED BY MAGE LAPEMIS

Rule One — The key purpose of the Guild is to enhance and refine the workings of magic, and to impart knowledge and training to younger mages as apprentices.

Rule Two — The Guild will be led by an elected Head of the Guild.

Rule Three — The Head of the Guild will be supported by an Inner Council and an Outer Council, member numbers to rise over time.

Rule Four — The Guild will work 'to protect by sun and moon' the mages of Axis and the humans who work with us.

Rule Five — The Head of the Guild has overall authority, and the code words to access the Staropal are to be known only by the incumbent Head of the Guild.

Rule Six — The Staropal will be concealed and only accessed in times of dire need, as decreed by the Head of the Guild and with agreement from the councils. The stone must be used for honest purpose and for the greater good.

Rule Seven — The humans who reside in Axis agree to work with and care for the physical needs of the mages, such as food, water, clothing and labour, in exchange for shelter and protection.

Rule Eight — Mages must only breed with other mages to keep the lines of magic pure. Accordingly, the humans of Axis must only breed with other humans.

Rule Nine — No mage or human shall pass outside the granite wall, unless ordered to do so by the Head of the Guild for special purpose.

Rule Ten — Others from outside Axis shall not be allowed inside the wall of granite, unless authorised by the Head of the Guild for special purpose.

Rule Eleven — Breaches of Guild Law will be judged by the Inner Council, with the final say by the Head of the Guild. Extreme digressions will be punished by obliteration or removal of power.

Rule Twelve — Mage power must only be used for sound purposes with honest intent. Use for personal ambition or evil intent constitutes a breach of the direst magnitude and will be punished in accordance with Rule Eleven.

THE ISLAND OF OSSILIS

Riverwood Province

PROLOGUE

'Ow!' Malach tried to bat his mother's hand away.

'Stand still. You must look neat.' Her grip tightened until her fingers pinched his shoulder and she resumed dragging the comb through his knotted hair.

'Why?'

'You're going to meet someone important.'

Scowling, Malach endured the rough drags of the comb through his hair. Who could be more important than his father, Chief of Riverwood? And why was she wearing her new dress of soft bunya skins? She also smelled nice, of orange blossom mixed with musk. Strange, when his father was away hunting, but he knew better than to ask.

'That'll do.' His mother squinted at him. 'Rinse your mouth and wash your face. Hurry.'

As soon as he spat out the water, his mother grabbed his hand and tugged him out of the cabin. Outside, she let go but glared at him to follow and walked away, taking the longest steps her dress would allow. He trotted to keep up, his spirits lifting when they passed through the outermost ring of stone and wood cabins and she strode towards the forest. Maybe he could climb trees while she met this important person, or lure a hawk to train as his own now that his arm was strong enough to hold such a bird.

His legs tiring, he trailed after his mother while she followed a narrow, crooked path among the towering pines, seemingly intent on passing right through Hanaki Forest. Was she going to the far edge, to the massive granite wall that Father had strictly forbidden them from going near? Rumours told that anyone who went close to the wall would be engulfed in fiery red energy and die instantly. The skin on the back of his neck prickled.

'Malach! Hurry!' Pausing, his mother pulled an object from her dress pocket.

Creeping closer, Malach rubbed his eyes and looked at the oval stone that was glowing a deep red. A warning or a summons? Was this the stone she kept hidden in the jar of cakes? She'd smacked him once when he took it out and held it up. The tips of his fingers tingled with the memory of the odd static he'd felt in the stone.

Shoving the stone back in her pocket, his mother took his hand. 'You must bow. Don't speak unless spoken to. Understand?'

When he nodded, her eyes softened.

'I want him to like you.' Bending over, she stared into his face, her nose almost touching his and her warm, mint-leaf-scented breath huffing over his cheeks. 'You're going to learn a big secret. Promise me you'll guard this secret with your life?'

A secret? He gave a solemn nod.

'My brave boy.' She patted his shoulder. 'Now you're old enough to learn, he may be interested in you.' Her dress rustling, she spun around and resumed walking.

By the time they reached the final row of trees, his mouth was dry and his feet sore. The dark pines cradled the air above, filtering the light into dapples of fidgeting shade; the ground was spongy with pine needles. Breathing in the scents of earth, pine and fungi, Malach peered out at the flat expanse of wild grasses stretching away from the trees and waving in the breeze. The grasses abruptly ended at the base of the ominous storm-grey wall. For an age, his mother stood staring at the wall, and Malach shifted his weight from side to side to ease the throbbing in his feet.

Something moved! His attention snapped to the bottom of the wall where it looked as if one of the rocks was rolling out into the grass. Heart racing, he stared hard while his mother patted her face with her hands and smoothed her dress. By the wall, something rose up and travelled towards them above the ground, but it was not a bird. His heart galloping, he frowned at the way his mother's lips parted and her eyes grew wide. That was the expression she wore when Father hauled her into their sleeping space.

Squinting at the approaching object, he saw it was a large black-and-white beetle, with a person riding it. His heart thumped. The beetle was massive! With fierce, jagged and curved horns. Malach swallowed. It must be awesome to ride. The tall rider was clad in brown robes, the face obscured by a hood.

'Don't stare,' mumbled his mother. 'Hold your tongue unless spoken to.'

Malach dropped his eyes, peeking through his eyelashes and listening to the hum of the beetle's wings as it landed on the grass. The brown-robed rider lifted a leg over the beetle's neck and slid down.

'Chinfe,' said a deep voice. 'Come.'

His mother stepped daintily towards the man and, after a heartbeat, Malach followed. He froze when the tall man stared at him, eyes glittering in a face in shadow.

'What is this?' the voice demanded.

Malach stopped, exposed amid the grasses, and glanced over his shoulder to judge how far it was back to the trees.

Approaching the imposing man, his mother slid her arms around his waist. 'This,' she said distinctly to the shrouded face, 'is your son. Now he's seven I thought you should meet him.'

The air whooshed out of Malach's chest. What was she talking about? Chief Magrin was his father. He would be the next leader of Riverwood when he grew up, and Father would train him. A roaring filled his ears. Then he understood the man was roaring.

'*My* son? What is this trickery?'

Mother's hand disappeared inside the cowl to caress the man's face. 'No trickery. He's yours.' Turning, she held her other hand out to him. 'Malach, come.'

Heart pounding, mouth dry, he hesitated. An invisible force buffeted him and in a single blink he stood in front of the man, looking up into a stern face glaring down at him. Squaring his shoulders, Malach stared back at the face with swarthy skin, coarse, jet-black hair and a black bristly beard. Sweat tickled the back of his neck at the static and power oozing from the man.

'Just this one, Chinfe, or do you have more surprises?'

Meekly, his mother said, 'No, my Lord Mage. Just Malach.'

'Does he show power? Never mind, I will read him.' The man pushed his mother aside.

Malach went numb when the man's gaze swept right *through* him. His head tingled and he squirmed at the sensation of gruff fingers prodding inside his mind. The fingers found the dark well in a corner, where he often found the willpower to do odd things, like call ravens to his outstretched hand, or move pebbles without touching them. The man's bushy eyebrows lifted and he grunted.

'So. The boy *is* mine.' The tingling eased and the man regarded him thoughtfully, then grabbed his jaw and yanked his face from side to side. 'He even looks like me. A shame the Guild Law on non-pure mages is clear. I must obliterate him.'

Stepping back, the man held up a hand with lines of red energy crackling and fizzling across the open palm. Knees quaking, Malach held his ground, hoping it would be quick: a warrior and hunter's death. He gaped at the writhing power in the man's palm. *This* was his father?

'Wait, my Lord Mage! No-one will ever know! He's yours to train in secret!' His mother flung herself in front of him, arms spread wide, and stood steadfast, protecting him.

The mage's brows drew together, his hand and the fearful red energy held aloft. 'Stand aside!' he roared.

His mother didn't flinch. 'He's a good boy, he's brave and he'll be strong and smart. Train him, Lord Mage. He is *yours*.'

Abruptly, the man released a bark of laughter and the crackling energies receded into his palm. 'You are full of surprises, Chinfe. A secret apprentice … the idea has merit. If he's good enough.'

'You won't regret this, Lord Mage.' His mother smiled.

'We'll see,' said the mage, directing his piercing eyes to Malach. 'Well, boy, would you like to be strong and powerful?'

'Like you?' Malach blurted. Oh no! He wasn't supposed to speak! Although the man had asked a question. Emboldened, he added, 'Can I ride on your beetle?'

His mother went to backhand him and her arm froze mid-air.

'Never discourage boldness!' snapped the mage. 'What did you say his name is?'

'Malach.' Mother rubbed at her arm.

The mage inspected him from head to toe, as if he were an interesting bug. 'Tend to my beetle while I spend time with Chinfe. After, I will take you for a ride.'

'Yes, Lord,' said Malach, bowing when he caught sight of his mother miming a bow with her hand.

Before he'd straightened up, the mage had grasped his mother's hand and was tugging her towards a tight knot of pines. Her giggles floated back and Malach turned away. Father would kill her if he found out. Wait, Magrin was *not* his father. *Promise me you'll guard this secret with your life?* Malach swallowed: Magrin would kill *both* of them in a heartbeat if he knew. Oh, but his *real* father was more powerful — a *lot* more powerful.

He shied away from the thought that his real father might also kill him, and he wouldn't even see his death coming.

Ignoring the noises coming from the copse, Malach approached the large beetle, which lifted its head and pushed its jagged horns at him. The reins were dragging loosely in the grass and, edging sideways, he grabbed these and took a hasty step backwards when the beetle waved its front pair of legs alarmingly close to his head.

Reaching inside himself, he drew on what he called his pool of luring potion and sent out calming thoughts. The creature stretched its head forward until the wispy antennae brushed the ends of his fingers. Standing on tiptoe, he stroked its face, marvelling at the tough carapace and the colourful glints in the glossy black surface.

He pulled the reins; the beetle baulked. He willed it to follow, and it did. Thrilled, he walked in circles, delighted at the creature's chirruping. Seeing a small green pine cone in the grass, he picked it up and offered it to the beetle. Its antennae brushed over the cone, then it reached up with its front legs and prickly feet took the cone from his fingers.

A breeze swirled around him and two strong hands plopped onto his shoulders.

'With some training you will do nicely, boy.'

Chapter One

Everand sat up as soon as muted light crept under the door curtain. Every muscle and bone in his body ached after the intense activity of the boat races and his wild ride on the river dragon. He scrubbed a hand over his face, sure he hadn't slept a wink, his mind and heart churning with emotions all through the darkness. Had he really chosen to stay in Riverfall and *not* return to the Mages' Guild in Axis?

His forehead pounded and he groaned. Why had he allowed the others to ply him with so much feeja wine at the feast?

The back of his head also throbbed mercilessly where Malach's eagles had torn out chunks of his hair. Unease pooled in his stomach. What would Malach do with the hair? His best guess was that the rogue half-mage would concoct a potion to subdue his powers. Malach would want revenge after having his plans to take control of the river dragon so soundly thwarted. Everand sighed. No time for such gloomy thoughts. As the scribe for the first-ever trade discussions between the four river provinces — correction, three provinces — he must stay focused.

Lamiya. A shiver of joy ran down his body. Dancing by firelight with her entwined in his arms had been amazing. His groin tingled and anticipation flooded him. Gorgeous, beautiful, brave and intelligent — and she wanted him to stay and be with her. His throat grew painfully tight. This was supposed to be a simple mission, not one where he lost his heart and decided to change his entire life! After just this sun of trade negotiations, he would go to Riverplain with Lamiya.

His stomach quivered with nerves. After only seven suns in the province there was so much he didn't know about her, or her people. He didn't even know how old she was. Younger than his twenty-six season-cycles? Probably, but not by much.

'Stop air-dreaming and get up.' Beram's voice came from behind him. The paddler was already rolling up his mattress.

'Air-dreaming?' Everand lumbered to his feet and began to roll up his mattress.

'Cloud-drifting, star-gazing, air-dreaming ... you were obviously thinking of Lamiya!' said Beram, wagging a finger at him. 'Atage and Lyber are relying on you to concentrate.'

Everand raised his hands in defeat.

'We're so happy you decided to stay. We like having you around, and not just because your magic is useful.' Propping his mattress against the wall, Beram grinned. 'I mean, instant warm water is nice, but we can heat it ourselves!'

Humbled, Everand nodded, still amazed that these people apparently liked him for himself. The eddy of nerves returned. The Mages' Guild would not release him lightly. Guilt flushed into him — by failing to return, he was betraying Mantiss, the Head of the Guild, who regarded him like a son and relied on him as a spy.

His mattress stored away, he hastily changed into fresh clothes, considering what was likely to happen next. The Guild wouldn't wonder where he was for another sun or two, until after the trade discussions. It wasn't his fault Mages Mantiss and Agamid had sent him to Riverfall without a communication sphere and no instructions on how he was to get back in to Axis through the wardspell. How was he supposed to tell the Guild that instead of finding squabbling people from different provinces, he'd uncovered an untrained half-mage and called a live dragon from the river?

He accepted the loaf and mug from Beram and chewed slowly, the unease threading through his stomach making the bread less palatable. The half-mage was cunning, unpredictable and a risk to the provinces. By failing to return to Axis as expected, he was consciously withholding this information from the Guild. The bread sat heavily in his gut. How culpable would he feel after whatever Malach did next?

'You look very serious for someone who saved our boat races from disaster,' commented Beram.

'Sorry. I was thinking about what Malach might do next.'

'You don't think he'll take his boat and team and just leave, as Atage asked?' Beram raised both eyebrows.

'It seems too easy, based on how clever and subtle Malach has been so far. Already, he's gained a concession by asking for time to repair their boat.'

'But Mizukaze rammed it!' Beram shuddered. 'He can't take a boat cracked by a dragon all the way back up the river.'

'Maybe so,' said Everand, 'and if he hadn't tried to shoot the dragon with his crossbow the boat would be intact.' Rolling his empty mug around and around in his hands, he said slowly, 'I agree, Atage had to grant them time to repair the boat, but I'll feel happier when they've actually left.'

'What else could Malach do, though?' Beram's brow creased with concern.

'Destroy the bridge. I thought that *was* his plan, to cause chaos at the end of the long race so that Atage would call off the trade discussions.' Everand shrugged. 'Malach has confirmed Riverwood will not trade, meaning they have no need for the bridge.'

Beram reached over to prise the empty mug from his fingers. 'Although we don't use it often, it is the only bridge across the Dragonspine River. It would certainly indicate a major divide between the provinces if it were destroyed.'

Watching Beram tidy up, Everand felt his forehead tighten and his head start to pound again. Malach could still destroy the bridge on his way home north — and he *must* have somehow acquired the potion that made creatures do his bidding and fight until victory or death. The rogue half-mage even looked and sounded *exactly* like Mage Beetal, his own former mentor and a reviled traitor to the Guild, who had originally developed the potion. Yet Guild Law prescribed that mages must only breed with mages … how could he confirm Malach's lineage?

With a shiver, he recalled Malach's final comment: *I know exactly who you are. You and I are not done yet.*

'Are you ready to go?' Beram hovered, twisting his hands together. 'You look worried.'

With a shrug, Everand said slowly, 'It seemed a good plan to ban Malach from the discussions, but now I'm thinking that if he were with us in Atage's meeting room we'd at least know what he was doing.'

'I could ask Acim and Zink to keep an eye on him and tell us if he does anything untoward,' said Beram, still twisting his hands together.

'Good idea. Tell them to interrupt the discussions to confirm when the Riverwood boat has left. Then we can focus properly.' Everand felt the tension leave his forehead.

'You go to Atage's dome ready to scribe and I'll find Acim and Zink and then join you.' Beram flapped his hands. 'Go!'

Stepping outside, Everand looked up at the heavy, grey sky and shook his head. When he'd first arrived, he thought the people's fervent belief that good races would bring a dragon to deliver rain for their crops to be nothing more than a fanciful myth. But the dragon came, and after five seasons of unending blue sky, the building clouds suggested rain. The mages had no idea about this kind of magic outside of the Guild.

He strode towards Atage's dome, the movement easing his stiff muscles, and observed that the town was already waking, with several traders carrying tables outside ready to display their wares. When he neared the domes assigned to the boat teams, his heart beat faster. Was Lamiya awake? He probed with his mind, and his lips quirked when he sensed her making her way to her dome door. She *always* knew when he was thinking of her.

Lamiya emerged and headed straight to the path to intercept him, a smile adorning her beautiful face. His spirits soared and when his lips met hers, a joy more powerful than any magic throbbed through him. Pausing for air, he crushed her against his chest and buried his face in her wavy, mahogany hair, absorbing the flowery scents. How was it possible she had chosen him? 'Lamiya, Lamiya,' he murmured.

'Everand, Everand.' She giggled.

He tickled her ribs and she squirmed. When she tilted her face up to speak, he sealed his lips over hers again, warmth flowing through his entire being. Painfully, he drew back. If only the trade discussions were over already.

'I know,' she said pertly, the blue tints in her grey eyes sparkling. '*After* the discussions.' She gave him a stern look. 'No more *after* anything else, busy mage.'

'Not if I can help it.' As soon as the words passed his lips, he knew further impediments were not only likely but imminent. Trying not to spoil the moment, he asked, 'No boat training?'

She leaned back, allowing his arms to support her weight. 'What, you think we haven't earned a rest?' Her dimples deepened. 'After being declared the best team at the races?'

Suppressing a smile, he replied seriously, 'You paddlers *live* for your boats. I can't imagine what else you'd do!' As affront crossed her face, he looked skyward. 'Will it rain?'

'I expect so.' Lamiya eased her weight off his arms. 'And I will be enjoying myself at the trading tables while you are locked inside a meeting scribing the records.'

'Speaking of which …' He kissed the top of her head. 'I'll look for you as soon as we're finished.'

'Enjoy.' Lamiya gave a mock yawn and then touched his elbow. 'Take good records. These discussions are important.'

No pressure. He could hear Mage Mantiss already: *This, dear boy, is precisely why we do not mingle with people or meddle in their affairs. Too easy to be assigned responsibility.* He sighed; he'd already stepped far beyond the bounds of the supposedly simple mission. But if he didn't intend to return to the Guild, did it matter? Now Mantiss was scowling in his mind's eye and growling: *It matters a lot. And you will be called to account.*

He swatted at the annoying pattering on his cheek before he realised it was Lamiya's hand.

'I see you're focused already. See you later, busy mage.' She tried to pout, but it became a smile.

Resuming his trajectory towards Atage's dome, he wondered what writing implements the people of Riverfall used. Probably feather pens and ink. Using magic to inscribe the records would be faster. Except he wasn't supposed to use his magic here; that would be meddling.

Atage's wife appeared in the dome doorway. 'Come in,' she said, flapping her hands. 'The others are waiting.'

Passing through to the meeting room, he assumed his seat was the place set at the table with sheets of finely sliced wood and two feather pens in a neat line. He glanced at the wall, enjoying the view of the ancient tapestry depicting a dragon boat racing a real blue-and-gold dragon across the lake at the river's source. The crafters had cleverly captured as a backdrop the silver threads of the waterfall cascading into the lake. He'd enjoyed listening to the history of the arrival of the first dwellers four generations before, recounted by old man Vogel, the oldest resident of Riverfall.

Arriving initially at Dragon Lake, the early people had named the dragon Mizuchi, meaning river dragon in their old tongue. Once the population grew, they'd moved south to the flatter and more arable lands alongside the river. A splinter group had gone further south, forming the next province of Riverplain. Old man Vogel had said the current trade discussions were especially important because many welcomed the opportunity to renew the bonds with their related people.

Atage's vision was clever — the trade discussions and the boat races were an ingenious way to bring the provinces together. The races had also enabled him and Lamiya to summon the river dragon, which transpired to be Mizukaze, *son* of the extinct Mizuchi. It seemed Mizukaze had remained elusive all this time, having no idea how to interact with the people of Riverfall.

Frowning, Everand thought of Mizukaze's reluctance to deal with him as a mage, the dragon growling that 'tricksy two-leg people with power' were not to be trusted. This implied the dragons had interacted with the mages before, but there was not a single reference to any connection with the dragons in the Guild texts. He recalled no mention of the creatures in any of his apprentice history lessons. What did this mean?

Folding down, he sat cross-legged on the plump cushion and nodded to each negotiator. The three from Riversea were clad in the team colours of gleaming white tunics and turquoise trousers. Their blond-green hair was bound in tight topknots, and Cowrie wore his chieftain's headdress of flowing white feathers from a sea eagle, the tips tinged grey.

Next to them were the negotiators from Riverplain. Luvu, the gruff older paddler, was flanked by Lepid and Lulite. They wore their team colours of vivid orange tunics and bright green trousers. Each had their hair tied back in a simple ponytail, adorned with a single red feather. Luvu grunted in greeting. Everand winced at the cool glance Lepid gave him, although he probably should have expected that. As Lazuli's older brother, Lepid was of course unhappy Lamiya had chosen him over Lazuli. Lulite, a good friend to Lamiya, gave him a shy smile and he smiled back; he would like to win her approval.

Present for Riverfall were the town leader Atage, his offsider Lyber and Tengar the team captain. The empty cushions at the fourth side of the table, where Malach and Torrap from Riverwood should have sat, felt ominous, a sign that Atage's vision was going awry.

With a rush of footsteps, Beram hurried in and took his place next to Everand. 'It is done,' he murmured. 'Acim and Zink have gone to the boat ramp.'

Wishing that his hovering unease would dissipate, Everand focused when Atage began to speak.

'Welcome, everyone. I hope this will be the first of many amicable discussions between our provinces, and the forging of strong friendships. My fervent wish is for us all to benefit from an exchange between us.' Pausing, Atage glanced Everand's way.

The records! Hastily picking up the longer feather pen, he selected the top square of thin-shaved wood. Concentrating, he wrote in flowing script: *Trade Negotiations Between the Four River Provinces*. He stopped. Should he scratch out four and write three, or record that four were invited?

'Ah,' said Atage. 'We should note that Riverwood was invited but declined.' To the rest of the table he explained, 'Apparently, they have no wish to trade with any of us.'

'Good riddance,' muttered Luvu. The others nodded.

Everand wrote that Riverwood had declined and felt a flush creeping up his neck when everyone watched while he added the names of the provinces and negotiators present, the feather making a scritch-scritch sound. If they were going to watch him scribe, it would take far too long. Subtly forming a spell of writing, he trickled it down his arm so the words flowed faster.

'Thank you for preparing detailed lists of what goods you can trade.' Atage held out a hand and Beram passed him three plaques. 'We need to decide matters such as how often we'll trade, where the trade will be held and how we set prices for the goods. We need a process for resolving any disputes, and a means of communication between us.'

Everand listed these under the heading of *Matters for Agreement*.

It was quickly agreed that the beginning of each new season would be a good time to hold inter-province trading. Tengar and Lepid interrupted each other in their enthusiasm to make sure boat races were added to the trading.

While the pair argued about how many races, and over what distances, Everand reviewed the conversation he'd had with Malach after the races. *You, of all people, should know the dragon can do much more than make it rain.* There had been a smug glint in Malach's almost-black eyes, and a subtle challenge. He rolled the feather pen between his fingers, thinking. The dragons had gone back to their lake at the river's source, near Mizuchi Falls, where the closest people were in Riverwood. Not ideal, but Mizukaze didn't trust Malach and would avoid him … However, that could change over time.

'Did you get that?' asked Tengar. 'The races are to be devised by the host province, and the details provided in advance.'

Everand wrote this down under his smaller heading of *Boat Races*.

'Well,' said Atage, 'this brings us to the order of host. There are four seasons and if the three of us rotate in the same order, each province will end up hosting in a different season. Is this acceptable?' Looking at Luvu, he added, 'That means Riverplain will be next. Does this suit you?'

The lines around Luvu's eyes creased in a smile and Lepid and Lulite shared excited grins. 'That'll suit us just fine, and north to south is an easy order to remember.'

That drew smiles around the table.

'Well, that's the first two items agreed.' Atage rubbed his hands together and turned to Beram. 'Can you ask Thulite to bring in brew and cakes?'

Sitting back, Everand thought things were going well. Without Riverwood, the discussion would progress faster and he could be with Lamiya sooner. She'd be enjoying herself at the markets, no doubt using the opportunity to chat to the artists from Riversea. He wanted to close his eyes and dream about the post-races feast and dancing by firelight with her in his arms.

How long would it take Malach's team to repair the boat? He swallowed, wishing Acim or Zink would arrive to report that Riverwood had left.

CHAPTER TWO

Lamiya combed her hair pensively. Everand was right; the team did live and breathe for their paddling and it felt strange not to be heading down to the river to launch Flight. Most of the men had left at first light, saying they needed to help catch enough fish for the dusk feast. Lazuli had gone with them without even looking her way. The comb snagged and tugged at her scalp. She'd hurt Lazuli. How could she make her peace with him?

Her mind leaped to thinking of Everand, and her pulse quickened. Being asked to glide and captain the Riverplain team had been honour, adventure and excitement enough. She hadn't expected to lose her heart to an unknown traveller, who turned out to be a mage from Axis in disguise.

Biting her lip, she couldn't believe how she'd been so immediately *aware* of him, and the overwhelming attraction that swamped her. She was drowning in currents of conflicting emotions: she wanted him, no doubt about that, just the thought of lying with him made her body quiver. Other times she was afraid of his powers. What could he do if something made him really angry? Her tongue smarted when she bit the tip of it, and her eyes watered.

Until the feast after the races, she'd been convinced that Everand would leave to return to his duties in Axis. The aloof mages didn't interact with the provinces, and everyone knew the granite wall was protected by magic that bestowed instant death on anyone who tried to breach it. Yet Everand had proven to be nothing like she'd imagined the mages to be. He was kind, caring … and willing to shoulder enormous responsibility on behalf of the Riverfall people, to the extent of risking his life.

It wasn't surprising that Atage had invited Everand to stay; she was astounded he'd chosen to say yes. A miracle beyond belief.

Lamiya put the comb down. The only sounds were the scratches from her bird's tiny feet while he hopped around on the table pecking at crumbs. 'Really? I didn't give you enough grain?' Whirr fluffed his wings.

Leaving her hair loose, she held out her wrist for him. Using the back of a finger to stroke the brilliant jade feathers of his back, she crooned, 'My other handsome friend is busy so you must keep me company at the trade stalls.' Whirr responded with a happy chirp, his eyes bright.

Walking quickly, she soon passed through the archway into the trading courtyard and then nudged Whirr inside her tunic to rest in his favourite spot between her breasts, where he wouldn't get jostled by anyone. Disconcerted, she saw the courtyard was packed and the trade tables were completely hidden behind dense rows of people inspecting and purchasing goods. On the raised dais, Clommus and his small band from Riversea played a lively tune that mingled with the general hubbub. Delicious aromas competed in the air and all the dining tables were already full. Not relishing the idea of pushing her way through so many people, she hesitated.

Perhaps she could purchase a gift for Everand, to thank him for buying her the magnificent necklace. Her heart raced. How had he *known* that was the piece she yearned for? She would wear it again at the feast this dusk. Her eyes grew misty: last dusk had been magical, just the two of them wrapped in each other, cocooned by darkness and firelight and oblivious to the crowds around them. A shiver chased down her back.

Taking a breath, she began to nudge her way through the press of bodies. What did one buy a mage? A mug? A thong to tie back his hair the intriguing colour of spun starlight? Her lips parted as she envisioned running her hands through his hair. Or maybe she'd ask Lattic to make Everand a paddle of his own. Imagining his face when presented with a paddle, she grinned. He clearly didn't like water. Or boats. Remedying this could be fun. How many times should she dunk him?

Elbowing her way to the Riverfall table, she admired the array of pottery. A mug at the back drew her eye: the blue dye swirled like the river passing between green fields. Everand might like that, but she'd have to carry it and it might get broken. There was a pile of cotton cushions next to the table, a sky-blue one with the stitched image of a fish attracting her attention. Tucking these ideas away as options, she wound her way to the Riverplain table.

Laza and Lopa were showing off the woven products to lines of people. Guilt twinged inside her; she should offer to help. A shadow fell over her shoulder and a solid paddler from Riverwood loomed next to her. She frowned. Hadn't Everand said they weren't going to stay for the trade discussions? Why was the man staring at her rather than at the goods? Unease forming, she tried to duck behind the trading table to avoid him, but a solid wall of people blocked her way. Standing on tiptoe, she waved to catch Lopa's eye, but her friend was busy.

Evading the man, she slid sideways through people until she reached the Riversea table.

'Lamiya! How be you?' asked Charonia with a warm smile. 'Be you still floating on a cloud after your victory?'

Making a show of rubbing her arms, Lamiya replied, 'It came at a price! But the team is most proud.' She smiled broadly, 'Especially when the competition was so strong.'

Charonia beamed at her while deftly receiving tokens from someone and handing over an intricate shell bracelet. 'Next time. I heard Cowrie say we be increasing our training.'

The woman turned to serve the next customer, choosing from several hands waving at her.

The burly paddler reappeared by her shoulder. Lamiya chewed at her lower lip. Could she ask Charonia for help? But the Riversea women were flat out serving people. The man pushed against her and, unbalanced, she merged back into the second row of people. Her pulse raced. That was deliberate! Detecting her anxiety, Whirr wriggled inside her tunic.

A second strong paddler loomed by her other shoulder, blotting out the light. A chill settling across her nape, she took a step back, the chill intensifying when the first man towered over her, his broad girth pushing her back another step.

'Riverplain glide,' the man said in a deep, gruff voice.

Mouth dry, she stared up at the bearded face: what did he want? She flicked her glance to the other man, who grinned, but it reminded her of a bird of prey.

'Come look at our boat,' said the first man.

Sensing a suppressed eagerness, Lamiya asked, 'Me? Why?'

The man's dark eyes glinted. 'You are captain of the winning team. Tell us how we can make our boat faster.'

Her gut shrieking at her to run, she leaned forward onto her toes ready to push off, but the men grabbed her elbows in vice-like grips and spun her around. Digging her heels in, she opened her mouth to scream. One shoved a rag in, grating it past her teeth. While she struggled to draw in air and not to gag, they hefted her up so her feet skimmed above the ground.

Kicking out, she battered the shins of the first man, ignoring the pain to her toes and the shocks jarring her legs. Grunting, the man squeezed her arm so hard the burning pain brought tears to her eyes. The two men squeezed together, hiding her, pressing her between their hard, smelly bodies. Wildly, she darted her eyes around. Surely someone would notice! She tried to squeal around the gag and they both pinched her so hard that she whimpered.

Purposefully, they juggled her through the crowds, with everyone annoyingly parting way and not even looking. The archway to the outer courtyard passed over them and the men hurried across the expanse of the next empty courtyard. *Everand!* She flung her fright to him.

Whirr squirmed and she conveyed, *Leave me. Get Everand. Atage's dome.* Whirr climbed out of her tunic. The man on her left grabbed at him with his free hand, but with a squawk Whirr dodged and flew off.

The man looked annoyed but the other man muttered, 'Never mind. It works.'

It works? What did he mean by that? Alarm shot through her: did they *expect* Whirr to bring Everand? Malach had planned this! How had she managed to get snared between two rival mages? One she loved; one she feared.

Using her tongue, she pushed repeatedly at the foul-tasting rag. Finally getting it to her teeth, she drew her tongue back and clenched her jaw ready to spit it out but the first man shoved it so far back in that she retched. The coarse material rasped her tongue and the inside of her cheeks, and it tasted weird. Her nostrils stung as she sniffed air in, trying to quell a surge of nausea. A bitter taste seeped into her mouth and her thoughts grew fuzzy. How could no-one have noticed? It wasn't fair. She struggled, but a strange numbness was creeping down her arms and legs and the strength in the men's arms was immovable.

The shadow of the final archway flitted above and then they were on the path leading south. It was disconcertingly empty; everyone was at the markets. As if seen from a long way away, she saw the river gleaming dully under heavy skies, the water sluggish and ominous. The men headed for the boat ramp and fear coursed through her. They were readying to leave! No, no, no! Feebly kicking out, she caught the shin of the man on her right.

'Give me a reason to beat you, woman. I'd enjoy that.' He thrust his face nearer, malice oozing from the cold glint in his eyes.

Lamiya sniffed air in sharp bursts, and her vision grew fuzzier. Forcing slower sniffs, she reached for her calling ability and projected what she could see to Everand. *Lamiya?* His tentative touch washed over her. *Help me!* His touch faded, his attention diverted. Her legs feeling disconnected, she hung limply between the men.

They reached the top of the ramp and at the bottom sat Raptor, ready at the water's edge. *Help them with their boat*, that was a good one, she thought. The cruel curved beak of the boat's eagle head leered at her while her captors approached the boat. The other burly paddlers waited in a tight knot. The knot split apart and Malach strode forward. Her captors dangled her in front of him.

Grabbing her chin, Malach yanked her face up to look at him. 'Boatwoman. You will seal your mage's doom.' He dropped her chin and her neck wrenched as the muscles failed to lower her head slowly.

She should say something, or spit at him, but the gag filled her mouth and her tongue felt swollen and fuzzy. There was a jostling and scuffling and four paddlers brought a struggling Acim and Zink to stand before Malach. Her heart pounded at the gash on Acim's head and the blood seeping down his face. Zink had one eye swollen shut, a puffy purple edge to it. Her curse came out as a moan.

Towering over Acim and Zink, Malach ordered, 'Go to Atage's dome. Tell Everand to meet me at the northern gate. Alone. If he doesn't come, he'll never see his boatwoman again.'

Acim spat in reply and Malach backhanded him across the cheek. 'Don't waste my time. Tell Everand to make sure no-one follows.' He backhanded Acim across the other cheek and blood gushed harder from the head wound.

A shriek went around and around in Lamiya's mind and she moaned again.

Zink stared one-eyed at her and asked, 'Are you alright?'

Malach belted Zink in the stomach and the paddler doubled over with a cry. 'No-one is to follow. Got that? Everand, alone — at the north gate. Go.'

The paddlers released Acim and Zink, who hesitated, giving her sorrowful looks.

'I said go!' roared Malach. 'Or do I need to send one of you as a body?'

Acim turned even paler and Zink took his arm. Mouthing 'good luck' at her, Zink led Acim away and they stumbled up the boat ramp.

Her eyes smarting, Lamiya sniffed. No crying in front of Malach. She sniffed again and tried to muster a baleful glare but Malach only laughed.

Deep sorrow filling her, she felt her courage drain away. Curse it! She should have known her glory in the races and her love for Everand were too good to be true. Her mind was growing annoyingly blank.

A rough, prickly sack was thrust over her head and total blackness descended.

Chapter Three

Everand listened to the banter around the table. What a surprise, they were discussing boat training. Except Atage, who sat back looking thoughtful. Was he also concerned about whether the Riverwood team had left?

A faint brush wafted over his shoulder, as if someone had tapped it, and Lamiya's face came to mind. He put down his half-eaten cake. *Lamiya?* Maybe he'd imagined the touch; wishful thinking. The brush across his shoulder came again, with a blurred glimpse of the dull grey river and the boat ramp. *Help me!* What was she doing there? He stiffened when blurred images jolted into his mind, tinged with a sense of panic: a boat waiting, burly paddlers mingling, the boat's eagle head leering coldly. Raptor! Still at the ramp. They hadn't left.

The image went pitch-black and he gasped. Had they hurt Lamiya? Heart hammering and chest taut with tension, he stared at the half-completed notes of the discussion. Could he leave and check on Lamiya? *Curse it.* How dare Malach use Lamiya to get to him. Turning to Atage, he said, 'Do you mind if I step out–'

'Shoo! Pesky bird!' Whirr zoomed into the room with Atage's wife in pursuit, flicking a cloth at him. 'Sorry. I'll chase it out.' She zapped the cloth, narrowly missing Whirr's tail.

The bird crunched into Everand's cheek, and he grabbed him and held him up in front of his face. Whirr peeped so fast he couldn't make head nor tail of the message. 'Calm down!'

Looking at Atage over the top of the agitated bird, he said, 'Sorry. Let me go outside for a bit and find out what's going on.'

Beram looked across in query whether he should go too, and Everand shook his head. 'Please carry on. I'll be back shortly.'

Rushing outside, he strode a few brisk paces away from the dome. 'Slow down! What happened? Where's Lamiya?'

A shudder rippled through the tiny bird and he shrilled a staccato series of cheeps.

'She's gone with the Riverwood men? Why?'

Whirr fluffed his feathers and peeped so fast he couldn't disentangle events from the bird's distress.

'Traveller!' someone called out hoarsely.

Everand looked up and his heart jolted. Acim and Zink were staggering towards him, supporting each other. His chest grew tight. What had Malach done? Putting Whirr on his shoulder, he reached out to steady the two paddlers. 'Are you alright? Did Malach do this?'

Acim grabbed his hand and leaned against him heavily, closing an eye against the trail of blood dripping down his face. 'He has Lamiya!' he croaked.

'We couldn't do anything,' panted Zink. 'We're so sorry, Traveller.'

'Start at the beginning, and make it quick,' said Everand.

Zink licked his swollen lips. His puffy eye looked painful and hot. 'We went to keep a watch on them, like Beram said. But they saw us and beckoned us to approach.'

'We didn't know what to do,' interrupted Acim,' so we went down the ramp.'

'The captain asked what we were doing, but his face … he knew.' Zink groaned.

'The paddlers grabbed us,' said Acim. 'We struggled, but there were eight of them against two of us.'

'I can see you fought back,' said Everand. 'Close your eyes,' he said to Zink. 'Let me heal your eye. Keep talking.' Letting go of Zink's arm, he placed his palm over the swollen eye, muttering a spell of healing. He eased the heat and inflammation away, then sent a cooling skin-repairing spell.

'Thanks,' muttered Zink, blinking his eye to test it. 'Then the other two paddlers appeared, carrying Lamiya. We're sorry, Traveller.'

'Now you,' Everand said to Acim, holding the paddler steady while he magically removed the blood and eased the head wound closed.

In a wobbling voice, Acim said, 'The captain gave us a message. He said you must go to the north gate. Alone.' Acim gulped and shook with distress. 'He, he said–'

'I can imagine what Malach said,' said Everand tightly. 'Go alone or I will never see Lamiya again.'

The two paddlers nodded glumly. On his shoulder, Whirr squawked and flapped his wings, the tips of the feathers tickling his neck. Footsteps sounded behind him.

'What's happening?' Beram rushed over. 'Have they left?' he asked, looking at Acim and Zink. 'What's wrong?'

Making his voice firm, Everand said, 'Malach has Lamiya. I must meet him, alone.' He held up a hand when Beram's mouth opened. 'Now. You must take over as scribe.'

'But–'

'I know you would help, but this is between Malach and me. It'll make matters worse if others go, or if we attack the Riverwood team.' Around a forced smile, he added, 'I can look after myself. I *must* go.'

'What do you want us to do?' Beram asked, wringing his hands.

Everand thought rapidly, which was difficult with Whirr fidgeting and digging his claws into his shoulder. 'I'm not sure what Malach plans. If I don't return with Lamiya soon, then wait one sun before you come looking for us.'

Scowling, Beram said, 'Wait a sun? Are you sure?'

Acim and Zink shifted uneasily, staring at Everand with wide eyes.

'Yes. You *must* finish the trade discussions. Don't let Malach interfere with these, or he has won.' He smiled wryly. 'I can't shoulder that guilt. And I want to find out more about Malach. Give me a sun.'

Clasping Whirr, Everand held his cupped hands out to Beram. 'Give Whirr to Lulite. She'll keep him safe. No,' he added, frowning at the bird, 'you can't come. Malach's eagles will eat you.'

Whirr sulkily tucked his head under a wing when Beram took him.

The distress of his friends beating at him, Everand took a step back. 'Apologise to Atage for me. I must go.'

'Good luck. Make sure you come back to us. With Lamiya.' Beram's throat moved in a large swallow.

'Good luck, Traveller,' echoed Acim, with Zink nodding beside him.

Clenching his fists, Everand spun around and strode towards the north gate. Curse Malach. The twists in this mission were becoming tiresome. A wave of dizziness swept over him. Lamiya! She must be terrified. Dear, beautiful Lamiya had chosen to be with him … and now this. His strides became choppy and he set his jaw. Malach wouldn't get away with this.

The northern courtyard was devoid of people or activity and he almost jogged across it before marching out through the north gate. Seeing no-one, he stopped to scan the area. The leaves of the cotton bushes stirred in a faint breeze. The river looked deep and dark under the heavy grey sky. Lifting his gaze, he observed the mountains far above the waterfall, their peaks shrouded in low clouds. Anxiety curled in his stomach, leaving an acidic burn. How could everything go so wrong so quickly after glorious races in sparkling sunshine and the joyful, carefree feast and dancing?

A head appeared above the riverbank. Malach and Torrap climbed up the last part of the bank and walked purposefully towards him. Where was Lamiya? He flexed his fingers, coaxing power into his arms and hands. Curiosity roiled amid his anger and dismay. What did Malach want?

Stopping three paces away, Malach raised a hand. 'Follow me if you want to see her again. Do not think to use your powers. If I don't return to the boat, my men will enjoy your woman.'

Beside Malach, Torrap scowled and rested a hand on the hilt of a long hunting knife hanging at his hip.

His heart pounding against his breastbone, Everand swallowed. No doubt Malach meant every word. With effort, he kept his face calm. He couldn't, wouldn't, abandon Lamiya. Malach was a devious coward and manipulative beyond belief — the similarities between him and the traitorous Mage Beetal were alarming. He stepped forward to take up position between them.

Eyes glittering with triumph, Malach spun around and headed directly back towards the top of the bank. Everand followed, with Torrap hovering annoyingly at his heels where he couldn't see him. Using a slow breath to draw in courage, he consoled himself that on his previous mission, Mage Beetal could have killed him on a number of occasions but he hadn't. He must have had a place, however small, in his former mentor's heart.

Well, he'd have to find a way to connect with Malach. He squared his shoulders: as well as rescuing Lamiya, he would use this development to confirm whether Malach was indeed Mage Beetal's son, and how that had transpired.

In the oppressive air, the river moved in sluggish eddies of dull greys and browns, looking even less appealing than usual. The waterbirds and insects were absent, silence riding the currents. Feeling a drop on his head, Everand glanced up. A raindrop hit him in the eye and he blinked. More drops fell and Torrap grunted.

When Malach paused at the edge of the bank, Everand saw Raptor waiting snug against the base. Heart thumping, he scanned the boat. *There.* The bundle of material and sack rumpled on the floor behind the last seat must be Lamiya. She wasn't moving. Was she unconscious?

Bile surging up into his throat, he clenched his hands, coiling his power. Forget learning anything about Malach, he should get her out of there. Could he translocate her out of the boat fast enough to then spin around and send a stun spell at Malach? Or should he drop Malach first? His chest burned with rage. Digging his fingernails into his palms, he ground his teeth. Decide! *Lamiya.* Get her away from Malach's men. A bead of sweat tickled his brow as he lifted his right hand.

There was a swish of movement behind him and the world went dark when Torrap dropped a sack over his head and yanked it down, pinning his arms and hands. The coarse material chafed and smelled awful. His nose twitched and his eyes watered: the sack was soaked in potion! His power ebbed, slithering back deep inside him. He flexed his fingers: nothing. *Curse it!* He should have been faster. Stupid, when he'd guessed Malach would try to subdue him.

He felt disconnected, adrift, weak. Was this how humans felt all the time? No, of course not, because they didn't know what it was like to have power. Why was he having these random thoughts? *Focus.* How was he going to save Lamiya without his power?

The sack buffeted him forward when Torrap and Malach grabbed the sides of it and nudged him down the bank. Intent on remaining upright, he slipped and slid down the slope, having no desire to do a face-plant into the boat or the water. He was jerked to a stop, the rim of the boat bumping against his knees, cold water slopping over his toes.

'Lift your leg,' instructed Malach. 'Higher. Move it forward.'

Everand complied, wobbling until Malach told him to lower his foot and his sandal touched the floor of the boat.

'Now the other one,' said Malach.

Trying to avoid stepping on Lamiya, Everand repeated the exercise. Both feet flat, he felt her bulk against his toes. Malach brushed past to take his position at the back of the boat. Did they intend to squish him and Lamiya between the last paddler bench and the glide platform? Cramping would be a severe issue before they got anywhere near Riverwood. The obnoxious odour inside the sack was making him queasy, and the motion of the boat was not going to help.

Strong hands pressed on his shoulders until he sat on the floor, his back resting against the boat side. His legs were crunched against his chest, with Lamiya curled up on his feet. He tilted precariously while the boat moved away from the bank and then swung upriver.

'Middle effort,' called Malach gruffly and the boat surged forward, the team working in silence.

Everand licked his foul-tasting lips, his stomach roiling from the boat rocking him from side to side and his legs already aching in the compressed position. An odd gurgling sound erupted in front of him, and Lamiya's weight flopped about on his feet. The gurgling increased, followed by a rasping sound. Panic shot through him.

'She's choking!' he shouted through the sack. 'Stop the boat and help her!'

The boat continued to surge in time with the strokes of the paddles, and the rasping from Lamiya grew worse. Imagining her turning blue and choking until she ceased breathing, Everand pitched his weight backwards and forwards, making the boat tip and tilt from side to side. Paddles clashed.

'Stop that!' roared Malach.

'No!' yelled Everand, pitching more wildly, the rim of the boat ramming into his shoulders. 'Help her or I'll tip the boat!'

The boat slowed. 'Folnak, help sit her up,' instructed Malach.

The boat wobbled with the new movement and the weight on his feet lifted.

'She's swallowing the gag,' said a new voice.

'Take it out,' said Malach.

Everand's heart pounded erratically until he heard Lamiya gulping and coughing. They'd *gagged* her? He ground his teeth. If only he had his power … Lamiya's coughing stopped and then she wriggled and bumped against his knees.

'Now what?' said the same voice. 'I can't hold her up.'

'I can hold her,' said Everand quickly. 'Prop her against me.'

After a pause, Malach responded. 'You know what will happen if there's any stupidity.'

'If you lift the sack a bit so I can stabilise her, that would help,' Everand said evenly.

'Do it,' came the welcome response.

Someone tapped his leg and a voice said, 'Part your legs so I can put her against you.'

Doing so, relief flooded him when Lamiya's back was tucked against his chest. Next, someone tugged the sack up to his elbows and he hugged the cold and trembling Lamiya. 'I'm here,' he murmured.

She pressed against him, and the hard boat rim pinched his shoulderblades. Resting his head against the top of hers, he so wished he could smell her wonderful essence over the bitter stink of the sack. 'I'm sorry,' he whispered. 'Sorrier than you can imagine.'

'Me too. This is my fault.' Lamiya sniffed and her hands groped for his.

Encasing her cold and clammy hands in his, he murmured, 'No, this is due to me.'

'Enough,' snarled Malach, and the boat moved forward.

Well, they were together, but not at all how he'd imagined.

Chapter Four

Rain fell steadily, and even with the warmth of Everand's body, Lamiya was wracked by shivers. A puddle was developing beneath her bottom, her throat felt raw from almost choking and her mouth still tasted like the foul rag. Worse was the relentless churning in her stomach. How stupid to let the Riverwood men kidnap her! And Everand had allowed himself to be taken — because of her. He had placed her above Riverfall and all the others.

She hung her head: how could she bear the responsibility of his sacrifice? His love was overwhelming and somewhat frightening. Her eyes burning with the threat of tears, she blinked rapidly. *Be strong.* Follow his lead of presenting a calm and challenging face to Malach, and pay attention to see if she could discover the reason for the odd undercurrent passing between them.

Against her back, Everand's chest was stiff and straight. What was he thinking? He'd made no attempt to save them or use his powers. Her forehead tightened. Was he unable to? Or was he biding his time, still intent on finding out things? How could she help? The boat continued north, the paddles splashed in a monotonous rhythm, the wild grass on the banks whispered as they glided by and she soon lost all sense of how far they'd travelled. The shadow cast by the bridge would be a marker, but in the rain that might not be discernible.

How long would it take her team to realise she'd gone? What would Riverfall do? Swallowing, she hoped they were continuing the trade discussions, although without Everand to scribe they must have realised immediately that something was wrong. Her guilt flowed stronger. They'd probably stop the discussions, and that would be her fault too.

Her shivers became trembles. When Everand caressed her hands and pulled her close, she longed to turn around and hug him properly, let him kiss away her fright. If they escaped alive, it would be another miracle. The dragons: could Mizukaze or Flight save them? But without his power, Everand couldn't summon them, not from their distant lake at the base of the waterfall. Could *she* call Flight? She reached for her calling ability but it slid away; she was too cold, too tired, too distracted.

Everand squeezed her and murmured, 'It's okay. Wait.'

'Slow the rate.' Malach's sudden command made her jump. They couldn't be at Riverwood already. Raindrops pattered on the sack, louder on the wood of the boat. The boat glided and raindrops ceased to fall on her, although she could hear them plopping into the river. It grew darker. They were underneath the bridge!

'Make for the bank as soon as we're past,' said Malach.

She heard the clunk-clunk of the oar directing the boat, and when Malach commanded a stop the boat slewed sideways. The long grasses and reeds on the Riverwood bank rustled and a waterbird hooted. Her pulse quickened: this bridge between Riverfall and Riverwood was the *only* land crossing between the eastern and western banks down the entire river. From early on in his mission, Everand had thought the bridge was at risk and he'd anticipated that Malach would destroy it during the races, but he hadn't. Were they going to destroy it now?

Her breath caught: that would make it harder for anyone to come and look for them! Unless they used boats and paddled straight across to Riverwood land. Malach wouldn't like that.

Easing in a shallow breath, she wished Malach would take the sack off. Fresh air would make her feel better, and she yearned to see Everand's face. Could he save the bridge?

The boat drifted and raindrops pattered endlessly into the river. Wondering what was Malach waiting for, she shuffled about trying to coax circulation into her numb legs that tingled with the threat of cramps. Everand copied her, giving her hands a squeeze. Damp seeped into her core and she clenched her teeth to stop them from chattering. Such a far cry from the glorious boat races in bright sunshine, which seemed a lifetime ago.

A new sound emerged; the beating of numerous large wings. Probably Malach's eagles, like the three that had attacked her and Everand at Dragon Lake by dropping boulders on them and annoyingly scaring away the river dragon just as it approached them. Her forehead pulled into a deep frown; Everand had exhibited plenty of power then, shielding them both and stunning the eagles so the two of them could get away. There *must* be a reason he was doing nothing now. He'd been on edge ever since Malach had arrived but how could they possibly know each other? Wasn't this the first time Everand had come out of Axis? Had he lied? There was definitely something he hadn't told her.

'Move the boat upriver,' came Malach's voice.

She swayed with the boat's movement and the beating wings vibrated the air, sounding like many more than three eagles. Dropping rocks onto the bridge would damage it but wouldn't destroy it, unless Malach could make the rocks explode. Everand was convinced Malach had magical power, evidenced by his ability to make creatures attack them. If so, the wooden bridge might not survive that.

'Turn the boat,' Malach ordered.

The change of momentum when the boat turned made her stomach roil and the sack cling to her head and face, the damp weave stinking potently. If she tried to take a deeper breath, the sack rasped her skin and snugged tighter over her mouth and nose. Everand coughed, perhaps having the same problem.

Malach spoke from behind them. 'I will remove the sack and you must swallow the liquid I give you. If not, the sack goes back on.'

'Very well,' said Everand.

What liquid? Did Everand know what it was? Lamiya's forehead began to throb. By the spirits, let Malach remove her sack too. Against her back, she felt Everand shrugging, presumably helping them to lift his sack off.

After taking a large gasp of air, Everand said evenly, 'Remove her sack.'

Heart thudding, she held her breath in hope. Malach didn't reply

'I'll swallow your potion when you remove her sack,' Everand said firmly.

She tensed. Would Malach hit him, like he had Acim and Zink? The paddler in front of her moved and the sack grated across her cheeks, leaving a swathe of stinging skin. Rain sprinkled onto her face, and blinking rapidly she gulped a breath and looked around. The boat was just upriver from the bridge, tucked in against the bank on the Riverwood side. Everand reached up to take a bowl from Malach, wrinkled his nose and then swigged down the contents. A musty, acrid aroma teased her nostrils.

'The taste could do with some work,' said Everand, wiping his mouth with the back of a hand.

Peering sideways, she saw Malach's eyes gleam with amusement. 'The taste is not important. Why don't you watch my eagles at play?'

Ignoring the raindrops plopping into her eyes, she gazed up at too many eagles to count circling above, each carrying a boulder in its talons. Malach stood relaxed at the back of the boat, watching his birds. Everand rubbed at her arms, warming them and perhaps also intending to reassure her.

'Watch,' Malach commanded. 'No trade. No contact.' The boat wobbled when he planted his feet and raised his arms in a wide V to emit an ear-splitting screech.

The eagles screeched in reply and formed into a long line of pairs. Running her tongue over her lips, Lamiya begrudgingly admired his skill with his birds. Thank the stars Whirr wasn't with her. The enormous brown and white eagles with curved beaks and raking talons were deadly.

Nuzzling her ear, Everand whispered, 'There's nothing we can do. It won't take long.'

Steeling herself, she gripped his hands. She'd wanted adventure. Well, that didn't come without danger, did it? The first pairs of eagles flew directly above the bridge, following the length of it, and dropped their rocks with uncanny precision. She flinched when the rocks hit the bridge and exploded in vivid bursts of thunder and orange-red flames. Smoke billowed and the centre of the bridge crumpled, broken slats and shards splashing into the river.

'Hold fast,' Everand murmured. 'Don't give him any satisfaction.'

Lamiya clenched her tongue while numerous pairs of eagles advanced over the bridge, the explosions booming and the echoes multiplying. *Copy his calm.* What could she learn? How did Malach exert control over these raptors? Did he have a calling ability similar to hers? Once the eagles had dropped their rocks, they peeled to each side and circled back to form up at the rear of the line.

She peeked at Malach, who stood erect with a small smile on his lips while he concentrated on communicating with his birds. Could they take advantage of this? She twisted her head to whisper to Everand, but when Malach glared down at her, Everand shook his head. Disappointed, she turned back.

How could Everand let this happen? The provinces would be changed forever.

Another set of eagles flew over and with cracks as if the ground itself was breaking, the massive tree trunks that formed the support pillars of the bridge broke and toppled. Waves washed away and the pillars crashed into the river. A moment later, the boat bobbed in the backwash. With a rumbling like imminent thunder, the stonework at the base of the bridge on the Riverwood side disintegrated and massive boulders and support beams slid into the water.

Lamiya's breath caught. Not only was the passage across the river destroyed, but the boulders and debris would slow the flow. What effect would that have downriver, with three provinces to traverse? Broken tree trunks, the wreckage from the bridge and rocks poked up above the frothing, gloomy eddies. No boat would be travelling that way for a while. Her heart sank and by the way Everand sighed, he'd reached the same conclusion.

Sadness welled in her heart as she thought of how much effort it would have taken the early people to construct the fine, sturdy bridge. Gone in a few heartbeats. She thought of Atage, so sincere in his efforts to bring the people of the four provinces together and to forge bonds and productive trade. All undone by this half-mage — for unclear reasons. Malach was ruthless, violent and horrible. She shuddered. Why didn't Everand do more? He was a full mage! Couldn't he make Malach disappear, or at least curb his powers? Why did he hesitate?

She twisted around to look at him but he gripped her shoulders firmly, turned her back around, then rested his forehead on the back of her neck. His lips tickled and his words buzzed against her skin.

'This is hard, I know. Wait. We must know more.'

He asked much, but he implied there was a bigger picture that she didn't understand. 'Know what?' she murmured.

The paddlers began to turn the boat back upriver and Everand took advantage of the noise and movement to brush his lips against her ear. 'I must confirm he's who I think he is. It's important.'

Leaning against him, she muttered, 'To your Guild?' It might not be important to the provinces.

When he nodded, fear flushed through her. He'd said he would stay in Riverplain with her, so why did he need to find this out for his Guild? Did he intend to go back, after all? Tiredness oozed over her. Too late to change her mind about adventure and intrigue, she was stuck in it now.

'Sorry. Yet another obstacle to our being together.' Everand snuck a brief kiss onto her nape.

'Enough,' snapped Malach. 'What do you think of my eagles?'

'Impressive.' Everand craned his head to look up at Malach. 'But it would be far more impressive if you could achieve that by yourself, without any eagles.'

Lamiya gasped. He was goading Malach!

Narrowing his eyes, Malach gave Everand an amused smile. '*That* is the point. You will find me a quick learner.' Dismissing him, Malach called out, 'Paddle strong. Head for home.'

So, Malach wanted Everand to train him! But how had he known a mage would come? By the way Everand's jaw was clenched, she could see he was thinking hard. Could he outsmart Malach? Were all mages this complex?

The boat picked up speed, heading due north.

Lamiya glanced back at the ruined bridge.

In shards, like her dreams.

Chapter Five

Despite the paddlers' efforts, the boat bobbed unevenly while the river adjusted to the change in flow and the conflicting eddies and currents formed by the wreckage of the bridge. They'd be paddling against the current, Lamiya observed. Behind her, Everand sat stiffly distant, distracted. Watching the choppy water surge past the boat, she decided that his cryptic comments to Malach held more barb than she understood.

Shaking herself, she sat taller and focused on the surroundings. The currents swirled and buffeted the boat and the team dug their paddles in with more force. Rain fell harder, and she rolled her shoulders to keep the numbing cold at bay.

After a while, she spied the tributary running away to the right on the Riverfall side. Chewing her lip, she remembered the smaller bridge across the tributary was deep inside Riverfall terrain and anyone trying to rescue them on foot or by cart would now have to go that way. Visualising the path she and Everand had taken to get to the lake, her spirits dropped. The path led to the eastern shore of Dragon Lake, but she didn't recall a path going to the western shore.

Closing her eyes, she brought to mind the rocky ledge they'd climbed to reach the lake. With water tumbling over the lip of the edge, crossing there would be treacherous. Unless … her heart skipped a few beats … unless any rescuers paddled straight across the river and came overland through Riverwood terrain. Could they achieve this undetected by Malach and his eagles?

Feeling the boat shift direction, she squinted. There was another tributary, running to the west, and the boat was turning into this.

'We enter Riverwood,' Everand muttered.

She gripped his hands and scanned ahead. The tributary narrowed and twisted through sharp meanders, and tall wild grasses on both banks blocked the view. After the fifth tight meander, they plunged between gigantic dark-green trees on both sides and she drew in the pungent scent of pines. The trees blotted out the sky and she shivered in the chill, shadowy air. The paddlers continued in disciplined silence and she absorbed the sounds of the breeze eddying through the trees and the shrill cries of raptor birds hunting. Another shiver shook her and goosebumps chased down her arms. Between the trees she caught glimpses of massive, solid rocks the colour of dark storm clouds.

'Granite,' murmured Everand. 'The hardest of all stone.'

She bit down the temptation to tease him about the appropriateness of the mages surrounding themselves with a wall of this hard and bleak stone. He was not cold and hard, and who was she to judge the aloof mages based on rumours and hand-me-down tales? Rain fell in large drops and she squirmed, her clothes squelching in the puddle she sat in. Cold seeped into her legs and lower back and she wished she were paddling to keep warm. As the glide, Malach would be getting cold standing at the back, and she surreptitiously glanced over her shoulder. His long cloak of eagle feathers, which repelled the rain, was keeping him snug.

The dense forest stretched along both banks in unusually straight lines above ground that was carpeted with slim, brown needles, and the odour of fungi and mushrooms hovered in the air. They passed a cleared square and she guessed they had milled those trees. Nervously, she eyed a granite outcrop which looked like shrouded people huddled together. In one copse, a flock of glossy, sleek, black birds with blood-red tail feathers was feasting on cones and emitting raucous cries. Her teeth chattered, and Everand rubbed her back and arms.

Ahead, water glinted through the trees. The paddlers slowed their rate and Malach nudged the boat to the right bank. Analysing the angle, she understood he was preparing for a hard turn to the left, towards the glinting water. There: a deep, narrow channel fed to the left, only two persons wide. In a well-practised move, the paddlers turned the boat hard left and they entered the narrow channel.

Lamiya stopped shivering and sat up to stare at the two granite statues looming on either side of the channel. When the boat drew closer, she saw large boulders had been positioned on top of each other to convey an impression of two sentinels guarding an entrance. An eagle perched atop the right-hand sentinel let out a shrill screech as the boat approached. A shudder chased down her spine and Everand tightened his arms around her.

The boat eased past the statues and a small lake opened up in front of them. Trees crowded the banks, and the water looked dark and brackish, with pine silt floating on the surface in random smudges. The boat headed towards a short, narrow, muddy shore and when the front of it glided onto the mud the pacers jumped out and pulled it further up, then held it steady while the team filed off.

Despite her keenness to stretch her legs, Lamiya forced herself to wait until Everand made a move. She took several breaths while he sat mutely, doing nothing.

Eventually, Malach snapped, 'You can get out.'

At that, Everand put his hands under her elbows and helped her to stand.

She wobbled, waiting for circulation to flow back into her legs and feet, and then she pulled him to his feet. Feeling awkward and clumsy, she stepped over the benches and climbed out of the boat, her heart quailing at the row of silent paddlers. Avoiding eye contact with them, she waited until Everand stood next to her, his face impassive.

Malach passed them and she went to follow but Everand stayed put. She planted her foot back down. Was he subtly goading Malach, or feigning obedience so they'd not be gagged or sacked again? If only she knew what he was thinking.

Over his shoulder, Malach commanded, 'Follow. Now.'

A burly paddler nudged Everand and when he moved off, she followed.

The group wove through the trees, treading along a narrow path. The pine needles were soft under her sandals and the rain seemed less, but this might just be the shelter the trees provided. The pine scent was invigorating, and colourful clumps of mushrooms and toadstools grew around the bases of the trees. A few of them had enormous, ochre bracket fungi sticking out like steps from the dark trunks, the larger ones looking almost solid enough to climb on.

They passed an enormous, cleared space where about twenty men, all well-muscled, swarthy and dark-haired like the paddlers, worked hard swinging axes. To one side of the flat area was a chaotic pile of firewood. On the other side men were shaving and shaping solid trunks into struts and beams.

One of the men put down his axe and called out, 'Ki, Malach!' The others copied the call and Malach raised an arm in reply.

After a while, they emerged into a large clearing and Lamiya peered up at the sky. The deepening purple haze suggested sun-fade was not far off. Focusing ahead, she saw sturdy stone and wood cabins, arranged in circles fanning out from a bright flickering mass. A bonfire! Nice! Her hands were blue from the cold. Most of the paddlers kept walking towards the cabins.

The tallest one, who seemed to be Malach's offsider, stopped and turned around, holding out an arm to direct them to walk to the right. Lamiya swallowed her disappointment. They were being taken away from the fire and the warmth to an area behind the rows of cabins. Everand touched her shoulder briefly and, with a sigh, she veered to the right and took longer strides to keep up.

Glancing forlornly to her left, she envied the people shrouded in long feather cloaks bunched around the fire. Hints of cooking wafted under her nostrils, making her stomach growl. Everand rubbed at his; with his tall frame he must be ravenous. Soon, her nose twitched with the smell of bird poop and wet feathers. Her dismay rose like bile as they passed the outermost row of cabins, people staring at them while they walked towards what looked like large, sturdy bird cages.

When they drew near, she saw birds of prey hopping about on the floors or clawing along branch perches. There were eagles, hawks and falcons. She shuddered; even these vicious birds should not be caged. Her flocks were free to roam and always came when she called them. Similarly, the hopeepa herds wandered the grassy plains and were only corralled when they were needed. How rough and uncaring these people were! Small wonder they didn't relish mingling with the other provinces; the different practices and beliefs would clash.

She looked at Everand. Although he kept his face blank, she had a strong sense of him analysing everything.

'Stop here,' said Malach.

Horrified, she watched the tall offsider open the doors to two empty cages at the beginning of the row. Her heart hammered against her breastbone. *Don't separate us*! The prospect of a long, dismal and cold dark-fall stretched before her.

'You, in that one. The woman in the other,' snapped Malach.

Facing Malach, Everand said, 'It'll be cold this dark-fall. I am cooperating, and if you put us together we'll be in better shape.'

Lamiya held her breath while Malach tilted his head to one side, considering.

'No,' he said brusquely. 'Torrap, put the woman in that cage.' To Everand he said, 'Being together next dark-fall can be your reward if you please me.'

Everand marched into his designated cage and the man called Torrap grabbed her elbow and guided her into hers. Once she was through the door he gave her a shove and she stumbled. The door thudded closed, and solid wooden bars grated into place. Managing to stop herself from falling, she spun around.

Entering Everand's cage, Malach passed him a small bowl. Everand took the bowl, squinted at the contents, then tipped it into his mouth and handed the bowl back.

Malach stood watching, then punched Everand in the stomach, making him cough and splutter. 'Drink means swallow,' he said roughly, before spinning on his heel and exiting the cage.

Torrap dropped the bars into place and the two men left without a backward glance.

As soon as they had disappeared into the darkening trees, Lamiya ran to the wall of latticed branches between their cages and grabbed the bars. 'Are you alright?'

Coming to stand on the other side, Everand put his fingers over hers. 'Yes, but he is too clever for words. It'll be a long and tedious dark-fall.'

'What did you drink?' Lamiya wriggled her fingers under the warmth of his.

'A foul-tasting potion that quells my powers.' Everand's face was in shadow but she sensed his scowl. 'I feel weak. Useless.'

Sorrow coursed through her. 'This is my fault.'

'Never, Lamiya,' he said fiercely, his fingers gripping hers in a pincer hold. 'I'm the one who's sorry. You're in this mess because of me. Who I am.'

Still not convinced it wasn't her fault, she said, 'Maybe you can tell me what's going on between you two. It'll help the time go by.' She tried to smile but her face muscles were too chilled.

'Lamiya, you are a delight.' The gloom and latticed wall made it impossible for her to see clearly, but it sounded as if he was smiling.

'First, let's warm up. I'm going to walk laps until it's too dark to see. Then we can trade tales.' She patted his fingers and stepped back.

Concentrating on the ground, she began a circuit, counting her steps. It took her twenty-five paces to walk along the side wall between their cages, and another thirty to traverse the length of the wall at the back. The land beyond the rear wall felt darker, denser. Due to trees and rocks? The wall on the other side was … she was halfway along when a bird battered against the barrier with its wings. Jumping sideways, she lost count.

Her heartbeat in her throat, she squinted, trying to see what type of bird it was. Too dark to tell, she tentatively reached out with her mind. Initially, she detected anger and defensiveness, but behind this her mind's eyes saw a sleek falcon with a white head, grey speckled feathers and a yellow beak. A handsome bird, it was furious at being caged and irritated by her proximity. She took a step back, but kept her connection.

The bird calmed, the wings grew still, and it clung to the bars cocking its head from side to side. *I mean you no harm,* she conveyed. *I would free you if I could. Do you have a name?*

The bird gave a screech and Lamiya smiled. *Plummet is a good name.*

She resumed walking and on her second circuit realised that all the birds were quiet, with their heads tucked under their wings to sleep. After five more laps it was too dark to see and she was bored. Making her way back to the wall between their cages, she called, 'Where are you?'

'Here.' Everand's lean shape emerged, barely visible.

Yearning for his touch, she grasped the bars, but just then bobbing lights appeared from the direction of the cabins, distilling into two flaming torches. Her heart galloped: what now? Two shadowy men stopped at the door to her cage. One held both torches while the other crouched down. Wood rasped across wood, and then came a clatter.

'Food and water,' said a voice. The torches moved to Everand's cage and the men repeated the process.

'What is it?' Everand asked. The men didn't reply and the cage fell into darkness when they turned around and went back the way they'd come. She heard Everand's footsteps moving towards his door, and the clatter of a plate. His words came out of the darkness, 'Eat it if you can. Keep your strength up.'

Reluctantly, she felt her way to the front of her cage and crouched. First, she used her fingers to explore the cage just above where the plate was. There was a flat wooden panel that she assumed they slid aside to feed the birds. Sitting down and leaning against the bars, she picked up the plate, cursing when hot liquid splashed onto her toes.

'A stew of some sort,' said Everand around chewing noises. 'Meat and mushrooms, I think.' After a few more mouthfuls he added, 'They won't poison us after all this effort. But it could be laced with a sleeping herb.'

Using her fingers, Lamiya picked up a chunk and sniffed it: meat. Disgusted, she dropped it on the ground and probed until she found cubes of vegetables: potato, taro, carrots. It would be better if these hadn't been cooked with the meat but she had to eat something. Her stomach clenching, she made herself chew slowly. Fish would be far nicer. Recognising the faint aftertaste as valerian root, she shrugged. Sleep would be welcome, and better than lying awake.

The jug proved to contain plain water and she sipped at it, leaving some for later. Done, she put the plate and jug down. Now she needed to relieve herself. How humiliating! At least it was dark. She crawled to the far back corner and squatted in the gloom, deciding to use the same spot each time. Finished, she edged to the other back corner that met with the common wall and sat down. The ground was damp, but it had stopped raining.

'Everand?' His clothes rustled as he approached her. Seated with her back against the rear wall, she lifted her hand to lap height and clutched the bars. Sounds told her he was shuffling into position, and his warm fingers found hers. She wriggled her fingers, loving the feel of him close by.

A thousand questions crowded into her head, but her eyelids were heavy and she felt her chin meet her chest. She yawned: the questions could wait.

Chapter Six

Everand sat in his apprentice chair, alarmed by the feral smile on Mage Beetal's face.

'What do you think of the creature from another world, my boy? Shall we kill her?'

Keeping his face calm, Everand eyed the slim woman seated on the rug in Mage Beetal's study. Clad in skins, and smelling somewhat like an animal, the creature was nonetheless human. The woman was tracing the patterns on the rug with a finger, eyes cast downward, too terrified to look at them. His mind raced: no doubt this question was another of his mentor's tests. However, his true mission, from his true master, was to find out what his mentor planned, and he couldn't afford to displease Beetal.

Shrugging, he looked his mentor in the eye. 'You could. But we may learn more from studying her.'

Beetal steepled his fingers and looked at him with amusement in his dark eyes. 'Study her. What could we possibly learn from such a ... primitive creature?'

Squashing his nerves, Everand said evenly, 'Well, she must be from another world. Don't we need to know where she is from and how she got here? And how she got past the wardspell?'

At that Beetal laughed, got up and poured himself a glass of red wine. 'Priceless, dear boy. She doesn't speak Ossilian, so how do you propose finding out anything?' Beetal drained his glass. 'Better we kill her now. Put her out of her misery.'

Everand swallowed. 'Give me five suns to see what I can discern and report to you. I will look after her.' Why, by all the stars, had he said that? Too late, Beetal was laughing at him — and nodding.

Someone was sprinkling water on his face in an annoying manner. Everand wiped it away. More water sprinkled and he flung his eyes open. He was not in Mage Beetal's study and the dream, no, not a dream, the memory, was dissipating. The damp seeping through his bottom told him he was sitting on the ground in a puddle, and his frantic glance about revealed he was inside a sturdy wooden cage, and it was raining.

Disoriented, he scrubbed at his face with both hands. A jolt jangled right through him at the sight of the woman huddled asleep on the other side of the cage wall, her fingers curled around the bar as if reaching for him! 'Elemar?'

The woman stirred and long, mahogany hair with blue and caramel threads tumbled over her shoulder. He frowned; Elemar had short, dark hair. The memory-dream evaporated like mist in warm sunshine. He was in Riverwood, held captive by Malach. With Lamiya. He scrubbed his face again. 'Lamiya, are you awake?'

Stirring, she lifted her head, her mouth opening in a large yawn. 'I feel terrible.'

He agreed; he was cold, stiff and even his bones were aching. 'Let's get up and move around before Malach arrives.' Placing his hands on the ground to either side of his legs, he pushed. He toppled forward, mud squelching up his nostrils when his face landed in a small puddle.

Lamiya snorted. 'Most elegant. Malach will be impressed.'

Pushing up, he got his feet under him. At least she'd retained her sense of humour. Wiping the water and dirt from his face, he said, 'Show me how it's done then, great glide from Riverplain.'

Her smile faded when she had to use the wall of the cage to pull herself to standing, her knees not quite straight. 'Ow,' she mumbled.

Shaking his arms and legs out, Everand forced a few wobbly steps. This was going to take a while.

'Paddler,' called Lamiya, 'five laps then warm-up drill. Go.' She set off at a brisk walk.

Watching her receding back, he admired her spirit and the way her hair rippled as she paced, an entrancing rich colour even when not sparkling in the sunshine. How had he managed to find a second beautiful and courageous woman? A second chance at love. On his first lap he used the energy from the movement to generate deep thought. Flexing his fingers and lengthening his stride, he tried to draw on his power.

After ten paces he felt it, although it was submerged and unresponsive. Encouraging. When Malach's potion wore off he'd be able to access it. He frowned and took jerky strides. How did Malach expect him to be able to train anyone in the use of magic without access to his power?

Rounding the back corner, he saw Lamiya striding out and swinging her arms up above her head, the muscles in her arms moving in an appealing way. In the other cages, all the birds of prey were perched on their branches, their beady eyes following her every move. Could she communicate with these birds? Could she persuade any to disobey Malach and help them?

The idea taking hold, he scanned the landscape. Behind the cages was dense pine forest. There were only six birds here, so where were all the eagles that had destroyed the bridge? Did they fly free, or was there a larger complex of cages somewhere? Where were the tree-moths and their cocoons? They must be nearby. The fourth time he reached the shared wall, he found Lamiya waiting.

'Follow my lead,' she instructed, standing with her legs apart.

Everand did his best to copy her while she enacted an impressive range of exercises, rolling her head and neck, then her shoulders, rotating her hips, then her ankles, swinging her arms up and plunging them down, then reversing and tossing from down to up. His breath came faster when she moved into motions as if she were pulling on a rope, followed by running on the spot, and then jumping up with both feet off the ground. He grew warm and started to breathe heavily.

'He comes.' She dropped her hands to her sides.

Drawing in a breath through his nose, Everand turned to observe Malach approaching the cages with Torrap striding beside him, and one of the other paddlers behind them. He stayed where he was, mid-cage.

Malach stopped at the cage door and jerked his head. A young paddler with an odd white streak in his fringe slid aside the grille and pushed a plate and jug through it, repeating the gesture in Lamiya's cage. Then the paddler straightened up and passed to Torrap what looked like sacks, which had been folded over his forearm. Everand's pulse sped up: surely not the sacks again?

When neither of them moved to receive their food, one of Malach's eyebrows arched. 'Eat. You'll need the energy.'

After the instruction, Everand moved forward and nodded at Malach before he picked up the plate and jug. Keeping his expression neutral, as if he ate cooped up in a cage every sun, he chewed the coarse loaf and washed it down with swigs of water. On balance, he preferred the Riverfall fare, but the loaf felt nutritious. A sideways glance at Lamiya told him she was keeping her eyes meekly downcast and also eating in silence. Good. He wanted to portray complete submission until Malach relaxed his scrutiny.

Suspicious, Malach frowned at him when he put his plate and mug neatly on the ground by the grille and took two paces back. Lamiya copied. Then he stood with his hands relaxed, pretending he didn't care what Malach said or did next, but he noted the questioning look Torrap gave Malach. When

Malach didn't produce the jar containing the quelling potion, his interest quickened.

Next, Torrap undid the bolts to his cage and held the door open. When he didn't move, the man beckoned impatiently. Everand stayed put and looked at Malach, who glared back with a crimson flush creeping up his neck.

'Come,' commanded Malach.

'Not without Lamiya.' He held his breath while Malach frowned, his expression so reminiscent of his former mentor. Abruptly, Malach nodded and Torrap moved across and opened the door to Lamiya's cage. When Everand stepped out of his cage, she stepped out of hers.

'If there's trouble, the sacks will be put back on. Is that clear?'

Everand gave a terse nod.

To the other paddler Malach said, 'You may go, Tiek. We'll be back before dark-fall. Tell Umit to prepare a shared meal for sun-fade and gather the people.' Tiek scurried away.

Malach then beckoned and strode past the cages, heading north. Everand fell into step behind him, with Lamiya following him and Torrap bringing up the rear. Glad of the brisk pace, which warded away the cold and gloom of the drizzle, Everand looked around. Before too far, they reached the tributary and Malach turned left and followed it.

After only a few hundred paces, Everand sharpened his focus. Ahead was a narrow wooden footbridge, crossing to the northern bank. Straight ahead on this side, massive boulders rose like a cliff face, and in the enormous pine trees on the hill behind these hung countless long beige cocoons, looking like elegant, paper-thin lanterns. His nostrils detected a musky odour. The tree-moth cocoons. Squinting at the closest trees, he realised the moths were there, perched in vertical clumps against the tree trunks, their dusty-brown, mottled wings blending in with the bark.

'Are the moths from Axis?' He posed the question to the long, feathered cloak on Malach's back, receiving only a grunt. With a shrug, he kept walking, allowing a small gap to develop when Malach stepped onto the wooden bridge so he could see where to place his feet. Guessing the wood was pine, he admired the impeccable woodwork, each slat and bolt perfectly aligned. The bridge had no railings, encouraging him to walk in the centre and in a straight line, the water burbling and foaming underneath.

On the far bank, the bridge fed into a worn dirt path that passed between stands of trees and increasingly dense and numerous clumps of granite. As the path grew steeper, the rocks outnumbered the trees and the boulders became craggier and larger. The weather had worn intricate crevices and edges, giving the look of wizened faces, and some had a dusting of pale-green lichen. Wishing the drizzle would ease, Everand wiped the water off his face. His damp clothes clung unpleasantly and chafed his skin, and the higher they climbed, the more a chill edge cut the air.

The brooding sky hung low overhead. It was difficult to discern without the sun, but he thought they were now headed east. To Dragon Lake and Mizuchi Falls? Did Malach intend to make him call Mizukaze? If so, that was why he hadn't been given more potion. He'd need a small amount of power and anyway, the sack Torrap carried was probably soaked in the quelling potion for any misstep. On the rocky, twisted path he had to choose carefully where to place his feet and more than once he almost rolled an ankle.

A swirl of wind enveloped him when they emerged onto a ledge and the land flattened. Goosebumps erupted along his arms, and his clothes clamped against his skin. When Malach stopped, Everand's feet slithered with the speed of his halt and Lamiya bumped into the back of him. Torrap came to stand on her other side, watching them intently. Running his tongue over his cracked lips, Everand worked saliva into his mouth.

Next, Malach stood with his feet apart, raised both arms high and wide and gave an ear-splitting screech. Lamiya flinched, looking so miserable that he burned to hold and comfort her, but they had to endure until he could come up with a plan. He forced a small smile, and her eyes brightened. The sound of wings came at the edges of the rushing breeze. Eagles. To protect Malach from him, or the dragon? Maybe both.

Torrap passed him a flask and Everand pulled the stopper out so he could sniff at the opening. Plain water. He took a drink and passed the flask to Lamiya. Torrap then gave both of them a handful of nuts and dried berries. Cupping her supply in one hand, Lamiya prodded the bits with a finger then pinched some up to pop into her mouth. Everand tried a few, the flavours a pleasant mix of sweet and savoury.

Rubbing at his cold arms, he looked up when five eagles arrived and circled above them. Three were massive brown eagles with white faces and white tips on their wings. Were these the same three that had attacked him and Lamiya last time they came to the lake? The other two were smaller, with storm-grey feathers and a white belly with brown speckles. The head and tail of the Riverwood dragon boat were carved in the likeness of these smaller eagles.

Malach gave another piercing screech and the eagles wheeled away towards the lake. 'Come.' Malach set off.

Everand gave Lamiya another tight smile before he hurried to keep up. If he succeeded in summoning Mizukaze, what would Malach do? Did he have the crossbow concealed under his massive cloak? A sharp rock stubbed his toe, and he limped until the throbbing eased. Curse it. He still couldn't predict Malach's moves. Just as he'd had trouble predicting Mage Beetal's plans, always forced to react as events unravelled.

Frowning, he now worried that insisting Lamiya come along was not a good idea. Beetal had used threats to Elemar's life to make him do things he desperately would rather have not. Rolling his shoulders against the stiffness setting in, he decided he'd have been distracted with worry if Lamiya had been left in the cage at the potential mercy of the Riverwood men.

Could he warn Mizukaze? He stubbed his toe again, ignoring the pain as an idea came. Or, could Lamiya warn Flight so the female dragon could warn Mizukaze? Were her skills strong enough to talk to the dragon from a distance? How could he convey the idea to Lamiya?

The air darkened when they plunged into a dense copse of the tallest, darkest pine trees he'd ever seen. When they passed below the branches, egg-sized drops of rain splashed on his head and sent trickling rivers down his face. With a mighty thud, an enormous pine cone fell to the side of the path and rolled to a stop at the base of the tree. Lucky that hadn't landed on his head! The barbs sticking up from the petal-like things looked deadly. The air was scented and muted and he rolled his shoulders again, discerning the gushing of the waterfall mingled with the breeze in the trees. They were nearly there.

When they exited the trees, a pebbly shore stretched to the large, grey lake. Water sluiced down the waterfall, noisier and fuller after the rain. Not the pristine silver it had been by moonlight; branches and leaves and mud were also coming down. His eyebrows lifted: could the dragon really have precipitated enough rain to cause this? It seemed implausible that the Guild did not know about these creatures with such ability in elemental magic.

Thoughtfully, he eyed Lamiya. Was her innate ability to summon birds another kind of magic, another form that the mages knew nothing about? The concepts would be an excellent research topic. He sighed. The researcher would have to mingle with other peoples — which the Guild would never sanction. In hindsight, no wonder Mage Beetal had become frustrated. There was so much more the Guild could do.

Lamiya tapped his hand. 'Malach asked you a question.'

Everand transferred his look to Malach. 'What did you say?'

Squaring his shoulders so he almost reached Everand's height, Malach said gruffly, 'How do you call the dragon? Teach me.'

Tilting his face skyward, Everand let raindrops splash on his face. The dark clouds were becoming patchy with lighter ones, indicating it might stop raining soon. He looked back at Malach, whose beard was bristling in rising displeasure.

'I need to understand how much you already know,' Everand said. 'Can we sit out of the rain?' When Malach opened his mouth to object, he hurried on, 'It'll be much faster to explain when I know what you've already learned and what spells you have mastered.'

Such surprise and interest reflected on Torrap's face that Everand wondered how much the people of Riverwood knew about their leader. Malach seemed to trust Torrap implicitly, but maybe he didn't want to reveal to others that he needed to learn, and didn't want anyone observing his mistakes. Glancing beside him, he found Lamiya was watching him with alert eyes. Good. She could watch and learn, and later help him analyse what unfolded.

'Granted,' said Malach stiffly, marching back towards the trees.

Torrap snarled and Everand strode after Malach, hearing Lamiya trotting to catch up.

Chapter Seven

Lamiya hurried over the slippery wet pebbles, watching Everand's erect posture as he strode behind Malach. It was like being snagged in a current, pulled along against her will. Wiping the rain off her face, she herded her scattered thoughts. Malach and Everand were going to discuss magic, and apart from being fascinating in itself, this presented an opportunity for her to understand Everand more. The conversation so far suggested that Everand knew considerably more than Malach — the extent of difference was about to be revealed.

A short way inside the tree-line, Malach stopped in a small clearing where the ground was carpeted with pine needles and there was a scattering of convenient rocks and a fallen log to sit on. Choosing the log, Malach gestured to a rock for Everand to sit on, and then told Torrap to fetch wood to make a fire. Lamiya suppressed a shiver; a small fire would be welcome. She sat on a rock opposite Everand, from where she could see both of their faces.

Torrap strode away through the trees and the two smaller eagles glided down to perch on the log next to Malach.

Gruffly, Malach said to Everand, 'Ask your questions with care. It'd be a shame if my eagles had to mark your woman's face.'

Her breath went down the wrong way, her throat clenched and she coughed and gulped, struggling to draw new air in. After a few tense heartbeats, she felt Everand looming over her and patting her back. Finally, her throat relaxed and she gasped in a breath. Sitting up, she smiled weakly.

Everand's warm hand rested on her shoulder and she received his thought: *Listen carefully. This is important.* At the same time, he said to Malach, 'I always choose my questions carefully.'

Her shoulder felt cold when he removed his hand and sat back down on his rock. In a deliberate move, she slid off her rock to sit on the softer ground, resting her back against it. Then she drooped her head to look as if she was dozing, watching Everand closely from beneath her eyelashes. *Listen carefully.* Did he intend to ask her opinion later?

Folding his hands in his lap, Everand said, 'First, I need to confirm you are a half-mage? Your father is a mage and your mother is from Riverwood?'

Malach laughed. 'I know who you are, and I'm sure you have worked out who I am. Is this important?'

'Yes,' replied Everand. 'There are no half-mages at the Guild and it means your powers may respond differently. I can try to teach you, but some of the proven methods might not work and I may need to … adapt my approach. You need to know this so if something doesn't work, you don't think I'm trying to trick you.'

Lamiya scrutinised Malach. There were no half-mages? This was consistent with the long-held tales that the mages kept to themselves. So, something unusual must have happened for him to be born. How intriguing.

'My mother was wife to the Riverwood Chief, but my father was a mage from Axis,' Malach said smugly.

Everand nodded slowly. 'How often did your father visit? Did he teach you spells on those visits?

'He came every second season.' Malach shrugged, 'Since I was seven, and old enough to learn.'

Lamiya suppressed a gasp. So, a mage *had* mingled with a human woman, and often. And the mages didn't know? She peered intently, trying to gauge Everand's reaction.

Although Everand kept a calm face, his fingers twitched. 'I see. May I ask how old you are now?'

Malach grunted, and said, 'Twenty-two.'

His brow furrowed, Everand seemed to be calculating. 'So, you've received around thirty lessons?' When Malach nodded, he asked, 'What was the nature of the lessons?'

Half-closing her eyes, Lamiya watched Everand's expression closely. Why didn't he ask who the mage father was? Did he already know? That might explain the odd undercurrent. Everand's expression didn't alter while Malach rattled off a list of things that included moving objects, reading spells, preparing a variety of potions, far-seeing, calling birds and other creatures. Was this a lot for thirty lessons?

'You gave orders to his transport beetle?' asked Everand. 'A large black-and-white stag-horn beetle? They can be aggressive.'

When Malach nodded, Lamiya noticed a tiny flicker cross Everand's brow. Was the beetle important? Was the colouring of this one distinctive somehow? It must be big if a mage rode on it. As big as the aggressive tree-moths? Oh! The moths must be from Axis, because all the river province insects were the size of a finger or a hand. Her birds ate them. Anxiety stirred within her: did Malach have an ally inside the Mages' Guild? Was *this* what Everand was worried about?

Sitting back, Everand gave Malach an intent look. 'You learn fast.'

'So my father said.' Malach compressed his lips.

Detecting the rising tension, Lamiya sat up straighter when Everand gave Malach a sad look. 'Did your father give you any of the potions? Or any magical artefacts?'

'Ask what you need to know, mage. Don't try to disguise it!' retorted Malach.

Everand stopped fiddling with his fingers. 'Did he give you the personality-adjuster compound?'

Around a slow smile of triumph, Malach said, 'So, you know about that.'

'Of course!' snapped Everand.

Had he just lost his self-control? Lamiya gulped. What *was* this compound? A tremor of fear ran through her while they sat glaring at each other. What had she got caught up in?

'Start my lesson,' said Malach in a thick voice. She couldn't decipher the contorted expression on his face.

Everand gave a short bow. 'Let's start with the calling, then.'

A twig snapped loudly behind her and she jumped when Torrap edged past, his arms full of kindling and a couple of short branches. She rubbed her arms while Torrap piled the wood in the centre of the small clearing. Then she stood up, selected a number of stones and rocks and helped him build a small protective circle around the wood. The sooner the fire was lit, the better. Torrap produced a stone flint from a pouch and coaxed a fire from handfuls of drier needles and some pine cones. Selecting a rock closer to the fire, she sat back down.

'Another thing,' Everand said, 'I've not actually ever taught anyone, because only the senior mages have apprentices. I'll have to remember how I was taught things, and then try to explain it to you.' He stood up and ran his fingers through his dank hair.

Lamiya looked away to hide her smile; he'd look much more impressive in his mage robe rather than a crinkled and sodden tunic smeared with mud.

'Calling is a matter of forming a visual image and then sending it to who or what you wish to communicate with. If you know the recipient's name, it's useful to start with that, as it helps attract their attention.' He paused until Malach nodded. 'If you want someone or something to come to you, rather than thinking the command "come here", you send an image of them approaching you.'

Her pulse quickening, Lamiya realised that was exactly how she called her birds! So, to the mages, this was a form of magic that had to be learned? How did she know how to do it? Briefly closing her eyes, she remembered her mother teaching her when she was small. Her lips twitched. Her mother had been able to call whole flocks from a great distance. She eyed Malach. How did he command his eagles if this wasn't what he did?

'Why?' asked Malach gruffly. 'If something should obey you, why not command it?'

Everand's eyebrows lifted. 'A command can be ignored. Did you always do what your father or mother told you to?'

'Don't get personal,' snapped Malach, but a flicker of understanding crossed his face.

Raising his hands in apology, Everand continued. 'An image is more compelling, and it's more like a request.' He shrugged. 'The dragon might not understand our words. If you send him an image, he's more likely to respond.'

Leaning forward, Malach asked, 'Is that how you got it out of the lake? How did you make it come to the boat races?'

Everand smiled, for a moment looking just like a wise teacher. Lamiya narrowed her eyes. She'd like to know how that happened, too. 'You know the answer. An eagle caught one of my message balls and gave it to you.'

Sitting back, Malach's features relaxed and he looked a bit more pleasant. 'You sent a series of images … the river, the pile of offerings, the boats … and the way out of the lake. Clever,' he said grudgingly. Then he frowned. 'Why did you show it the path?'

Lamiya felt her eyebrows rise. Was *that* what Everand had been doing when they had gone by cart with him to see the bridge? She'd thought he was admiring the scenery from the bridge, while he'd been composing messages to the dragon! She shivered with a thrill of excitement. He could put messages in a ball and send it across distances? Maybe he could teach her that.

'Nobody had ever seen this dragon.' Everand rolled his shoulders. 'I thought it was a myth.'

'But you and your woman saw it,' Malach said smugly. 'And I saw you and knew you had power.'

A hint of a blush appearing on his neck, Everand said, 'Anyway, I realised that being a river dragon, it might not have wings.'

'Wings!' Lamiya blurted, and then clapped her hands over her mouth, her mind filling with the idea of majestic soaring dragons.

'On another world there are enormous, winged dragons. They come in a variety of colours.' Everand smiled fondly at her, his eyes a deep, deep blue.

Lamiya's mouth dropped open. Had he just said another *world*? She massaged her temples with her fingers. How could he know all these things when he wasn't much older than she was? The mages were not supposed to leave Axis, yet he'd been to another world? A wave of dizziness broke over her, and she saw that Malach looked uncomfortable. She almost felt sorry for him as the extent of difference between him and Everand became clearer.

Her heart twisted. She wanted to know Everand better … and he was far more complex than she'd realised.

'Let's try it,' said Everand. 'Think of something you'd like Torrap to do and project the image to him.'

Torrap, who had been sitting on the log near Malach, stood up so quickly that he lost his balance and fell backwards over the log, landing with a thud on the pine needles, his sandals waving in the air. Lamiya contained her smile while the burly hunter righted himself.

'Perhaps you could ask him to do something more practical,' said Everand dryly.

Malach guffawed. 'So, you do have a sense of humour.' His face turned stern. 'My father said you did not. "Boring and strait-laced beyond belief," were his exact words.'

When Everand's face became absolutely devoid of expression, Lamiya's heart thudded unevenly and she frowned. Malach's father *knew* Everand? Well, maybe that wasn't a surprise, as the mages probably all knew one another. But why would his father have discussed Everand with Malach? Her forehead began to throb.

Everand's eyes grew a rich shade of azure, and he said slowly, 'Think what you want Torrap to do, and then tell me if he has done it.' The tips of his fingers twitched, slightly.

'Very well,' said Malach, giving Everand an equally flat stare.

Lamiya held her breath while Malach looked at Torrap, who fidgeted as if he wanted to bolt as fast as his legs could carry him. The hunter showed courage, standing with his hands clenched at his sides. Abruptly, his eyes widened, he turned and walked a circle around the small clearing and then came to sit down on the log again. Malach looked smug.

'Good,' said Everand.

When Malach turned to stare at her, his eyebrows pinching in concentration, Lamiya froze and her mouth went dry. *No! Leave me alone!*

Everand clapped his hands together loudly and Malach's attention diverted to him. 'Shall we go to the lake now?'

In answer, Malach stood up, rubbing his palms on his trousers.

Even though her knees were shaking, she noticed how Torrap looked at Malach warily. Would the people of Riverwood want to follow a leader with powers they couldn't see or understand? She chewed her lower lip. They'd probably be too afraid not to. Straightening his cloak, Malach set off and Everand beckoned to her with a small smile.

In single file, they marched through the trees and crunched across the pebbly beach. She stared at the ripples lapping against the shore, the water becoming a darker grey-brown where it grew deeper. The surface gleamed brown-silver in the weak light and the waterfall crashed into the lake in a churning pond. A deep shiver travelled through her.

Peering coyly through her eyelashes, she saw how straight and tall Everand walked and her heart lifted. Every now and then, he turned slightly and smiled to encourage her and she admired the calm set to his face, as if danger did not exist. When his dark-blue eyes fixed on her, she clenched her fingers and pushed down the longing to run into his arms. Would Malach honour his word and let them be together this dark-fall? A breeze moved dank strands of hair against her cheeks and she felt the touch of the spirits. They would escape Malach's clutch, she just knew it.

On reaching the edge of the lake, Everand and Malach stood stiffly, both waiting for the other to speak. With a sigh, she stared across the lake. Where were the dragons? The surface rippled in the breeze, the water a dense shifting mass under the heavy skies. Close to the shore a silver fish jumped and disappeared with a splash. Her attention was drawn to the centre of the lake, where the water seemed deepest, darkest, and an eddy washed away from a disturbance. Glancing up, she saw Malach was speaking to Everand, but she let the words wash over her, her mind focused on the lake.

Half-closing her eyes, she reached out, visualising the orange-green dragon with the red mane. *Flight? Are you there?* An image came of the two dragons curled up on the lake bed, the tail of Flight swishing a hello. Was this what her mind wanted to see, or was she actually seeing it? She sent an image of Flight rising to the surface, briefly splashing with her tail, then submerging again.

Holding her breath, she waited, Everand's voice tumbling around her while he gave detailed instructions to Malach.

Pushing away the question about why he was saying so much, she fixed her eyes on the centre of the lake. There! A small wash surged away when an orange-scaled tail broke the surface, glistened for a heartbeat, then sank silently back below the surface. She rubbed her eyes and looked at Everand, who gave her an imperceptible nod. Her heart thudded loudly. He'd wanted her to try!

Malach had his back to her, but he spun about, his eyes narrowed. 'What did you do?'

'Nothing.' She kept her eyes downcast.

'Try now,' Everand said firmly to Malach. 'This will be more difficult due to the distance and the water in between, but give it a try.'

Malach glared at her before he turned to face the lake. The back of her neck grew cold, and she looked over her shoulder at the large brown eagles flying above the trees and heading towards them. Their talons scratched over the pebbles when they landed behind Everand. The two grey eagles then flew out of the clearing and came to land behind her.

'See?' said Everand. 'You've already mastered calling your birds.' When Torrap stepped beside him, shook out the sack and held it ready to throw over him if necessary, he added, 'And your man here. The dragon is larger and wilder. You need clarity and a vivid image.'

The air closed in around Lamiya, stifling breath and thought, while Malach stretched his arms out in front of him and stared at the centre of the lake. Her heart thudded hollowly against her breastbone and she wished Whirr were snuggled there. Was this wise, teaching Malach to call the dragons? What would Malach do if he failed? She swallowed: what would Mizukaze do if he came? A gust of breeze swirled around them and Malach straightened his arms, his mouth moving.

A larger ripple washed over the pebbles, receding with a hiss as the water drained between the stones. Lamiya felt the disturbance in the centre of the lake, sensed the two dragons uncoiling from the muddy bed and rising, bubbles seeping from their mouths. Malach scowled with effort. The dragons were nearing the surface and a larger ripple brushed over the shore, rolling smaller pebbles with it.

The corners of Malach's mouth curled up in the start of a smile. Lamiya felt sad. How could the dragons respond to him? He was not a good man. She thought of how Flight had raced in the body of her boat and of the harmony, grace and power of skimming over the water together. Malach wanted to control them. To do what? Nothing good.

Danger! Don't come, she thought to Flight. She sensed the dragons pause, sensed their noses touch as they communed. Her heart skipped unsteadily. They had heard her.

'Ach!' Reeling back, Malach flung his arms up protectively.

'What happened?' Everand looked alarmed.

Spinning around, Lamiya saw Mizukaze's massive blue tail with gold spikes rise up and thwack down onto the water, sending up a fountain of muddy brown spray. Ripples sped towards them and crashed over the pebbles, tumbling pebbles and small stones at her feet. 'The dragon is angry,' she said to nobody in particular.

Everand raised a hand. 'Wait. Think. You connected, which was the objective.'

Malach looked a trifle pale and Torrap hovered behind Everand, tossing the sack between his hands. A massive rumble shook the clouds and Lamiya looked up, alarm jolting her at the clouds collecting in a broiling mass of dark grey. Large drops splatted against the pebbles, hitting her head and sliding unpleasantly down the back of her neck. Her heart hammered; was Mizukaze doing this? A fork of lightning flung down, striking one of the closest trees, which exploded into a ball of flame.

'We must leave!' Everand pushed Malach towards the trees.

Massive, stinging hailstones pelted them as they scurried back under the trees to the clearing. Her heart singing, Lamiya skipped behind the men. For now, the dragons were safe from Malach.

Back at the clearing, Everand stepped in front of Malach. 'What happened?' When Malach hesitated, he said urgently, 'What's wrong with the dragon?'

Rain hissed through the trees and Lamiya's clothes clung to her skin, but she was warm inside. Hah! Not everything was going Malach's way. She averted her face to avoid smiling at the way Torrap looked wild around the eyes and Malach simply stared back towards the lake.

Abruptly, the rain stopped. Steam rose from the carpet of needles and filled the air with the pungent scent of freshly wet pine and fungi. She inhaled, the crisp scent helping to clear her head.

'Give me the quelling potion.' Everand held out a hand.

Was he mad? Lamiya felt her eyes grow wide. If his powers had returned, why wasn't he taking advantage of it so they could make their escape?

'Quickly,' he said when Malach fumbled with the pouches strung along his belt. His eyes met hers, offering an apology.

She dipped her head: she trusted him, even though she had no idea what he was doing. As soon as Malach handed him the small flask, Everand drained it, wiped his mouth and handed it back. Weak sunlight filtered through the glossy green branches, highlighting the mossy lichen on the rocks. Mist coiled up and the clearing was transformed into a pretty sanctuary.

The potion took hold and Everand swayed. 'It is done. Tell me what happened.'

With hunched shoulders, Malach sat on the same log as before.

Lamiya perched back on her rock. This would be interesting. How would Malach explain? Looking around, she saw his eagles had vanished.

'First,' said Everand, 'tell me, did you convey the images? Did you reach the dragon?'

'Yes. It heard me,' Malach said gruffly.

Everand spread his hands. 'A dragon in a rage is not a good thing. Is this because of what happened at the boat races? Or is there something else?'

'I made it angry before the races. It hasn't forgotten.' Malach rubbed his bristly beard.

'What did you do?' asked Everand.

Lamiya was impressed with his efforts to coax Malach into talking without making him lose his temper. If Mizukaze was angry *before* the races, this could be significant. When she and Everand first found the dragon, he had been brimming with fury. Maybe it wasn't only because they'd dared to go to his lake and call him! Curiosity rising, she watched Malach closely.

'I tried to call it, which it ignored, and then I left it some offerings.' Malach shrugged.

'For a start, the dragon is a male, called Mizukaze. You need to be more respectful.' Everand jerked upright, his face tight with worry. 'Offerings … You didn't put the compound on those offerings, did you?'

Cold seeped over her. Was Everand referring to the same potion that he thought had been used to make the tree-moths aggressive, a jumping fish attack their boat and a viper bite Ejad? Poor Ejad would have died if Everand hadn't used magic to heal him. Her stomach did a somersault. What would happen if a *dragon* ate that potion? Malach was insane.

Malach gave a tight nod and Everand ran his fingers through his hair. 'He didn't eat it?'

'No,' admitted Malach.

His face earnest, Everand leaned forward. 'Listen to me. *Never* use that compound on the dragon. If you succeed, he's likely to kill your entire people. You are closest to the lake.'

'My father had an army of the beasts at his command. Why not me?' spat Malach.

'Your father controlled one mature dragon and that female dragon controlled the others. He was immensely powerful; you are not. If you anger this young dragon, he'll be unpredictable and uncontrollable.'

'You are here to teach me!' Malach roared.

Lamiya massaged her brow. An army of dragons controlled by a leader dragon? Everand had seen this? And he knew all about this potion already. *Wait.* That was how he'd worked out someone was using magic! She hadn't understood why he'd been so unsettled by usually benign creatures becoming aggressive.

Dismayed, Everand sat back. 'I couldn't control this dragon if he were in a fury. I barely managed to negotiate with him before.' He looked at Malach sadly. 'This compound angers whatever takes it beyond reason. It causes rage until sated … or death.'

'Don't try to trick me. This compound is the path to power.' Malach clenched his hands into fists.

Concern ripped into her. Maybe Everand shouldn't have been so hasty in asking Malach to quell his power! How had Malach obtained this compound? And did he mean the path to magical power, or the power to control others? Her mind buzzing with questions, she saw the way Everand's jaw tightened and his eyebrows furrowed. Why were they ducking and weaving around what they both obviously needed to discuss? Should she say something?

Resting his hands on his knees, Everand said levelly, 'We need to talk more about that — but one thing at a time. Can we talk about the dragon first?'

Malach's eyes grew dark but he unclenched his hands, rested them on his knees like Everand did and ground out, 'Tell me how I can win over the dragon.'

With a grimace, Everand asked, 'So, you left an offering laced with the compound. Was this about five seasons ago?'

At Malach's stiff nod, his frown cleared. '*Finally*, I understand what is happening here.'

Lamiya jumped up so fast dizziness surged through her and her vision blurred. Five seasons ago … that was when it stopped raining. 'You!' she croaked. Anger strangled the words she wanted to hurl at Malach.

Everand stood and then paced in a circle. 'At the races, Mizukaze wanted to ram your boat and eat you. He referred to "slimy tricksy not-spice fish", which must have been your offering laced with the compound.' Still pacing, he waved his hands around. 'If the dragon can indeed control the rain, then you angered Mizukaze so much he withheld the rain for all this time — five seasons — to punish the people.'

Yes! Everand was confirming Mizukaze had caused the drought. Because of something Malach had done! Hadn't the dragon known that the people of Riverfall and Riverplain would be affected too? Maybe not, given the dragon had never left Dragon Lake — until the boat races. What a strange series of events.

Hands by her sides, she curled and uncurled her fingers. The fact that the even younger dragon, Flight, had bound herself to *her* boat and come to the races too was surely not a coincidence. A shiver chased across her nape. No-one had seen the dragons for generations, and now there was a male and a female dragon together. She and Everand had a lot to talk over when darkness fell.

A bigger shiver crossed her nape. Was it also not a coincidence that she and he, a mage, were so undeniably attracted to each other? She shook her head, urgently wanting to dispel the feeling of being moved around by unseen forces, and focused on the discussion.

His face animated, Everand paced briskly. 'Mizukaze is a relatively young dragon and didn't know there are different provinces and people. He intended to make all the crops fail in revenge.'

As he passed by, he glanced at her. 'That's why when we approached him at the lake he was aggressive. But we were different, giving him the idea that not all people were tricksy.' He gave Malach a dry look. 'Then your eagles dropped rocks on us and him, reinforcing the tricksy part.' He threw his hands in the air. 'It's a miracle he came to the boat races at all!'

Lamiya took a step forward. 'Not a miracle. He trusted *you*.'

Malach bristled, but she remained standing and glared at him. She was right; Mizukaze had come willingly to Everand. He gave her a guarded look and a thought deep inside prodded at her: *You were in front; you were the one with your hands in the lake.* She took a breath. Could *she* have called the dragon? Everand had called her the dragon caller. Blinking hard, she sat down.

'I think, deep down, Mizukaze wanted to come. He *wanted* to race the boats and hear the drums beating.' Everand paced around the sodden and blackened fire. 'But Riverfall didn't know he was not the same dragon their ancestors had raced and worshipped. Mizuchi, his mother, died. She had told Mizukaze about the offerings and races, but Riverfall had stopped visiting the lake so he didn't know where the people were.'

Facing Malach, Everand said sternly, 'You can't trick a dragon. A battle dragon is a lethal and ruthless beast.' He sat on a rock and folded his hands in his lap. 'You have lost the dragon's trust. Is there another way to achieve what you want?'

Understanding filling her, Lamiya swallowed with difficulty. He hadn't taken the chance to escape because he still held the interests of the provinces in his heart. His final question was clever: he couldn't deflect Malach if he didn't know what the half-mage wanted. Her heart bounded with admiration. Everand might look like he didn't know what he was doing, but he did. She was right to trust him.

Drops pattered down from the trees into the silence, and the rays of sunlight grew bolder, casting pale gold beams into the clearing. A bird chirped.

Malach rose to his feet. 'We will go back. I will think on what you have said.'

If she hadn't been gazing at Everand, she'd have missed the stiffening of his shoulders when Malach added, 'After sun-fade you will tell me about my father.'

Wiping her hands down her damp tunic, Lamiya breathed out. They had survived this event.

And at sun-fade she would get to find out exactly what was going on between these two.

Chapter Eight

Mage Mantiss opened the door to let Mage Agamid in. The senior mage brushed past him and Mantiss peered out. The purple haze of dusk was rapidly changing to the solid greys of dark-fall. By the time Tiliqua arrived, it would be dark enough for them to carry out their plan.

'Take a seat and have some wine while we wait.' He ushered Agamid through to the dining area, and pulled out his usual chair at the head of the table.

'You still haven't heard anything, then?' asked Agamid.

'No. We should have given Everand instructions on how to return, but he is resourceful enough that I expected he'd find a way to let us know when he was ready.' Mantiss shook his head.

Agamid sat back, stroking his trim brown beard. 'If we have kept count correctly, the trade discussions would have been held last sun. Even if he took one dark-fall to rest, I would have thought he'd have tried to reach you by now.'

'Let's hope he is safe. If between the three of us we can't bring him home, I'll have to reveal to the Inner Council what we've done and have them assist us. Not ideal.' Mantiss tilted his head at a knock on the door. 'Tiliqua is here.' He went to stand up but heard the swish of Elytra's dress as his wife went to the door.

Tiliqua strode in, taking the longest steps her robe would allow. 'Still no word?' Her fine blonde eyebrows were pinched with concern.

Waving a hand telling her to sit, Mantiss closed his mouth on his reply when Delma, the head of the kitchen, entered with a tray of glasses and a jug of white wine. The bulky cook bustled around the table filling their glasses and gave him a sideways glance, perhaps wondering why they were silent, then hurried out.

Mantiss took a sip then put his glass down, concentrating on containing the tremor in his hand so it didn't wobble. The cursed weakness was becoming increasingly difficult to conceal. 'First, we will translocate to the rooftop landing area above the beetle stables. Nobody will be there in the dark.'

He looked across at Agamid. 'We need you to create a small gap in the wardspell. I have turned off the alarm, so Tiliqua and I can reach through the gap with mind probes to locate Everand. Did you bring the map?'

Agamid produced a rolled-up parchment from the folds of his robe.

Her eyes reflecting sharp interest, Tiliqua leaned forward. 'Can I see? So I understand properly where you sent Everand?'

While Agamid unfurled the map, Mantiss watched his daughter's face as she absorbed the details. She was thrilled when he had opened up to her, only two suns ago, divulging the real reason for Everand's absence from council. Her enthusiasm at being invited to assist was gilded with a personal interest in Everand as a potential partner, but nonetheless, she possessed a keen, analytical mind and extraordinary ability and power for a woman. Regret pinged through him that he hadn't confided in her earlier. Perhaps he should have trained her covertly alongside Everand. Two parallel spies. Too late now, but as these events unfolded, he could see how far her ability reached.

'We translocated Everand to here.' Agamid placed a finger on what looked like a large flat area of land next to a wide turn in a long, broad river. 'The map is long outdated, but this is where the man Beram said the main town of Riverfall is. I forget its name. This is where the boat races and trade discussions were to be held, so Everand should be in the town somewhere.'

Tiliqua inclined her head elegantly, the plaited coils of blonde hair glinting shades of gold in the light from the room orbs. 'So, we should search almost due east from here, and start as soon as our probes cross the river. It looks straightforward enough.'

Hoping her confidence was not misplaced, Mantiss gulped down the rest of his wine and pushed up from the table. Standing too, Agamid and Tiliqua followed him to the hallway, where they held hands to form a triangle. Mantiss uttered the translocation spell. After a brief shimmer of air and a drop in temperature, the three of them stood on the rooftop landing pad of the marble building that housed the beetle stables on the eleventh floor. A light breeze carrying a faint peaty odour ruffled Mantiss' robe.

Turning to face east, he appreciated the shelter from the coolish breeze when Agamid and Tiliqua came to stand on either side of him. Agamid raised both arms, his purple sleeves hanging down, and mouthed a complex spell.

Mantiss pushed aside the insistent, niggling concern that they were breaching Guild Law. As Head of the Guild, he was authorising their actions as necessary for the greater good. The Guild needed to hear Everand's report on what was happening in the provinces! For a while, unease had been steadily growing in his mind that something was happening beyond their great protective wall. The man Beram turning up out of the blue to seek Guild assistance had been the deciding factor in his inner debate whether the Guild should peek outside its cocooned life.

Above and before them, some distance away, the dark sky crackled with lines of purple and blue energy, and a yawning diamond shape about the size of a head formed.

'It is done,' said Agamid, a bead of sweat rolling down his forehead.

Mantiss took Tiliqua's hand and they raised their free arms, directing their hands and minds at the dark space Agamid had created. In harmony, they intoned the spell to create a strong mind probe. Aware of Tiliqua coiling her probe around his, feeding in her strength, Mantiss then sent it forth. For several breaths, his mind saw only darkness, with a sense of land rolling away far below. Then silver light from the rising slip of moon glinted off water. The river. He sent the probe straight ahead and, after a few more breaths, the glinting water ceased.

Dropping his mind probe lower towards the earth, Tiliqua's probe following, he found faint greys and silvers reflecting off the rim of a tall wall. The town was walled? His mind perceived the dark, open spaces of courtyards, then the glow and warmth of numerous clay domes. Surprise eked through Tiliqua's touch that the people lived in short, squat houses. It would be convenient if Everand were standing outside somewhere, hoping they were looking for him.

Together, they skimmed their minds over the town. Mantiss' legs began to shake with exertion and without the support of Tiliqua's youth and strength, he knew he would already be struggling to hold the spell. They'd have to be fast.

'The courtyards and gates,' he murmured.

Probing with care, they came across an occasional person walking into or out of a dome, but of Everand there was no trace. Mantiss bit back a curse. They didn't have the magical strength to search inside every house. And, of course, he'd told Everand to keep his powers a secret, meaning there would be no convenient residual trail of magical energy to latch onto. He felt a surge of determination from Tiliqua, and their probe roamed over the domes at the southern end of the town.

The essence from one of the southernmost domes felt familiar. Beram's home? He probed down closer, but the dome was empty. No Beram, and no Everand. Mantiss released a sigh. His arms were beginning to shake and his concentration was waning.

'I can't feel him. At all,' whispered Tiliqua, sounding disappointed.

'No. We must retreat. For now.' Mantiss pulled his mind probe back to sweep over the courtyards one last time. Ceasing the probe and releasing the magical energy, he took in a deep breath and dropped his arms. His legs threatened to give way, and he had to shuffle a few steps to cue the muscles to hold him upright.

'Father! Are you alright?' Tiliqua put a supporting hand underneath his elbow.

He patted her arm with his other hand. 'I am getting too old for this level of exertion. I will be fine after a rest.'

As tall as he was, Tiliqua peered into his face and arched an eyebrow.

'Closing the gap now,' said Agamid, waving his fingers in a sinuous pattern. 'Let's hope nobody noticed the line of energy.'

His head heavy on his neck, Mantiss nodded, thinking that if it had been Everand creating a gap in the wardspell, he would have had the foresight to insist they make their energy signatures invisible. He should have thought of that! But in their favour, it was dusk mealtime when every mage should be inside. With sheer willpower, he drew deep and muttered the code to reinstate the alarm to the wardspell.

The muscles in his legs quaking in an unwelcome warning that his supply of power was spent, he asked Agamid, 'Can you translocate us back to my dome?'

'I'll do it,' said Tiliqua crisply, reaching out to grasp their hands.

In a few blinks they were back in the warmth and cosy orb light of his dining area. Grasping his elbow again, Tiliqua guided him back to the dining table and Mantiss sank gratefully onto his chair. Before he could decide what to say, Elytra entered and took her chair at the table, and almost immediately Delma and a kitchen girl appeared carrying trays with their meal.

'More wine?' Delma asked.

'Please.' Mantiss eyed his shallow bowl of chunky potato and pumpkin stew. 'A good red, perhaps.'

Once everyone had fresh glasses of wine and had started on their stew, Agamid said, 'What next?'

Mantiss put down his knife and fork. 'If we don't hear from Everand by sun-high, I will have to enlist the Inner Council. We can't leave him out there, and we'll need the strength of the others to broaden the search.'

'Do you think he's travelled to a different province? Why would he do that?' Agamid asked, frowning.

'We did ask him to resolve this dispute and to find out as much as he could about the provinces, but given the provinces were all gathering in Riverfall I didn't expect him to move anywhere else. It's a possibility, though.' Mantiss stabbed at and then chewed on a chunk of sweet, yellow pumpkin. Trust Everand to take his task to the broadest extent. His spy was, at times, overly devoted and serious.

Pausing with a potato speared on her fork, Tiliqua spoke. 'You could send me. I could look for him.'

The breath caught in the back of Mantiss' throat. An audacious suggestion. A tempting solution. He looked around the table. Agamid gave a subtle shake of his head and Elytra looked horrified, whereas hope shone from Tiliqua's eyes. After a deep, slow breath, he said, 'That is a most generous and bold offer. But one I can't accept.'

When her spine stiffened, he suppressed a wince. 'I've transgressed enough as it is by sending Everand outside the wall. My only reasonable justification is that he has been outside the wall before, when he was spying on Mage Beetal for me. I can't possibly be forgiven the transgression of sending two mages outside Axis. The council would regard *two* covert breaches of Guild Rule Nine as unconscionable.'

Tiliqua looked down at her fork and then placed the potato into her mouth. Lips compressed with worry, Agamid looked from her to him.

Willing his daughter to make eye contact, Mantiss said gently, 'I'm sorry, Tiliqua dear. But I would prefer not to have the council annoyed at you. I need you to be in a position of influence.'

Nostrils flaring, Tiliqua held her head high. 'Very well.' Her eyes narrowed. 'I like the sound of a position of influence.'

As Mantiss reached for his glass of wine, beneath the table his knees shook and he firmed up the contact of his feet on the floor. Already, the younger mages were jostling for position, sensing weakness and the possibility for change. What would they make of his revelation about Everand's mission? He took such a large gulp that the red wine seared his throat and his nostrils zinged with the acidity.

With Agamid, Tiliqua and Everand standing by him, and probably Saiphos, former apprentice to Agamid, he held loyal sway over half the Inner Council.

It was the other half he worried about.

Chapter Nine

Everand watched the feathers in Malach's coat ripple while they trudged back across the wooden footbridge. His stomach growled, reminding him he hadn't eaten since the handful of nuts and berries offered on their way to the lake. But he wasn't really hungry. Beside him, Lamiya strode out with her mouth compressed to hold back the thousand questions she no doubt wanted to ask. He sighed. He'd have to answer to Malach first and then Lamiya.

They walked down the track leading to the raptor cages and the birds' shrill cries filled his ears. Would Malach honour his word that he and Lamiya could be in the same cage? He had cooperated, but he refused to beg. Dusk was falling, and up ahead the dancing orange light from a bonfire flickered above the roofs of the stone cabins. Glowing embers drifted into the darkening sky, and he remembered that Malach had told Tiek to gather the people. A chill passed across his neck. Malach wouldn't parade him and Lamiya in front of everyone like captured prey, would he?

While they rounded the corner of the first cage and approached the open door, Everand grabbed Lamiya's hand and then marched them both into the cage. He took six large paces before he turned, still clutching her hand. When Malach stopped by the door, Torrap gave him a questioning look. Lifting his chin, Everand stared defiantly until Malach nodded at Torrap, and the man slid down the crossbars with loud clunks, locking them in together.

'A cloak to share would be welcome,' Everand said, but the two turned their backs and left, swallowed up by shadows when they passed through the trees.

'Don't look,' said Lamiya before she bolted to the back corner.

He kept his back turned, waiting to use the other corner to relieve himself when she was done. Anger sparked inside him. This was supposed to be a simple mission. Not one where he was caged like an animal and reduced to squatting in dark corners. The disregard for life Malach exhibited was disconcerting. Were all hunters like this? The people from Riverplain and Riverfall were gentle, peaceful people. Why was Riverwood so different?

'Your turn.' Lamiya reappeared out of the gloom.

After going to 'his' corner, he crouched by a puddle and rinsed his hands. Then he took Lamiya's elbow and guided her to the outer wall nearest the forest, but close enough to the door so they could see if food and water were brought. Sliding to the ground, he sighed and took the weight off his aching legs and feet.

When Lamiya sat beside him and leaned against his shoulder, he slipped an arm behind her shoulders, pulling her closer. She was so brave and stoic. Fatigue washed over him and he was glad when she nestled against him but didn't speak. Closing his eyes, he let his head droop.

He jerked awake from his dream of running a hot bath, his heart thudding against his chest bone. Torchlights were bobbing among the trees. Lamiya jolted awake and he gave her a reassuring squeeze. Peering into the light spilling from the flaming torch, he recognised the long cloak of eagle feathers. Malach held two brands aloft while Torrap and Tiek opened the cage door and put down plates, three flasks and a folded object that might be a blanket. His stomach gave a loud rumble and Lamiya elbowed him in the ribs.

Lumbering to his feet, Everand watched Torrap reach up and put a torch in wooden holders to either side of the cage door. Tiek spread a coarse blanket a few paces inside the door, under the spilling light, then Malach came to stand on the edge of the blanket and Torrap bolted the door. Everand's eyebrows lifted when the other two men departed, a single torch showing their progress through the dark maze of tree trunks.

'Eat. We will talk,' said Malach.

Everand walked stiffly to the blanket. Picking up two plates, he handed one to Lamiya and chose a corner of the blanket to sit on cross-legged. Malach put the flasks in front of them and sat cross-legged facing them, his face a mix of shifting shadow and mottled orange light from the torches behind. The plate was warm, and Everand's nose twitched at the aromas of roasted meat and baked potatoes.

'This first.' Malach handed him a small flask of the quelling potion.

Everand swallowed the liquid and placed the flask on the blanket. His stomach growled, and Malach gestured to his plate. He picked up the chunk of meat, which had small leg bones in it, and bit off a mouthful. He didn't recognise the flavour, but it was tasty enough.

'This is a bird.' Lamiya glared at Malach accusingly. 'I won't eat it.'

Everand almost choked on his mouthful.

'What do you think my raptors hunt?' Malach laughed.

Should he encourage her to eat? Everand chewed, thinking. How offended would she be? *Very.* With a sigh, he reached over, took the bird leg from her plate and added it to his, ignoring Malach's guffaw of laughter. To deflect the focus from Lamiya, he asked, 'What would you like to speak about?'

Good humour in his face, Malach tipped forward. 'Tell me about the mages and my father.' Sitting back, he took a long pull from his flask.

The crisp tones of a wine teasing his nose, Everand slowly finished his mouthful, considering where to start. Lamiya picked at her food, but he could tell she was listening intently. This was an opportunity to tell her more about himself, something he'd had little time to do so far.

'Stop me if I'm telling you what you already know.' He ate one of the potatoes, liking the crispy skin and strong spices. 'There are one hundred and thirty mages in Axis. Male mages outnumber female mages by a factor of two or three. Mages do not readily produce children, often bearing only one child, or sometimes none.'

Malach nodded. 'Where does the power come from?'

Choosing another potato, Everand chewed thoughtfully. 'Mages only partner other mages because we are born with innate, but latent, magical ability.'

'If you only partner mages, who else lives there?' interrupted Lamiya.

Slowly, Everand said, 'There are also more than two hundred people. They work willingly for us doing the menial tasks, such as growing crops, to leave us free to focus on our magic.'

'The mages. You said latent ability.' Malach waved his flask at Everand.

'We are born with ability, but it is unrefined.' Everand tilted his head. 'As far as I know, there is no record of how we came by it. The Mages' Guild works to study our abilities and the spells that enable us to direct and control it. Our power is … submerged. It must be drawn to the surface and then trained to come when we need it, and in the form we require.'

'Some are more powerful than others?' asked Malach.

'Yes,' said Everand. 'Some mages are particularly strong and learn faster than others.' He took a deep breath. 'Your father was one of these.' The torches flickered and hissed, and Malach and Lamiya stared at him expectantly. Malach flapped a hand at him to continue.

'Mage Beetal was a member of the Inner Council of Ten, a position of responsibility in recognition of his ability.' Everand tilted his head to one side again, observing Malach's face. 'He showed power from an early age, but ...' he chose his words carefully '... from the outset he was innovative and wanted to experiment.'

He reached for the flask on the blanket and took a cautious swig of the liquid. It was wine, the flavour strong and a tad bitter. He rolled it around his tongue, thinking Mage Beetal would have liked it, given his propensity for wine.

'You were his apprentice,' said Malach flatly.

Sensing Lamiya's eyes on his face, Everand nodded. 'I was assigned to him when I was twelve.'

'What do you mean, assigned?' asked Lamiya.

Looking at her, Everand said, 'My father died and my mother vanished. Because I was twelve, not a small child, I was given my own quarters and assigned as an apprentice earlier than is usual.' Turning back to Malach, he said, 'My mother was the most powerful female mage known. The Head of the Mages' Guild felt I should study under a mentor with suitable ability, and he chose Mage Beetal.'

Pushing down the memories of his clandestine meetings with Mage Mantiss in the Guild library, he didn't say he had also been assigned to spy on Beetal because the Guild did not trust him. Lamiya's hand crept onto his knee.

'So, what happened?' grunted Malach. 'Why is my father dead?'

Ruefully eyeing his empty plate, Everand tried to rein in his galloping emotions. Would it be a mistake to show regret? Or would this help him to connect with Malach? Putting his plate down, he sipped more wine before he met Malach's dark and impatient eyes.

'You may not believe me, but I wish it were otherwise.' He spread his hands open. 'Your father was strong, intelligent, imaginative and … ambitious.' Malach's eyes glittered, but he didn't interrupt. 'He felt the Guild was stifled, limiting the use of our powers when so much more could be achieved.'

'He said this to me.' Malach tapped his fingers against his flask. 'He called them buffoons who couldn't see past their own noses.'

'That sounds like him.' Everand smiled. 'He wanted to change the Guild, open it up. So, when the previous Head of the Guild died, Beetal applied for the position.'

Malach sat up, his surprise evident even in the dim light.

'He was challenged for the leadership by Mage Mantiss, and because the mages were uncertain about Mage Beetal and felt threatened by his opinions and suggestions for change, Mantiss won easily.'

'I don't understand,' said Lamiya, leaning forward. 'What did he want to do that was so threatening?'

Everand looked at Malach, but he nodded, allowing her question. How much should he reveal? He wouldn't lie to Malach, but he didn't want to set in motion events that could see a repeat battle for power. 'For starters, Mage Beetal wanted to visit other worlds.'

Lamiya gasped. With a shrug, he continued. 'He was insatiably curious, wanting to explore, see what other worlds were like and perhaps learn of other abilities.' He frowned. 'But travel outside of Axis is strictly forbidden. Our land is protected by a lethal wardspell that stops others from entering — and also prevents us from leaving.'

Her face glimmering in the torchlight, Lamiya sat bolt upright. 'So, it's true! Anyone who touches the wall is killed?' Before he could agree, she rushed on, 'Wait! Did you say you are not allowed out? How … bizarre. How did you get here, then?'

'Impudent woman,' snarled Malach. 'Know your place!' He raised a hand threatening to strike her, but looked at Everand. 'Answer the question.'

'Guild Rule Nine states that a mage must not travel beyond the wall without sanction from the Head of the Guild. Mage Mantiss *asked* me to go, to protect the Riverfall races.' He flexed his fingers in his lap. 'It takes great power to part the wardspell, and two senior mages had to do this for me to go through. They then sealed it behind me.'

Sadness welling, he added, 'A feat your father achieved all on his own. He created a rift in the wardspell and went to another world. That was his undoing.' Eyeing Malach in query, he added softly, 'We were unaware he'd also travelled far closer to home.'

Malach took a long drink from his flask, and Lamiya fidgeted and fiddled with her fingers, burning with questions. Eventually, Malach put the flask down and clenched his hands. 'He said you betrayed him.'

Warmth crept up Everand's neck and into his cheeks. 'Mage Beetal was called to account in front of the Council of Twenty. I gave evidence to confirm he'd created the rift and taken me to another world. In other words, he had breached Guild Law.'

His face growing tense and dark, Malach snapped, 'Why? Why not join him?'

Misery and doubts rising, Everand swallowed. 'Your father made some good points. But he had no boundaries. He'd concocted the personality-adjuster compound, raised a secret army of dragons and murdered some of the people on the other world. Innocent people, who were no threat to him.'

Bile rose in his throat at the memory of being astride a young dragon while it snatched up a primitive village woman on the world of Terralis. Avoiding Lamiya's horrified look, he focused on Malach. 'The Guild was afraid he would travel to Chrysalis, the world of our ancient enemy.'

'So?' snapped Malach, but he looked intrigued.

Everand shook his head. 'I tried to dissuade him, but your father went to Chrysalis regardless and ...' He stopped short.

He must *not* mention that Beetal had taken the Staropal, the powerful artifact containing unfettered power that the mages could draw upon. The Staropal was safely buried deep beneath the marble tiles of the Great Hall, able only to be raised with a secret password known to the incumbent Head of the Guild. For nearly two generations, the power already drawn had been decreed sufficient. No, Malach did not need to know about this.

Meeting the glittering fury in Malach's eyes, he said slowly, 'I wish he hadn't gone. He was overpowered by the farseers of Chrysalis, ruthless half-moth and half-woman beings with magic exceeding ours. They were intent on conquering Axis and absorbing all our power.' Misery roiling inside him, he finished the tale. 'They forced Mage Beetal to open the wardspell for them and their army, and a battle was fought in the Guild Hall.' His voice wavered annoyingly.

'At the last, I believe your father realised what he'd done — but it was too late. The mages were losing the battle, with twenty already dead and others severely injured. Your father tried to redirect the wrath of his dragons to alter the outcome, but one of the farseers realised he'd changed his mind and killed him. We mages did not harm him.'

'You cared for him!' said Lamiya, sitting back and staring at him.

He brushed her face with his fingers. 'He was my mentor for a long time, and I hoped for most of that time that I could deflect him.' Turning back to Malach, he said, 'Consider carefully. The call of power is alluring, but there is a point at which it becomes all-encompassing and destructive.'

'You underplay your role,' said Malach tightly. 'What would have happened if my father hadn't left after your Guild's petty judgement of him?'

A cold shiver chased down Everand's arms. Malach *was* as astute as his father. 'Under Guild Rule Twelve, which states that power must only be used for sound purposes with honest intent, he would have been charged and punished.' He hesitated. 'Given the extent of his crimes, under Guild Rule Eleven, he would most likely have been obliterated.'

Lamiya gave a strangled gasp and looked at him with wide eyes.

'So,' said Malach, 'your betrayal was key.'

Everand hung his head. Mage Beetal had set the course with his actions but he had also offered him a place by his side, and he'd chosen loyalty to the Guild. There was no getting away from that. It seemed fitting that he was being called to account by Beetal's son.

The darkness grew to a deep velvet-black around them. The rain had eased, but high clouds obscured the moon. The torches sputtered and fizzled, sending sparks into the inky air. Lamiya's fingers stole onto his knee and gave it a squeeze — he would be glad of her company this dark-fall. How could Malach not kill him after this confirmation that he had betrayed his father? Everand's face muscles tightened. Ironically, he still didn't know what this ruthless half-mage actually wanted.

His pulse quickened, but he kept his head down. Was it possible the half-mage *didn't* have a grand plan? What if, initially, Malach had only wanted to sabotage the trade discussions because Riverwood didn't wish to trade? Could it be that simple? Not quite. Malach had already tried to influence the river dragon. He wanted to command dragons and have power — like his true father — but he didn't know enough about his power.

Everand's heart raced. His arrival had given Malach the opportunity for a replacement mage to train him. As a bonus, he was the disloyal apprentice and here *alone*, giving Malach the chance to avenge his father's death. If he were Malach, he'd grasp these chances with both hands. Wanting to put his face in his hands and groan, he instead drummed his fingers on a knee and swallowed painfully around the knot in his throat.

The Guild was right: the mages should *not* meddle in the affairs of people. What if a different mage had been sent? Another mage might have annihilated Malach at the first hint of magic — problem solved, return home and close the wardspell tight. But he had hesitated. For *personal* reasons. Would the provinces suffer because of his indecision? His head feeling light and vacant, he lowered his eyes.

'Are you alright?' Lamiya's beautiful face was creased with worry.

A dark shadow loomed over him.

'You deserve to die.' Malach's rough voice came out of the gloom. 'But first you will teach me. Sleep on that, betrayer.' Malach marched to the cage door and Torrap emerged from the trees to let him out.

The bolts thudded back into place with the sound of finality.

Chapter Ten

Grinding his teeth, Malach strode away from the cage. Torrap threw him a sharp glance, which he ignored. The mage was irritating, speaking in riddles and innuendo. The woman was more annoying, constantly interrupting with questions. But she had served her purpose; bringing the mage to Riverwood. Why would his people ever want to mingle with the likes of her?

'What next?' asked Torrap.

Slowing his stride, Malach considered. Torrap was his most trusted hunter and he could confide in him more. Tree trunks flitted by, briefly lit by the glare from their torches before receding into darkness. Ahead, an orange glow rose from the bonfire. Tiek had gathered the people as he'd asked. 'The mage confirmed his identity,' he offered. 'And his role in my true father's death.'

Torrap gave a grunt. 'Good you captured him, then. Why is he here?'

'Good question,' Malach acknowledged, slowing down more. 'He said it was to protect the boat races, so Riverfall must have somehow asked for help. I can't see a mage miraculously coming out of their warded granite cocoon just in time for the races and trade discussions.'

'No,' agreed Torrap. 'And he tried to disguise who he was.' The hunter caught at his elbow, his face intent in the flickering light. 'Do you think the Guild knows he's here? Or is he acting alone?'

Stopping, Malach looked up through the gently waving branches at the glimpses of dark sky. Fluffy clouds obscured the moon and stars, shrouding the light as if concealing secrets. 'Another good question. He implies the Guild would obliterate me for not being a pure mage, but if that's the case why send only one mage? Something isn't right.'

'What will you tell the people?' asked Torrap. 'They should know you have extra abilities.'

Malach tapped his fingers against his thigh. 'Perhaps. But they won't like that I'm not Chief Magrin's son. For now, they only need to know that we won't be trading with the other provinces. Let them absorb that first.'

'They also won't like that you have deceived them for so long, and the longer you leave it …' Torrap frowned.

'True. But I want to gain more power first so I can impress them. I will tell them. Soon.' When Torrap shrugged and didn't look convinced, Malach put a hand on his shoulder. 'You give me good counsel. Let me see how much I learn next sun.' He moved off along the shadowy track.

To his relief, Torrap remained silent for the rest of the walk. His hunter was astute; he'd chosen well who to confide in. If only the races had gone better and he'd won the dragon over, then he could have made his announcement supported by power and victory. He ran his tongue around his teeth. Another sun, maybe two, to gain enough power to awe his people and bring Everand to his knees. Then he would reveal everything. He strode faster.

Taking his position at the front of his gathered people and next to the bonfire, Malach waited while Torrap slithered to his place in the front row of hunters and sat down. Behind them, hundreds of eyes glinted in the firelight, all fixed on him. Above, luminous, fluffy clouds glowed in front of the moon they concealed, as if trying to prevent it from beaming light down on his speech. He took that as a sign of encouragement to proceed with his covert plan.

'My people, we return successful from Riverfall,' he began, roving his gaze over the team of paddlers. 'Our paddlers did well, and Raptor strove alongside the best teams on the river.' He flapped a hand and the team punched their fists in the air and shouted, 'Ki!'

His people cheered, the firelight shining on smiling, relaxed faces.

'As for the trade discussions, we made clear our intention not to join in. We have no need of these peoples!'

His people clapped and hooted, eyes dancing in the firelight and teeth gleaming white in wide grins.

When everyone fell quiet, he added, 'To be sure of no more unwelcome meddling, we destroyed the bridge! No-one can step onto our lands now. We are free to get on with our lives as before.'

The smiles faded and an awkward silence hovered over the gathering, people shifting uncomfortably. Only the keen eyes of his paddlers and hunters remained fixed on him. Working saliva into his mouth, Malach chose what to reveal. 'We brought back two prisoners.' He paced by the bonfire, gathering energy into his steps. 'One of these is an undercover spy mage.'

A gasp went up and several of the women put a hand over their mouth. His hunters sat taller, eyes narrowing and expressions alert.

'Because we live closest to the great stone wall and the elusive mages of Axis, I captured him so we can find out why he's here.' He spun to face them all. 'The woman is bait to make the mage talk.'

A murmuring rippled along the rows of people, many frowning and fidgeting. One of the older women, a friend of his mother's and influential among the womenfolk, opened and shut her mouth.

Looking directly at her, he said, 'Ask your question.'
'Will we be safe, Chief Malach?'

'I will keep you all safe, Hemma.' He firmed his tone. 'The mage wants to learn about us, so we exchange information. He is teaching me useful things.'

'He's not dangerous, then?' Hemma persisted.

Malach wanted to roll his eyes and tell her to quieten down. '*All* mages are dangerous. This one is powerful, but he will do as I bid because I have his woman. I also have a special recipe to contain his power.'

Hemma narrowed her eyes and the older women around her muttered among themselves. In the front row, his hunters looked impressed.

'Trust me, as your leader I work in your interests.' He out-stared Hemma and after a few heartbeats, she lowered her eyes.

There was surreptitious fidgeting and shuffling but no-one else dared challenge him, so Malach spread his arms open, palms upwards. 'We celebrate the return of the team and warding off interference.' To Tiek, he commanded, 'Break out the wine!'

People scrambled to their feet and the older women disappeared into a nearby cabin and returned carrying trays loaded high with sweetmeats, spiced nuts and dried fruits. Tiek and Folnak lugged two large tubs of wine into the clearing and placed these in the space in front of the bonfire, while the younger women brought trays of mugs.

Malach felt a smile form when one woman gave him a sly glance as she put down her tray, and he watched her walk, hips swaying, back to the others. She was pleasing to the eye and curved in all the right places. Maybe he'd take her to his cabin later.

Accepting the mug Tiek offered, he took a large swig before approaching the paddlers, who were gathered together. He clapped each man on a shoulder, praising their efforts. Mahog, the oldest, gave him a shrewd look, as if he sensed there was more to the captive mage than had been said. Malach gave him a nod and moved to the next group. The hunters were in good cheer and saluted him with their mugs, having been against trading with the other provinces from the outset.

After three mugs of wine, he ambled to the collection of older women. They fell silent and looked to Hemma, who inclined her head. 'Chief.'

'Good feast,' he replied. An awkward silence stretched out. Thinking of the excitement of the women paddlers over the trinkets from Riversea, he realised the women might have enjoyed products from other provinces. They'd get over it. He raised his mug at Hemma and moved on.

The air grew a chill edge and his people looked relaxed, chatting in groups. The tubs of wine were empty, and the food trays lay discarded with only a few crumbs left. He roamed his eyes over the gathering. Where was the young woman with the curves? She was flirting with Tiek. He grunted. Never mind. He'd be better off planning what to do next with Everand. Catching Torrap's eye, he indicated he was leaving. 'First light,' he mouthed at the hunter.

His breath misted with orange hues from the dying bonfire as he walked away. On reaching his cabin door, he hesitated. Should he sneak along the winding path to observe the mage and boatwoman? He shook his head. Enough of them! Entering his cabin, he lit two candles, rinsed his mouth and crawled under his skin blankets. His tongue was fuzzy with the aftertaste of wine and his limbs felt pleasantly loose.

Lying on his back, he put his hands underneath his head and replayed Torrap's questions. Was Everand here just to protect the races? Did the Guild know he was here? Yes. Everand had said senior mages had to part the wardspell for him. A thrill running down his chest, he remembered Everand had also said his father could do that all on his own. He *knew* his father was special and Everand had confirmed this, even if unwittingly.

Torrap's other point was far more troubling. If the Guild suspected he existed, or someone like him with magic, and wanted to obliterate him, why not send a group? His thoughts looped, always returning to the same question. *Did* the Guild know about him? Maybe not, considering how surprised Everand had looked when they first saw each other at the boat ramp.

Could his father possibly have kept his existence secret for so long? That would be an incredible feat of deception, but Everand had admitted his father was powerful and clever. Curse the Guild — and Everand — for taking his father. Heat prickled his skin and memories of Mage Beetal crowded his mind. The bristling beard, sharp, glittering eyes, crackling power and energy. The quick mind and drive for purpose and knowledge.

He looked like his father; could he be as powerful and commanding? With Everand's help … perhaps. If the slippery apprentice could be controlled. So far, Everand had been astoundingly compliant. Was that because he had the boatwoman as leverage? He reviewed their conversations so far. No, it was more than that. Everand was curious and wanted to know more about him. He came across as indecisive, as if biding his time. His hunter instincts advising caution, Malach swallowed then yawned so widely that his eyes watered. Caution was easy; it was knowing when to be bold that took more judgement.

Allowing his eyes to close, he welcomed the dream of striding by the lake in a brown robe, strong and oozing power.

Like his father.

Chapter Eleven

Everand listened to the breeze rustling through the upper branches of the trees, just audible above the cheery background burbling of the tributary. A faint orange glow lit the sky beyond the forest of trunks, and he assumed Malach was speaking to his people. Exploring fingers found his hand and unclenched his fingers, one by one.

'Let's move back to the wall,' said Lamiya, her voice floating from the gloom. She pulled on his hand, urging him to stand and follow. Something clattered under his feet. Malach had left the plates on the blanket. The blanket. He reached down to grab it and dragged it with him, the plates and flasks tumbling onto the ground.

'Here,' said Lamiya.

Putting out a hand, he felt the coarse lattice of the cage wall. Turning his back to it, he draped the blanket around his shoulders. 'Let me sit and hold you,' he murmured, sliding down the wall, pulling some blanket under his bottom and spreading his legs. Lamiya tripped over his ankle and then positioned her back against his chest and snuggled into him. With a deep sigh, he rested his chin on top of her head, loving the way her hair tickled. He hugged her close, and she grasped his arms.

'Everand ...' she said tentatively.

He tensed. Not more questions! Didn't she ever grow tired?

'Thank you.'

'For what?' he mumbled.

She hugged his arms against her. 'For trying to help us. For coming for me.' When she shivered, he felt the reverberations against his chest.

Words failed him. How could he not have come for her? He didn't deserve her reprieve; Malach had only taken her because of him. But she knew that, and she continued to follow and trust him. Emotion rolled through him; he so wanted her.

Extracting a hand, he swept her hair back over her shoulder, feeling the soft, silky strands and seeing in his mind the shining mahogany waves with hints of caramel and blue threads. His fingers caressed the elegant line of her neck, which he so adored. Warmth eddying through him, he planted a kiss behind her ear. She wriggled and drew in a sharp breath. Travelling down her neck, he planted a series of soft kisses, enjoying the way she pushed back into him.

Heat gathered in his groin and he paused, resting his lips against her silken skin, breathing in the essence of her. Was this wise, when they couldn't follow through? Not here in this cage. His mouth had other ideas and he licked the side of her neck, delighted at her low moan. Brushing his lips over her skin, he travelled up her neck. She moaned again and twisted in his arms. Her lips touched his chin, nibbling gently and moving higher. Teasing, he lifted his chin and then gasped when she ran her tongue up his throat and hot desire bolted through him.

'Lamiya,' he croaked. Her tongue rasped up his throat again and a deep, husky groan started in his groin and gushed up and out through his lips. Any restraint fled and he pressed his mouth onto hers and kissed her for all he was worth. Distantly, he felt her arms sliding up around the back of his neck, and then she pulled him down even harder. He slipped his tongue into her mouth and touched her tongue, shuddering at the moan that rocked her. Her arms tightened and the tip of her tongue wandered into his mouth, exploring.

Barely able to breathe, he was lost in heat and a crashing desire to run his hands over all of her, to get to know her every fold and curve, to part her legs and drive himself into her. *Not now! Not here, not like this.*

When the pressure in his groin became unbearable, he sobbed into her mouth and tore himself away, resting his head on top of hers and crushing her against his chest. Trembling, she pressed against him. Kissing the top of her head, he waited until his body calmed.

As his breath steadied and his heart slowed, his mind jumped into action. *This* was what had been between Elemar and Rhyan, the chestnut-haired warrior from her world who came to fetch her. Twice, Elemar had given herself to him — out of gratitude for saving her life and perhaps some affection — but what she'd shared with him was *nothing* like this. The two times he'd made love with Elemar it had been a tender, respectful sharing. But she could *never* have chosen him when she felt *this* for Rhyan.

Playing with Lamiya's hair, he conjured an image of Elemar's warrior face and cropped dark hair. *Farewell, Elemar. I understand, now. I thank you and release you from my heart.* He kissed the top of Lamiya's head again; this was where his heart was meant to be. If he lived long enough.

Lamiya crawled her fingers up his chest to caress his cheek. 'You're thinking again. I can tell.'

'Mmn,' he murmured into her scalp. 'Nice thoughts.'

'Good,' she said smugly.

'Get some sleep,' he mumbled. 'Who knows what Malach has planned for us when it grows light.'

Slipping her fingers into his, Lamiya whispered, 'We will escape, won't we?'

'We must.' He couldn't promise her more, but Malach hadn't killed them yet, just as Mage Beetal hadn't killed him or Elemar despite multiple opportunities. Even though he knew it wasn't yet expedient for Malach to kill him, perhaps the half-mage was also reluctant to do so. Especially given his link to Malach's father. Holding onto this notion, he let sleep claim him.

☾

His rapidly beating heart jolted him awake. It was pitch dark. What had woken him? The moon was only halfway down her arc, a pale shadow behind the gauzy, drifting clouds.

'Wake up,' Lamiya hissed, shaking his arms.

Running his tongue around his teeth, he wished they had some water to rinse away the bitter remnants of the wine. In his arms, Lamiya was wide awake and simmering with nervous energy, but peering into the gloom he saw nothing untoward. His ears only detected the babbling brook and the whispering of the pine needles.

'I can sense Whirr,' she said urgently.

'Whirr?' The bird was far away in Riverfall. What was she saying?

'He's nearby.' Lamiya's fingers pinched his arms. 'Lazuli! They're coming for us!' Her voice wavered.

Alertness flooded into him and he reached for his power to extend his senses. It hovered tantalisingly beyond his reach and he flexed his fingers in annoyance. 'Are you sure?'

'Yes! Their presence is getting stronger. Let's go to the door.' Scrambling to her feet, she started to edge along the wall.

Keeping the blanket draped over his shoulders, he stood up and followed: his turn to trust her. At the door, she fidgeted, shuffling her feet. He squeezed his eyes tightly shut then opened them wide and stared into the dark silhouettes of the trees. Hunched shapes drew his attention and he gazed hard, concluding after a few breaths the shapes were rocks. Skimming his eyes around the space, he found nothing out of place.

He swept his gaze back. Wait! The clump of rocks now looked closer. Or was he imagining what he hoped for? His lips twitched when the rocks shuffled several paces closer, the grey outlines wobbling. Letting the blanket fall to the ground, he put his hands on Lamiya's shoulders, whispering, 'You have good and brave friends.'

A small object hurtled out of the darkness. Whirr flew through the bars and thumped against Lamiya's chest. His excited peep was cut off when she pinched his beak to keep him quiet.

'What about the caged birds? Will they make a noise?' Everand said urgently. Under his hands, her shoulders moved in a shrug.

The moving rocks reached the edge of the trees, gliding soundlessly like shadows. Impressive. Two shadows approached the cage where he stood, and he jumped when white eyes suddenly gleamed in the darkness. They had blackened their faces!

'Traveller!' said Beram. 'Let's go.'

Everand waited while Beram and the other shadow eased the solid bars out of their keepers and the cage door opened. Lamiya stepped lightly through the gap and was enveloped by the other shadowy figure. Lazuli.

When he followed her out of the cage, in the darkness Beram's warm hands grasped his.

'This way,' said Beram.

A loud screech sounded behind them, and Everand froze. Another screech split the air and the talons of the raptors clacked as the birds moved on their perches.

'Help me release them.' Lamiya fumbled for his hand.

Hesitating, he whispered, 'Won't they attack us?'

'They despise their cages. Plummet told me.' She tugged at his hand.

Plummet? Never mind, trust her. Lazuli and Beram hovered by the first cage while he and Lamiya slipped along the row of cages, brushing their hands along the wooden rails to guide them. At the third cage, a sleek bird with a white face and grey body flew out of the darkness to grip the bars with its talons and cock its head at Lamiya.

'There, my lovely, we'll free you,' she murmured. 'Tell your friends to be quiet and allow us to pass, and we'll free all of you.' The bird snapped its beak. 'Help me,' she said over her shoulder.

He slipped the bars up and she pulled the cage door ajar. Plummet swooped out the small gap, banked tightly and flew back over the cage to disappear into the trees.

'Let's close all the doors. Let Malach wonder what happened.' Lamiya's teeth flashed white in a grin. 'That'll teach him to cage things.'

Every one of the freed raptors dipped a beak in salute at Lamiya before flying silently into the trees — away from the cabins and village. Still, Everand worried that the free-roaming eagles would discover them and alert Malach. There was a lot of ground to cover before they reached the river, and it might be light before they got there. Frowning, he followed Lamiya back along the cages. Maybe he'd be able to access some of his power by the time it grew light. Being attacked by numerous eagles would be an unpleasant way to die. The back of his head throbbed at the memory of two eagles tearing out clumps of his hair.

Back at the first cage, they slid into step behind Beram and Lazuli. By squinting, Everand discerned that they wore long dark-grey cloaks, black tunics and ankle-length black trousers and soft boots. He felt distinctly visible. When they merged into the trees, three more shadows rose from the ground.

Ejad, grinning wildly from his sooty face, handed him a long grey cloak. Larimar tapped his elbow in greeting before passing a cloak to Lamiya. The other shadow stepped close and before he could react, Mookaite slapped a mixture of mud and ashes onto his cheeks and smeared it all over his face. Glancing sideways, he saw Lamiya's face was already black and she was tying a grey scarf over her hair. With a finger to her lips, Mookaite positioned him and Lamiya in the middle of the line. They set off, weaving their way through the trees and threading past clumps of boulders, followed by Beram and Ejad with Larimar guarding the rear.

The bubbling of the tributary grew louder, and Everand understood they were skirting the village of cabins and making their way towards the small lake and channel. Had they brought a boat that far? How had they got past the shattered bridge and debris in the river? While he walked, he rolled his shoulders. His bruised feet protested at yet more walking, but it was good to be out of the cage. When they reached the tributary, Lazuli swung right, leading them along it until they got to the narrow channel the Riverwood crew had used to take their boat into the small lake.

Lazuli held up a hand to halt the group, and Mookaite said over her shoulder, 'You'll need to balance well or crawl.'

Dim moonlight gleamed along a narrow, solid surface — they'd felled a tree and dropped it across the channel. Everand's mouth went dry when Lazuli ran lightly across. Mookaite walked calmly across and, tentatively, Everand stepped onto the tree trunk. It felt stable enough, but the curve of the trunk promised a dunking if his feet slipped. Fixing his gaze firmly on the far bank, he took a breath and strode out. Halfway across, his balance wavered and he ran, using the momentum to carry him to the far bank. He jumped off and stumbled onto his hands and knees.

'As elegant as usual, I see,' Lamiya said, completely poised as she stepped off the trunk.

Brushing the grass off his knees and hands, he watched Ejad run lightly across. To his surprise, Beram and Larimar then grabbed the far end of the tree, and Lazuli and Ejad took hold of the nearer end. Between them, with a few grunts, they tipped the tree trunk and wedged it diagonally in the channel. When they crossed, Beram and Larimar jumped up and down to push it below the water's surface, until only a few gnarled branches poked up.

'Two can play at that game,' said Lazuli sourly. 'They'll have to carry their boat to launch it now.'

Clever. That would slow any pursuit, especially if Riverwood didn't realise the tree was there until they tried to take the boat down the channel. The others moved around like silvery outlines of hollow ghosts and, looking up, Everand saw that to the east the sky was already growing silver with the hint of approaching light. Putting a finger to his lips, Beram jerked his head in a diagonal direction, indicating they were to head across country through the long grasses. Everand nodded, trusting they had opted for the fastest route, but they'd be exposed and more vulnerable in the open grasslands.

Mookaite passed around flasks of water and everyone took a few mouthfuls. While wiping his mouth, Everand noticed the men's cloaks sat awkwardly over their backs, as if they had hunches. Curious, he lifted the edge of Beram's cloak. A bow and pouch of arrows, the newly shaved wood showing palely in the grey light. A tinge of grief coursing through him, he lowered the flap of the cloak. So, it may yet come to violence.

Lazuli swept his hand in the direction they were to take and took off at a swift run. The others drew in a breath and charged after him. With a gasp, Everand forced his legs into a run. The paddlers were fit. How far did they intend to keep this pace? After the initial burst, Lazuli settled into a steady lope. Even so, Everand struggled to keep up, ignoring his aching feet as they quickly left the last of the trees behind.

The waving sea of grasses all looked the same, and the seeded heads brushed against his knees and thighs, leaving stinging scratches. Wondering how Lazuli knew where to go,

Everand kept his eyes firmly locked on the heels of Mookaite, following her exact path. Sweat trickled down his neck and under his arms, and still they ran. When Lazuli veered a few paces to the right, he glanced up and realised that the colourful speck ahead was Whirr, guiding their path. The boat must be at the river, ready to take them across. Clever. They had halved the distance that would have been required if they'd paddled all the way.

The grasses changed from waving grey stalks to dancing yellow-golds and greens and the sun rose directly ahead, casting those ahead of him as fleeing silhouettes. As he'd anticipated, they were running more or less due east on a trajectory that would take them to the river a bit north of Zuqart, to the Riverwood bank opposite the waterwheel. A strange birdcall sounded ahead and Whirr shifted to the right, with Lazuli altering course too. A figure rose up from the grasses and Everand smiled when Acim slapped hands with Lazuli and fell into step in second position. Were they nearly there? His feet hoped so. His tunic clung soddenly to his back, but at least he was warm.

His thighs burned from the sustained effort, and as soon as he brushed sweat away from his eyes, more sweat dripped. The gold-green grasses swayed in an endless sea. Surely, they must be near the river by now. His legs stretched out of their own accord and the ache in his thighs eased. His feet, however, slapped the ground harder. They were running downhill. Another of the strange birdcalls sounded and Zink emerged from the grasses, grinned at him and Lamiya, and fell in behind them.

The downhill slope steepened and Everand's heart beat wildly at the glimpse of the blue band of river. They were going to make it unchallenged!

Just then, Lazuli looked over his shoulder and sped up. Cursing, Everand lengthened his stride, his feet protesting loudly and his breath coming hard in his chest. Whirr banked, wings blurring as he hurtled to reach Lamiya.

'The eagles!' shouted Lamiya.

Shoulders tensing, Everand fought the urge to turn around to look. Driving with his arms, he fought to keep up while the group bolted down the slope. The water glimmered an enticing blue, but they were not safe just because they had reached the river. He shook his head, scattering drops of sweat, and squinted. There! Two more people by the water's edge, holding the blue-and-gold dragon boat adjacent to the bank. The carved dragon head and tail just poked up above the reeds.

Gasping for air, he slid to a stop when the others did. At the boat, still three hundred paces away, Tengar and Lulite were staring grimly back up the slope. When Everand began to twist around to look too, Beram and Mookaite grabbed his arms and pushed him.

'You and Lamiya in the middle,' Beram snapped.

Drawing in ragged breaths, Everand crouched and pulled Lamiya close to him while the others formed a protective circle. His mouth tightened when the others unslung their bows and tugged arrows out of their sheaths. A cloud of enormous brown-and-white eagles swooped down the slope; far too many to be felled by arrows.

A cold shiver running down his arms, Everand reached to his innermost core — and his power simmered and shifted, sliding around while he tried to grasp it. He moaned in frustration.

'Are you alright?' Lamiya's frightened question reached him.

Clasping both of her hands, he faced her. 'Help me call my power!'

She squeezed his hands and he felt her presence infusing him, her courage seeping through the touch. Trying again, he travelled down the lines to his pool of power and coaxed it to come. It slithered around, as if sulking from having been quelled. Lamiya sent a surge of energy through his hands, telling it to behave.

A snort of laughter went up his nose and he grabbed handfuls of power. Drawing shiny, vibrant power to him, his chest expanded while he summoned the spell of warding and threw a protective dome over the circled group. A heartbeat later the sky went dark with the mass of eagles flying above. A volley of rocks and stones rained down, bouncing off the shield with cracks like lightning and rolling down the sides like rumbling thunder.

The others stared at him in wonder.

'Can we shoot through it?' yelled Lazuli, hefting his bow in his hands.

Curse it! He should have thought of that. Coaxing more power to him so he could adjust the shield, he sweated with concentration when the shield wavered and wobbled. Around him, the others murmured uneasily, watching him with anxious eyes. It was as if he were back at the beginning of his training, when he could only do one thing at a time and his power threatened to slide away at the slightest excuse.

After what seemed an eternity, he adjusted the warding so that it would allow objects to pass outwards. More sweat trickled into his eyes. 'Lamiya, tell me what's happening so I can focus on the shield.'

'The eagles are circling. They will dive in at us.' She squeezed his hands.

'Can you warn me? Can you talk to them?'

Her hands anchored in his, she was silent for a moment. Then her hands trembled. 'No. Their minds are beyond reach. They are intent on killing.'

Everand sighed. So, Malach had used the personality-adjuster compound before he sent the birds, or he'd honed their aggression through training. 'Tell the others they must kill them.'

'They come!' gasped Lamiya, and chaos erupted.

As if in a bubble, he bent his will to the shield, hearing the others' yells, the zing of arrows and the thuds of eagles battering against the barrier. Closing his ears to the cacophony, he fumbled for more power. Thank the stars, it responded and he fed crackling fire energy into the shield. The smell of charred feathers wafted, and a roaring and fizzling added to the chaos.

A shudder rippled through Lamiya and her sorrow eked through her hands. Suddenly her fingers pinched his and she screamed, 'Lulite!'

Distracted, he opened his eyes, his heart racing. 'What?'

Snatching her hands away, Lamiya stood up. 'Lulite and Tengar! The boat!'

Unthinking, he stood too and swept his gaze around him. The others stood with their sides heaving, lathered in grime and sweat. A circle of dead and dying eagles spread out from the perimeter of the shield. Broken arrows lay scattered on the ground as well as buried in birds. When he turned to face the river, the shield wavered annoyingly, and he fed more power into it.

Alarmed, he gasped at the sight of six eagles harrying Tengar and Lulite while they tried to keep hold of the boat. Lulite was hauling on a mooring rope looped around the dragon neck, her shoulders hunched protectively, and Tengar was wielding the glide oar as a weapon, fending an eagle away from her back.

With a shriek, Lamiya sprinted towards them. Curse her! He dropped the shield and charged after her. Drawing power while he ran, he reached her side just as an eagle swooped in, talons stretched out, screeching fit to wake the dead. Anger surged down his arms and the eagle exploded in a ball of flaming feathers.

A few paces away, with a loud thwack, Tengar hit the eagle attacking Lulite. When it dropped, stunned, Tengar hammered the oar blade on its head, its screeches pitiful as it died.

The four remaining eagles circled cautiously. Ready for them, Everand flexed his fingers, trying to dampen down his anger so he could think straight.

Breathing hard, Beram and the others joined them and reached into the boat to grab their paddles. 'Four left,' said Beram, sounding tired.

Everand looked at the empty pouches. They were all out of arrows. 'Maybe. This is only half the number of eagles that destroyed the bridge.' Decided, he hurled a fire bolt at each eagle, until none circled.

Beram ran his hand over his face, leaving an interesting array of white and black streaks. Ejad, Acim and Zink cheered, and Lamiya hugged Lulite.

Holding up a hand to get their attention, Everand said, 'Don't board yet. Malach knows where we are. Better we face the next attack while we're on firm ground.' Tremors were running down his arms and legs from the exertion and he set his jaw, worrying whether his reserve of power would be sufficient.

Sunlight now cascaded over the river surface and the sea of grasses waved in vivid golds and greens. Above, far up the slope, the dark line of trees stood like soldiers guarding the hilltop.

Malach was not done yet.

Chapter Twelve

Hugging Lulite tightly, Lamiya gasped, 'I thought I'd never see you again!'

Her friend stepped back and grabbed her arms. 'We were so afraid for you. We had to stop Lazuli from swimming across the river to go to your rescue!'

Whirr peeped a warning from inside her tunic and, tearing her gaze away from Lulite's dear face, Lamiya saw the others were all staring up the slope with expressions of disbelief and horror. Her breath caught in her throat. 'What is *that*?' A line of eagles was visible on the skyline, but the object in the centre drew her focus.

'Go! Stand next to the Traveller.' Lulite gave her a rough push, her face pale.

Already, Everand was looming beside her, his forehead pinched in a fierce frown. 'Malach comes.'

Shading her eyes with her hand, Lamiya squinted up the slope. The weird object flying down the hill distilled into four eagles carrying a sturdy branch, two at each end. The body and legs dangling down in the centre belonged to a person hanging onto the branch — Malach. Fear rippled through her at how incredibly strong and determined Malach was. Another line of eagles followed and, her fear multiplying, she scanned the grasses. Were his men coming too? They'd never get away in the boat now. She slipped her hand into Everand's.

Once Malach had halved the gap, Everand spun her to face him. 'You must stay here. Promise me.'

Her entire being went cold: he intended to challenge Malach! Grabbing his arms, she said, 'No! Don't go!'

Unpicking her fingers from his sleeve, Everand passed her hands into Lulite's, saying, 'Make sure she stays here. Your lives depend on it.'

Lamiya squirmed, tugging to extract her hands from Lulite's grip, but her friend held her so tightly her knuckles were going white. When Everand planted a kiss on her forehead, her heart panged as if it were breaking. After a tense smile, he stepped away and began to stride up the slope. Her feet tried to follow, but Lazuli and Larimar came to stand on either side of her, their shoulders brushing hers. Lazuli gave her a grim smile, his eyes bright amid an array of mud, ashes and blood.

Horror rising, she fixed her eyes on Everand's back as he toiled up the slope, aligning his path to greet Malach. The protective shield around him glinted with all the colours of a sky-arch, and he was curling and uncurling his fingers, drawing power. Her throat was clenched so tightly she could barely breathe.

The line of eagles fanned out and the four eagles carrying the branch flew to just above the ground, hovering with majestic, slow flaps of their wings. Malach stretched his feet down, stood squarely and released the branch. The eagles set down on the grass, barely visible except for the tops of their heads above the rustling and waving grass stems. Without a word, Malach balled his fist and a dark crimson bolt flew at Everand.

Lamiya's heart stuttered: he could do that? A blue bolt flew out from Everand's hand, crashed into the crimson one mid-air, and both dissolved into prisms of crimson and blue, tinkling down like petals dropping. The others murmured and Lamiya's lips twitched.

Nudging Larimar aside, Lulite hung onto her arm. 'Will he kill him?' she asked, eyes wide.

'I don't know.' Lamiya's heart hammered so fast her ears were ringing. 'He wanted Everand to train him!' But Malach's face was like a thundercloud and he looked angry beyond reason.

Giving her a wilder look, Lulite said, 'No … will Ever-what, the Traveller, kill *him*?'

Fear crashed through Lamiya. *Would* Everand kill Malach? She wouldn't have thought it possible but now, with the paddlers and her at risk, would Everand kill a person? Her stomach twisted painfully. Could she love him if he did? Or would she be afraid of him? Her heart melted. This was a defining choice for him. How could he bear it, to be faced with one difficult decision after another? She could see the bands of muscle in his neck and shoulders were corded with tension.

'Well?' Lulite gave her arm a shake. 'Will he?'

'Not unless he has to.' Lamiya shook her head.

Lazuli gave her an intent look, his eyebrows pinching together and causing new patterns in the mess on his face. 'How will we escape if he doesn't?' He blew out a breath. 'How does the Riverwood man have this power? I don't understand.'

Twisting her hands, trying to contain her nerves, Lamiya said, 'I will explain … later.'

'There is much I would like you to explain.' Lazuli gave her a terse glance.

Around a swallow, she said, 'I will. All of it.'

'Count me in,' said Lulite dryly. 'I'd also like to know what's going on!'

Such dear and loyal friends! Warmth spread through Lamiya and Whirr fidgeted inside her tunic, his feathers tickling her chest. A sharp crack sounded and she jumped. Everand had deflected another bolt from Malach mid-air and crimson, blue and silver shards drifted down, sparkling in the sunshine.

Malach squared his shoulders and roared, 'Surrender and I will spare your little friends!'

The 'little' friends shifted restlessly, gripping their paddles. Tengar muttered, 'Audacious, considering the Traveller has more power.'

Yes, thought Lamiya, but what had Everand once said? *He is not bound by the Guild constraints, as I am.* That was it. She so admired his integrity and clear set of values — things Malach did not possess. She chewed her lip, worrying that his integrity might not help him now.

Everand said evenly, 'I ask again, what do you want? What are you trying to achieve?'

'Good question,' said Lazuli grudgingly.

'Yes,' muttered Ejad. 'This is seriously disrupting our training!'

The others laughed in a brief release of tension and Lamiya gave the young paddler a fond smile.

Hearing their laughter, Malach's face tightened in fury. 'You are to train me!' he snarled at Everand.

Calmly tipping his head to one side, Everand said, 'That part I understood. For what purpose?'

'To be a mage. Like my father.'

Lamiya held her breath. That wasn't what Everand was asking, but did it matter if they could reach some agreement? That seemed to be Everand's style: solve this dilemma and then prepare for the next one.

'If I do train you, will you leave the people of Riverfall alone?'

Her pulse beat in her throat. Surely, he wouldn't submit to Malach! Grief ripped through her: he had said he would go to Riverplain with her. She shivered. She couldn't, wouldn't, go to Riverwood. Not again. 'No,' she whispered.

'Look to the crest,' murmured Lazuli.

While the silence stretched interminably, the outlines of Riverwood men appeared along the ridge above — many more than the boat team, and all carrying spears or crossbows. A shudder rippled across her shoulders. If Malach didn't agree, they'd *all* be forced to kill. How had it come to this?

Everand stepped closer to Malach and Lamiya strained to hear what he was saying.

'Choose wisely. My power has returned and you threaten my friends.' When Malach didn't respond, he spread his hands. 'I am your *only* chance to learn. Any other mage from the Guild would despise you, for they are not fond of your father.' Frustration edged his words. 'Choose, Malach, before your men arrive and it's too late. Lead them wisely.'

'You would do this?' asked Malach gruffly.

Lamiya's chest ached when Everand took another step towards Malach and she could only see his back. Suddenly, his words bounced in her head and she could also hear Malach! He was projecting to her. Noticing that Beram's face was screwed up in concentration, she tapped him. 'You can hear him?'

'I can. We are to witness whatever is agreed.' Beram shrugged. 'Or *not* agreed.'

She focused back on Everand, who inclined his head and said sincerely, 'I *will* teach you because you are the son of my former mentor. You deserve the opportunity to reach your potential and to know what kind of mage he was. I'll tell you more about Mage Beetal and the Guild — but I insist you use your power more wisely than he did.'

'And if I don't agree?' rasped Malach.

If only Malach would see reason! Lamiya held her breath. Everand was being entirely fair, so why, by all the spirits, was Malach being so obstinate? What was wrong with him?

'Your eagles and men will be adrift without their leader. And if they seek to avenge you, they'll find the other river provinces united in more than a trade agreement.'

'You threaten me,' Malach snarled.

Of their own accord, Lamiya's hands flew to her mouth. Had Everand just told Malach he would kill him? *No, no, no.* She almost couldn't bear to watch. Whirr poked his head out of her tunic and snapped his beak.

'No,' said Everand. 'I answered your question as it was asked. I prefer we reach agreement.' He tilted his head. 'There's one more thing you must know: the Guild will not sanction your existence, or me teaching you. We must be discreet, or we will *both* find ourselves facing the ire and might of the Guild.'

'Why would you risk this?' asked Malach, his words brittle with suspicion.

A smile laced Everand's reply. 'You know why. I have chosen to follow my heart and remain here in the provinces. If I were to return to the Guild and tell the mages about you, you'd have no choice and no opportunity to learn.' He shrugged. 'For the last time, I ask you to choose.'

Lamiya's heart skipped and thudded erratically. He would stay, as he'd promised! But what Malach said next would define both of them — and what happened here. Around her, the others stood rigidly, sensing the critical moment had arrived even if they couldn't hear the words. Tengar scowled so hard she thought his face might crack. Time seemed to slow while Everand and Malach faced off, and the waves moving through the grasses showed Malach's men were picking their way down the slope.

Suddenly, Malach raised an arm and Everand promptly lifted his, blue power crackling in his palm. Lamiya couldn't take her eyes away. *This was it.* Bile rushed into her throat: he was going to kill Malach.

Malach dropped his arm sharply and the Riverwood men stopped where they were. Then he flung his arm wide and the curve of eagles lifted up from the grass, banked and flew away up the slope. When Malach repeated the dropping motion with his arm, his men sat down where they were.

Hope pulsing through her, Lamiya swallowed painfully. This was too good to be true.

'Wise choice.' Everand bowed.

'You'd better not try to deceive me. Bring your woman to make sure you stay focused.' Standing taller, Malach glanced her way.

An icy chill shivered through Lamiya, but Everand shook his head. 'There are things I must do first. I will come to you in … four sun-ups.'

'No. Come with me now.' Malach grunted and clenched his fists.

Everand looked down the hill at her, and then back at Malach. 'No. I have a promise to honour. You have my word. I will come to train you in four sun-ups.'

'You expect me to let you go now and trust you will come? I'm not a fool!' Shaking a fist, Malach advanced a step.

'You have my word. Wait for me on the shore of Dragon Lake at the fourth sun-up.'

'You ask much.'

'I'm not the only one asking much,' snapped Everand. 'You've shown me what you're capable of, and I'm sure there will be consequences if I don't come when stated. Let's leave it at that.'

Malach spat on his hand and held it out. Intrigued, Lamiya watched Everand do the same, although distaste eked through his words. 'Until the fourth sun-up.'

When Malach turned around and marched up the slope towards his men, Lamiya released a long, slow breath. Why didn't Everand simply fell the man now? That would end all the trouble. She sighed, knowing he'd never even contemplate doing such a cowardly thing. But what if Malach tried to trap him when he went back? She shook her head. Why was everything always so complicated?

Everand loped down the hill and when he reached the group she held back while the others cheered and clapped him on the back.

Finally, his eyes met hers — and they were filled with misery, not triumph.

CHAPTER THIRTEEN

Before Lamiya could say anything to Everand, Tengar yelled for the paddlers to board and everyone began to wade through the reeds to the boat. If only they were alone so she could talk to Everand! How could they get to know each other when they were constantly surrounded by people and caught up in reacting to events?

'I'll glide,' Tengar said. 'You and Everand sit in the back row. The others will paddle.'

Fatigue coursed through her limbs now the danger had passed, her feet were numb and she was suddenly sleepy. For once, she plodded over the benches rather than skipping over them, and eased onto the last one. When Everand settled beside her, she leaned against him. 'Well done,' she murmured.

'Maybe,' he said shortly, slipping his arm around her waist.

On Tengar's command, the boat ploughed out into the middle of the river. The waterwheel loomed progressively larger as they powered straight across to the Riverfall side of the river before Tengar turned the boat and they paddled briskly south towards the boat ramp. Despite having had no sleep, the crew paddled strongly, the boat skimming along the water. At least the more direct route was shorter than when she was kidnapped and taken north, and the boat was running with the current. Before too long, the walls of Zuqart came into view.

Despondently, Lamiya looked at the pink walls of the town gliding by. The colourful tents had all been packed away and the town was quiet. What had happened at the trade discussions? She must ask Lulite for the details. When would Riverplain host the races?

Her neck gave a warning twinge, threatening to cramp, and she became aware of Everand's head leaning heavily on her shoulder. His eyes were closed and his face was relaxed in sleep! Adjusting her position to better take his weight, she reached over to hold the hand resting in his lap. His fingers felt cold; he was probably exhausted. A smile tugging at her lips, she reflected that as a scholar of magic this was probably the most exercise he'd ever done. Maybe he'd enjoy training with her and the team and growing fitter.

She felt her eyebrows pull into a frown. He'd said he had a promise to honour. Was he only going to Riverplain because he'd said he would?

Stirring, Everand adjusted his head on her shoulder and murmured, 'I'm looking forward to seeing where you live.'

Startled, she muttered back, 'Can you read minds even when asleep?'

He let a few heartbeats go by. 'Your body gave you away. Such tension for such a small person.'

'Nice,' she said. 'For someone with such a heavy head!'

He squeezed her fingers and his mouth twitched. A longing to kiss the twitch away arose and she released another sigh. Perhaps she should learn how to block her thoughts; it could be awkward to be read so easily all of the time. A groan escaped her when his lips etched into a smile. 'Stop it!' she hissed.

'You're distracting me,' said Tengar from behind. 'Let me focus to bring the boat in.'

Lifting her gaze, she saw they were level with the boat ramp and Tengar was already lining Mizuchi up. Atage and Lyber and a number of townspeople were hurrying along the path to the ramp and a lump lodged in her throat when they waved and cheered. The boat slid in straight, and she had to persuade her jelly-like legs to stand up.

As soon as they were on the ramp, Atage rushed down to grasp Everand's hands. 'Are you unharmed? We're so relieved to see you back!' Spinning around, Atage grabbed her hands. 'You too, Lamiya. Are you alright?'

She nodded, flustered by the attention as others crowded around and shoulders were clapped and hands slapped. Their rescuers were heroes and Acim, Zink and Ejad basked in the attention, grinning like idiots and giving sweeping bows to everyone.

Mookaite took her arm. 'You and Everand must come to my dome so I can check you over. Some herbal brew will do you good.' The healer paused. 'I'll tell Beram. You can meet with Atage after.'

Hesitantly, Lamiya said, 'I must find out what my team wants to do. They're probably anxious to go home.'

Peering up at the sky then back at her with a frown, Mookaite said, 'It's still early. See you soon.' She moved away to murmur in Beram's ear.

Considering what to say, Lamiya approached her paddlers. Clasping each of their hands in turn, she said, 'I can't thank you enough.' They fidgeted modestly and she fought back tears of humility. 'Seriously, you were all so brave.' She sniffed when Lulite brushed at her eyes with the back of her hand.

'Luvu said we should bring you back or not bother to return.' Lazuli gave her a strangled smile.

'He did?' She was astonished that the gruff paddler should have said any such thing. Looking around, she asked, 'Where are the others?'

'Packing up the dome,' said Lulite gently. 'They're keen to leave now you're safe.'

'Fair enough,' said Lamiya.

Lulite added, 'Luvu said he'd glide. We can paddle Flight home with eight paddlers. You and the Traveller … should go in the cart with Lapsi.' Lamiya opened her mouth but her friend continued, 'It has been decided, Lamiya. The other carts have already left.'

Humbled, Lamiya swallowed. 'I am grateful. We can eat and get changed before we go?'

'Of course,' said Lulite with a tired smile. 'We all need a good wash!'

Reaching up, Lazuli scraped a wad of ash and mud off his face and flicked it onto the ground. His eyes narrowing, he looked at her and said, 'I could dunk you in the river to speed the process up.'

Taking a step backwards, Lamiya smiled. 'Warm water would be nicer!' Her stomach grumbled alarmingly. 'And I'm famished. Malach's courtesy leaves a lot to be desired.' She shivered. 'He served roasted bird for us to eat!' Whirr peeped indignantly, and the disbelief on the others' faces made her laugh.

'Did you eat it?' asked Larimar, looking queasy.

She shook her head, not telling them Everand had eaten her portion as well as his own.

They moved off as a group and she gave Everand a brief wave, given that he was deep in conversation with Atage and Beram. He sketched a wave back with one hand.

☪

Soon clean, dressed in fresh clothes and her tummy pleasantly full of savoury loaves and grilled fish fillets, Lamiya walked to Mookaite's dome humming. Her paddlers had tumbled over themselves in excitement to tell her that Riverplain would host the next inter-province races and trade gathering. Already, they were proposing a challenging mix of races and activities. Her pulse lifted thinking about the new drills she might devise. Lazuli's idea for a backwards race was clever, and would need some practice. His other suggestion for the straightest race without the glide would prove interesting too.

Perhaps even better, two seasons after their turn, the races would be hosted by Riversea. How wonderful it would be to go to Riversea and see the ocean and the massive sandhills. Best of all, Everand would be with her and they could share new scenery and learn about other people.

Scents of lavender and roses wafted out from Mookaite's dome. 'May I enter?'

'Come in,' called Mookaite cheerfully.

Pushing through the curtain, she found Beram and Everand seated at the low table sipping mugs of brew. Apart from giving her a nervous smile, Everand looked refreshed and the dark-blue tunic he wore accentuated his eyes. Mookaite motioned for her to sit and placed a steaming mug in front of her.

Beram spoke. 'We're discussing whether in four sun-ups Everand will go straight from Riverplain to Riverwood to see Malach, or come here to visit us on the way.'

Her eyes rocketing to Everand's face, Lamiya pushed down a kernel of anxiety that he intended to go through with his promise to Malach.

'If you come here first,' said Mookaite seriously, 'we can tell you if anything unusual has happened since you left.'

'I don't like it,' Beram rumbled to Everand. 'But I understand you must do this.'

With a kind look, Mookaite said to her, 'You're welcome to stay with us when Everand trains Malach, if you'd like.'

Surprised, Lamiya nodded, feeling her cheeks warm.

'When will you come?' Beram asked Everand.

Looking pensive, Everand said, 'The sun-fade before I start Malach's training, so three from now. We'll come by magic to save time.'

'Why did you choose four sun-ups from now? Is this significant?' Mookaite asked, putting her mug down.

With a wry smile, Everand replied, 'I was thinking on my feet. I doubted Malach would agree to any longer, and I need some time to think this through.' He gave Lamiya a nervous look. 'And I promised Lamiya I'd go to Riverplain.'

Beram slapped a knee and then drained his mug. 'Well, my friend, let's fetch your things before Lapsi arrives with the cart.' The two men stood and left.

Trying not to squirm under Mookaite's speculative look, Lamiya focused on sipping her brew.

'How do you feel?'

Sensing the question was about more than her bodily health, Lamiya hesitated and blew on her brew before she said, 'Fatigued, relieved, happy … and incredibly nervous.'

Mookaite smiled warmly. 'Take it easy, on all accounts. Your body needs to recover more,' she waved her hands, 'from the travel, the strenuous races and all your adventures.' Her look became serious. 'You've been in frightening situations. You must give your mind and spirit a chance to absorb this.'

That was a good point, Lamiya thought, and something she hadn't considered.

Stretching across the table to take her free hand, Mookaite said earnestly, her brown eyes filled with kindness, 'Everand adores you, Lamiya. This is clear from the look in his eyes and the way his face softens whenever you are nearby. You are a lucky woman.' She squeezed Lamiya's fingers. 'Take this part easy too. He is a powerful mage, but he's also a young man not much older than you. He, too, is being tumbled about like a pebble in an eddy. Be kind to each other and do not rush.'

Tears prickling the backs of her eyes, Lamiya gulped down her mouthful of brew, trying not to choke on it. Mookaite was so wise!

The healer stroked the back of her hand. 'You have good instincts. Follow them. You're also one of the bravest people I've met.' Flashing her a smile, she added, 'You need each other … you yearn for each other … just remember you're both dealing with tense and difficult situations as well.'

'Thank you.' Lamiya bowed her head and then sat quietly until she heard the rumbling of the cart wheels drawing close. Nerves abounding anew, she stood up.

At the curtain, Mookaite enveloped her in a fond embrace and kissed her cheek. 'May the winds follow your boat, Lamiya, and the sun shine on your heart.' Her eyes glinted. 'Come back with Everand and talk more with me. I'd like that.'

Beyond words at the healer's generosity and caring, she hugged Mookaite tightly, hurriedly stepping back when Whirr gave a protesting peep at being squashed inside her tunic.

'Let's go, Lamiya!' Lapsi called from the front of the cart. 'We have a long way to travel.' The two hopeepa stamped their hooves and flapped their ears.

Beram and Everand came striding up, and Beram placed a bundle on the back of the cart that she assumed were several changes of clothes for Everand. She gave Everand a shy smile, her heart racing when he looked at her and wiped his hands on his trousers. Was he nervous too? She felt an eyebrow arch. *Be kind ... he is also a young man.*

'Well, Traveller,' she said brightly. 'Are you ready to see Riverplain, the most magnificent of all the river provinces?'

The others laughed and Everand gave her a warm smile, his eyes turning an amazingly deep blue, before he climbed up onto the cart.

Lapsi patted the seat beside him, 'Up here, Lamiya.'

She watched Everand get settled on the platform at the back of the cart, wedging his lean frame between his bundle of clothes and a range of goods purchased from the trade stalls. Then, understanding that Lapsi wanted to talk to her, she climbed up and perched beside him. Lapsi flapped the reins and the hopeepa moved off at a brisk walk. Twisting sideways, she waved a cheery farewell to Mookaite and Beram, who stood with their arms around each other.

The cart passed through the courtyards, people pausing whatever they were doing to wave goodbye. Soon, her face felt stiff from so much smiling. The cart rumbled out through the southern gate and when they passed the boat ramp she said a fond farewell to it, the start of the glorious races.

'We did well, didn't we?' She grinned at Lapsi.

'It'll be difficult to do better at the next races,' he said wryly.

For a long while, Lamiya sat quietly taking in the scenery, which looked different from her perch on the cart as opposed to being in the boat. Whirr poked up out of her tunic, and his feathers tickled when he turned his little head this way and that. With the back of a finger, she stroked the top of his head and he gave a happy cheep.

'We're going home, my little guardian.' What would Everand make of her flock? Hopefully, he'd be impressed and as amazed by the array of colours and plumage as she always was.

The southern fields of crops ended and the cart travelled between the river, a blue-grey under the patchy clouds, and the start of the grassy plains. Realising that Everand hadn't said a word, she twisted around and peered down. He looked to be in a deep sleep, propped up by his bundle of clothes. A strand of starlight hair had fallen over his face, and she wished she could lean over and tuck it back behind his ear. Her gaze lingering, she pondered Mookaite's words. With his face relaxed, Everand did indeed look younger, but still disconcertingly desirable with his high cheekbones and strong, chiselled jaw.

Catching Lapsi watching her, his lips compressed in a thin line, an eddy of nerves washed through her: what would her people think about Everand being her partner?

'Is it alright that Everand comes to see Riverplain?' she asked softly, crossing her fingers that Everand wouldn't wake up and listen in.

His grey eyes turning darker, Lapsi gave her an assessing look. 'Opinion is mixed. Some worry that trouble will follow. Others don't mind, for he is honourable and personable enough.' He shook the reins to nudge the hopeepa into a faster trot. 'Mainly, we worry for you.'

Lamiya felt warmth stealing up her neck and across her cheeks.

Putting the reins into one hand, Lapsi patted her knee. 'Lulite tells me not to worry, that the Traveller would die before he let any harm come to you.' He took his hand away. 'But still.' He glanced sideways. 'Lulite wants you to talk with her. Part of her celebrates for you, part of her fears for you.'

Feeling chastised, Lamiya twisted her hands in her lap. She *had* told Lulite she'd talk to her about this matter of the heart.

'Lazuli is predictably upset, and he has those who side with him.'

'I know. I must talk to him.' Lamiya swallowed and bowed her head. 'Did everyone expect I would partner with Lazuli?'

'Yes and no. You two look to be a good match, but those who know you well could see that his feelings were stronger.' Lapsi shrugged. 'We thought maybe you needed more time to grieve for your parents, but now we see this wasn't so.'

Heat burned her cheeks and she fiddled with her fingers. 'It's hard to explain. Lazuli is my best friend, other than Lulite. He's like a brother, and my heart didn't change the way his seemed to. I feel awful I didn't notice how much his feelings had changed.' She paused. 'I was too absorbed with the races and the opportunity to glide the team. Do you think Lazuli will ever forgive me?'

'Tell him all of this. Lulite and I value you both and would see peace between you. Besides, we need the front and the back of the boat in harmony.' Lapsi gave her a kind smile.

Lamiya winced, conscious of the possible effect on the team. For a while she watched the water moving in the river, thinking about what she could do or say to make it easier for everyone.

From the way the river curved, they were nearing the tributary marking the boundary between Riverfall and

Riverplain, and the cart would need to veer inland to cross the bridge.

They swung around the last of the curve, and she spied the boat ahead and Luvu's solid back at the stern, holding the glide oar. Her spirits lifting, she sat up straighter.

Lapsi smacked the reins down and the hopeepa broke into a lope. The cart drew alongside the boat and when Luvu glanced over, she waved cheerfully. The paddlers lifted their paddles in salute and her heart soared.

Then the boat disappeared around the bend and the cart swung to the left to follow the inland path. The pair of hopeepa maintained the faster lope, eager to reach their herd.

'What should I do?' she asked Lapsi, hanging onto the seat rail while the cart bounced along the narrower path. Already the grasses were changing from the shorter, sparser pasture of Riverfall to the taller more varied mixture of alfalfa, rye and meadow grass of Riverplain.

'You'd be wise to take the Traveller to meet the province guides and explain who he is. Ask their permission for him to remain as a guest.' At her look, Lapsi added, 'In the meantime.'

'A good plan.' She sighed. 'Besides, I imagine word has already spread from those who reached home before us.'

'There is that,' said Lapsi.

Suddenly, her mouth felt bone dry. The cart bounced around another bend and the ground sloped downwards, leading to the tributary. Ahead, the wooden bridge fanned across the water. A hand grasped the railing at the back of her seat and she looked over her shoulder to see Everand sitting upright.

'Good timing,' she said. 'We're about to enter Riverplain.'

Chapter Fourteen

Everand pulled himself to standing, one hand on the back of the seat, the other massaging his sore neck. They were travelling through wide, flattish grasslands, moving away from the river. Now that he was awake, he couldn't find a comfortable spot between the sacks of things with hard shapes that felt like pottery, and bolts of colourful cloth. Wobbling to keep his balance, he asked Lapsi, 'Can I sit at the front too?'

Lapsi nodded and Lamiya smiled, shuffling across to make room. Balancing against the movement of the cart, he stepped over the seat rail and plopped onto the bench. The hopeepa were loping swiftly downhill towards a narrow band of river. When he shaded his eyes with a hand, he saw the bridge.

'Once we've crossed the bridge, we'll be in Riverplain,' explained Lamiya. 'This tributary is known as Dragonscale Creek.'

'Tell me more.' The more he understood before he met her people the better.

Tilting her head prettily, Lamiya said, 'After the bridge we enter the plain, where most of the hopeepa herds live. They graze the grasses, and we harvest some to make dry hay for the cold-season.'

Everand tried to recall what he knew of the team. 'So, Lepid, Lazuli and Levog breed hopeepa? And some of the people who arrived later with the other carts?'

'You remember well. Six families breed, train and care for the hopeepa.' Watching his face intently, she added, 'Lepid and Lazuli breed the strongest and finest hopeepa, and their animals are highly prized for breeding to improve the other herds.'

There was an undercurrent of tension in the way she fiddled with her fingers. Was she telling him to be careful around the brothers because they had standing in her province? 'I see.' Perhaps it would be best if he didn't say anything else.

Looking at Lapsi, he said, 'You are a fisherman?' When Lapsi nodded, he asked, 'Where do you fish?'

'Mainly in Dragonfoot Lake, which is near the village where most of us live. Sometimes we also travel to the river to catch different kinds of fish.'

'Larimar is a fisherman too?' Everand thought he remembered Lamiya telling him the pacer wanted to breed exotic colourful fish. He frowned. What should he do about his own exotic fish, Mizu, still in stasis in his rooms at the Mages' Guild?

'You're frowning.' Lamiya touched his knee but quickly withdrew her hand, conscious of Lapsi.

'My fish was sick and I put her in stasis to come on this mission.'

'What is this stas-thing?' asked Lamiya, and Lapsi also looked at him keenly.

Rubbing his jaw, he considered how to explain. 'I used magic to pause time around the fish so I could heal her when I return.' He stopped short: he wasn't going to return.

Her eyebrows creasing together, Lamiya gave him a troubled look. 'Is your fish important?'

'I'd like to get her and release her into a lake here. She is a beautiful silver fish with red patches.' Drumming his fingers on his knee, he wondered whether he would now get the opportunity.

Lapsi gave him an approving look, but Lamiya's frown deepened. Changing the subject, he asked, 'What sort of houses do you live in?'

After a pause, when Lamiya didn't speak, Lapsi said, 'We make squares from mud and rushes and stack these to make the walls. The roofs are made from a lattice of branches covered with bundles of thick grasses and rushes.'

Surprised, Everand thought these homes sounded quite different to the Riverfall pink-orange clay domes. From the old man Vogel's recounted history, the people of Riverfall and Riverplain shared a common ancestry, and he thought Vogel had said it was only two generations ago that the people had divided, with the more land-and-animal-focused group coming south. This was long enough for observable differences to emerge? Mantiss had asked him to find out about the provinces and, so far, his observations suggested the people were all quite different. Then he remembered he would not be delivering his report. He forced his spine and shoulders straighter; no use dwelling on his decision.

At the bridge, the hopeepa dropped back to a walk and their hooves clopped a merry tune as they crossed. The wood was a lighter colour than the other bridges he'd seen and the slats were narrower. He couldn't see many trees nearby, just waving grasses speckled with hints of vibrant colour. 'Where did the wood for the bridge come from?'

Lapsi answered. 'There are spirit trees near the hills before the cliffs. We fell the trees and shape the wood there, then bring it by cart to where we need it.'

Spirit trees? He guessed the tree trunks were white, rising like spirits from the ground. Elemar and her people had believed in spirits that lived in trees and rocks. He recalled how her face had lit up when she'd tried to explain these to him. Could he learn about the people of Riverplain fast enough not to offend anyone? Peeking sideways, he found Lamiya's face was marred by a slight frown. Was she nervous about introducing him? Perhaps she was anxious about what he would think of her lifestyle, given that it must be far simpler than that of the mages.

He lifted a hand to run it through his hair, caught the movement and put his hand back in his lap. The one time that Mage Beetal had taken him to Elemar's world of Terralis, he'd shuddered at the wild landscape and the fierce, primitive, warrior lifestyle — and had felt no desire whatsoever to stay there. He'd assumed Elemar would remain in Axis, with him. Unease travelled through him. Would he feel differently about Lamiya's people, or was he deluding himself that he could remain here?

The hopeepa finished clopping across the bridge and as soon as their hooves reached the path, they took off at a trot. While the long legs of the hopeepa covered the ground, Everand thought hard. What else did he need to know? Leaders — who were the Riverplain leaders? The trade negotiators had been people from the boat team.

'Who leads your province, and what should I call him? Or her,' he added hastily. Lamiya and Lulite were held in high regard so he shouldn't assume the women held a lower status.

Speaking slowly, Lamiya said, 'We call them the Riverplain Guides. The honour is passed down from parents to children, as long as the spirits approve and the guides are not tainted or tempted by evil spirits.'

Fidgeting on the bench, Everand worried that this sounded uncannily similar to Elemar's village. Worshipping other beings was an unfamiliar concept for the mages, who believed only in themselves and the power of magic. From his study of some of the older books in the library, he was aware that cultures on other worlds often believed in deities or spirits outside of themselves. He hadn't considered that such beliefs might be held on their own world of Ossilis! The books were old, given that two generations had passed since Mage Thrip had travelled outside of Axis.

He drummed his fingers on his knee, realising he'd thought this kind of worship was an ancient practice. After the trouble Thrip had caused, the Guild laws were reinforced and the councils combined their power, augmented by the might of the Staropal, to create the wardspell to seal Axis. No updating of the books.

'When we reach the village, I'll take you to meet the guides. U-Mali and U-Lumin are partners, and the role of guide has passed down through U-Mali's family since her grandmother.' Although Lamiya smiled, her eyes held clouds of doubt.

Lapsi gave him a sympathetic look. 'They are kind and wise people. They guide us well and always listen to our views.' He looked fondly at Lamiya. 'Our glide has brought great glory to the team and our people and they'll be pleased to see her.'

Everand took in their smiling faces, but unease coursed through him and he wiped clammy hands on his trouser leg. Lamiya was special to her people and they'd watch him carefully to make sure no harm came to her. Was her ability to call birds a marker of distinction? This mission had more meanders in it than the river itself! Every time he thought his path was growing straighter, another curve appeared.

Life inside the Mages' Guild was ordered and highly controlled. Concealed away from any other influence, the mages pursued their learning and magic, surrounded by every comfort they required. Although the Councils of Ten and Twenty debated matters, the Head of the Guild always had the final say. A vague discomfort lurking, he thought about how often Mage Mantiss had nudged them in a specific direction, always acting to preserve the equilibrium of Axis.

Lamiya tapped his knee. 'Don't worry. I'm sure the guides will like you.'

'Are those hopeepa?' he asked, spying a clump of animals wandering through the tall grasses.

'Yes, they are from Lepid or Lazuli's herds,' said Lamiya. 'We'll see their yards and training arena soon.'

When the hopeepa pulling the cart let out loud bellows, the grazing hopeepa lifted their heads and a couple called back.

Many of the creatures were clustered around dense-leafed bushes with splashes of red flowers, stretching their necks out to tug at flowers or leaves. Others stood with their front legs splayed to reach down to eat the grasses.

Lamiya pointed to a grid of sturdy wooden-railed yards, all empty. Next to these was a large circular yard with high railings. 'That's Lazuli's training arena. When the hopeepa are two or three seasons old, he takes them in there and gets them used to being handled. They're not taught to pull the cart until their bones are properly developed at two full season-cycles.'

Just outside the arena two hopeepa stood facing each other. One bellowed and charged at the other one, its horns aiming for the chest. Everand jolted straighter when the second hopeepa lowered its head and the two sets of horns clashed. Tails swishing, the creatures pushed at each other, grunting and bellowing. 'What are they doing?'

'Young bucks testing their strength.' Lamiya gave him a broad smile.

Unnerved, Everand stared while the creatures grappled, broke loose and charged each other again. One raked the flanks of the other with its horns. 'Will they hurt each other?'

'Sometimes. Lazuli will check them and tend to any injuries.' She shrugged, adding softly, 'Last year he had to kill one that was injuring the others. He was most upset.'

Everand rubbed her knee briefly. 'Do you eat the meat from them?'

'Never!' gasped Lamiya. She and Lapsi both paled and gaped at him.

He raised his hands in apology, wondering what they did eat if they didn't like hopeepa meat or bird flesh. Just fish and vegetables? The cart rumbled south, the bellows of the young bucks fading, and Everand tried to make sense of the geography. Although he couldn't see it, Dragonspine River must run steadily south to their right. There was a wide expanse of grassy plain, dotted with bushes and hopeepa, between the path and the river. To the left were more grassy plains, but he discerned bands of trees and hills rising in the distance. The eastern sea must lie beyond the hills.

'Most of us live in the south, near Dragonfoot Lake,' said Lamiya. 'The land is rich for us to grow fruits, vegetables and herbs, and we're closer to the bushes and trees that the birds like.' She waved her hands about and Whirr peeped, still tucked inside her tunic. 'The lake is full of fish. We use the reeds and stronger grasses for our roofs and other materials, and we can train and swim in it.' She slid him a sly look. 'I can teach you to swim, if you like.'

About to reply that he didn't need to know how to swim, he closed his mouth. If he were to live here, he probably did need to know. No doubt she wanted to teach him to paddle properly too. 'That would be useful,' he said, straight-faced. 'You never know when the boat might tip over.'

She punched his arm and Lapsi laughed.

'We're almost there,' said Lapsi, pointing ahead.

The roofs were difficult to distinguish from the surrounding grasses, but Everand made out slightly different coloured round shapes. A glittering, vivid blue caught his eye; the lake. A thousand questions crowded his mind and his mouth ran dry. Should he bow to the guides? Where would he sleep? Would he be permitted to stay with Lamiya? He peered at her from under his eyelashes. Probably not. Perhaps they'd need to be formally partnered first. Should he ask? *No, too soon.* He rubbed his palms along his trouser legs.

There was also the matter of Lazuli. The handsome pacer was unlikely to give up so easily. On his home ground and surrounded by friends, would the pacer stand up and object to his presence? So far, Lazuli had been restrained, just tense and hovering protectively around Lamiya.

'When will the boat arrive?' he asked, annoyed that his voice cracked.

Breezily, Lamiya said, 'Not long after us.'

Looking away, Everand hoped he'd at least get to meet the guides before the boat arrived with Lazuli. Last time he'd had to compete for a woman's affection it hadn't gone well. Two warriors from Terralis had spent an entire season seeking their own flying horses so they could travel through Mage Beetal's sky rift, purely to retrieve Elemar. Around a swallow, he remembered the suppressed fury in the chestnut-haired warrior's steely eyes. Rhyan had been cautious around him, but he suspected that was only because Elemar had told the warrior that he'd use his magic to obliterate him if he challenged for her.

Being a mage held some advantages, but it didn't solve the problem and he'd left it to Elemar to choose between him and Rhyan. His glance stole sideways. Lamiya sat tall and proud, her beautiful face gleaming with anticipation as she neared home, her luxurious, mahogany hair falling in soft waves. His heart pounded.

Clenching his fists, he resolved that this time he would not stand meekly back and hope that Lamiya would choose him. He'd stand his ground and make his claim.

What would happen then, he had no idea.

CHAPTER FIFTEEN

Approaching the narrow channel on foot with his men, Malach ground his back teeth together. His eagles flew above, heading back to their beloved high trees. Anger washed through him: most of his flock had been killed and it would take considerable time and effort to train new birds.

Behind, his men marched in silence and he imagined them exchanging glances. He had lost much face in attempting to recapture the mage and his woman, Torrap now knew that Chief Magrin was not his father and others probably suspected. Would anyone challenge him for the right to be chief, claiming his inherited position was void? He snarled: let them try. His men now knew he possessed some abilities in magic. Hot shame burned across his nape. His men also knew the other mage was stronger, and that he needed to be taught how to wield his power. More honour lost.

Pausing at the edge of the channel, he eyed with distaste the half-submerged log and the muddy, foaming water rippling over the gnarled surface. It would have to be moved so they could get their boat through the narrow channel and out to the main river.

'Arrange a group to remove this mess.' No sooner had Torrap nodded than he swung his gaze to Mahog. 'Gather the people in the meeting circle so I can speak to them.'

'Now?' asked Mahog.

'Yes, now,' snapped Malach, spinning around and walking nimbly across the bits of log protruding above the water. A muddy ripple washed over his feet, soaking his sandals. Not caring, he headed to his cabin. It would take a while for his men to cross the log in single file, and he wanted to get his thoughts in order.

He flung open the cabin door and threw his cloak onto the floor in a corner. Curse Atage and the people of Riverfall! Why couldn't they have let everyone be? Why poke their nosey, do-good fingers into his territory? He must deter others from coming to the lake to visit the dragons. How could he train the dragons to obey him if the creatures were off frolicking with these pesky people and their boats?

Yanking the thong from his topknot, he shook his hair out and dragged the bone comb through the tangles. The tugging brought back the memory of his mother making him presentable to meet his real mage father when he was only seven. He braided his hair and secured it in a neat topknot, recalling how excited he'd been to discover he wasn't like the others: he was better. Although his mage father had only visited every second season, the training had been progressing nicely. He'd learned enough about magic to whet his appetite, but not enough to properly control it.

His forehead throbbed. He had flourished under Mage Beetal's attention — and then, after only a handful of visits, his father had been assigned a Guild apprentice. From then on, whenever he fumbled over the spells, his father would sigh and tell him his mage apprentice had mastered it. He clenched his hands, feeling the pulse beat through the vein in his neck. It hadn't been long before he loathed the Guild apprentice.

His gaze rested on the oval summoning stone his mother had used to know when the mage would visit. The stone remained obstinately dull grey. His mind's eye replayed the imagery conjured by Mage Beetal's tales of his secret army of winged dragons. His father had promised to give him a dragon of his own, if his bid to become Head of the Mages' Guild were successful. Closing his eyes briefly, he recalled the time, when he was ten, that his father's lesson had been to take him to Dragon Lake, telling him there was a dragon living in the water. He'd been so thrilled when his father called the dragon and its head had breached the surface, but the dragon had refused to approach, sliding under the waterfall instead.

Since then, he'd trekked regularly to the lake by himself and the dragon had remained annoyingly elusive despite his efforts. His mouth twisted, a bitter taste crawling across his tongue. The dragon had responded to Everand. He smashed his hand down on the table. Meek and mild on the surface, Everand was as slippery as a fish. His father had underestimated his apprentice. *He* would not make the same mistake.

Stripping, he used a cloth to wash his face and torso, then dressed in his best hunting garb of bunya skins. Tightening the hide belt and slipping his long knife into its sheath, he resolved to send his favourite pair of eagles to see what the people of Riverfall were doing now. See what the mage was doing. He ground his back teeth again. What did Everand need to do before he came in the promised four sun-ups?

Anxiety slithered into his stomach: was the delay to give Everand enough time to betray him to the Guild? Hadn't he said the other mages would despise him as the son of the traitor Mage Beetal? Tapping his fingers on the knife sheath, he tried to replay word for word what Everand had said. The mage had seemed sincere when he said *he* was the only chance for him to continue his training.

Malach tilted his head. Would Everand really renounce the Guild for this scrawny boatwoman? Maybe. Using the woman as bait had proved far easier than he'd expected. Curse *her* people for coming to free them. Would Everand have stayed with him longer otherwise? Everand had said that he wanted to talk more about what had happened to Mage Beetal — and also stated that he hadn't been the one to kill Mage Beetal, nor had any other mage, but that a creature from elsewhere had. A groan of frustration escaped Malach's lips. His father should have explained his plans more. And let him help.

Staring unseeing at the cabin wall, he reviewed Torrap's astute questions. Why had the Guild sent just Everand? Why send anyone at all for minor upsets to boat races and trade discussions? When his spy eagles had reported that a messenger from Riverfall had set off to the south, he'd thought his strategy of constant upsets had worked, assuming that the messenger was going to Riverplain and Riversea to announce the cancellation of the races and discussions.

Instead, the eagles had tracked the messenger to the southern part of the granite wall and reported that the man *disappeared* through the wall. He drummed his fingers on his knife sheath. That had thrown him.

Nothing had happened for several suns so, reluctantly, he'd taken his boat and team to Zuqart and devised a new plan to destroy the bridge at the end of the long race. But when he got to Zuqart, this 'traveller' had been there. He'd perceived the submerged power immediately and, more incredibly, the mage exactly matched his father's description of his Guild apprentice! Curiously, everyone else seemed to think Everand was a random human traveller from Axis.

He snorted and rolled his shoulders. At least he'd forced Everand to reveal himself. But why was he here? Why had the Guild responded to what must have been a request for help? Something strange was occurring. He focused on the grey oval stone sitting dully on the wooden shelf. Did it work two ways? Could he use it to connect to a mage inside the Guild? Instinct suggested this was not a good plan, not if Everand spoke the truth. He clenched his fists, digging his nails into his palms. The Guild was as elusive as the cursed river dragon.

How could he find out whether a broader strategy was underway? Did Everand know, and could he make him tell? All was not lost; he still had an opportunity to advance his training in magic.

Retrieving his cloak of eagle feathers and dropping it over his shoulders, he went to the door. He would prepare his people for conflict and wait to see if Everand arrived when promised. And if he didn't, the tree-moths would enjoy an excursion to destroy the cotton crops. His lips twitched at the thought of how much his men would enjoy kidnapping the boatwoman again if Everand betrayed him — and he'd leave her at the mercy of his hunters.

Adjusting the cloak on his way to the meeting circle, he heard the murmuring of numerous voices. Pleased, he found that the entire village was seated in neat half-circle rows on the far side of the fire pit. As usual, the men sat cross-legged in the front four rows and the women sat behind, with the children huddled between them. Torrap and Mahog sat in the middle of the first row. Taking his customary position next to the fire pit, Malach stood squarely and raised his arms.

'My people, I want to tell you of great events.' He lowered his arms and two hundred faces watched him expectantly. 'For a long time, we've lived our lives untroubled by what outsiders do. This is changing.' Striding two steps forward, he looked into the faces of those in the front row, his strongest hunters. 'Riverfall tried to bring the provinces together. We deflected this. We destroyed the bridge across the river and declined the offer of trade. We do not need them!' He shook his fist.

Torrap and Mahog raised their fists and shouted, 'Ki!' Everyone copied, shouting enthusiastically and he felt an eyebrow lift when even the smallest child waved a pudgy arm.

Once everyone fell quiet, he let the anticipation build for a few breaths while he paced along the line of the front row. 'I also told you we'd captured one of the powerful mages from Axis.' He paused while people shifted uneasily. In the back row, a small child wailed. 'You saw my men and eagles set off earlier. This was because the mage escaped during dark-fall due to the meddling provinces.'

Gasps and murmurs rippled through his people. He bowed his head, counted to three, then looked up.

'The men that were there saw me spar with this mage. Using magic.' A tense hush settled over the huddled people. Another child wailed. 'The mage will return to train me.' Commanding silence, he held up a hand. 'For countless seasons, I have borne a secret.'

He roamed his eyes over the gathering, and in the front row Torrap's eyes glittered in anticipation. Malach spread his hands. 'From a young age I was sworn to secrecy by my mother, Chinfe.'

The expressions of some of the older women tightened, especially those who were his mother's friends.

'As my men recently observed, I have unexpected abilities. This, my people, is to our advantage.' Pausing, he gave a grim smile. 'My mother attracted the attention of a mage from Axis, and I am the result of *that* union — not of her partnership to Chief Magrin.'

A wave of muttering passed through the people, many turning to look at others, and a few men reached to their hips, groping for a weapon.

Pacing, Malach continued in a loud and strong voice. 'I have deceived you. But Chinfe swore me to secrecy. Even after her death, I held this close to my chest, honouring her wish.' Satisfied by her shocked expression, he nodded at Hemma. 'Now, with trouble looming, you need to know. You *must* know.' Stopping, he spread his hands open, palms up, and tilted his face up to the deep, dark sky.

'Magrin had no other offspring, and as the son of an immensely powerful mage, who better than me to lead you?' He flung his arms open wide, and the fire suddenly sparked and sent a stream of hissing embers skyward. 'Especially now, when strange events unfold around us.'

He twisted his wrists and more glowing embers coiled up into the sky, adding to the sombre mood. Leaning forward, he spoke fast and earnestly. 'Unprecedented, the Mages' Guild sent a mage to Riverfall. We don't yet know what this means.' He smiled at the look of fright on the faces of many, but not his hunters, who watched him sceptically. Torrap regarded him with narrowed eyes, and he realised he must explain what had happened to Magrin to win them over fully.

Adjusting his cloak over his shoulders, he roamed his look over his people, then gave a wise nod. 'Chinfe was clever. She concealed her dalliance with this mage. Unaware, Chief Magrin raised me as his son, training me to succeed him — and on his visits the mage gave me training in magic. For a time, I had two fathers.' Regret pinged through him. 'I have been prepared to be your leader, *and* I have been trained in the basics of magical power.'

He clasped his hands in front of his body. 'As you know, ten seasons ago, Magrin and Chinfe disappeared. I was there. Magrin followed Chinfe and me to her meeting with the mage on the edge of Hanaki Forest. Great warrior and hunter that he was, Magrin challenged the mage.' Taking a breath, he said sadly, 'Despite his courage, strength and skills, Magrin was felled by a bolt of magic.'

A few women put their hands over their mouths and others stared in horror. Hemma glared at him through narrowed eyes.

'Chinfe, running to try to deflect Magrin from his fateful challenge, was also caught by the massive energy of the death bolt.' He kept his voice steady despite the shudder that threatened.

Memories rushed in of how, for a few awful heartbeats, he'd thought Mage Beetal would kill him too, to remove all evidence of his secret affair. He'd stood, shoulders squared, waiting for the death blow. Instead, the mage had given him a look of almost apology and came to rest a hand on his shoulder.

Still feeling reprieved, he recalled the pressure of the mage's strong hand, the intense look on the stern, swarthy face.

With effort, he brought his focus back to the gathering. 'The mage truly cared for Chinfe and he buried her in their favourite copse of pines, while I buried Magrin nearby.'

Some of the older women wiped their eyes and when a child started to cry it was hushed by a nearby woman. The men looked troubled, but so far none challenged him. Now he must appear sympathetic but also strong. He spread his hands open again.

'The mage told me to keep what had passed a deep secret. He also told me he'd keep training me.'

A confused silence followed and many people frowned. Some glanced around anxiously, as if they expected this powerful mage to suddenly appear.

'At that time there was dissension in the Mages' Guild. My true father visited just once more and told me he'd been betrayed by others.' Several people gasped. 'The mage that I captured confirmed that my mage father is dead, killed in a Guild battle.' His people didn't need to know the complex relationships. They didn't need to know Mage Beetal had been branded as a traitor. He swept his gaze over everyone.

'We stand on the brink of a precipice. The mages are coming out of Axis to meddle in our lives. I have brought us this far, this second mage has agreed to continue to train me and I will pry more information from him.' Raising his arms again, he brought his speech back to the beginning. 'I will gain in power to protect and lead you. As warriors and hunters, we must increase our weapons training and fortify our lands for we do not know what comes!'

Practising what Everand had shown him, he sent a mental command to Torrap and Mahog, suppressing a smile when the two men immediately stood and rattled their knife sheaths. 'To Malach!' The rest of his men scrambled to their feet and raised clenched fists. 'Malach! Ki!'

Malach sent another mental command and his three remaining eagles soared into view, dim moonlight reflecting off their massive wings, circling above with shrill cries. The fire flared in a tower of bright hot flame, showering the air beside him with a thousand glowing sparks, and in the shadowy space beyond, with one voice his people chanted his name.

A roaring filled his ears: he had them.

Chapter Sixteen

Mage Mantiss waited until the members of the Inner Council had stopped shuffling and murmuring to one another. Everand's vacant chair seemed to glare at him from between Saiphos and Caimanops. 'Let's start, shall we?'

Pelamis leaned forward, looking pointedly at Everand's empty chair and opening his mouth to speak.

'First,' said Mantiss firmly, 'we will complete the allocation of the four apprentices. Tiliqua has ascertained their preferences in readiness.' Glowering at Pelamis, he said, 'I know Everand was going to do this. The second matter for discussion is his whereabouts.' Satisfaction threaded through him when Pelamis leaned back and exchanged a sideways glance with Simoselaps. Oh yes, they could wait until he was good and ready.

He waved a hand at Tiliqua, inviting her to discuss the apprentices. As agreed, she went into great detail about their backgrounds, abilities evidenced so far and their preferences for the focus of their training. The council would be bored and keen to conclude the meeting long before they reached the matter of Everand's whereabouts. Seated beside him, Agamid's eyes glinted with amusement and Tiliqua, while maintaining an austere expression, was no doubt enjoying her role.

After a while, a red flush began to creep across Pelamis' face. The young mage had snapped out his choice of apprentice as soon as Tiliqua paused for breath. Agamid and Tiliqua had chosen theirs, and then Tiliqua had spent an inordinate amount of time subtly coaxing the shy and reluctant Neelaps into offering to take the last apprentice, saying it would be good for the Guild to have another mage so interested in agriculture.

'Surely, we can move to the second matter for discussion?' barked Pelamis eventually. Next to him, Simoselaps nodded.

Placing his elbows on the table, Mantiss clasped his hands together and glanced around the table. 'Is everyone satisfied we have finished allocating the apprentices? No more questions?'

'There weren't any questions,' said Pelamis.

Mantiss bestowed a fatherly smile upon the young mage, who flushed a deep crimson. 'Well then, I declare that matter closed and we can move to the next matter. I thank Tiliqua for her efforts and sound report.' When he nodded at Tiliqua, she lowered her eyes, he suspected to hide a smile.

Toying with a bracelet of chunky precious stones, Menetia said somewhat haughtily, 'I think we can move on, Mantiss.'

'The second matter is Mage Everand's mission.' Seeing their interest sharpen, Mantiss took in a breath. 'Everand, at my request, has gone to a nearby river province.'

Pelamis bolted upright. 'A breach of Guild Rule Nine!'

'And without council endorsement,' added Simoselaps, his brown robe rustling with the waving of his hands.

Agamid leaned forward. 'I remind the council of the precise wording of Rule Nine: No mage or human shall pass outside the granite wall unless ordered to do so by the Head of the Guild for special purpose.' He stroked his beard. 'Mantiss said Everand went *at his request*. In accordance with Rule Three, the Head of the Guild is *supported* by the councils, not directed by the councils.' Agamid sat back.

'Semantics!' spluttered Pelamis. 'Explain the mission.'

'Very well,' said Mantiss, speaking slowly, as if to a child. 'Let me remind council members that we are here in Ossilis due to Mage Lapemis and ten others fleeing violence and near annihilation some four generations ago.'

'Is this relevant?' asked Menetia. 'We know the history.'

'We would be wise to learn from our history.' Mantiss inclined his head.

'Which generated Rules Nine and Ten about avoiding interaction!' Pelamis almost shouted.

Squashing his relief that Pelamis was responding exactly how he'd anticipated, Mantiss said, 'Indeed. And unplanned and *unsanctioned* external interaction, *not* authorised by the incumbent Head of the Guild, has almost undone us. Twice.' He found the steel to glare at Pelamis. 'Precisely why I *chose* to send Mage Everand, and him alone, to find out what is happening in the provinces that surround us.'

'Why now?' asked Menetia, her bored expression belying a quick mind.

'I confess,' said Mantiss, 'that I was beginning to worry about whether we should update our knowledge. I firmed my decision when a messenger caught our attention and asked for help.'

'How, when no-one can enter Axis?' Saiphos looked confused.

'Resourceful, the province man threw rocks at the granite wall to trigger the alarm and at Mantiss' request I went to investigate,' interjected Agamid. 'It seems the provinces were about to initiate inter-province trade, and someone was trying to sabotage this.'

'An audacious move to try to contact us,' said Mantiss smoothly. 'I decided, in conference with Agamid, that we should find out more and *then* convene the council.'

Pelamis looked around the table, trying to garner support. 'Why send Everand? Why not me, or any one of us?'

Keeping a straight face, Mantiss replied, 'Ah, I'm so glad you asked. Because young Everand is the only mage to have *already* breached Rule Nine. Have you forgotten that Mage Beetal forced him to travel to another world?'

A red stain rising up his cheeks, Pelamis said, 'Where is Everand then? When does he report?'

Clasping his hands together more tightly, Mantiss cleared his throat. 'Unfortunately, the province trade negotiations have just passed and Everand has not returned. I had hoped to have him present to give you all a detailed report ...'

On cue, Tiliqua leaned forward. 'Is he safe? Do we need to look for him?'

'Are more mages going to travel?' said Pelamis slyly. 'Are you going to authorise more breaches of Rule Nine for special purpose? Such as retrieving the incompetent Everand?'

Before Pelamis could volunteer, Mantiss responded, 'No. What I ask for is council assistance to send a combined mind probe to find Everand and translocate him home.' When several mages moved to speak, he held up a hand. 'Everand is strictly undercover. We are not meddling with the provinces because, apart from the original messenger and the town leader, nobody knows there is a mage in their midst. We *must* keep this secret. I propose we use our combined powers to recover him before anyone else realises.'

A heavy silence loomed over the table. As instructed, Agamid and Tiliqua remained still and quiet so they couldn't be accused of collusion. Mantiss waited. How would the council vote?

'Is this a formal motion?' asked Menetia eventually.

'Thank you, Menetia. A good idea.' Mantiss smiled at her and sitting taller, tugged the sleeves of his robe down and said clearly, 'As Head of the Guild, I move that the members of the Inner Council assist me to form a combined mind probe to locate Mage Everand, who is on an endorsed mission, and to bring him home. All those in favour? Anyone wish to speak against the motion?'

After some fidgeting and shuffling, everyone, including Pelamis, nodded.

'Thank you all,' said Mantiss. 'Let us break to refresh and I will sound the summons to reconvene the council after high-sun meal.' Keeping his face neutral, and wishing the subtle tremors in his legs would subside, he remained seated until everyone except Agamid had departed.

'You haven't lost your deft touch,' said Agamid, hazel eyes warm with amusement.

'Maybe so, although the combined probe could reveal more than I would prefer. I need you and Tiliqua to conceal my weakness.'

Raising an eyebrow, Agamid gently asked, 'You think it's getting worse?'

Mouth dry, Mantiss nodded. 'The healers have no clue. Unless you decide you could manage the position, we need Everand home so we can start to groom him.'

'He has the ability, but the others don't like him … can such an aloof loner be a leader?' Agamid said, his features twisting in a grimace.

'That, in part, is why I sent him on this mission. Alone. With no support, he must somehow mingle with and persuade the people of the river provinces to listen to him.'

With a fond smile, Agamid stood. 'This is exactly why I never accept your challenges to a game of strategy stone. I am never able to anticipate when your coloured stones will have mine surrounded!'

Smiling, Mantiss replied, 'Indeed. I have only been beaten twice — both times by Everand.'

When Agamid laughed, Mantiss felt his humour fade.

What, precisely, was his clever and strategic spy doing?

Chapter Seventeen

Slowly, the round thatched roofs grew more distinct, and Everand appreciated the way their subtle shades of green and yellow blended into the surrounding scenery. The cart trundled over a crest and he gasped at the long, oval lake of turquoise water nestled in a dip surrounded by green, gold and purple reeds.

Noticing that Lamiya was watching his face, he said, 'Stunning.' She beamed at him.

Hordes of brightly coloured things flew up from the bushes near the water. He thought they were butterflies, but when the myriad colours sped towards them, the chittering and cheeping corrected his impression. Magnificently plumed birds swooped around the cart, and Whirr wriggled out of Lamiya's tunic and flew up to join them. The birds darted in close to Lamiya's head and flitted away again.

Growing dizzy, Everand counted at least ten types: tiny yellow ones with red beaks; turquoise, jade and yellow ones like Whirr; red, grey and white ones with long narrow beaks and leaner bodies, and an array of birds with bell-like calls and feathers in every hue of a sky-arch.

When Lamiya held out her arms, she was instantly buried under excited, cheeping birds. Her smile stretching from one ear to the other, she looked radiant, tilting her head this way and that as she listened to them. A lump clogged his throat: how could someone this special possibly love him? Finding Lapsi's grey eyes regarding him with a hint of sympathy, he shrugged. Yes, his heart was captured, well and truly.

The cart passed the first cluster of houses and people tumbled out of doorways, wiping hands on tunics or aprons. 'Lamiya! Welcome home!' cried multiple voices. Many people looked at him with open curiosity but smiled in welcome and he smiled and nodded back until his face ached. Lapsi gave one-handed waves as he deftly steered the fidgety hopeepa towards an elongated, oblong roof that nestled close to the lake. Lamiya threw her arms up, tossing the vibrant flock into the air. The birds circled once before flitting away to the bushes.

She tapped his knee. 'We're going straight to the Meeting Place. The guides are waiting.'

Pushing down a rush of nerves, he wondered whether the birds had told her this.

Peering at him through thick, curved eyelashes, she murmured, 'Relax. Be yourself.'

He swallowed. What else could he do, anyway? Distracting his mind from the pending meeting, he looked at the village. The way the wide eaves jutted out from the walls, presumably to keep rain from seeping into the houses, made the sloping thatched roofs resemble giant straw hats. The doorways and windows were screened by woven strings adorned with vibrant feathers mingled with pretty, coloured pebbles. Similar to his impression of Riverfall, he sensed a close-knit, peaceful community. But there was a major difference: the town of Zuqart was enclosed by a high wall whereas the Riverplain houses were scattered across the grasses.

'Which one is your home?' he asked Lamiya.

She pointed to the far side of the lake. 'Over there, in a grove not far from the lakeshore.' Moving her finger, she indicated a couple of roofs near the entrance to the lake. 'Lulite and Lapsi live there, as do a few of the fishermen.'

The cart swung towards a tributary that fed into the lake. 'Is that another river?'

Lamiya nodded. 'Dragonleg River. It's just wide enough to bring our boats down, but it's quite deep. The boatshed is on the northern shore, where there's a nice flat beach to bring her in.' Her lips twitched. 'It's an excellent swimming area.'

He gave her a dry look. 'I can hardly wait.'

She laughed, her eyes shining with amusement, and Lapsi snorted.

When the ground levelled out, Lapsi tugged on the reins and said, 'You two can get out here.' After a pause he asked, 'Where do I put Everand's things?'

Lamiya gave Lapsi a brief hug. 'Can you put them in your home for the moment? See you in a bit.' Turning to him, she said, 'Ready?'

Wanting to say 'no', he wiped his clammy palms one last time and clambered down from the cart. Lamiya jumped down lightly and took hold of his elbow to spin him around. His mouth dropped open at the structure before him.

They were standing at the back of the building, which was perched lengthways along the lakeshore to take in the view. The building was structured for light, air and space with both long sides left open with no walls. Thick grey tree trunk supports rose at intervals, carved into half-circle dips at the top, where medium-sized logs were set in and stretched across to support the roof. Narrow trenches ran down the sides to channel water around the building, bordered by attractive grey and white pebble paths.

Squeezing his hand, Lamiya led him towards the nearest path. While they scrunched their way down the gentle slope, he roamed his gaze over the tranquil lake and the appealing array of shrubbery. 'Do you ever get tired of looking at this view?' he asked, his voice rasping.

'Never. It changes with the seasons and the colour of the sky, but every view is calming and pleasing.' Lamiya tossed her head and her mahogany hair rippled over her shoulder, making the turquoise threads in it shine just like the lake.

Yes, Everand thought, every season would bring a fresh perspective of beauty. His pulse beat strongly and he already felt so *alive*. He could also imagine waking up to this view every sun-up with Lamiya cuddled in his arms. Lamiya's world was completely different from Elemar's world. He *could* live here. *With her*. He should tell her that.

Tugging her to a halt, he said softly, 'Riverplain is magnificent. I like it already.'

A range of emotions crossed her face before she smiled coyly and said, 'Good.'

He wanted to kiss her and sit by the lake with her in his arms, for an eternity. She shivered and her eyes grew darker. Surely, she was thinking the same thing.

'The guides are waiting,' she murmured and let go of his hand to resume walking.

With a sigh, he followed her down the path and around the corner to the front of the Meeting Place. Something plopped onto his foot and he looked down as a small squat creature jumped off his foot onto the path then hopped towards the water, making croaking sounds. A bird hooted from amid the reeds.

Lamiya stood waiting at the bottom of stone steps that climbed to the centre of the structure. Above the steps was a formal entry: two smooth grey trunks supported a straight darker crossbeam, the outer ends of which were angled down to give a neat, crisp look. In the middle were elegantly carved symbols of waves and feathers.

Matching his pace to Lamiya's, he ascended the steps and the Meeting Place opened out before him, the interior cool and dim under the thatched roof. Lamiya reached down to tug off her sandals and placed them on a narrow wooden bench on the right-hand side. He copied and lined his sandals up, nudging them to the very back of the bench because they hung over the edge. Next, Lamiya turned to where there was a large stone bowl filled with crystal-clear water.

Picking up an ornate wooden ladle, she dipped this into the bowl and poured water over one hand, and then the other, letting it run down into a second bowl placed below the first one. 'The water purifies your spirit before entering this sacred place,' she whispered.

Acutely conscious that the province guides were watching him, Everand took the ladle and tried to mimic Lamiya's elegant movements. As the cool water washed over his hands, he felt his heartrate slowing. He resisted the urge to splash some over his face to remove the grime of travel. Carefully putting the ladle back in position, he watched Lamiya closely.

Clasping her hands together in front of her chest, she bowed from the waist. He copied. Her feet soundless on a rush mat floor, she stepped into the building and walked forward. Following her, he marvelled at the soft feel under his feet and the intricate work in the tightly woven mats. The whole floor was covered in equal-sized oblong mats, with embroidered cloth edges and uniform weave. Most impressive.

Glancing up, he drew in a breath at the neat latticework across the roof supporting the sloping thatch above it. Movement caught his eye and he turned his head fractionally to observe an ornament swaying in a light breeze. A string hung down from the roof, feeding into a woven circle of rushes dyed a deep blue. The circle had lines across it, reminding him of a spider's web, and below it hung thongs of pale-blue feathers and clear stones that glinted as they caught the light.

'To capture any evil spirits,' whispered Lamiya. 'Eyes front.'

Heart thudding against his breastbone, Everand looked at the two people seated three paces away. Both were clad in simple grey tunic tops, the woman with a pale-blue skirt, and the man with green trousers. The only signs of their importance were the ornate braids in their grey, wispy hair, and the necklaces made of precious stones the same turquoise as the lake. When Lamiya bowed again, he bowed low too, his mouth running dry.

'Dear one, welcome home,' said the woman, rising from her chair and clasping Lamiya's hands in hers. 'The spirits and winds guided your boat well!' The woman looked ancient, crevices of wrinkles forming around her deep-set eyes and mouth as she smiled.

'You have made us all proud,' said the man, stepping forward to also clasp Lamiya's hands.

A deep pink hue adorned Lamiya's cheeks and her eyes sparkled. 'Thank you, dear guides.' She blinked rapidly. 'The team performed beyond my wildest dreams.'

'A great team, with a talented captain.' The guide grasped Lamiya's hands again, peering deeply into her eyes, and Lamiya blushed an even darker pink.

The guide's eyes widened. 'I see,' she murmured. 'It is true then.' Her gaze shifted to Everand and bright, bird-like eyes looked straight into him. Before he knew it, she stepped sideways and took his hands in hers. Her skin felt leathery, cool and dry, like a reptile. 'Mage Everand of Axis, welcome to Riverplain.'

Everand gave a short, stiff bow, difficult with the woman still gripping his hands, the top of her head only reaching his chest. 'Thank you for allowing me to visit.'

For a long time, the woman kept hold of his hands and he looked down at the top of her head, at the finely braided grey hair and the pale-blue feathers hanging down behind each wrinkled ear. He risked a glance at Lamiya, seeing that she and the man waited, motionless and silent, as if they were all paused in time.

A tingling set up in his fingers, moving up his arms, and he felt a presence infusing him, quietly measuring him. His mind began to respond to invisible questions, similar to a Guild truth-read. Without thought, he raised a blocking shield, pushing the guide back. The tingling in his fingers increased and he perceived a gentle admonishment. Awe filling him at the guide's subtle power, he swallowed. To win Lamiya he had to allow this disconcerting intrusion. Lamiya trusted these guides: so should he. Closing his eyes, he dissipated the mind block and allowed the memories that were called to surface.

Fleeting images came of his training under Mage Mantiss and Mage Beetal; his protection of Elemar, and letting her go; the meeting with Mantiss, Agamid and Beram and his volunteering to go on the mission; falling into the river and seeing Lamiya standing up at the back of the boat; taking her with him to call the river dragon.

The images containing interactions with Malach wavered, tinged with anxiety, before shifting to his wild ride on the dragon Mizukaze; being captured and taken to Riverwood; their rescue and his stand against Malach and his promise to return to train the half-mage. The guide's presence hovered there, picking through his conflicting emotions about Mage Beetal and Malach as if she were wading along a rocky streambed.

The final image was of Lamiya standing before him, eyes wide, lips parted in a smile, mahogany hair stirring in a breeze. A bead of sweat trickled down his brow and, amazed, he opened his heart to show how much he wanted to be with Lamiya. A final question: yes, if needs be, he would die for her.

Cool air washed over his hands and he swayed. With a rustle of cloth and feathers, the guides returned to their seats. Everand stood blinking, the present returning in increments: the sounds of the birds and croaking creatures, the air moving under the roof, the feel of the mat beneath between his bare feet, his heart beating, his breath going in and out. Lamiya standing beside him. The woman guide gestured with a tiny hand to a green cushion in front of her chair.

'Please, sit,' said the man, his voice deep for his aged frame.

His legs feeling light and far away, Everand lowered himself to sit cross-legged on the cushion. Lamiya knelt on her cushion and then sat back on her heels.

The man leaned forward, his long grey hair, adorned with red feathers, tipping forward. 'Welcome, Mage Everand of Axis. I am U-Lumin.' The man smiled, revealing gaps where several teeth should have been. 'I look forward to hearing about Axis. We can always learn from others.' He sat back.

Everand nodded at U-Lumin and looked at the woman, who was regarding Lamiya thoughtfully. He admired Lamiya's poise and patience as she sat waiting for what would be an important judgement.

'Dear heart,' began the woman, and Lamiya straightened imperceptibly. 'Your choice is sound. Your instincts and inner sight have guided you wisely.'

Lamiya's shoulders heaved in a sigh and Everand's heart beat more quickly. Were they referring to him?

'Mage Everand's heart is pure and he is not tainted or tempted by evil. However,' the bright eyes flitted to him, 'his spirit is not yet complete. Further trials await him, and his resolve will be tested. You must both be brave and strong.'

Everand felt dizzy. Further trials? His spirit was not complete? Was she referring to Malach? His desire to break away from the Guild? He latched onto the reference to both of them needing to be brave and strong. Did that imply Lamiya would be with him? Sweat trickled annoyingly down his brow, but he dared not wipe at it.

Bowing so low that her nose brushed the matting, Lamiya murmured, 'I understand, U-Mali guide. Thank you.'

'Dear one,' continued U-Mali, 'you have far more ability than you yet know.' Her face softened and the wrinkles seemed shallower. 'Your mother is most proud of you. *We* are most proud of you. Mage Everand will help you, just as you will help him. The spirits have brought you together for a reason.'

A glinting tear fell from Lamiya's eye and disappeared into the matting. The old man watched her, a frown creasing his forehead. A breeze eddied through the space and the ornament hanging from the roof swung with its passing, the pebbles clinking and tinkling.

U-Mali raised a gnarled hand. 'The spirits are speaking: your path will be difficult and clouded, but we wish you well.' She dropped her hand and the breeze died, the tinkling sounds fading to be replaced by the croaking of the lake creatures. 'Go now, and settle Everand in.' The guide's gaze shifted to him. 'Mage Everand of Axis, we would speak with you again soon.'

Everand bowed. 'Thank you, U-Mali and U-Lumin.'

Lamiya rose smoothly to her feet, pausing while he stood and, after a final bow, they reversed from the guides. At the steps, she repeated the pouring of water over her hands, he followed suit and they retrieved their sandals. When Lamiya bounced down the path, he followed ponderously, his feet heavy with uncertainty.

On reaching the edge of the lake she spun around. 'They like you! You can stay!' She quivered with excitement.

'I can?' Utterly drained, he ran a hand through his hair. 'You might have warned me I'd be read like that.'

'I didn't know. I thought it would be a simple welcome and U-Mali would ask to read you later.' Lamiya's smile slipped and she shrugged. 'This is better.' Chewing at her lower lip she said seriously, 'It means everything that the guides approve. So much has happened, is still happening, that I might have doubted.' Her eyebrows pinched together and she stepped towards him. 'Do *you* have doubts?'

His heart melted. 'Lamiya,' he said huskily, 'if we ever manage to spend any time alone together, I will show you how few doubts I have!'

Her smile was as searing as the sun coming out from behind a cloud. Then she tilted her head. 'I hear shouting. I think the boat is arriving!'

With a sigh, Everand swallowed his disappointment. Already, they were obliged to be surrounded by people. Perhaps the Riverplain spirits had a warped sense of humour and these deflections of all romantic opportunities were an extended form of test? He shook his head: what was he thinking?

'Come on, we must greet the team.' Lamiya touched his hand and then set off along a well-trodden dirt path that skirted the lake.

Taking a deep breath to gather courage, he took long strides after her. She was heading for the flat beach, and numerous villagers were making their way down the slope towards the lake. Rounding a curve, he saw the far end of the lake was further away than he'd anticipated. His breath caught at the stunning turquoise waters, growing darker as they reached the distant purple-green smooth hills. The sky was a pale, wan blue. He yawned. Wait, it was still the same sun of their rescue but it felt like an age had passed, and they'd had no sleep. Small wonder he felt drained.

With courteous nods, people fell into step around him and he had a strong impression that everyone already knew who he was. Most of the people had blond hair of varying length with shades of gold, a few had brown hair and a handful had dark hair like Larimar. Their skin was fairer than the people of Riverfall, but their facial structure and body build was similar. The majority wore simple cloth tunics and skirts or trousers, and most had feathers in their hair or wore thong and feather necklaces or bracelets.

The track widened and the ground levelled off into a broad, flat beach. A little away from the shore was a long, low, mud-brick building, the wooden doors propped open. Those around him cheered and waved at the boat approaching the beach.

Narrowing his eyes, he thought again that the boat looked *faded*, as if it had lost its vibrancy after the dragon peeled away from it at the end of the long race in Riverfall. The dragon head looked subdued, more wooden. Would they build a new boat? And would Lamiya coax another dragon from it? So much for the Guild thinking it understood how magic worked.

He edged his way to the front row of people, where he could see Lamiya standing apart to greet her team. Someone nudged their way beside him.

'You met the guides, then?' Lapsi asked, an eyebrow raised.

Unsure what to say, Everand just nodded. Surely, it would be better for Lamiya to tell her people what the guides had decreed.

Flight's prow slid onto the beach and the paddlers raised their paddles and called 'Yo!' Lazuli and Larimar leaped out to cries of welcome. The rest of the team got out, more stiffly than usual, but then they'd paddled a long way and without sleep due to their rescue mission. Lamiya hugged each paddler as soon as they reached the beach. His eyebrow lifted when even the gruff Luvu gave Lamiya a warm return hug. Lapsi ran to embrace Lulite, who looked pale and shaken.

Lazuli turned around and waved at a number of people. Everand stiffened when the paddler's gaze fell on him. Before he could even nod in acknowledgement, Lazuli dropped his paddle and took jerky strides towards him, his face dark with anger. Everand hastily moved away from those around him.

'How could you put her in such danger?' Lazuli shouted, thumping both hands against his chest.

Everand tried to grab Lazuli's hands but the man was too furious, too quick, and a flurry of fists connected with his ribs. Bracing himself, he grabbed again and another series of fists pounded painfully into his sides.

'It was your fault!' spat Lazuli, his face twisted with hate. 'She could've been killed! Go away and leave her alone!'

An uneasy muttering started in the crowd, and he clenched his fingers so he wouldn't hurl a bolt at Lazuli, or raise a protective shield. He must fight fairly. Lamiya disentangled herself from Luvu and began to run towards them, but to his relief Lapsi and Lulite intercepted her.

Nodding at them, he called out, 'Wait, Lamiya. Please.' He had to deal with this. By himself.

Space opened up behind them when the rows of people backed away, and Lazuli launched at him. He managed to get his hands up to deflect the blows, but then Lazuli dropped a shoulder and swung an arm in an arc. The fist connected with the side of his face and pain shot through his jaw. Fury surged through his chest.

'Enough!' he snarled. 'Lamiya makes her own choices.'

'Fight like a man! You have no claim here!' yelled Lazuli, positioning his weight ready for another assault.

Everand shifted his balance onto his toes, his legs protesting at yet more activity. Lazuli sprang, swinging his fist, and Everand leaped to the side and pushed Lazuli's back as he went past. The pacer stumbled but righted his balance and, faster than imaginable, twisted and leaped again. Everand grabbed Lazuli's arms and they pushed and shoved against each other. The pacer was strong! But he had the advantage of height, so he dug his heels in and pushed back.

Soon, they were both shaking from exertion and sweat ran from their faces to drip onto the pebbly shore. Lazuli would not give, and Everand worried about what would happen if his feet slipped. The man was so determined!

'Lazuli,' he gasped. 'Listen. This just happened.'

'You lured her!' growled Lazuli. 'Leave her be.'

'That's up to her. Not you. Not me.'

'No!' Lazuli shoved harder.

His feet starting to slide backwards, Everand braced himself against Lazuli's ire. They'd have to fight this out until one of them gave.

'Go back to Axis. Stop interfering!' Lazuli ground out, eyes narrowed to fierce slits.

Interfering? When he'd come to help the provinces at *their* request? Anger coiled in his stomach and pumped his arms with rage. He leaned his shoulders into it and gave Lazuli an almighty shove. The pacer stumbled backwards and, heads and shoulders hunched, they circled each other. Watching Lazuli's feet for the indication of a leap, Everand flexed the fingers of his right hand and clenched it, ready.

Lazuli jumped, hands outstretched, and Everand swung his arm as hard and fast as he could. The skin tore off his knuckles with the force of the connection with Lazuli's cheek, and the pacer stumbled sideways. He kicked at Lazuli's ankles, and the pacer fell. A red film crossed his eyes and when he blinked he was straddled across Lazuli's chest, his fist plunging towards Lazuli's face. With sheer force of will, he pulled the punch sideways. His hand thudded into the ground beside Lazuli's ear, the pebbles ripping more flesh from his knuckles. The stinging was excruciating.

'Curse you!' he shouted, adjusting his weight on Lazuli's chest and pinning the paddler's arms down.

Wriggling, Lazuli shouted, 'Get off me! Fight properly!'

'Like your young hopeepa? Pushing and shoving?' Everand just stopped the words 'like savages' from passing his lips.

Teeth bared in a feral snarl, Lazuli's handsome face contorted until it was unrecognisable.

'Stop it. Be still,' Everand hissed. 'End this honourably! You're spoiling a triumphant return.' When Lazuli continued to wriggle furiously, he put his mouth right by the closest ear. The heat rising off the pacer was incredible. 'Lamiya won't think more of you this way. She values you. Keep it that way.'

His steely eyes becoming focused, Lazuli grunted. 'You'll never hurt her?'

'Never,' said Everand firmly. 'You have my word.'

'I'll kill you if you do,' said Lazuli, his eyes a deep storm-grey.

'Fair enough.' Taking Lazuli's silence to mean they had an understanding, Everand got up and reached down to help the paddler to his feet. Lazuli ignored his hand, rolled to the side, stood up and stalked back to the boat with his shoulders held rigid.

Everand stared at the pebbles by his feet. What would they all think? Were the guides watching from their high Meeting Place? His mouth compressed; they'd hardly approve of him now. Lamiya! What must she be thinking? He peered up coyly to see her standing stiff with tension, staring at him with her mouth open. A wave of nausea rolled through him. Among the silent crowd, nobody moved.

He had just undone every good thing he had achieved since his arrival. Lazuli was right: he should stop interfering and go back to Axis. Fixing his gaze on the grove of vegetation at the far end of the beach, he set off that way, his strides growing longer and faster.

He should have done better.

Been better.

Chapter Eighteen

Her heart thumping uncomfortably, Lamiya stood staring at Everand's receding back; his steps were getting faster and jerkier. After giving her a sour look, Luvu turned away to help the others with Flight. Should she go after him? Leave him be? Anxiety curdled in her stomach. Lazuli would *never* forgive Everand, or her, now. Her arms trembled with exhaustion. The fight was the last straw. How could they do this to her? What was wrong with them both? And Everand stalking away without a word? How dare he!

A shiver wracking her, she took a step along the beach, then stopped. What to do?

'Look out, Lamiya!' called Larimar.

She moved backwards out of the way while the team carried Flight past, nobody looking at her. With infinite sadness, she watched Flight's tail disappear into the dim shed. How could it have come to this after such joy and glory? She wanted to wail and rend her clothing. The spirits approved of Everand, the guides had said, and now *this*? She rolled a pebble around with her toe. How could she fix things? Light footsteps approached and Lulite's warm arm slipped around her shoulders.

'Give him some space. Go to Lazuli.' Lulite gently brushed a strand of hair away from her face. 'Lamiya, you know what you need to do.' Her friend's expression was brimming with concern.

Swallowing painfully, Lamiya nodded.

'That's our glide,' said Lulite with a brief smile. 'Come by later and we'll share a calming brew.'

Her legs and feet devoid of any energy, Lamiya trudged towards the boatshed. Inside, the paddlers were bantering happily and wiping Flight down with soft cloths. Eight faces looked up at her entry; one remained firmly turned away. Silently, and with brief nods, except for Lepid who scowled, everyone put down their cloths and crept out of the shed. Lazuli remained standing by Flight's head with his back to her. She wrung her fingers together but tilted her chin up. So. He was going to be difficult.

Drawing in a deep breath, she walked around the boat to face him and on seeing his grazed raw cheek, already swelling an angry purple, her anger melted.

'Oh no,' she reached a hand up and he flinched away. 'That must hurt.' The misery in his eyes brought tears to hers. 'I'm sorry. For everything.' She tried a shaky smile but Lazuli just stared, cold and aloof. Not at all the exuberant pacer she knew and loved. *Try harder.* Swallowing her sense of failure, she took his cold hand in hers.

'Please, Lazuli. You're my best friend. I'm so sorry I didn't realise your feelings for me had changed.'

'Do you love him?' barked Lazuli, his hand unresponsive in hers.

Forcing herself to meet his troubled eyes, she mumbled, 'I think so. I've not known him long, but I think so.' She gave a small shrug. 'I didn't look for it or expect it, it just happened.'

'How do you know he hasn't cast a spell on you?' Lazuli asked bitterly. 'Could you not love me?'

'He wouldn't … but you know that.' Softly, sincerely, she said, 'I do love you, Lazuli. You are my best friend, my brother, my pacer! I can't help that I feel a different love for Everand.'

'What if he wasn't here? Would you love me like that then?' His steel-grey eyes bored into her.

Chewing at her lower lip, she debated how to answer this all-important question. Bringing his cold, limp hand to her lips, she kissed it. 'Maybe. But we can't change what has happened.' It wouldn't help telling him that the guides had approved of Everand. 'Can there be peace between us?'

He yanked his hand back and ran it through his snarled hair, bits of grit sticking up in it. 'I don't know. I wish things were otherwise.'

Clasping her hands in front her, she felt she could ask for nothing more. 'I understand. I'm sorry.' She smiled forlornly. 'I wish for your friendship. When you're ready.' Mustering her dignity, she walked quietly from the shed.

She found the others sitting on the beach a discreet distance away. Mustering more courage and dignity, she walked slowly towards them and stopped when they all looked up at her. 'I'm sorry for all the trouble …' her voice wavered and she had to take a breath. 'You are the best team ever.'

The paddlers scrambled to their feet and pulled her into a group hug, everyone patting her on the back. 'Give him time,' said a few.

'Look out for Lazuli?' she requested, sniffing. 'We need him!'

'Indeed,' said Luvu, his voice gruffer than usual. 'This festival and the events associated with it have caught us all by surprise.'

Searching the circle for Lepid's face, she gave him an apology with her eyes, relieved when his expression softened and he gave her an imperceptible nod. Theirs would have been a wonderful strong family to join. Regret burned into her but, as she'd said to Lazuli, things had passed that couldn't be undone now.

'Er, Lamiya,' said Larimar shyly. 'There are some strange noises coming from down there …' He jerked his head to the far end of the beach, where Everand had gone.

She felt her eyebrows rise. What did he mean? A sharp crack resonated from the distant grove, echoing across the water.

'Good luck,' said Luvu with a grunt. The team gave her anxious but sympathetic looks and dispersed back towards the boatshed.

Fixed to the spot, she stared toward the grove. What was Everand doing to make that sound? Facing an irate Lazuli had been one thing; facing an enraged Everand who seemed to be losing his grip was another thing altogether. Another sharp crack rent the air and the grove foliage shook and wavered, as if in a gusting wind.

Garnering her resolve, she began to walk. If she couldn't face Everand when he was like this, how could she possibly love him? Brushing her hair back over her shoulders, she straightened her tunic and walked faster. This was it: if she couldn't face and appease him, she'd need to rethink. But the guides seemed to think the match was a good one, perhaps even destined. She shook her head. She'd have to decide for herself, follow her instincts, as tempting as it was to run back and tell Lazuli she'd changed her mind and take the safer, known option.

Taking a breath, she told herself to be bold and remember Mookaite's words: *He is a powerful mage, but he's also a young man caught up in events.* So be it, she'd address Everand as a young man and forget he was a mage.

At the edge of the grove of bushes she paused, listening to the eerie hush surrounding the area, the absence of bird or insect calls. The wildlife was frightened. If only Whirr was with her, so she could send him in ahead. But he wasn't. Schooling her face to a calm expression, she brushed past the branches, inhaling the scents rising from the leaves and flowers.

Emerging into a small clearing, she found Everand pacing in a circle with his fists clenched. Around the edge of the clearing, large rocks lay in jagged shards. Her lips twitched. So that was what he was doing! He hadn't noticed her arrival.

'Nice,' she said and he spun around, rigid, to stare at her. 'Did you break all these rocks by yourself?'

'I might have.' He jutted his chin, aloof and defensive.

Going to a pile of shards, she picked one up, noting the sharp, clean lines of the break. 'Do you feel better now?'

His mouth tightened. 'I do not.'

Her eyebrows lifted. He was far from his usual controlled self. *Treat him like a man ...* 'I see,' she said, edging closer. 'Do you need more rocks? Shall I fetch some?'

Glaring down his nose at her, he snapped, 'It's not funny, Lamiya.'

Instinct telling her to keep bantering until his sense of humour returned, she hefted the shard in her hands. 'I can see that. Exploding rocks looks most serious.' Turning the shard over, she added, 'But look how neat the lines are! We can probably use this somehow.'

His eyes grew a deeper blue and he opened and shut his mouth. Twice. She smiled, and he looked disconcerted. 'I thought you might like to help Larimar breed exotic fish, but perhaps you'd rather be in charge of exploding rocks?' Pacing in front of him, she added, 'Yes, that might be better. We don't have anyone else with this skill.'

'You're making fun of me,' he said stiffly, flexing his fingers in a worrying way.

'Me?' She stopped right in front of him and widened her eyes in mock innocence. 'Would I do that?' She shook her head. 'That would be most unwise, especially with a great and powerful mage.'

'You ...' he threw his hands open, 'you are impossible!'

Dropping the shard, she swiftly stepped into his arms and slipped hers around his waist, relief swamping her when he put his arms around her and crushed her hard against his chest. She felt his chin rest on top of her head. Tightening her grip, she listened to the thudding beat of his heart against her ear, waiting until the erratic rate slowed and the rigidity eased from his body. His arms were trembling, and he was taking slow, deep breaths to recover his equilibrium.

Lifting her head from his chest, she leaned back and looked up. Her heart wrenched at the lost expression on his face. He'd always been so strong, so self-assured, so able to reason through everything.

'Everand?' When she touched his cheek, he gazed deep into her eyes, the pain etched in his far greater than she'd expected.

'This is not me. I don't know who I am,' he whispered.

His anxiety howled at her senses. He didn't know where he belonged. She floundered; maybe she didn't either. Partnering with an outsider … she was entering the unknown too. How could they help each other if they were both adrift? She needed to see water to think properly. Taking his hand, she said, 'Let's go and sit by the lake.'

Using her free hand to part the foliage, she found a narrow dirt trail and followed it, taking him further away from any likelihood of meeting others. The bushes gave way to reeds, and soon she found a secluded spot where the reeds led to a short grassy bank above a narrow beach. Small waves lapped soothingly over the pebbles and the lake stretched before her, turquoise and azure in the golden light of the sun hovering close to the horizon. The sun's warmth lingered on her arms and the top of her head.

Sinking down onto the grass, she tugged him down beside her. When he put his arm around her, she nestled against his shoulder, letting out a slow sigh. For a while she watched the light playing on the water and the coot birds waddling among the reeds. A large fish jumped, flashing silver, disappearing in a cascade of silver droplets. Several more fish leaped up and skimmed across the surface.

A submerged shadow seemed to follow them and she squinted, trying to see better. What *was* that? A brief perception of hidden power floated by, and then dissipated. The lake became still again.

Suppressing a shiver, she sighed. Should she coax Everand to talk, or just kiss him? The latter was more appealing. She reached up to tilt his jaw towards her, waiting until his eyes lost that faraway look and focused on her. She parted her lips and, before she could blink, he leaned over and closed his mouth over hers. Delight washed through her and she melted against him as his kiss grew earnest, his lips soft and warm. Linking her arms behind his neck, she let him support her while he lowered her to lie on the grass. He paused to look into her eyes, querying whether this was agreeable to her.

For answer she pulled him down on top of her, feeling his warm lean body melding over hers, his legs brushing between hers. Desire shuddered through her, mirrored in his body. A lock of hair escaped his ponytail and fell forward, tickling her face. She tucked it behind his ear, watching his eyes grow darker and infinitesimally bluer.

'This is who you are to me,' she murmured.

His lips quirked and he planted butterfly kisses down her cheek, her jaw, nuzzling his way down to her neck. She kneaded his back with her hands, wanting more. Remembering their cuddle in the cage at Riverwood, she rasped her tongue up the side of his neck, enjoying the texture of his skin and the salty taste. He gasped, so she did it again, smirking when he gave a deep groan. His body was gaining in heat, and hers responded. Her breasts aching and tingling, she arched against him and he groaned again. Between her legs was a pool of throbbing heat, and she felt a pleasurable slipperiness there. An eddy of nerves gathered in her stomach: was she ready for this? There would be no going back.

Panting slightly, he lifted his head. 'What is your custom? Should we wait?'

Curse his restraint! Disappointment gushed through her, but he was right, difficult as stopping now was. 'Yes,' she whispered. 'The guides would wish it.'

'I thought as much,' he murmured with such tenderness her heart ached. He kissed her neck, mumbling, 'I don't wish to wait, but if I want to stay …'

Between her legs throbbed dully and she swallowed tightly. How long would they need to wait? But, she acknowledged, those who knew her well would know if she gave herself to him. They would read it in her eyes.

Everand's focus grew distant and he bolted upright, pulling her with him. Her heart raced when he formed a protective shield over them and said urgently, 'Close your eyes. Lose your presence!'

What? Why? She tried to sink into herself.

He hunched over her, head bowed, lips working. A translucent shield grew into a thicker dome over them. A ripple of energy passed over it, came back, and passed over again. Frightened, she huddled into herself.

After a time, he said, 'You can open your eyes now.'

'What's happening?' she cried, grabbing his arm.

'I felt a mind probe. The Guild is looking for me.' He held her arms, his fingers almost pinching. 'I'm not sure I was fast enough with my block. They will come for me.'

'Why?' She gripped his arms, terrified that he would fade before her eyes.

His eyes the shifting colours of deep turbulent waters, he said slowly, 'My mission here is complete because the races and trade discussions are over. The Guild expects me to return, to report what happened here and resume my duties.'

'Would it matter if you didn't return?' Surely, there were plenty of other mages and they didn't need Everand.

Shifting his weight to sit more comfortably, but keeping the shield in place, he said, 'A good question. I am but one of the Inner Council of Ten, and the others could continue their research, administration and work without me.' The colours in his eyes swirled, darker blue taking prominence. 'But mages are not allowed outside the Guild and we are not supposed to mingle with non-mages. The Guild would rapidly lose control of the magic if this were to happen.'

'How? If the mages are powerful and people are not, how would the Guild lose control? Control over what?' She frowned, her mind struggling to follow the nuances.

Everand stroked her fingers. 'More good questions. I assume the Guild is worried about dilution of the magic, given that although we are born with power we have to be trained. Malach could be a test of what would happen, but they won't want to know.'

'Why does your Guild remain secluded? You could interact but not breed …' A flush stole up her neck.

'True. But Mage Beetal and I are not good examples, are we? Imposed isolation removes all temptation.' After a grimace, Everand frowned. 'It's also to do with our magic, and our access to an additional source of it. I don't think the wardspell was always in place. But two generations ago a different mage, and then again only recently, Mage Beetal, travelled outside the wardspell. Both times, the Guild was invaded as a direct result — and very nearly lost. This doesn't encourage a relaxation of the laws.'

Sitting straighter, Lamiya drew in a breath. If this were the case, why had they sent Everand in response to Beram's request? 'But they sent you here.'

'You see so much, and so clearly.' He reached over to stroke her cheek.

'I do?' Thinking of U-Mali's strange comment about the spirits having brought them together for a reason, she shrugged. 'I might see, but I don't understand.'

'Neither do I. Every time I think I grasp what's happening, something shifts.' He tilted his head. 'From the outset, when they dropped me *into* the river and you nearly paddled the boat over the top of me, this mission has not gone right.' His mouth twisted wryly. 'I should have asked many more questions before I volunteered. But I was sent urgently because the other mages were about to arrive and Mage Mantiss didn't want–' He turned whiter than the trunk of a spirit tree.

'What?' She grabbed his hands. 'What? You've just realised something important.'

'What if the interruption was contrived? To stop me from asking questions?'

Her heart thudded in her ears. Was he saying the Guild had manipulated him? 'Tell me what happened. Did they know you'd volunteer to come?'

'Mantiss knows me well.' A tremor passed through his hands. 'I've been a spy for him since I was orphaned at twelve. He and Agamid called only me to the meeting with Beram. They *knew* I would offer to go.'

'What could this Mantiss gain by sending you?' Lamiya shifted her weight to deflect the threatening pins and needles.

'That,' said Everand, 'is the part I'm not sure I fully grasp. He said he thought it was time we found out more about the nearby provinces. Maybe Beram's arrival prompted him … or maybe he was already thinking this.'

Trying hard to see the bigger picture, she tapped her fingers on her knee. Not having magic outside the Guild seemed fundamentally important to the mages. Far more important than boat races and inter-province trade. 'Is it possible they thought Malach, or someone like him, existed?'

Everand's fingers twitched. 'I don't see how … although Mantiss and Agamid had already met with Beram before they summoned me. What could Beram have told them?' He gasped. 'The attack by the gigantic tree-moths! Beram might have already told them about that *before* they summoned me.'

'Yes,' she said, following his line of thought.

'I should've seen it earlier. The gigantic tree-moths are what made me think someone with power could be involved, but I thought Mantiss and Agamid didn't know about them!'

'You could ask Beram if he'd already told them.' Reluctantly, she added, 'When you go to see him on the way to Malach.'

'I could. If Mage Mantiss suspected someone like Malach existed and wanted me to prove it, they will be most keen to hear my report.' He gave her a grim smile. 'If I tell them Malach exists, confirm that he has magical ability and, worse, confirm that he is the illicit son of Mage Beetal, their retribution will be swift and final.'

'They will kill him without question?' A cold shudder ripped over her. '*This* is why you want to understand Malach. You want to see for yourself if he deserves death. You are undecided.'

'Yes,' he said miserably. 'But I'm likely to be the only one who is undecided.'

'Oh.' Her heart swelled for him. 'I see. You worry that you disagree ... your value is different ... But you are being fair, giving Malach the benefit of the doubt.'

'You see me in a positive light I'm not sure I deserve.' He shrugged. 'I thought I was comfortable at the Guild, that I belonged there. But maybe I've *always* been apart, being a spy, pretending to be other than I am, concealing my true purpose. I deceived Mage Beetal for a very long time. I tried to conceal myself when I reached Riverfall.'

His eyes looking sad and fatigued, he rubbed at a band of muscle in his jaw. 'Maybe all this shows that I am just a shell, and I don't know who I am, or where I belong.'

'Stop!' The word came out louder than she intended. 'Look at me. Being a spy is your ... *outside*. Beram, me, Mookaite, the others ... we see your *inside*.' She poked him in the chest. 'We see *you*, Everand, no longer of Axis. We trust *you*.' A subtle presence hovered at her shoulder, her mother, U-Mali, U-Lumin, and she felt a soft push. 'You need to trust yourself! To be who *you* want to be. Not what anyone else wants you to do. Or be.'

Slowly, he raised his head, his eyes a deep azure with light behind them. 'You give me heart, Lamiya. I can try.'

A wave of gladness, chased by exhaustion, washed over her. Navigating a turbulent river with an unbalanced boat would be easier than trying to chart her way through these currents associated with feelings! Managing a smile, she said, 'No more breaking rocks?'

'That I think I can promise.' The humour sparkled in his eyes. 'Unless of course the people of Riverplain decide that is truly where my skills are best applied.'

'I'll ask them,' said Lamiya, glad to be back on surer ground. 'We'd better get back before they send out a search party.'

Chapter Nineteen

Everand watched the way Lamiya moved briskly along the dirt track, her muscles working smoothly, her thick mahogany hair bouncing with each step, the caramel and blue threads glistening in the light. The ache in his groin was throbbing unmercifully. How could he be so entranced by a woman he'd known for a mere nine suns?

Clenching his jaw, he wondered how and when the guides would decide he and Lamiya could be together. Properly. What more did he need to do? Should he ask her to partner him? Was she ready? The ache intensified and he bit down a moan. The way her body had responded to his, and the way she'd arched into him! He scrubbed at his face with both hands. She seemed ready. Was *he* ready? He was ready for the lovemaking part, no doubt about that, but was he ready to commit to her *and* a whole new way of life?

'Stop thinking so much,' she said pertly over her shoulder and strode faster.

Stop thinking? Already, he didn't have enough time to think everything through! His legs pulsed with fatigue and he wished it were dark-fall so he could sleep. The outside and the inside of him — the concept was intriguing. As was her comment about *allowing* himself to do the things he wanted to do. Difficult, when he'd spent his life following directions charted by others, and applying his stealth to deliver what was perceived to be right.

Her clarity was blinding: his conflict sprang from the disconnect between what he *wanted* to do, what he thought was fair and just and what the Guild *expected* him to do. He wanted to stay; the Guild wanted him to return. He wanted to find out more about Malach, give the half-mage a chance; the Guild wanted to obliterate Malach. He sighed. The *allowing* part was not so easy.

A branch swung back to thud against his chest and he bumped into Lamiya's back when she pushed through the last of the foliage and stopped dead. He put his hands on her shoulders, peering over them to see why she'd stopped.

'There you are!' said Lulite, apparently waiting for them. The woman glanced keenly at them both. 'Are you alright?'

'Fine,' said Lamiya, blushing and slipping a glance at him. 'We should collect Everand's things.'

'About that,' said Lulite, taking Lamiya's hands. 'Everand may stay in your hut, but I will also stay with you.'

So, they were to be supervised. Everand's lips quirked. That would make it easier to exercise restraint.

'Thank you,' said Lamiya. Sliding another look at him, she said, 'I'll speak with the guides soon. But let's get settled in.' She yawned.

Lulite laughed. 'Me too. These adventures are exhilarating but they're also exhausting!'

The two women linked arms and set off along the beach, leaving him to follow. The boatshed was all closed up, and a couple of children splashed and swam in the water. Remembering Lamiya's promise to teach him to swim, he shuddered with apprehension. Up the slope, the thatched roof and elegant gateway of the Meeting Place held a commanding position. Were the guides still seated there? Was this the inner conflict that U-Mali had seen when she told Lamiya his spirit was not complete? His head ached. Lamiya was right: too much thinking.

The path twisted around the water's edge and he saw a bridge ahead. It sat high above the water, neat wooden steps leading up to it. At the bottom step, Lamiya took his hand and they climbed up together. Once at the centre of the bridge, he leaned on the sturdy railing to look at the lake and distant hills, their pastel greens and purples soothing in the fading light.

Lamiya squeezed his arm. 'We're headed to that clump of huts. Lapsi and Lulite live in the first one, and their fishing boat is moored there.'

Now that he looked, he saw the small fishing boats nestled among the reeds. Further along the lake shore were fruit-bearing trees. He became aware of chirping and peeping, and the erratic movement of birds in the foliage. A solitary hut blended in just before the trees. 'Your home?'

'Closest to the birds.' Lamiya's eyes sparkled.

'Come along,' said Lulite. 'I could use a nice brew.'

Ignoring the tremble in his legs as he descended the steps, Everand followed the women, who walked surprisingly briskly given how much activity they'd already done. A chill passed across the back of his neck. Was that another probe? He must have led the Guild a merry chase. They would have searched for him in Riverfall, but by then he'd been kidnapped and was in Riverwood, his powers quelled by Malach's potion.

Then he'd travelled swiftly south. There was no reason for the Guild to look for him in Riverplain … He stopped. He'd expended a stupid amount of power breaking rocks! If they were searching with the combined power of the Inner Council, they'd have detected that energy. The probe had felt as if many minds were woven into it. Did that mean Mantiss and Agamid had told the council about his mission? Had his failure to make contact prompted Mantiss to act? Cursing, he scrambled a shield over himself. He shouldn't have let it lapse.

'What is it?' Lamiya asked, her forehead pulling into a frown.

'Another probe. The sooner we reach your home the better.'

They wound their way along the path until they reached a couple of thatched houses, the doorways facing the lake, and paused for him to pick up his bundle of clothes from Lulite's home. Tucking the neat package under an arm, he waited while the women hugged.

'See you soon,' Lamiya said.

Lulite gave her a look. 'I'll leave food ready for Lapsi and gather a few things. You get that brew ready!'

When they passed the next home, Lamiya said, 'This is Larimar's hut. There he is!' She waved cheerfully at the reeds by the shore, where Larimar was working on one of the boats with Lapsi. The next two homes belonged to Lattic and Lopa separately. 'Although,' Lamiya whispered, 'that may change. Lattic's wife died trying to give birth to their first child many seasons ago. Recently we've noticed he seems to have his eye on Lopa.'

'What do they do?' asked Everand.

'Lattic is a builder and he makes the mud bricks, with Luvu mainly. He's the best thatcher we have and also carves the paddles for the team.' Warmth in her voice, Lamiya waved her hands around. 'Lopa is a weaver. She grows grasses and herbs as well as breeding birds. Hers is the nearest home to mine.' She tilted her head prettily. 'They're both shy and will suit each other.'

Everand watched her thoughtfully. The people knew each other well and were aware of what everyone was doing. That would take some getting used to. Although the mages knew what each of them was studying or working on, and the two councils met regularly, they took no interest in others' personal lives — which had allowed Mage Beetal to have an extended affair with Malach's mother without anyone noticing!

Grimacing, he reflected that even he, the often-present apprentice, hadn't noticed. He'd need to learn to see people in another layer. Lamiya had already shown him how valuable this was.

Coming to a stop, she gave him a nervous smile. 'Welcome to my home.' She swept her arm towards the hut.

'Thank you.' He bowed with a flourish.

With another nervous smile, she pushed aside the feathered thongs hanging in the doorway and disappeared inside.

Relaxing his shield, he swept his gaze over the turquoise lake and the smooth hills huddled around the far end as if they were protecting it. The setting sun cast golden glints on the water and the air teemed with myriad aromas: fruits, water, flowers, grasses and a musty scent that might be the reeds. Something ran tickling down his neck and he slapped at it, turning to find Lamiya holding a long feather and grinning. He held his arm out and she nestled against him.

Moving behind her, he put both arms around her middle and rested his chin on her head, still absorbing the view. 'Your home is beautiful,' he murmured.

'You like it?' She leaned back into him.

'I would very much like to live here,' he mumbled, meaning it.

'If you're sure … we must speak to the guides soon.' She hugged his arms tightly.

Tugging her soft, silky hair over her shoulder and to one side, he bent to nuzzle the side of her neck. His groin immediately throbbed and she trembled. 'Very soon,' he agreed. She twisted around and tilted her mouth towards his. He melted his lips over hers, a deep sigh passing through him. Just as well they were going to be supervised.

Something flashed by his ear. He jumped and Lamiya broke away with a laugh.

'Whirr!' The bird zoomed around her head with scolding peeps. 'Be nice.' She wagged a finger.

The bright bird perched on his shoulder and trilled loudly, disconcertingly close to his ear.

'Whirr welcomes you,' said Lamiya, looking amused.

'I see. Thank you, Whirr.' Everand held up the back of his hand and Whirr ran down his arm to perch there, his tiny talons gripping uncomfortably. 'How am I supposed to kiss you now?'

'I have an idea for a game.' Stepping closer, Lamiya tickled his ribs. 'Let's see how long you can hold Whirr in that perch for.'

Squirming this way and that while she tickled him unmercifully, moving up and down his ribs, he endeavoured to keep his arm out. Every time he thought about making a grab for her, Whirr peeped and she tickled him harder. 'Enough!' He tossed his arm and Whirr flew off. Did these people never rest? He'd have to get fitter.

Lulite stepped past Lamiya, saying, 'I can see I'll have to make the brew myself.'

Heat stained his cheeks at the way Lulite arched an eyebrow at him. Then she trod neatly past them and disappeared into the hut. Heart thudding, he felt like an unruly child; something he'd never been.

'Well,' said Lamiya, hands on hips and with a mischievous smile, 'mages are ticklish.'

No smart reply came to mind and he turned to admire the lake again. Lamiya leaned against him while he watched the deep orange-gold glints playing on the rippling surface. The colours reminded him of the dragon that had peeled away from her boat at the end of the long race. How had that happened? Unless the dragon had already been in the lake? But then how had it become one with her boat?

'Is there a dragon in your lake?' he asked.

When Lamiya peered up at him, he swallowed at the way the setting sun highlighted the blue tints in her hair, mirroring the sunlight on the water. 'We haven't seen one. Why do you ask?'

'There is Mizukaze, and before him his mother Mizuchi, in Dragon Lake in Riverfall. The ancestors knew of the dragon and raced their boats against it. Riverplain also has a dragon-shaped boat. Is this because you had common ancestors and a common boat tradition? Or is there a dragon here too?'

'We spend a lot of time on or near the lake. Although ...' she stared across the water, her face softening, 'sometimes I wonder. There are times when I'm sure I sense another presence.' Her face brightened. 'We could look for it.'

'I can't help but wonder how the dragon Flight became infused in your boat. Perhaps her spirit entered the boat from a real dragon in the lake?' He held Lamiya at arm's length and looked into her face. 'Or did you conjure the dragon from the *intent* carved into the wood?'

Her mouth dropped open. 'Would that even be possible?'

'I don't know, but you have an ability that defies definition.' He kissed the top of her head. 'You are special in more ways than your people know, although your guides sense it.'

Her eyes widened. 'Is that what U-Mali meant when she said we could help each other?'

'Maybe.' He smiled.

'Because I am a nice person,' came Lulite's voice from the doorway, 'I have made a mug for everyone.'

'We'd better go in,' murmured Lamiya, linking her arm around his elbow.

The feather thongs tickled when he brushed through them. Inside, Lamiya's hut was the same size and shape as Beram's dome, but instead of being rosy-pink clay the walls were brown and yellow oblong bricks made of mud and straw. The floor was covered with the same impeccably woven mats he'd seen in the Meeting Place, but Lamiya's mats had a cheerful turquoise cloth edging. A low table, carved in the shape of an elongated feather complete with fine lines etched into it for detail, sat in the centre. Next to it were plump cushions in bright yellows and greens.

His gaze rested on the tiered shelves, lined with an assortment of bowls of seeds, nuts and berries. There were also woven baskets filled with fruits or feathers. Along another wall several cooking utensils hung from hooks. The orderliness and bright colours matched Lamiya's personality.

'Sit,' said Lulite, fluffing up a yellow cushion for him and then putting a mug of brew and a plate of seed-covered cakes in front of him.

Everyone was doing everything for him, but these people were not assigned to work for mages, like at the Guild. 'That smells good.' Feeling awkward, he asked, 'Can I help with anything?'

Both women raised their eyebrows at him.

Lulite turned to Lamiya. 'A man who offers to help inside the hut? *Now* I see why you like him.' They both laughed.

His cheeks warmed and he took a sip from his mug, hiding behind the steam.

'You're a guest for now,' Lamiya said. 'But I'll remember your offer later.' She briskly laid out bowls of seeds, nuts and green-leaf vegetables. He wasn't surprised when she added a small, flat bowl with black, brown and green seeds for Whirr. Next, Lamiya lit candles, placing these in small wooden alcoves scattered around the walls, while Lulite retrieved baked fish wrapped in aromatic leaves from her basket.

A dull ache permeated all of his muscles and he longed to lie down and close his eyes. Letting their chatter wash over him, he ate his food and drank another mug of brew.

With a kind smile, Lamiya picked up his empty bowls. 'Sleep now?'

He helped roll out the two mattresses, placing them as far apart as possible. The light weight promised a filling of soft feathers. Uncertain, he hovered to see which mattress he was to sleep on. Would Lamiya lie next to him, or would the women share a mattress?

'Perhaps you need to go outside for a moment?' Lamiya touched his elbow.

He stepped outside and moved away from the hut to relieve himself. The rising moon cast a swathe of silver-white across the lake and a soft silvery outline on the hills. The croaking creatures were making a loud chorus and an insect was emitting a click-click-click noise. Mesmerised, he stood in the darkness until he heard a soft call from Lamiya.

Back inside, in the dim light from the sole candle, Lulite was snug under a blanket on the far mattress. Shyly, Lamiya prodded him towards the other mattress. Still clothed, he sank onto it with a sigh and she lay down beside him and pulled the blanket over them. She'd changed into a loose tunic for sleeping, but he was too exhausted to check whether Beram had packed one of these in his bundle.

'Sleep well,' said Lulite around a yawn.

As soon as his head fell onto the cushy pillow, he struggled against the weight of his eyelids. Lamiya lay curled up with her back against his chest. He wanted to stroke her hair but his arm was too heavy, and he'd barely planted a kiss on the back of her head before darkness swooped over him.

He dreamed he was in his quarters at the Guild. The moon was high in the sky, the marble tiles of his room sparkling with threads of silver and white. Through the arched window a spray of stars winked against the inky velvet sky.

Mizu was still in stasis in her tank in the corner. He propped open the lid of the tank and stood on tiptoe to reach in. Holding a pod of the gel in both hands, he admired the fish's red and silver scales and intricate gauzy fins and tail. Mizu was just like the fish he'd seen in Dragon Lake, so she must have come from Riverfall or Riverplain. How had Mage Beetal acquired her? A gift from Malach's mother? Why else would the impatient and ambitious mage keep the fish?

Everand? Mage Mantiss called him. He looked up. He was alone in his quarters. Besides, mages did not conduct meetings in the dark.

Why was Mizu sick? Did she miss being free in a lake? 'Would you like to go home, Mizu?' Her tail twitched. Heart beating faster, he repeated the question. He was sure the tail had moved.

Everand?

Not now, he thought, irritated at Mantiss' interruption.

Everand? Is that you? Mage Agamid.

Lifting his head, he wondered why both Mantiss and Agamid were calling him. 'I will take you home,' he murmured to Mizu, easing the gel pod back into the tank. Closing the lid, he spun around at the sensation of people standing behind him.

He was alone, but the sense of others was tangible.

Everand, report.

Everand?

Everand, is that you?

We found him?

Alarmed, he opened his eyes. A lone candle spluttered, the wick almost burned down. He was lying on a mattress on the floor in a hut. Something moved right beside him and he jumped.

'Everand?' A woman's voice. He bolted upright. He was in Riverplain with Lamiya but the energy of the mages was intensifying. The shield! Curse it! He'd forgotten to raise the shield! He leaped up and away from Lamiya — they must not find her.

'What's happening?' Lamiya sat up, the candle casting shadows over her face.

'Stay there!' He held up a hand, warding her away. 'The Guild has found me.' A rustling noise told him Lulite was also awake. He gritted his teeth against the tingling that was spreading over his entire body, prickling and probing.

Everand, get ready, Mage Mantiss instructed.

In the gloom, his arms and chest crackled with lines of green energy, immediately joined by purple ones. Then orange, blue, turquoise, beige and crimson lines joined in and the pulling, tugging, prickling became painful. Curse it! The *full* Council of Ten had combined power to translocate him back to the Guild. *Now.*

In despair, he looked into Lamiya's dark, horrified eyes. 'Don't search for me. I *will* find a way back.' Throwing a glance at Lulite, he said, 'Keep her safe.'

Groans escaped his lips when the pulling and crackling became agonising, and the walls of the hut shimmered in the familiar swirls of translocation.

The hut faded to grey nothingness and enduring, he grimaced.

Thank the stars he was fully clothed!

Even if these were basic and none too clean.

Chapter Twenty

The pain was excruciating when the council yanked him back through the wardspell with none of the consideration shown on his outward passage to Riverfall. Muscles clenched, Everand arched in agony, fearing that his heart might actually stop. The taste of iron crawled into his mouth. *Curse it.* He'd bitten his tongue.

Anger snaked into his stomach. So sneaky of the Guild to force him back in the middle of dark-fall. Would Lamiya ever forgive him? Surely, she'd understand what had happened.

The swirls whirled faster and faster, and he detected the marble walls of the Great Hall materialising around him. *Think! You're a spy! Now you must conceal yourself from those you serve. You can do this: you did it before.*

He landed on his knees on the silk rug below the dais. Putting a hand down to steady himself, he kept his head bowed while he drew a breath. A circle of mages' feet surrounded him, accompanied by gasps and mutters. Footsteps approached, and a strong hand took his arm and hefted him to his feet.

'Welcome back! Are you well?' Mage Agamid peered at him.

Bowing stiffly, Everand replied, 'Yes, thank you, Mage Agamid.' Reluctantly, he looked around the circle, all too aware of the power receding into the mages' fingertips as they recalled their energy. Mage Mantiss gaped at him and Tiliqua stared, relief and alarm warring on her face. Some of the younger mages looked pleased, but he suspected this was because their magical recall had worked rather than it being a reflection of pleasure to see him.

Bowing deeply to Mantiss, he said, 'Master. I was wondering how I was going to get home.' The last word jarred.

'Everand, my boy, where have you been?' Mantiss rushed forward and took his hands, arching a silver eyebrow. 'You were not where we expected.'

'It's a long story,' said Everand, hoping the council would give him some time to recover. *To think.* He glanced surreptitiously at the impassive faces, and his heart sank. They expected him to say more.

'I adopted the disguise of a traveller to conceal my powers.' He gave a self-deprecating shrug. 'So, when the boat races were finished, I travelled to the next province, consistent with the disguise. I thought it might be useful to find out more about the other provinces.'

At that, several of the mages raised their eyebrows, their expressions suggesting they thought this a frivolous idea.

'Besides,' said Everand contritely, clasping his hands together, 'I was sent in such a hurry that we didn't make arrangements for my return after the mission.'

Mantiss looked a tad uncomfortable. 'Never mind, you are home now. What can you tell us? Did you find out who was trying to sabotage the races?'

Everand did not like the intense look accompanying the question. Did Mantiss know more than he was saying? 'I did,' he replied slowly. 'One of the four provinces didn't wish to take part in inter-province trade. Their leader decided that if he upset the boat races it would bring disgrace and a loss of trust to Riverfall.'

His knees began to shake. Deciding that a faint from exhaustion could be a useful reason to delay his report, he relaxed his leg muscles and toppled dramatically to his knees, allowing his head to almost hit the rug before snapping his hands into position to save himself.

'Everand!' Agamid hurried to help him back to his feet. 'You look exhausted.'

'Sorry! I haven't slept much the past three dark-falls.' Looking down at his grimy tunic, he added, 'And I badly need a bath and some clean robes.' He leaned on Agamid's arm more than he needed to.

'Is that what the odour is?' asked Neelaps, wrinkling his face. Beside him, Pelamis smothered a smirk.

'Could we reconvene?' Agamid asked Mantiss. 'Surely the report can wait until it is light?'

'Yes, of course,' said Mantiss, looking around at the council members. 'Thank you all for helping to retrieve Everand. The Inner Council of Ten will reconvene straight after breakfast.'

Everand hung onto Agamid's arm while the other mages bowed to Mantiss and departed with a colourful swishing of robes. Tiliqua looked back over her shoulder, her expression pensive. Mantiss stood staring at him as if he wanted to extract the information directly from his mind. He must deflect any prospect of this, or Mantiss would see far more than he wanted to reveal. His heart skipped in relief when Agamid spoke.

'I'll take Everand to his quarters and tell the kitchen to send food and drink for him at first light.' Agamid paused. 'Do you wish to speak after that or shall I see you at the meeting?'

Letting his head droop, Everand listened keenly. So, there was additional information passing between these two. He must be careful.

'Thank you, Agamid,' said Mantiss firmly. 'Perhaps you could join me for breakfast?'

'Yes, I will,' said Agamid, before squeezing Everand's arm. 'Come along, let's get you some rest.'

Everand allowed Agamid to lead him from the Great Hall, and as they crossed the massive silk rug he became aware that Agamid was breathing shallowly because his clothes really did smell. He straightened up and moved away a little. 'Sorry.

Being a traveller has some distinct disadvantages, one being that these people do not have hot baths.'

'I can see you have had some adventures,' said Agamid quietly while they walked along the crushed pebble path between the buildings.

'There is much to tell,' said Everand, not having to feign a large yawn. 'Everything is jumbled and my report will make more sense after some sleep.' When they reached the entrance to his building he turned and said with a short bow, 'I'll be fine from here. I appreciate your help. See you at the meeting.'

Wearily, he climbed the stairs to the ninth floor, the circular marble staircase eerily quiet. On reaching his door he hesitated. These rooms had been his home for a long time and he'd never anticipated that he might live somewhere else. With a small smile he imagined Lamiya touching his elbow and saying, *too much thinking*.

The crescent-moon-shaped handle registered his identity and the door swung open. He stepped inside and the room felt just like his dream: through the window the moon was high in the sky, with a spray of stars spread across the inky sky. The marble tiles sparkled with threads of silver and white, and a moonbeam highlighted the fish tank in the corner near the arched window. His fatigue falling away, he crossed the floor in large strides and opened the lid of the fish tank.

As in his dream, he scooped up a pod of the gel with Mizu embedded in it. A lump rose in his throat. How could he have expected this beautiful fish to live in a contained space? He melted the gel, ignoring the water splashing over his feet and puddling on the floor. Bending his will, he scanned the fish.

After three passes, he could find nothing wrong. Frowning, he sent a mind communication to the fish's pretty head. *Mizu, would you like to go home?* He added an image of the lake outside Lamiya's hut, with the soft hills cradling the eastern end and the colourful reeds along the lakeshore.

He nearly dropped Mizu when she twitched, the scales cold and slippery across his palms. A glassy eye rolled to look at him and an image of Dragon Lake came back to him. She was from Riverwood! *Tell me how you got here.*

Astounded, he received moving images of swimming through deep lake water, going to the surface for tasty morsels, being scooped up in a net of woven reeds and a woman's face peering into the net. The woman's gruff expression bore a resemblance to Malach, and the clothes were those worn by the people of Riverwood. Mizu was plopped into a jar and carried, then put into a clear jar where she could see out.

The next impressions were of a grassy area and being handed to a tall mage in brown robes. The image of Mage Beetal bending to passionately kiss the dark-haired woman made the back of his neck prickle. This was not a side to his mentor that he'd seen.

The following images were familiar, seen by the fish from inside the jar in its place on the corner of Mage Beetal's desk in his study. Astonishingly, his mentor had remembered to feed the fish and occasionally even looked at her. Mizu finished by showing him entering the study and bowing to his mentor.

'Very funny,' he murmured. The fish flopped on his palms, needing to be back in water. 'I'll take you to this new lake as soon as I can,' he promised, lowering Mizu back into the gel and dissolving it, pleased when Mizu blew bubbles and swam laps. He dropped in some ant eggs and closed the lid. One problem solved. Communicating with the dragon Mizukaze had taught him much.

He sat on the bed, the absence of Lamiya a powerful ache. His arms felt empty without her nestled against him. Yawning widely, he decided that being clean could wait and set a wake-up spell to sound before first light. Collapsing on top of the covers, he passed out.

☪

The wake-up bells jolted him out of a dreamless abyss. Rosy rays of light were peeking through the window. His neck felt like a block of wood from lying in one position for so long, and he groaned as he sat up. Gazing at the tank, he sighed in relief when Mizu swam to the side and blew bubbles. Good, he hadn't dreamed that part. His spirits sank when he remembered the imminent summons, and the odour of dust and sweat pervading his nose reminded him he needed a bath. A soft knock came at the door.

He stumbled off the bed and crossed the floor, finding he'd slept with his sandals on, and opened the door with some trepidation. A girl in a blue dress and simple apron stood there, a tray of breakfast in her arms. She dropped her eyes and curtsied.

'Thank you,' he said, taking the tray and thinking she didn't look familiar. The girl flushed, trying hard not to look at his odd outfit, and curtsied again.

'Will that be all, Mage Everand?' she asked.

'Yes, thank you … what is your name?'

The girl paled. 'My name?'

Everand frowned. Perhaps she thought he was going to make a complaint. 'You know my name; I'm just trying to be polite.'

Looking confused, she murmured, 'Melida, sir.'

'Thank you, Melida, for bringing breakfast so early.' He winced when she curtsied again and fled. Were all the humans this shy around the mages? The warm breads and stewed fruits smelled divine and he hurried to his table to devour them. The pot of tea was strong, just how he liked it, although the slice of lime made his bitten tongue sting unmercifully.

The sun's rays were already turning yellow so he ran a hot bath and lowered his battered body into it. Letting the steamy water ebb his tensions away, he tried to map out what to say in his report, but his mind refused to focus. With a sigh, he clambered out of the bath.

Clad in his second-favourite azure robe, he'd barely brushed and bound back his hair when the summons chime sounded. After taking a deep breath, he set off. Three floors down, he met Saiphos emerging from his rooms. The mage, formerly apprenticed to Agamid, smiled.

'I'm looking forward to your report,' said Saiphos. 'It will be a change from the usual agenda.'

Everand remembered that Saiphos had been keen to help when they were trying to counter Mage Beetal's actions before. Of a similar age, perhaps Saiphos also felt there was scope for some change. 'I suppose so,' he replied blandly. They trotted down the last flight of stairs and he asked, 'Has anything unusual happened while I was away?'

'Not really. Unless you count Mantiss deciding to remodel the antiquity room in the library.' Saiphos' crimson robes rippled with his shrug.

'Really?' said Everand. The antiquity room was where the oldest, original texts were housed. What would happen to the old texts? To the knowledge that was perhaps not imparted to the apprentices? He would like to see if there were any more detailed records of the arrival of the mages in Axis. Going on what Saiphos had just said, he should do this sooner rather than later. 'I see. My report might just be more interesting than that.'

Saiphos looked sideways at him.

Everand lengthened stride along the pebble path until his colleague had difficulty keeping up and was breathing heavily when they reached the steps to the Great Hall. Resisting the urge to bound up the steps to show off his new fitness, he walked up. Crossing the rug briskly, he found most of the council was already gathered.

On reaching the top of the dais, Everand bowed to Mantiss and Agamid, waited until Saiphos took his seat on Mantiss' right and then pulled out his chair to sit on Saiphos' right.

Seeing that Tiliqua was watching him from her seat directly opposite, he gave her a small smile.

While they waited for the last two to arrive, he glanced at the faces around the table, observing his fellow council members with fresh eyes. The battle with Mage Beetal and his army of dragons, and the death or demotion of Beetal's allies, had led to a significant refresh of the Inner Council. Mantiss was by far the oldest, and Agamid and Menetia were the only others with hints of grey in their hair. Not present yet, at thirty-five, Simoselaps would be the next oldest. Caimanops was thirty — and Tiliqua, Neelaps, Saiphos and Pelamis were all in their mid-twenties, like him, and had not long completed their apprenticeships. Mage Beetal would have been pleased at this possibility for fresh, more flexible views.

When Tiliqua's cool blue eyes continued to assess him, he decided he'd need to be careful around her. His cold and aloof mother had been incredibly powerful, and he suspected that Tiliqua also held extraordinary power. Her interest in him presented a further complication. Mantiss often referred to him as 'my son' and was probably hoping he would marry Tiliqua and make the title formal. Now knowing this would never be possible on his part, he should avoid too much contact with her.

Pelamis and Simoselaps rushed in together. As soon as they were seated, Mantiss leaned forward and placed his hands on the polished mahogany table. 'Thank you for convening so early. As you know, identifying and assessing any risks is a key role of the Inner Council. This is why I asked Everand to help the river province in need, and to find out as much as he could about all the river provinces over the eight suns required. To this effect, I'd like us to hear Everand's report directly. Then we can discuss whether there are any perceived risks.'

'This is the only agenda item for this special meeting,' added Agamid.

Everand steeled himself. They expected a full and detailed report; this was going to be difficult. Already, Simoselaps, Pelamis and Tiliqua were focused on him intently. He breathed in through his nose. Where to begin? Perhaps he could bore them with too much detail and force them to ask questions, which would hopefully be wide of the mark.

'Perhaps you'd like to start, and then we can ask questions.' Mantiss flapped a hand at him.

Locking his fingers together and adopting a sincere expression, Everand said, 'First, thank you for bringing me back. I can recount what happened from when I was sent to the province of Riverfall. I'm not sure how much the council already knows, so I'll set the context.'

'Keep it brief,' said Agamid pleasantly.

Everand described how he'd arrived in the town of Zuqart in the province of Riverfall seven suns before a festival was due to be held, which included racing boats to induce good rainfall for their crops.

Neelaps interrupted, his eyes twinkling with interest. 'What sort of crops?'

Playing to Neelaps' interest in agriculture, Everand said, 'They grow a wide array of crops, such as kapok cotton for clothing, wheat, fruits, vegetables and nuts. They're also keen fishermen–'

'We get the idea,' snapped Simoselaps. 'This is not a geography lesson. You can discuss growing and planting things with Neelaps later. So, what was the risk?'

'The boat races were to be followed by trade negotiations. The risk turned out to be that one of the provinces, Riverwood, didn't wish to participate in inter-province trade. They tried to sabotage the races and discredit the leader of Riverfall so the trade discussions would be cancelled.'

Simoselaps waved a hand brusquely, his beige sleeve swishing across the table and his brown eyes conveying impatience. 'What did they actually *do*? Focus on the risk, Everand.'

'They destroyed some crops, injured some of the boat paddlers and I thought they'd try to destroy the bridge across the river between their province and the others.'

'Why?' asked Agamid.

With a small shrug, Everand said, 'As far as I can tell, the Riverwood culture is very different to the others. They wanted to be left alone.'

Menetia threw Mantiss an exasperated look, her brown hair coiled in so many layers on top of her head that Everand couldn't count them. Her bracelets clinked when she waved an elegant hand. 'Does this have anything to do with us, Mantiss? I fail to see why it is a matter for the council.'

'I agree,' snapped Simoselaps. 'This seems minor.'

Pelamis leaned forward. 'Mage Mantiss, you said you sent Everand to ascertain whether there were any risks. Is there anything you were concerned about? This all seems most odd to me.' He scowled. 'Why meddle at all?'

Bold questions! Keen to know the answers, Everand held his breath.

Clearing his throat, Mantiss responded, 'Everand has left out a few points that might be of interest. The attacks on the crops were carried out by gigantic moths. This was reported by the messenger from Riverfall, and is a key reason why I sent Everand. Boat races and trade between provinces hold no interest whatsoever for us.'

Glancing around the table, Mantiss paused to stare at Pelamis. 'As you say, we don't meddle. The Guild annals clearly record that the first mages used magic to magnify the size of the insects in Axis — so how did such large moths come to be outside of Axis?'

Mantiss rested his elbows on the table and steepled his fingers. 'The messenger reported the moths were aggressive and focused in their attacks. Accordingly, I conferred with Agamid, and we felt we should confirm there was no magic involved, as unlikely as this appeared to be. Everand is adept at gathering information, so let's hear what he has to say.'

When all eyes swivelled to him, Everand's stomach churned: curse it, Mantiss *had* suspected magic was involved and hadn't said anything! Had Mantiss kept quiet because he worried there was inside involvement again? Or did he suspect there was someone with ability outside of the Guild, as unlikely as this seemed? Mantiss looked uncomfortable, his thin shoulders tensed and his face drawn.

Saiphos flapped a hand. 'What are you implying? That someone from Axis was involved? Why would they be?'

Everyone looked back at Mantiss, and Everand took the opportunity to skim their faces. Agamid seemed uncomfortable, Tiliqua annoyed. The others appeared confused, except for Simoselaps and Pelamis, who were regarding him through narrowed eyes. Of the nine, he guessed only three might be prepared to hear his views about a fair trial for Malach. Agamid was a fair man, but intensely loyal to Mantiss. Neelaps and Saiphos were also fair and less self-focused than the others.

The biggest threats were Simoselaps and Pelamis, who were rapidly gaining in boldness. Would they take the opportunity to discredit him and dislodge him as Mantiss' perceived favourite? Next along was Tiliqua, who would be objective and analytical, but how would she react when she understood he had no intention of pursuing a marriage to her? He gave a tight swallow. She and Mantiss would be offended, and would everything he'd done so far be sufficient to offset his master's disappointment? The hairs on the back of his neck shivered, as if brushed by a chill breeze.

Giving him a steely look, Mantiss said, 'Everand, get to the key points, if you please.'

He was trapped, unable to conjure a credible alternative. Maybe if he revealed the story bit by bit, he could gauge how much they knew. Resigned, he spoke evenly. 'Initially, I thought it was a petty inter-province squabble and wondered why I'd been sent. Then I saw the large moths and realised that someone must be influencing the moths, as well as other creatures, to attack the town and paddlers of importance.'

Spreading his hands on the shiny table, he added, 'As implausible as it seemed, I worried that someone was using magic.' He looked directly at Mantiss. 'The strategy was reminiscent of Mage Beetal's subterfuge. My mentor concocted a special compound to influence others, and I found traces of this in one of the attacks.'

Now that he held everyone's undivided attention, he said modestly, 'For a while I hesitated, thinking I was making connections where there were none. I also had no means to report back, and I couldn't bring myself back through the wardspell.' He shrugged. 'And I had been sent without the council knowing, so I could hardly lob rocks at the wardspell to trigger the alarm. I assumed Mage Mantiss had a strategy to recall me.'

He paused for effect and waited while Mantiss shuffled on his chair, but then flapped a hand at him to continue. There was no getting around it.

'Then, just before the races, the Riverwood boat team arrived. Their captain was the spitting image of Mage Beetal.' The collective gasp around the table was satisfying. Playing the drama, he added, 'Worse, this man looked straight at me and instantly recognised me as a mage, despite my disguise.'

'By the stars! How could this be?' Mantiss croaked.

Sadly, Everand said, 'Mage Beetal deceived us all one more time. The half-mage is his son.'

'Beetal rutted with a *human*?' said Menetia, her mouth twisted in disgust. 'He was more insane than we thought!'

'Does the son have power?' asked Agamid, creases of concern around his eyes.

'Yes, but limited training.' He would make it look as if it was Malach's fault, not his, for failing to return to the Guild. 'One of the reasons you couldn't find me was this half-mage kidnapped me, took me to Riverwood and was trying to force me to train him.'

'How did that happen?' demanded Tiliqua, anger flashing in her eyes. 'You're a fully trained mage! How could someone with basic training overpower you?'

Meeting her look, he replied, 'He made a quelling potion and his men threw a sack over me that was soaked in it. They forced me to keep swallowing the potion for two suns, which is why you couldn't detect me.'

Tiliqua's eyes narrowed. 'You allowed someone to drop a sack over you? I find that unlikely.'

'Are you disputing my word?' Everand asked, sitting taller. 'I was supposed to conceal my powers and ability, on Mantiss' orders.' He looked at Mantiss. '*Under no circumstances, none whatsoever, must you reveal your powers.* I am certain that is what you said.'

Mantiss had the grace to look uncomfortable.

'But you just said he knew you were a mage!' Tiliqua glared at him. 'How did you escape then?'

'I was rescued by frie– by people from Riverfall and Riverplain because they were grateful for my help in preventing disruption to the races. Then they took me further south, away from Riverwood, to keep me safe.'

'We're getting off track here,' said Simoselaps. 'There are several questions arising.' He ticked them off on his fingers. 'First, did you confirm he is Mage Beetal's son? Two, how did this happen? Three, how much power and training does he have and four, is he a risk?'

'If I may,' said Pelamis smoothly, 'none of those points matter. Guild Rule Eight is quite clear. Non-pure mages are not allowed, and if any are found they must be obliterated, under Guild Rule Eleven. Is that not so, Mage Mantiss?'

Most around the table nodded and looked relieved at such a simple solution. Everand swallowed. Should he propose his alternative, or pretend he was comfortable with the Guild Law? Before Mantiss could reply, he leaned forward and said, 'I think Simoselaps' questions have relevance. I can confirm this half-mage is indeed Mage Beetal's son.'

Simoselaps gave him a curt nod.

'It seems Mage Beetal met with the mother a few times and gave the boy some basic training.' Everand shrugged. 'He might have passed his son some compounds, such as the personality-adjusting one and the one to quell power. I don't think this half-mage has sufficient skill to make them.' As long as they didn't ask for a name, he would avoid giving them one.

Agamid put his hands on the table, his hazel eyes troubled. 'How did Mage Beetal get there, do you know? Is there a breach in the wardspell?'

'I'm afraid I don't know.' Everand shrugged apologetically. 'Beetal travelled through the wardspell and then via a sky-rift to get to Elemar's world. As you know, we found and closed that rift, but I don't know if he created another one closer by.'

Looking intently at Mantiss, he said firmly, 'My capture represented an unforeseen opportunity. I was planning to give the son a few basic, harmless skills while I found out more. I didn't try to escape because I was aiming to win his confidence. Unfortunately, the Riverfall people rescued me before I could find out enough. And then the council brought me back.'

Deliberately keeping his head bowed and clasping his hands together, he added, 'I'm sorry my report is not as complete as I would like. I would have liked to be able to answer all of Simoselaps' questions.'

'Not at all, Everand, not at all,' said Mantiss. 'You did well, and you have uncovered that the Guild has a risk that must be addressed. Although this is unexpected, it proves it was a good thing we decided to see what was occurring around us.' Mantiss' voice grew stronger. 'The council must vote. What action do we take from here? Proposals, if you please.'

'Obliteration,' said Pelamis firmly.

'I concur,' said Menetia in a bored tone, toying with a bracelet.

'I also,' said Tiliqua, but she was looking at Everand, not Mantiss.

Caimanops shifted in his chair. 'I think Everand has a point. Should we try to find out more? If we obliterate the son, we lose the chance to learn how this happened and whether there is another breach somewhere.'

Hope sparking in his chest at one dissenting voice, Everand jumped in quickly. 'Another factor to consider is whether we should bring this half-mage to the Guild. Or does the council propose to annihilate the man without trial and in front of his people? Wouldn't that create the risk of the river province people retaliating?'

Agamid's eyes glimmered and Neelaps looked at him thoughtfully. Saiphos stirred beside him, and Tiliqua looked taken aback. The others frowned.

'I see we have a few factors to consider. If we set out to capture him, do you know where this half-mage is?' Mantiss appeared disconcerted, stroking his wispy silver beard with a shaky hand.

'I know where he lives. Riverwood is the northern-most province.' Everand paused. 'I should warn you that his people are fierce hunters and trained warriors. They are also loyal to their leader and will not lightly let us take him.'

'You seem to have a knack for finding these barbaric people,' muttered Tiliqua with a scowl.

Agamid turned to Mantiss. 'We should take a break and reconvene to discuss strategy. These are serious matters and we need some time to form our opinions before we vote.'

'I agree,' said Mantiss slowly. 'I ask you all to consider the situation and be prepared to offer solutions. I will recall the council after the high-sun meal.'

With a rustling of robes and quiet chatter, the council members stood up and pushed their chairs in. Everand clunked his chair back in against the table before he could be asked to stay behind.

'Infinitely more interesting than a library makeover,' muttered Saiphos, walking beside him as he crossed the rug, heading for the doors.

'You should hear about the boat races,' replied Everand, thinking some time alone with Saiphos might prove fruitful.

'I'd like that,' said Saiphos before he turned away and walked down the wide wooden steps.

Everand looked across the neat, verdant lawns. So, Mantiss and Agamid *had* suspected something was amiss when they sent him on the mission. And they had kept that from him. But they *had* looked surprised when he declared Malach's existence. Was there something else they were worried about? How could he find out? In the meantime, the council's views were not promising for Malach, but he had bought some time.

How best to use it?

Chapter Twenty-One

An awful hollowness pooling inside her, sapping all thought and energy, Lamiya sat turning her empty mug around and around in her fingers. At first light, Lulite had made her a brew accompanied by a plate of fruits and sat with her, making sure she forced these down. Then her friend had left to see Lapsi, saying she'd return later.

A burning, acidic taste flowed into her mouth and she gagged, wanting to throw up. Perhaps a walk by the lake would calm her nerves. With shaking fingers, she put the mug down and pushed up to her feet, glad when Whirr flew onto her shoulder and rubbed his tiny head against her cheek.

Wandering to the edge of the water, she stared longingly across to the far side, but the boatshed stood silent and closed, the beach stretching deserted along the shore. She clenched her fingers. A rigorous paddle would be a useful distraction, but the team needed to regather their energy. Her feet chose the path towards the distant hills and groves of fruit trees. With a peep of approval, Whirr fluffed his wings. Flooded by an urgent longing to be surrounded by her birds, Lamiya quickened her steps.

Forcing her mind to be in the present, she peered at the fruit trees, noting the myriad shoots promising new leaves and the balls and ovals of forming fruit. At the grove of feeja trees, she leaned in to sniff at the impressive spread of tiny red flowers, boding well for a bountiful crop. Her mouth watered at the thought of eating her favourite fruit, the taste a strong and exotic mix of sweet and tart that exploded over the tongue.

At the final row of trees, she hovered, gently fingering the delicate baby fruit. Lopa had experimented by crossing feeja tree grafts with the green-tang fruit. The hundreds of tiny, crisp, green fruits brought a smile to her lips. This would be the first season the fruit was large enough to eat, and Lopa was still debating what to call it.

Whirr peeped loudly and the trees in the next grove were transformed when hundreds of vividly plumed birds rose from the leaves and descended to where she stood. Laughing in delight, she raised her arms out wide and was immediately covered in chattering, fluffy, bustling bodies. The noise drowned out further thought. Sensing her sadness, the birds took it in turn to greet her by rubbing the tops of their heads against her chin or a cheek. They were all there: the green finches with blue faces, the grey striped ones with vivid red tails, the bright yellow canaries, the brown grass finches with white faces and black throats and the ones with black rings around their eyes and chests that looked like tiny owls.

'You are doing wonderful work,' she told them. The bountiful budding crops were evidence of the birds' meticulous work protecting the trees from grubs, weevils and flying insects. A melodious chorus replied and then she asked, 'What about the nut trees? Would you care to show me those?'

She ambled to the next grove with a cloud of coloured wings fluttering around her, creating tiny eddies of air. Standing in the shade of the taller trees, she peered up at the clusters of nuts while the birds showed off, zipping in and out of the branches and hovering near neat nests perched almost invisibly in the higher branches. Every type of nut was doing well, even the round, creamy ones with the shells that were so hard to crack. Would she ever be able to prepare her favourite sweet dish of stewed feeja fruit laced with ground nuts for Everand?

A wave of loss crashed over her. Her heart raced, her vision narrowed and she struggled for breath. How could he be wrenched away from her like that? Whirr fluffed at her face with his wingtips until she realised the ghastly rasping sound was her breathing. Closing her eyes, she drew in deep breaths, her lurching, hammering heart slowly growing steadier with each one.

When she opened her eyes, her feet drew her further east along the lake, toward her family's shrine. Her soul fluttered in her chest; her parents' guidance was exactly what she needed. Walking slowly, she trailed her fingers through the lower leaves of the trees, seeking reassurance from their soft, wispy touch brushing her fingertips. The birds flew back to their tasks, except Whirr, who returned to her shoulder.

Ahead, the hills loomed larger, the green mounds rising like breasts, calling her to come nestle in their comfort. Coot birds waddled among the reeds and noisy ducks splashed at the water's edge with their young.

The path grew narrower and fainter when she reached where few people went, the grasses and weepy willow trees stretching almost to the lake's edge. The rhythmic rippling of the water soothed her further. Her soul fluttering once more, she approached the dense stand of willows. At the opening to the circle of trees, she bowed respectfully to the cairns of stones on either side.

'Spirits of my ancestors, grant me entry,' she murmured.

A breeze stirred the branches, the long leaves whispered a sibilant greeting and the hanging pebble chimes tinkled a welcome, an approval to pass. Her sandals soundless on the soft, verdant grass, she stepped into the small grove and in another three strides was kneeling before the stone shrine, the drooping willow leaves a green cocoon around her. A shudder wracked her and she struggled to contain her sorrow. Whirr flew to the base of the shrine and watched her with beady eyes.

To the left of the shrine was a small wooden bowl and ladle. She never quite understood how it was always filled with fresh water, but accepted this was so. Picking up the ladle, she scooped out pure water and trickled it over one hand and then the other. Then she put the ladle down, dipped her hands into the bowl and splashed handfuls of the cool, calming water over her face, enjoying the aroma of earth and leaves that enveloped her.

Taking a steadying breath, she faced the cairn of rocks, built of sufficient soul stones to now reach head height when she knelt. Beginning at the base of the tower and murmuring each name with respect, she read the names of her ancestors carved into the ornate grey stones, until she reached the top two. Bands of sorrow snapped across her chest and her breath caught, snagged in the memory of how the fierce pyre had taken her parents' physical bodies away and released their spirits into the sky.

Afterwards, she had scoured the lakeshore for an entire sun, seeking suitably elegant rocks to represent her mother and father. Then she had sat with Lattic, grateful for his silent personality and watching with a broken heart while he carefully chiselled the names into the rocks in a neat, elegant script. *Lestaya. Azuri.*

'Mother,' she whispered, 'taken far too soon, I greet your spirit and humbly request your guidance.' Completing a small bow, she murmured, 'Father, taken far too soon, I greet your spirit and wish you well in the afterlife.'

Her hands resting in her lap, she searched inside for the pool of still water, her calling pond, and imagined the pool growing deeper, more compelling, and subtle tendrils of mist reaching out. Head bowed, she eased in slow and even breaths.

The dangling willow branches danced sibilantly and air moved across her face in a feather-light caress. The feathers on the top of Whirr's head flattened as if he'd been patted, and he peeped. The presence of her mother infused the grove and hints of the lily scent her mother used to splash on her wrists teased Lamiya's nostrils.

Before she could deflect it, a massive wave of grief — both old and fresh — enveloped her and she bent over, sobbing so hard that her chest and throat hurt. Finally spent, she took a shuddering breath and sat straighter. The breeze flowed over her head and down her hair, just like her mother used to stroke her hair.

'Mother,' she rasped, 'I miss you so much. I need you for I am … adrift.' She imagined Lestaya, clad in her pale-green tunic and darker green skirt, wavy golden hair coiled above her head, picking up her skirt and settling onto the grass in front of her. Warm air brushed over her hands. *Tell me.*

'It is too much,' Lamiya began. 'First you and Father, so ill for so long, and I could do nothing to help you.'

You loved us. That was enough, dear daughter. We miss you too.

'And now, just as I find someone to love, to be with, he is wrenched away. I fear they will kill him and I'll never see him again.' Her words turned into a wail.

Lazuli? Something happened to Lazuli? The spirit of her father oozed around her and a light touch patted her shoulder. He'd always liked Lazuli. Fresh grief assailing her, she remembered how many times Lazuli had come to sit with her father in his illness, chatting away about hopeepa breeding and paddling training.

Hush, dear. Not Lazuli, her mother's spirit admonished. *As wonderful as Lazuli is, he is not the one to love Lamiya.*

Surprise tingled through her. 'You know about Everand?'

Is that his name? Close your eyes and show him to us, daughter dear.

Lamiya closed her eyes and drew upon her favourite memories of Everand: seeing him in the river the first time;

going to Dragon Lake in the dark; him riding Mizukaze and saving the races; being kidnapped to save her, standing so tall and powerful to challenge Malach. She blushed when her mind added the feel of his mouth on hers, his arms around her and the way he nuzzled at her neck, and how warmth grew between her legs.

I see. Her mother's spirit seemed amused. *He is most handsome and noble.*

Humph. He doesn't like boats, her father's spirit grumped.

'I plan to remedy that,' said Lamiya.

I perceive great power. Her mother's spirit was thoughtful. *Lamiya, dear heart, you have grown tremendously in your ability already. You truly love him, which is well, as you two have been put together for a reason.*

A shiver chased down her neck as her mother echoed the words of U-Mali. She hadn't asked for any of this! But neither had Everand. Perhaps their reward for whatever they had yet to do was each other. If he came back. Noticing that Whirr was watching her with his head tilted to one side, she gathered her courage and asked, 'Can you foresee what I have to do?'

The grove was silent, holding its breath, until eventually the leaves fluttered on the branches.

Sadly, no, dear daughter. Your path is shrouded in mists. You must hone your visions and calling ability. The only thing I can see is that you will be the next Riverplain guide.

'What?' The truth of it rammed into her and she swayed. U-Mali and U-Lumin's daughter had died as a child and they had borne no other — their line of ancestry was over, and a new guide would have to be found. Her heartbeat boomed in her ears. Could it be her? Surely, there was someone else? The pebble chimes swirled and tinkled, sounding as if her parents were laughing.

You should see your face! We always knew you were special, and not just to us.

What I don't understand, came her father's presence, *is what the fearsome beasts are for? I thought we called birds, not massive, scaled creatures?*

Lamiya felt her mouth drop open and hastily snapped it shut. Was her father referring to something that had already happened, such as the calling of Mizukaze or Flight, or were there more dragons to come? Everand had asked whether there was a dragon in her lake. Did he also think there were more dragons? The essence of her parents began to fade and she held her hands out, mutely pleading for them to stay just a little longer.

Take care, daughter. Be brave and true.

A last eddy of lily scent wafted under her nose and then the grove was still, cool and silent. The sounds of the lake returned, the rustling of the reeds, the calling of the waterbirds, the clicks and chirrups of insects. For a while she sat watching the flickering beams of light playing over the soul stones of her parents. The beams highlighted the threads of pink she had so admired when choosing her mother's stone, whereas her father's stone had more sombre threads of silver and dark blue.

Her skirt was damp beneath her clasped hands, and although her body felt heavy, it also seemed cleansed. Balancing on her knees, she used the ladle to wash her hands again, then stood and kissed her mother's engraved name, feeling the cool rock brush her lips. Then she kissed her father's name. Whirr flew up to sit on her shoulder, ready to leave.

Hope beating in her heart, she stepped slowly from the grove. Her parents had approved of Everand and foresaw a future for them.

He *must* find a way back.

He had promised.

Chapter Twenty-Two

Hearing the slap of the other mages' sandals descending the steps behind him, Everand set off down the path that led to the Guild library. His stomach grumbled, but he'd missed so many meals on his 'simple' mission that forgoing one more wouldn't hurt. Striding quickly to deter any of the others from walking with him, he glanced at the lawns and gardens. A vibrant array of flowers and manicured green lawns rolled away from the path, giving a sense of space, but now the gardens seemed somehow too neat and too tidy compared to the river and open landscape of Riverfall and Riverplain.

His chest throbbing painfully, he thought of Lamiya's hut and the stunning views from her door. He imagined her standing there smiling at him, and the ache intensified. How soon could he find his way back to her? The council was moving faster than he'd anticipated. Would the library reveal any clues about what could be worrying Mantiss and Agamid?

The five-floor dome of the library rose before him, the white marble bouncing the sun's rays into his eyes. He powered up the external polished redwood steps, eyeing the symbol of the Staropal hovering between two book outlines etched into the wooden frame above the door. The star-shaped bronze plaque didn't do justice to the magnificent, head-sized stone filled with swirling colours that was buried deep below the floor of the Great Hall. The plaque represented the knowledge and wisdom held in the library, but the Staropal was far more than that.

Passing under the doorframe, Everand recalled snippets from his history lessons that were part of his apprentice studies. Mages were born with power, which required training, but there was further power contained in the Staropal. The founders of the Guild had discovered the stone buried deep in the eternal spring, and had reportedly taken the finding of the magnificent stone as a sign they should settle there. From early on, the stone had been buried and warded, only accessible through a special word spell known solely by the incumbent Head of the Mages' Guild.

The battle had been fought in the Great Hall itself, where Mage Beetal had forced Mage Mantiss and the Outer Council of Twenty to raise the Staropal. Then his mentor had taken it, a foolish move that had only alienated the Guild further. In an even more stupid move, his mentor had taken the Staropal with him when he travelled to Chrysalis in search of greater knowledge.

Everand scrubbed at his jaw, trying to ease the frustration tensing the muscles. Listening had never been one of his mentor's strong points, no matter how persuasively he'd tried to reason with him.

In an entirely miraculous stroke of good fortune, the farseer in Chrysalis that captured Mage Beetal had forced him to use the stone to create a sky-path for their army, and hence he'd had to bring it back with him when the Chrysalids invaded the Guild. Everand's forehead throbbed with a deep frown. How had his mentor managed to retain control over the stone when surrounded by three powerful farseers? Was it possible they couldn't wield the stone or access its magic? If so, that would explain why they hadn't killed Mage Beetal.

When mages were dead and dying and all had seemed utterly lost, his mentor *finally* listened to his pleas to save the Guild and redirected the wrath and might of his army of winged dragons to the Chrysalids.

Pushing down a rush of sadness that it had been too little, too late, Everand considered what had happened next. After Mage Beetal was dead and the Chrysalids were defeated, Mantiss had buried the Staropal again, with extra layers of wards and protection. Mantiss had also added an alarm to the wardspell to deter any further breaches. All hundred mages had been gathered, and in a strident voice Mantiss had declared there would be no further access to the stone, and no extension of powers. The Guild would work to refine their existing powers through research and experimentation — and for the past eight seasons this had been the case.

Tripping over the top step, Everand hurriedly righted himself. Where had the Staropal come from in the first place? How did it get to be in the eternal spring? Rapidly scanning through his memories, he couldn't recall a single mention of this. History simply said it was found in the spring, concealed in a rocky cranny. His forehead prickled with tension. If there was only one stone, then it was unlikely to be a natural phenomenon. How had it been created? Or, more importantly, by whom? Had nobody researched this?

'Everand! I haven't seen you for a while.' The librarian appeared in the hallway and greeted him warmly.

Bowing, Everand said, 'I have been busy, Mage Hydrelaps.' Straightening, he decided to get to the point. 'I hear some changes are planned for the library?'

'Yes. Mantiss decreed we should clear the antiquity rooms to make way for new research.' Hydrelaps wrung his long hands together.

'Saiphos mentioned this. I was hoping to take a look at the antiquity collection to see if there were any books I'd like for my own collection — in case Mantiss allows us to choose.'

Hydrelaps lifted his sparse red eyebrows and hope sparked in his green eyes. 'Of course. It would be excellent if some of the ancient texts could be preserved. Follow me.' With a swish of blue robes, the librarian set off across the grey-tiled marble floor.

Everand followed, breathing in the smell of the parchment maps and books, wood polish and hints of dust, and admiring the way the lights played upon the floor from the tall stained-glass windows. Hydrelaps kept the building in excellent order, and books never failed to be on the shelf they were supposed to be. Apprentices were rostered on to assist and anyone who didn't meet Hydrelaps' exacting standards soon knew about it.

Even the study rooms on the higher floors were always neat, welcoming places to attend classes or borrow books and conduct research. The sun-filled room with a view of the Bellflower gardens and pond was his favourite.

Whenever he spent time in the room, Hydrelaps always thoughtfully asked the kitchens to bring him refreshments. He liked and respected the librarian with the narrow face and sparse beard who was so considerate and devoted to the acquisition and safe storage of all valuable knowledge.

They swiftly passed the shelves of books for alchemy, then those for defensive spells and tactics, and next came several shelves devoted to healing. That knowledge had been useful when Ejad was bitten by the viper and Everand was glad he'd paid attention in those classes. Suddenly missing Ejad's infectious enthusiasm, he faltered when the faces of Beram, Mookaite, Tengar, Atage and the others crowded into his mind. He missed them all. It was an infrequent emotion and he was surprised at its strength.

The door to the room of antiquity was closed. Hydrelaps placed his hand over the leaf-shaped handle, fashioned from a tawny wood that stood out against the rich redwood door. Entry was restricted to the Head of the Guild and the librarian, and Everand felt humbled by Hydrelaps' trust. The librarian had observed him meeting Mantiss in here from time to time. Was this the basis for such trust? Following Hydrelaps, he stepped into the cooler, dimmer room with a musty aroma of truly old books and parchment. Motes of dust hovered as if time had stilled around them.

'Is there any facet of history in particular that I can help you with?' asked Hydrelaps.

Guessing that the nature of his requests would be passed back to Mantiss and that Hydrelaps wouldn't leave him in the room unattended, Everand debated for a moment before bringing a smile to his lips. 'Mage Mantiss sent me to a neighbouring province to resolve a minor dispute and, having observed how different the people are to us, I've become interested in how and when the mages settled in Axis.'

When Hydrelaps raised both eyebrows in astonishment, Everand paused. Trying not to look too keen, he then offered, 'Perhaps I can tell you about the lifestyle of the provinces in exchange for your guidance on the oldest texts?'

The librarian cleared his throat. 'An unusual request, and of course the texts must not leave this room.' Hydrelaps squinted at the shelves. 'I suppose I could do some dusting and polishing while you peruse the books. When do you plan to start?'

Allowing his face to fall in disappointment, Everand replied, 'I'm in between council meetings and was hoping to spend a short time here now.'

Hydrelaps raised his eyebrows again. 'Very well. Wait right here while I fetch a duster.' He spun around and hurried out of the room, leaving the door open.

Sorely tempted to rush to the books in the furthest, darkest corner of the room, Everand remained put. He couldn't afford to lose Hydrelaps' trust so early. Enhancing his senses, he roved over the shelves, ascertaining the titles on the spines of the books. Those on the first five shelves he was familiar with from various stages of his studies. He paused at the glass-doored cabinet containing the rolled-up maps, thinking that what maps were kept in there could be revealing.

Nagging intuition kept pulling his attention to the remote corner, to where an ornate and gnarled bookcase built from ancient oak trunks held items on a single shelf. The other shelves held only dust. The slim books looked crumbled and musty, indicating they hadn't been used for a long time. Could he ask to see these without raising suspicion? He transferred his attention to the shelf of books adjacent to the oak bookshelf. *Boats?* The library held books about the construction and navigation of *boats*? His breath caught in the back of his throat.

With a slap of sandals, Hydrelaps strode back into the room with a large cloth duster in one hand and a bottle of polish in the other. He looked relieved to see Everand standing exactly where he had left him. 'Thank you for waiting. Have you thought of a topic?'

'Well,' Everand said slowly, as if thinking, 'a key feature of the nearby lands is a large river. These are water-based people and they even hold boat races. Do you have any texts on boats?'

'Boats? Let me see …' Hydrelaps twirled the cloth, the yellow material shedding particles of fluff to dance in the air with the motes of dust. 'Ah yes. We do have a small collection. This way.' He walked towards the bookcase almost at the far end. 'Are their boats made from wood?'

'I believe so. The most interesting ones have wooden heads and tails fashioned to look like dra– mythical creatures.' Everand swallowed. Why had his instinct been not to say dragons?

Stopping dead, Hydrelaps spun to face him. 'I would like to see that!'

'Those are the boats they race,' said Everand. 'It's quite a sight, with ten paddlers to a boat plus a steering person and a drummer.'

'A drummer!' exclaimed Hydrelaps. 'How fascinating.' He faced the bookcase. 'This is our modest collection. Let me know if you find any illustrations of those boats and show them to me.'

'Thank you. I will,' Everand said, nodding.

'I'll be over there.' Hydrelaps indicated the bookshelves across the aisle.

Everand skimmed the titles on the spines. *Seafaring Vessels. Fishing Vessels. Ship Warfare. Boat Construction. Sails, Ropes and Oars. Navigating Winds and Tides.* Given the inland nature of Axis, this was quite a collection. Oh, yes. Their teacher of ancient history had mentioned briefly that the mages had originally come from across the sea. He felt his eyebrows tug into a frown. The coverage of the voyage and arrival was so brief he'd forgotten about it.

Carefully, he extracted the navy book with the title in gold letters about seafaring vessels. The cover was made from an animal hide, desiccated and taut with age. An odd smell lingered and he wrinkled his nose as he pried the front cover open and ran a fingertip over the yellow, crinkled parchment. It was coarse to the touch, crisp against his fingers.

He turned to Hydrelaps. 'Should I wear gloves? These books feel fragile.'

Pausing with the cloth in his raised hand, Hydrelaps' face scrunched up and he sneezed. 'My apologies! These shelves do indeed need a dust. Gloves?' His sparse eyebrows drew together. 'That would be a good idea. Shall I fetch some?'

As tempting as it was to encourage the librarian to leave the room again, Everand said, 'No, I can create some. Will thin silk be appropriate?' At Hydrelaps' nod, he put the book down flat on the shelf and, looking at his outstretched hands, created snug gloves of fine silk, coloured a pale sky blue. He added an invisible thin shield beneath the fingers. This way he would leave no trace of what he touched.

When Hydrelaps resumed dusting, Everand picked the book up again, smoothed the parchment down and turned the inside title page over. The words were sculpted in a spidery, cursive script and the language was flowery, barely recognisable as Ossilian. He skimmed the page containing the specifications of what types of wood were required, then turned the page. His interest sharpened at the fine line drawing. The vessel looked large, and the body of it sat high above a crinkly line representing water. Two tall wooden masts rose from the deck and large triangular cloths stretched from these. The names allocated to the parts of the boat said they were called sails.

Reflecting for a moment, he decided it made sense that people travelling across large expanses of water such as a sea would not paddle or row. Various ropes and hawsers were attached to the sails, and the objective was to harness the force of the wind to move the boat. There was no requirement for boats like that in Axis, so it wasn't surprising the topic wasn't covered in the history lessons. He carefully prised open the rest of the pages, but the entire book was devoted to technical aspects of boat construction and there was no reference to when and why these boats were sailed.

Gently replacing the book, he eyed the other titles. *Ship Warfare* ... why would mages need a book about this? He crooked a finger in the top of the spine of the red cover and eased the book out. His heartrate increased. On the cover inlaid in pressed silver was a boat reminiscent of the dragon boats, except the boat was longer and bigger with ... he counted rapidly ... fifty paddlers on each side. The ornate carved wooden head drew his eye. Surely, that was intended to represent some great sea serpent? The gaping jaws, sharp teeth, bulging eyes, short horns and spikes made the creature look fierce.

Opening the book, he quickly became absorbed by the numerous diagrams in neat, sharp lines despite the age of the text. People with spears and crossbows sat behind the head of the serpent and another armed group sat at the rear. He thought of Malach standing at the rear of Raptor hefting the crossbow. The bows were similar. Or maybe there was a limited choice for functional design of this weapon.

Entranced, he read the strategies for warfare at sea. The crews carried long ropes with grappling hooks to pull another boat closer, and short ladders so they could board it. There were pages devoted to techniques for ramming another boat to capsize it depending on the swell of the waves, the wind direction and speed and the sea currents.

The final pages showed strategies to deter the great sea serpents, with long spears and balls with sharp spikes that could be thrown. His mind played the scenes vividly for him and he sighed, wishing the topic had been covered in his studies. Turning to the last page, his heart skipped: a map.

His fingers tightening on the book's cover, he glanced at the librarian, who was meticulously lifting each book to sweep the cloth across the wood underneath. Looking at the map, Everand mouthed a memory spell and fixed the page in his mind so he could study it in detail later. A sideways glance told him Hydrelaps hadn't noticed the subtle draw of power.

The place names were hard to read because the ink had faded and so the ornate letters had gaps in them. The map showed a large and long, head-shaped landmass surrounded by oceans. At the margins of the page were edges of what were islands, or the distant reaches of other landmasses. He made out an 'O' as the beginning of the name of the landmass. Ossilis? The word looked to be the right length and the last letter resembled an 'S'.

He held the book a little further away, trying to recall the map that Agamid had taken to the initial discussion with Beram. Was it similar? Wavy blue lines ran down the map, not quite in the centre, a little towards the eastern edge.

Astonished, he realised the rivers and lakes made a pattern akin to looking down on the outline of a dragon from above. There was an oval lake feeding into a plateau that looked like a dragon's head. Dragon Lake and Mizuchi Falls? A narrow band of water fed from the southern end of the lake, forming the dragon's neck. This ran for a way and then two tributaries fed in from the west and the east, resembling forelegs, and the river widened to look like a sinuous dragon body.

Excitement shivered through him. Surely, the western foreleg was the tributary that led into Riverwood, and the other one was the narrow river at the northern boundary of Riverfall? At the southern end were two more tributaries that looked like a dragon's hind legs, and when the river reached the sea at the bottom of the landmass, it coiled and fanned out like a tail. The province boundaries were not marked. He looked again: there was also no feature indicating the granite wall that surrounded Axis, nothing at all to represent the existence of the Guild.

The nape of his neck tingling, he closed the book and jumped. His neck had been trying to alert him to the rhythmic slap of approaching footsteps.

Agamid strode into the antiquity room and stopped short. 'Everand! Why — I didn't realise you were in here.' Curiosity burned in the mage's hazel eyes.

Clutching the duster and leaving a trail of floating yellow fluff behind him, Hydrelaps bustled over. 'Mage Agamid, welcome. Can I help you?'

Still looking at Everand, Agamid said, 'Mage Mantiss asked me to fetch the large map again for the Inner Council of Ten discussions.'

'The one you borrowed before?' clarified Hydrelaps.

'Yes, that one.' Agamid looked at the book in Everand's hands and his eyebrows rose.

Thinking quickly, Everand held the book up to show the cover to Hydrelaps. 'This boat is similar to the province racing boats I mentioned, except it looks bigger.'

'Let me see.' Hydrelaps scurried towards him, forgetting Agamid's request.

Stifling a smile, Everand passed the book to Hydrelaps. 'This boat has more paddlers, but the design with the carved head is similar.'

'What a monster!' exclaimed the librarian. 'You didn't see one of those, did you?'

Technically, he hadn't seen a sea serpent, so Everand shook his head.

'Did they use wooden sticks like this?' asked Hydrelaps, running his fingers over the silver image.

'Paddles,' said Everand. 'Ten paddlers to a boat.'

'Ahem!' Agamid cleared his throat loudly. 'The map, if you would, Hydrelaps.'

'Oh, yes! Immediately.' Hydrelaps thrust the book back at Everand and rushed to the bookcase containing the maps, fumbling in the folds of his robe for the key to the glass doors.

'Why are you reading about boats?' asked Agamid.

Slipping the book back onto the shelf and dissolving the fine gloves before he turned around, Everand said, 'I was looking at the pictures rather than reading. I found the boat races interesting and was surprised to find our library holds books on the topic.' He shrugged then dropped his hands by his sides.

'Why are you in this room?' Agamid peered around at the old shelves and the musty books.

Warmth crept into Everand's cheeks. He should adhere to the story he'd already told Hydrelaps. 'I heard the council is considering redoing this room. I was wondering what would happen to the old books and, if they were going to be destroyed, whether I might be allowed to keep a few. I was going to ask Mantiss.'

Around a level, assessing look Agamid said, 'I see. And are there?'

'If no-one else is interested in the ones on boats, I'd like one or two of those. This is the only shelf I've looked at.' Everand lifted his shoulders nonchalantly.

'Your map, Mage Agamid.' Hydrelaps held out the rolled parchment respectfully.

Agamid reached for the map and tucked it under an arm without taking his eyes away from Everand's face. 'Mantiss is about to reconvene the council. You might as well walk with me.'

Chapter Twenty-Three

With a satisfied grunt, Malach pushed the skin blanket back. 'Go now,' he said to the young woman on his mattress. Standing, he cricked his neck from side to side and stretched his arms out, smiling thinly when the woman's gaze dropped to his groin. 'Come back at dark-fall.' She'd been bold and had pleased him; he could go another round with her. Her shapely curves had fulfilled their promise.

The woman snatched up her clothes, dressed and left with a final sway of her hips. Scratching at the itch in his groin, Malach went to the tub in the corner, dipped the ladle deep and scooped cold water over his body. Refreshed and the itch dispatched, he dressed in his short-sleeved tunic and knee-length trousers, tightened the leather belt and attached the sheaths for his best knives.

With care, he tipped more of the personality-adjuster compound into the clay jar, watching the rich crimson liquid ooze into the jar mouth before pressing the wooden stopper in tight. Putting this in the soft pouch he reserved for it, he tied the strings to attach it to his belt.

Peering into the larger jar on the shelf, he frowned when he saw the potion was running low. The notebook his father had given him didn't contain the spell to make more and Everand would probably refuse to make it, even if he knew the recipe. Never mind. If things went well, he could force Everand to show him how to use mind control to achieve the same outcome.

Briskly, he filled pouches with berries, nuts and strips of dried bunya meat. Grabbing his shorter cloak from the peg next to the door, he swung it over his shoulders and stepped out.

Shoulders back, he nodded to those he passed and made a direct line for his raptor cages. When he strode into the clearing, Torrap was already there, watching the two new warrior hawks fly around their cages testing the bars for an escape route. Curse the impudent boatwoman for freeing his other birds! Now he had to start again.

As soon as he held out his hand, Torrap bent down to pick up a wooden board with strips of fresh, pink bunya flesh on it. Unstoppering the jar, Malach slowly tipped a drop of potion onto the meat. Torrap juggled the board carefully, slid aside the door to the feeding hole and nudged the board into the cage. They repeated the exercise for the second cage.

'Should we step back?' asked Torrap.

'No. The birds must get used to me. They will eat.' Malach eyed his new catches. The warrior hawks were sleek, agile hunters. Both females, the grey feathers along their back and wings were a shade lighter than those of the males, their cream chests and bellies speckled with grey-brown freckles. The females tended to be sharper-minded, and besides, the people of the other provinces were too used to seeing his eagles now and these smaller birds would attract less attention.

The bird in the second cage relented first, dropping to the floor to peck at the flesh strips. The darker rings around this one's eyes distinguished her from the other hawk.

Crouching, he was pleased when the bird stared at him but did not fly off. 'I name you Swift,' he said. The bird shook herself, settled her feathers and pecked at the empty board. 'Give her some more,' he said to Torrap.

He stood and moved to the first cage. It took a while, but the other bird eventually approached the food board, clacking her beak several times before gobbling the flesh in swift grabs.

When he crouched, the bird hopped backwards and clacked her beak. He held a hand out for Torrap to put a strip of meat in it, then poked this through the bars and waited. The bird stretched her neck and flapped her wings. She was cautious, but looked more aggressive. Eventually, the bird hopped forward and ripped the meat from his fingers.

'I name you Strike,' he murmured. Standing, he wiped his hands down his trousers. The next feed would be easier. Losing trained birds back into the wild had wasted time and valuable potion.

'The moths?' asked Torrap.

After a cursory nod, Malach skirted around the edge of the cages and took the narrow, shaded path that led to the crop of granite boulders below the copse of ancient pines. He grew warmer as the path climbed, and munched on handfuls of nuts and berries. Torrap followed in silence. Three suns until Everand returned. Which spells did he most need to be taught? What information did he require?

He licked his lips, the gritty aftertaste of the nuts clinging to his tongue. Was his father's demise eight seasons ago in any way connected to why the Guild had sent Everand now? The slippery apprentice hadn't suggested this, but it seemed a possibility given that the mages never left Axis.

Using well-known handholds to lever his body up the granite face, he had sweat beading on his forehead by the time he pulled himself up the last rocky ledge. When Torrap arrived beside him, he asked, 'How many cocoons did we count last time?'

'Thirty-six,' Torrap said promptly.

Moving forward with Torrap beside him, Malach scanned the weighty branches of the ancient pines. The foliage spread away from the branches like chunky dark-green fingers gnarled with age. No sunlight made it through this canopy, and the air was moist. The pervasive scents of pine, mould and fungi were not enough to disguise the musky stench of the moths. A shiver chased down his arms at the cool air tingling against his skin and drawing his cloak tighter, he gazed at the massive cocoons hanging from the branches.

The moths had chosen a group of five ancient pines in the middle of the copse for their nursery. Elongated, beige, paper-like lanterns were suspended from the middle branches by sticky silvery threads. The cocoons, as big as a person and glistening with strands of sticky substance, jiggled on their threads with the movement of the caterpillars readying to hatch. Good. He'd lost too many moths in the last two attacks on Zuqart. Curse the Riverfall boat captain and his ability to organise men.

The closest tree trunk quivered when the moth clinging to it shifted in his presence and the outlines of the wings became visible. The musk cloying his nostrils, Malach admired the camouflage; the dusty wings laced with veins and bark-like lines blended in with the knobbly trunk. Moving quietly, he stepped through the rows of trees.

Enthralled when he'd first found a couple of moths four seasons before, he'd learned the hard way about the dust they shook from their wings when threatened. His face and arms had blistered and burned for several suns and he'd seen their potential as a weapon. The moths had arrived after his mage father ceased to visit, so he was unable to confirm that they'd come from Axis. However, given the similarity in size to the beetle his father rode, this seemed likely. Perhaps a pair of moths had somehow followed his father through the wall and found the copse of trees to their liking.

His father had never explained how he travelled through the granite wall and had strictly forbidden him and Chinfe from approaching it. Although of late he'd yearned to approach the wall to look for his father, he'd resisted the temptation, deeming the risk too great. Perhaps after Everand had taught him more magic he could reconsider.

Turning to Torrap, he raised an eyebrow.

'I count forty-two,' said Torrap.

'Good. We'll return in four suns to feed potion to the larvae.' Malach started off along a narrow trail leading away from the trees. The ground squelched under his sandals, the gloomy shade not yet dried from the recent rain. Fresh fungus and mushrooms sprouted in an array of colours: white, grey, red, purple and gold. His mouth watered. The purple ones made an excellent stew.

'Where now?' asked Torrap.

'Dragon Lake. I have some spells to practise.'

He navigated the twisted, narrow path towards the lake in silence, although he suspected Torrap had many questions. Leaning forward, he drove with his legs up the slope leading to the lake. It might be useful to have Torrap's perspective on the unfolding events.

When the ground drew level again and they entered the forest on the western shore of the lake Malach strode out, enjoying the energy coursing through his body. He felt strong and relaxed after sex with the woman. Remembering how he'd seen Everand flexing his fingers to draw power, he crunched and spread his fingers while he walked, focusing to summon his power. By the time he emerged onto the pebbly shore, his fingers were prickling and he felt magical energy coiled inside, waiting to pounce.

Stopping about twenty paces from the water's edge, he scanned the grey expanse. Mizuchi Falls tumbled into the northern end of the lake in a dull incessant roar and the air was misty with spray. His breath steaming in front of his face, he scanned the lake but it revealed no hint of the two dragons.

He focused on the centre. Were the dragons coiled up on the lake bed there, where it was deepest? Licking the moisture from his lips, he considered: should he try to call the dragon? It hadn't gone well last time, but what if he was respectful, like Everand suggested? Maybe leave this until last. Perhaps the beast would appear of its own accord.

'My friend,' he began, noting surprise flicker across Torrap's face, 'we have three suns until the mage said he would return to continue my training. I want to test my skills and decide what training I need most.'

Looking pensive, Torrap nodded.

'That fool Atage's idea might have started out simple, but he's set unprecedented events in motion. As the chief, I must chart a safe course for Riverwood.' He paused but, taciturn as ever, Torrap said nothing. He frowned. The man was too subservient. 'I'd appreciate your insights.'

Torrap's heavy brows lifted and he shifted from foot to foot.

'Speak, man!' Malach said more curtly than he intended.

In a deep and measured voice, Torrap said, 'You're right. Riverfall erred when they went to the mages. They saved their boat races, and the other provinces will trade with one another, but a mage has come out of Axis and we don't know what that means.' He tapped his fingers against his thigh. 'I don't think Riverfall knows what this means, either.'

Malach fumbled in his pouch and offered Torrap a handful of nuts and berries. 'Go on.'

Still munching on the nuts, Torrap said, 'I now understand why you captured the boatwoman and the disguised mage.' He shrugged. 'You succeeded in disentangling us from inter-province trade, but the greater risk is what this mage may do. And what the other mages will do when he returns to Axis.'

Meeting Malach's eye, Torrap continued. 'I see why you want to increase your skills, because I imagine the mages can only be deterred by magical power.' His face grew troubled. 'But what if ten or twenty mages come? I can't see how we could hold out against them.'

'Why would they come? What do they have to gain?' Malach tapped a foot on the pebbles.

'Do you think they want the dragon?' Torrap looked at the lake water.

'I don't think that's it. I don't think Everand knew there was a dragon here when he was sent.' He quashed the surge of irritation that the annoying Everand had not only communicated with but had also *ridden* the dragon. 'And he left the dragon in the river, having negotiated an agreement between it and Riverfall.'

'That's true.' Torrap scuffed the pebbles with his toe. 'What else could they want?'

Malach's gaze drifted across the blue-grey water and a hard knot formed in the pit of his stomach. No matter how hard he tried, he couldn't put aside Everand's candid statement that the Guild would obliterate him if they found him. Everand didn't seem to agree with this action, or he'd have tried to destroy him during his escape. His head began to pound.

Torrap cleared his throat. 'I can think of one thing they might seek.'

Reluctantly, Malach raised his eyes to meet Torrap's dark ones.

Torrap pointed a chunky, calloused finger. 'You.'

'Everand, curse him, suggested as much. But how could the mages know about me?' The knot in his stomach burned searing hot. Had his father betrayed him to the Guild before his demise? Bile filled his mouth and he had to focus to listen to Torrap.

'Do you think Everand was sent to find you?'

'Hard to say. He recognised me immediately, but then he was apprenticed to my father and I look like him. He seemed taken aback, though.'

Rolling a pebble around with a toe, Torrap asked, 'Why didn't he kill or capture you? Why leave you here knowing you had power?' He looked up. 'Where is he now, anyway?'

'My eagles said he went to Riverplain with the boatwoman.'

'Riverplain? Not back to the Guild? Do you believe he'll come back as promised?' Torrap said tersely.

'This is the heart of it. My gut tells me to believe him. He comes across as sincere, but he is the apprentice who betrayed my father, so who can tell.' Swallowing, he gazed once more over the lake. A breeze eddied across the surface and goosebumps rose along his arms.

'Is it possible …' Torrap spoke haltingly '… is it possible Everand didn't know he was sent to find you? That he thought he was simply coming to deter a petty province squabble?'

Laughter bubbled in Malach's stomach, displacing the hard knot, then fountaining up to burst from his lips. 'It would explain much.' There was such a ring of truth to it that the idea settled firmly. 'Everand was so … *bumbling* and uncertain around me I thought it was a clever façade, but what if he actually didn't know what to do?' He laughed again.

'I see the concept amuses you,' said Torrap with no hint of a smile. 'However, this means someone else is manipulating Everand.'

Malach's laughter died. That, too, had an awful ring of truth to it. No wonder Everand had floundered. Did he suspect he was being manipulated? He must. The lanky love-struck mage might bumble about but he wasn't stupid. The Guild wouldn't have chosen him to send on the mission if he were.

'So,' said Torrap, demanding his attention. 'Do you trust Everand?'

'I'm not sure. A good test is whether he comes back when he said.'

'In the meantime, practice is a good idea. As is fortifying our village and increasing weapons training, which you've already started.' Torrap gave a nod of approval, his hand sliding to his sheathed dagger.

Unease slid through Malach, but his hunter was right: they could only work with what they knew. His focus sharpened. Was that a ripple in the centre of the lake? Another ripple ebbed outwards, and water slopped over the pebbled shore.

A bigger ripple circled, and the blue dragon's head breached the surface.

The creature fixed its enormous golden-yellow eyes fully on him and, with a gasp, Malach bent over in a deliberate, respectful bow, feeling the air move beside him when Torrap bowed too. He straightened up to see the dragon's gaze was still fixed on him, its ears pricked. Slowly, the dragon subsided under the water, the tips of its ears vanishing without a ripple.

Malach's heart thudded loudly in his ears. That was a start. If he could train the dragon and its mate ... surely a dragon would be able to fend off a mage? He swallowed a ball of regret. If only he hadn't tried to trick the dragon before. Now he'd have to work harder to gain its trust.

The dragon trusted Everand.

Was this a sign that he should too?

Chapter Twenty-Four

His feet feeling as if they had rock weights on top of them, Everand followed Agamid from the library. Curse it, his trip to the antiquity room had been discovered already. He'd have to follow through and ask Mantiss whether he could have any of the ancient books. How could he stall the council for more time? A flurry of ideas bombarded him while he crunched along the pebble path.

Halfway along, he realised by the way Agamid was looking at him that he must have missed a question. 'Sorry, what did you ask?'

'Are you recovered now?' Agamid peered at him closely.

'I'm still tired,' admitted Everand. 'I missed many meals on this mission and there was far more strenuous activity than I'm accustomed to.'

'You do look a little drawn. I imagine you're glad to be back,' Agamid said with a kind smile.

'I did enjoy my hot bath and having food delivered to my quarters. Things I took for granted before.' A neutral answer seemed best.

'You must come to my estate for the dusk meal soon. I'm curious to hear more,' said Agamid with another kind smile.

'I'd like that.' Everand just stopped himself from adding 'any excuse for a good meal'. The people of the river provinces enjoyed this kind of banter but the mages would find it impolite.

The air around him thickened and he suddenly felt stifled. *Focus. You must influence this meeting.*

Glancing sideways, Agamid asked, 'Did we send you to the right place? That's the first time we have translocated a person so far.'

The words tumbled out. 'You dropped me *in* the river instead of next to it, and a boat almost rowed right over the top of me.'

His purple robes flapping around his legs, Agamid stopped dead and nearly dropped the rolled-up map, just managing to clench his arm against his side in time to catch it.

'I hate being wet, and the water was cold,' Everand added.

'You sound annoyed,' said Agamid tentatively.

'With such limited information and no planning, the mission was difficult.' The look on Agamid's face! The mages wouldn't suspect he wanted to go back to the provinces if they thought he hated it there. Everand drew his eyebrows together in a deep frown. 'Next time, I will ask many more questions before I volunteer! Still,' he shrugged, 'I'm back, and the races and trade discussions went ahead.'

'You did well.' Agamid pursed his lips and resumed walking.

Everand trailed Agamid up the steps to the Great Hall, energy beginning to fizz through his veins and his mind clearing. Crossing the silk rug with his head held high, he allowed himself a quick glance down at the artwork. Was the current council as noble as the mages depicted in the battle on the intricate rug? The powerful beings from Chrysalis who had invaded twice with their armies were clearly a threat, but was Malach, a solitary half-mage?

He mounted the steps to the dais and saw that the council members were already gathered in a riot of colour around the gleaming mahogany table. Sitting down, he placed his hands in his lap and observed the subtle glance Agamid gave Mantiss.

'Saiphos will record the decisions we make.' Mantiss passed paper and a pen to Saiphos.

From his adjacent chair, Everand watched Saiphos write the purpose of the meeting as a heading.

'The Inner Council must make four decisions. First, what the fate of this wild half-mage is to be; second, how this fate will be enacted; third, where; and fourth, when.' Mantiss spoke distinctly and firmly. 'Agamid will count the votes for each proposal, with a majority of eight required for each resolution to be passed. Any dissenting votes will be noted.'

Mantiss waited until each council member had nodded and replied that they concurred.

Everand's heart raced.

'What is to be the fate of this half-mage?' Mantiss posed the first question.

Pelamis said, 'I move for obliteration as per the Guild Rules.'

Several heads nodded.

'Any gainsay?' asked Mantiss.

In the ensuing silence, Everand gritted his teeth, trying to dismiss the thought of Lamiya gaping at him, her beautiful face screwed up in horror. *How can you let them do this?* Looking down and breathing through his nose, he tried to summon the courage to ask whether any other options could be discussed. Peering up through his eyelashes, he found everyone was watching him. There'd be nothing to gain by arguing Malach's sentence, and plenty to lose. *Bide your time.* He gave a small shrug.

'The first resolution is carried,' announced Mantiss, and Saiphos scribed the result.

'The second question is how. Opinions, please.' Mantiss glanced around the table.

To Everand's surprise, Tiliqua spoke. Her blonde hair was plaited and coiled on top of her head, giving her a stern look and making her even taller than she already was. 'The entire Inner Council should conduct the obliteration. It is the responsibility of all of us, having voted, and to make sure it is done properly.'

The majority nodded but Saiphos sat with his pen poised mid-air, and Neelaps and Caimanops looked uncomfortable. So, not everyone was completely at ease with the prospect of obliterating someone. Sadly though, these three mages were not strong enough to dissent. Curse it, neither was he. The muscle at the back of his jaw tightened.

'I move that the entire Inner Council of Ten be responsible for the obliteration of the half-mage.' His silver eyebrows drawing together, Mantiss looked at Everand. 'Does he have a name? We should be clear about who we refer to.'

'His name is Malach,' said Everand tightly, 'of Riverwood province.'

'Let me reword this,' replied Mantiss. 'As the incumbent Head of the Mages' Guild, I, Mage Mantiss, move that the entire Inner Council of Ten be responsible for the obliteration of the half-mage Malach of River …'

'Riverwood,' supplied Everand.

'… Riverwood province. All in favour say so.'

Around the table, each mage said they concurred, with Pelamis and Simoselaps speaking the fastest and loudest. Just how keen were they to wield their powers? When Mantiss' look rested on him, Everand nodded stiffly. Noticing that Agamid was giving him a long, steady look, he lowered his eyes again. Two resolutions passed; two to go.

'I appreciate your prompt decisions,' said Mantiss. 'The next one is where the deed of obliteration should be enacted. The choice seems to be whether we obliterate this … Malach … in Riverwood or whether we bring him back to the Guild. Who wishes to speak to either option?'

Simoselaps leaned forward and placed his hands on the table. The mage's brown hair and eyes, beige robes and goatee beard made him look like a snake in the grass. The way he flicked his tongue over his lips didn't help. 'I vote we obliterate the half-mage in his home province. Bringing him here seems an unnecessary risk.'

Pelamis promptly concurred, Menetia and Tiliqua nodded and the others said nothing.

Sitting straighter, Everand said, 'Can I make two points? If we choose to obliterate Malach in Riverwood, then all ten members of the Inner Council must travel there. Do we need any other mages as independent witnesses, given that the council acts on behalf of the Guild and thus all mages in Axis?'

Narrowing his eyes, Mantiss opened and then closed his mouth.

'Second, as I said before, the people of Riverwood will not stand back and let us kill their leader. More blood will be shed.'

Satisfied with the discomfort on a few faces at his deliberate use of the words 'kill' and 'blood', Everand sat back. They must acknowledge this was not a research experiment — they intended to take a life. He detected disappointment in the way Mantiss' eyebrows drew down in a scowl, deep rings of wrinkles gathering around his eyes. Most of the others regarded him with aloof expressions. Saiphos held the pen mid-air again and stared with his mouth open.

'What do you propose?' asked Agamid evenly.

'I have an idea that also addresses the fourth question of when.' Everand took a breath: this was it, his best gamble. 'Malach is expecting me to return to Riverwood on the third sun-up from now to continue to train him. We can expect him to be at the nominated place, anticipating my appearance. What if three or four of us go then to subdue and capture him, and transport him back to the Guild?'

A quick glance around the table confirmed that he held everyone's attention. 'He is unlikely to take others with him to the training because it would show his people that he has weaknesses.'

'In other words, set a trap?' interjected Neelaps.

'Yes.' Out of sight under the table, Everand clenched his hands. 'If we translocate just before first light, the others can hide in the trees. I could distract Malach with an exercise to practise, and then we can take him. He'll just vanish and his people won't know what happened.' He unclenched his hands and rested them flat on the table, looking at Mantiss. 'This also gives us time to arrange all the necessary protocols, and to agree who will be witnesses.'

Agamid ceased stroking his beard. 'Let me unfurl the map so we can see precisely what Everand has in mind.' He leaned down to retrieve the map that was propped against his chair and placed it on the table.

Saiphos and Tiliqua helped hold it open by placing their hands on the corners.

When he ran his eye over the map, Everand's chest throbbed as he thought of the real river, the town of Zuqart, his friends in Riverfall. *Lamiya*. His throat tightened painfully; his longing must not reflect on his face. Deliberately frowning, he stood up and leaned over the map.

'Riverwood is the northern-most province.' Everand traced his finger over the shaded area representing the pine trees and granite boulders. 'The people live near here, in stone and wood cabins.'

Neelaps leaned over the map, his face lit with curiosity, and Caimanops put his elbows on the table, his thirst for knowledge clear. With a brief smile, Everand said, 'I can tell you more about the provinces later, if you like.'

'Focus, if you will,' said Mantiss curtly, and Agamid gave him an unfathomable look.

'Let me think …' said Everand, pondering the map. His instinct nagged him to adhere to the agreement that he meet Malach on the pebbly shore by the lake. But what if the dragons appeared? Would the mages harm the dragons? They'd been terrified of Mage Beetal's dragons. Conversely, that could be useful. When the mages realised that he'd deceived them, would he need the dragons to protect him?

'Here by the lake,' he pointed, 'is a broad, pebbly shore. I told Malach to meet me there soon after sun-up. He often goes to the lake, but it is a hike from his village and his people don't go there.' He moved his finger to point to the dark band representing the edge of the forest. 'The trees are large and dense, so three mages could readily conceal themselves among them. Here could work.'

Looking directly at Mantiss, he said, 'But we must remember that Malach can detect power. I suggest we wait until I've given him a complex exercise to divert his attention.'

Steepling his fingers, Mantiss glanced at the map before resting his eyes on Everand, as if trying to see into his mind. Keeping his face neutral, Everand waited. Best not look too keen.

Finally, Mantiss asked the others, 'Views?'

After a short but animated discussion, as Everand hoped, nobody had a better idea.

'Very well,' said Mantiss. 'I move we vote on the third resolution, which is that four of the Inner Council, including Everand, go to Riverwood to retrieve this Malach and bring him to the Guild. Those in favour?'

Everyone quickly concurred and Saiphos recorded this decision.

Somewhat pointedly, Tiliqua asked, 'What do we do with this man-mage when we get him here?'

'Let us finish voting, Tiliqua,' Agamid replied quickly. 'A valid question, but we still have time to establish the next steps.'

Everand lowered his eyes. The mages could discuss this next step all they liked; he hoped it wouldn't be required.

'Who will go? I am happy to.' Pelamis glanced sideways at Everand.

Agamid sighed. 'Thank you, Pelamis. We will get to that part too. Mantiss?'

'And the fourth resolution: I move that we vote on the proposed timing of the third sun-up from now, in accordance with Mage Everand's pre-arranged meeting with Malach.'

The tension in Everand's neck and shoulders ebbed away when the motion was carried. He had bought valuable time. Discreetly, he eyed the others. If it were up to him, who would he take? Certainly not Pelamis, but that might now be a given. Could he suggest Agamid, assuming Mantiss wouldn't want to go himself? He found he was being regarded steadily by Agamid's hazel eyes.

'May I ask …' he waited until he had Mantiss' attention. 'May I ask if Mage Agamid would like to lead the party to Riverwood? I'd be grateful for a senior council member to be present.'

Sitting straighter and with a brief flicker crossing his eyes, Agamid turned to Mantiss. 'If you agree, I will go. I propose the four be me, Everand, Pelamis and Saiphos.'

A sharp clatter broke the silence when Saiphos dropped the pen on the table, staring at Agamid with his mouth wide open.

'Does it have to be four, or can I go too?' asked Simoselaps, giving Pelamis a sour look.

The others looked at him, but Everand lifted his shoulders and said, 'Agamid is the senior mage. It's up to him to decide whether four or five of us go.'

Agamid bestowed him with yet another unreadable look before turning to Simoselaps. 'I think four will suffice, given we want to travel undetected. But I leave the final decision to Mantiss.'

Saiphos fidgeted with the pen and opened his mouth, no doubt to offer his place to Simoselaps, but he was silenced by a stern look from Agamid. Hope beat in Everand's chest that Agamid did not entirely approve of the whole resolution and wanted Saiphos, his former apprentice, to be there because he would follow orders without question. Did Agamid anticipate that Pelamis might need to be stopped from doing something rash?

Finally, after a long pause, Mantiss said, 'I agree that four mages will be sufficient. Saiphos, stop twitching and record that Agamid, Everand, Pelamis and you will go to subdue and retrieve the half-mage Malach on the third sun-up from now.'

'Shall I roll up the map?' asked Agamid. 'Is the meeting finished for now or do you want to resolve the finer details too?'

While they again waited for a decision, Everand observed that Mantiss looked strained and somewhat tired. Perhaps the unprecedented serious decisions were taking their toll, especially so soon after the last battle, during which his master had been severely injured.

'That is enough for now. We have time to review the details.' Mantiss' voice strengthened. 'Thank you all.' His expression softening, he added, 'I take this opportunity to formally thank Everand for his role. His ability to uncover plots and risks to the Guild is exceptional, and we are grateful for his skills. Saiphos, make a formal record that the council thanks Mage Everand for his work.'

Squirming on his chair, Everand bowed to hide the flush he was sure was staining his cheeks. A hefty dose of guilt rising, he couldn't force any words from his mouth to respond.

Chapter Twenty-Five

Lamiya burrowed into the mattress and pulled the blanket higher. Warmth crept up her back, and strong arms wrapped around her, pulling her into a long, lean body. Gentle fingers prised her hair away from her neck and tucked it over her shoulder. Velvet, warm lips brushed across her nape and a shiver tingled down her entire body. Butterfly lips worked their way down her neck and nibbled at her shoulder. Warmth pooled between the tops of her legs and she arched backwards. Her breasts ached for his touch and she willed him to explore *all* of her body. Rolling over, she reached out but her fingers found only a feathery mattress.

She flung open her eyes: it was dark and she was alone. 'Everand?' she whispered into thin air. He'd felt so real. Was she dreaming? Her breath caught: or was she far-viewing his dream about her? Liking that idea, she snuggled down again.

Ten breaths later, she sat up. Sleep banished, she needed activity to dispel the ache pulsing through her. Lulite's gentle snores reached her from the other side of the hut. Her friend had insisted she wouldn't leave her alone this dark-fall. Suppressing a yawn, she slipped from under the blanket and groped for her over-tunic. Hauling that over her head, she rose silently. A brew would be nice, but her tinkering about in the dark would wake Lulite.

She eased her way through the curtain and walked barefoot to the edge of the lake, feeling the crunchy stones give way to cushiony grass and then gritty dirt when she reached the shore. Sitting down, she hugged her knees and rested her chin on top of them. The water glistened pale grey with the waning of the moon and a hint of coming light; the air was still and carried a moist scent and touch, suggesting it would rain soon.

Closing her eyes, she reached out with her vision and saw dark clouds forming above Riverfall. Mizukaze's doing? It would take a while for the rain to reach Riverplain, so the team could probably complete their training session without getting wet.

Her gaze moved to the eastern end of the lake, where the hills huddled a darker grey, waiting for light. Her heart beating steadily, she acknowledged a strong pull to the hills. Scratching her chin on her knees, she considered what had happened in the grove. If she was to be the next guide of Riverplain, this meant she had skills far beyond those she'd already found. She must trust her instincts, and hone her calling and far-seeing if she was destined to lead and advise others.

When she brought an image of Everand to mind, her pulse sped up and her body throbbed with need. *No*, she told her body. *Focus on him. His essence.* Stillness crept over her mind and body, as if time and space rolled around her while she sat perched by the lake. Memories of her brief time with Everand flashed by. Amid these, Malach's raptor-like face loomed at her and she shivered. Smoothing her frown, she freed her mind to roam and asked her inner guide: what do you see?

A blanket of calm oozed over her and her shoulders drooped, her chest expanding and relaxing as the vision unfolded. Thousands of birds swooped and formed long ribbons against a cloudless sky. The lake roiled and bubbled and a presence hovered below the turmoil. Not Mizukaze, something even bigger. Her mind wanted to retreat: she coaxed it to stay. The presence dissipated and red petals showered onto the water to swirl in the current. A fish jumped and she was hypnotised by its glassy eye, travelling with it to the depths of the lake to hover outside a dark, yawning cave.

Fear reached into the corner of her mind, but then a radiant light, refracting all the colours of a fresh sky-arch, beamed out of the chasm. An enormous pearly egg rolled to the dark entrance. The egg cracked, and a tiny orange-and-green-scaled face peered out. The vision shifted, and she saw her parents cradling a newborn baby. *What?* Was that her? She forced her forehead to relax. *Don't analyse, accept.*

Next, water swirled and rippled, washing away from the prow of Flight as the boat skimmed across the lake. She stood at the rear, the wind in her hair, working the oar, while the orange-and-green dragon swam underneath the boat. The dragon swam closer and then dissolved upwards into the bottom of the boat. She chewed her lower lip. So, that *was* how the dragon they called Flight got into the boat! Her mind tried to rush away, a thousand questions forming. Closing these down, she brought her focus back to nothingness, allowing the vision to continue its embrace.

The final image came, of her entwined in Everand's arms, dressed in her skirt the colour of moonlight and her turquoise tunic, white flowers braided into her hair and cascading down her back. The intricate shell necklace glinted at her collarbones. He wore his azure mage robes. A deep sigh floated through her and a soft pressure touched the top of her head, like a kiss.

Opening her eyes, she smiled. The meaning of parts of the vision was elusive, but the ending was wonderful. Her smile slipped when she pondered the image of Malach. His aura was so dark that her heart cringed, advising her not to like or trust him. However, Everand seemed determined to give the half-mage a chance, and if Malach's future hung in the balance perhaps having someone trust him would make a difference.

A knot of unease grew. Based on events so far, it was more likely that Malach would take advantage of Everand's trust. She scowled. Would Everand detect any duplicity? Possibly not, but she could keep alert and warn him.

A waterbird hooted from the reeds, bringing her focus back to the here and now. Across the lake, the roof of the boatshed on the far shore gleamed faintly with the arrival of dawn, and the water reflected a blue-grey hue. To the east, silvery beams cascaded over the hilltops and spread tendrils of light down the slopes, as if reaching for the water lapping at the foot of the hills. A breeze blew from the west, lifting her hair and caressing her cheeks, urging her to go east.

She replayed the image of the pearly egg cracking to reveal a baby dragon, almost immediately overlaid with the vision of her parents with a baby. That *had* to be her. Were the two births pre-destined? Had they occurred at the same time, or was the vision just showing her a connection? Then there was the view of the dragon Flight rising up through the water to infuse herself into the body of the boat. After the races, the dragon had greeted her as if she knew her. But then, come to think of it, she'd felt like she knew the dragon. This couldn't be mere coincidence. What did it mean?

Go east to find out, her inner guide whispered. Mind made up, she stood and shook the grains of grit from her tunic. Training first, then a long hike east, whether it rained or not.

Reaching her hut, she pushed through the feather curtain to find Lulite seated at the low table, a plate of fruit and nuts sitting in front of her and both hands clutched around a mug. The drummer did not look her usual spritely self. Lamiya poured a mug of brew and sat opposite, taking in Lulite's pale complexion and hunched posture. 'Are you alright?'

Lulite nodded and gripped her mug tighter.

'Not hungry?' When Lulite compressed her lips and turned a shade paler, Lamiya worried. Then she guessed. 'A child? When?' So, this was why Lulite had swapped from paddling to the less strenuous drumming at the festival! She'd wondered, but had been so focused on her role as glide and team captain that she'd neglected to ask.

'Next cold-season. We've been trying for a while.' Lulite managed a smile.

Scurrying around the table, Lamiya enveloped Lulite in a fierce hug. 'This is wonderful!' Guilt swamped her. 'You should have said!' Holding Lulite at arm's length, she scolded, 'You could've been killed rescuing me!'

'I wasn't sure then, but now … I am.' Lulite wrinkled her nose. 'You can have my fruit.'

'Does Lapsi know?'

'Oh yes, he's thrilled.' Lulite groaned. 'Speaking of which, he and Lattic will come to fetch us soon and I'd rather not train this session. I hope this queasiness wears off.'

'Me too. You must stay with Lapsi from now on. I'll be fine.' Lamiya hugged her.

Lulite squeezed her hand. 'Everand will come back. I'm sure of it.'

'I'll make you another brew. Try to nibble at some star-fruit.' She busied herself making more brew and preparing a plate of berries and nuts. Light chatter seemed to help Lulite, whose colour improved and she began to nibble at the fruit.

Lamiya swallowed the last of her brew and went to her clothes rack, tucked along the back wall. Dismayed, she stared at the grimy pile of cloth at the base of the rack. How could she have forgotten to wash her team tunics! Grabbing clothes a similar colour, she dressed rapidly and had just finished brushing her hair when voices approached outside. She tapped her fingers on her thigh. Whirr was absent, no doubt preening in front of female birds. Deciding to leave him behind, she picked up her paddle, gave Lulite a pat on the shoulder and headed to the door.

'Yo, Lamiya!' called Lapsi, giving her a brief smile before hurrying to Lulite.

'I'm fine.' Lulite waved him away. 'But I'll rest this session. You have enough paddlers without me?'

'I'll wait outside,' Lamiya murmured, and pushed through the curtain to greet Lattic and Lopa, who were hovering on the grass. Both gave her happy smiles and her spirits lifted; it would be good to get back in the boat.

Lapsi emerged and set a brisk pace along the track around the lake. Following, Lamiya stifled a smile at the way Lattic and Lopa kept stealing glances at each other. Then warmth crept into her cheeks: was this what others did when she and Everand were hovering around each other? No wonder the team felt awkward.

'Yo!' The others called when they reached the shed.

'Where's Lulite?' asked Lepid.

'My fault,' she said loudly, when Lapsi looked uncomfortable. 'Lulite needs to rest because we chatted until too late.' Lapsi gave her a grateful look and the others shrugged and resumed what they were doing. Nobody asked where Everand was. Did they all know that he'd left? What had Lulite told them?

Luvu spun around and walked purposefully towards her. 'I'll glide this session. Will you be paddler ten?' He hesitated. 'We can discuss technique, and the team wants to talk about ideas for the races when we host the festival.'

She searched Luvu's grim face: was the team replacing her as glide? When she peered past him the others suddenly became busy and Lazuli's mouth tightened as he looked away, a tense set to his shoulders. Was that it? Would it be easier for Lazuli if she wasn't in charge of the boat? Were they uncomfortable because Everand had gone and they didn't know why or what to say? Come to think of it, she didn't know how to explain it, either. She twisted her paddle in her hands.

His expression softening, Luvu said gruffly, 'It'll be alright. Give them a chance to absorb everything.'

Swallowing her disappointment, she said, 'I understand.'

'You're still our champion glide. Let's see what fancy ideas the team has for the next competition.' The older paddler's face brightened.

The team carried Flight to the water and when everyone lined up to board, she realised they were a paddler short and she'd be in the last row by herself. 'Which side do you want me to sit?'

'Try the right,' Luvu replied. 'We'll be a bit unbalanced, but it's only training.'

Settled onto the bench behind Lepid, she flexed her fingers and realised how good it would be to paddle instead of being the glide. Digging her paddle deep, she enjoyed the pull along her body and the feel of her muscles strengthening while Luvu took the boat out to the centre of the lake and they did a long warm-up. When the boat passed the western end of the lake, she glanced up at the Meeting Place and wondered if U-Mali and U-Lumin were watching. Then Luvu called for a lift and she threw herself into the training, loving the pull and release of her muscles, the air rushing past her face and the boat skimming along the water.

Luvu took them back past the boatshed and called for a break. 'Right,' he said. 'Suggestions for what races we'll hold as host.'

'We need a long race,' said Lazuli, twisting around. 'The full length of the lake and back.'

'We could start and finish just below the Meeting Place,' added Larimar.

'I agree,' said Lamiya. 'We need a glory race, and finishing in front of everyone will be wonderful.'

'Anyone disagree?' asked Luvu. Everyone shook their heads. 'Carried. Another idea?'

Lattic raised his paddle and said, 'What about a race with turns? The lake is wider than the river so we could race over a square, which will test the boats' turning skills.'

Impressed, Lamiya asked, 'How will we mark the turn points?'

Lattic looked over his shoulder. 'People in fishing boats. Then we can make sure nobody interferes with another boat's path.' She beamed at him and he gave a shy smile back.

'I like it,' said Luvu.

'That's two serious races. What about some short fun ones? Like the ones we were discussing before?' Lazuli's eyes sparkled with enthusiasm.

Lamiya pivoted to catch Luvu's attention and whispered, 'Should we make Lazuli the race organiser for the festival? He has great ideas.'

With a grunt, Luvu straightened up. 'A mix is a good plan. Team, shall we make Lazuli the chief race organiser?'

'Yo!' Everyone lifted their paddles and Larimar patted Lazuli on the back.

Grinning broadly, Lazuli looked back at Luvu. Then his gaze dropped to her, and she smiled and gave a respectful nod. His grin faded, but his eyes rested on her for a breath before he turned around.

'Paddles up!' called Luvu. 'Enough sitting about chatting. Let's do some proper work.'

The rest of the drills passed in an enjoyable blur, and soon they were carrying the boat back into the shed. As she helped settle Flight into place, the first drops of rain sounded on the roof. The team closed the doors and prepared to make a run for their huts. Lamiya broke into a jog, raindrops pattering on her head and along her bare arms. No longer distracted by paddling, the tug to go east was an incessant whisper in her core.

On reaching Lulite and Lapsi's hut, she slowed to a walk and hovered by their door. There was no response to her call, so she poked her head through the curtain and saw Lulite lying curled up on a pile of cushions, soundly asleep. With a smile, she withdrew and jogged on. By the time she reached her hut, her hair was slimy and cold down her back and her tunic was clamped to her. Rain ran down her face into her eyes and her sandals squelched.

She bounced into her hut and ducked when Whirr divebombed her head.

'I see,' she said, laughing. 'You only love me when it's wet outside!'

Whirr swooped at her head again. She filled a bowl with seeds, and he greedily pecked at these while she peeled off her wet clothes and hung them to dry where it wouldn't matter if they dripped. The tub of water was still warm from the earlier mugs of brew, so she grabbed a cloth and sponged herself down. Her skin tingling with energy, she chose dark-green ankle-length trousers and her favourite burnt-orange tunic with long sleeves. The colours reminded her of leaf-fall season.

To keep the worst of the moisture out, she fetched from its peg her feather cloak with a hood and then prepared pouches of loaves, strips of dried fish and a sliced feeja. Whirr hopped across the table and cocked his head at the cloak.

'Long walk. You coming?' Whirr fluffed his wings. 'So, seeds for you and more nuts for me.'

Strapping on her woven grass belt, she tied the pouch strings to it, deeming she had enough to give her energy until dark-fall. Rain hissed steadily on the thatched roof. Should she wait for it to ease? It might not, judging by the spread of cloud that had drifted in. *Go, go, go,* murmured the whisper. She frowned. What was the hurry, other than she'd thought of the idea? She stilled her senses and her pulse throbbed once … twice … thrice … and her instinct said to go *now*.

With a sigh, she settled the cloak over her shoulders and tied the drawstrings firmly. Whirr flew onto her shoulder and then crawled inside the front of her tunic. Drawing the hood over her head, she tugged it forward to protect her face and marched out through the door before she could change her mind.

The curtain feathers parted and she slapped into an immovable object.

'Ooph!' The air left her chest and Whirr screeched and scratched her with his feet. What the …? Taking a step backwards, she came face to face with Lazuli.

'Sorry,' he muttered with a grimace. 'I wasn't expecting you to charge out like that!' Curiosity filled his grey eyes. 'Where are you going?'

'What are you doing here?' she asked at the same time. He looked hurt, so she added, 'Come in. You look half-drowned.' She reversed into the hut and lowered her hood. Lazuli followed hesitantly, water dripping from his hair and eyelashes. Retrieving the damp cloth, she handed it to him.

'Thanks.' He wiped his face and arms and stood awkwardly, turning the cloth over in his hands.

Pushing down the niggling whisper about the distant hills, she looked at Lazuli. Dare she hope he'd come to repair their friendship? He looked miserable and lost. She felt as if she were split into two people: one niggling about time passing and the other trying to work out why he was here and what she should do about it.

She sighed. 'Have you eaten?'

Looking hopeful, Lazuli shook his head. 'No ... but you were going somewhere?'

'Sit.' She pointed to the moss-green cushion he usually sat on when he visited. He sat mutely while she fetched a plate of food and a mug of half-hot brew. Sitting back down, she waited while he ate. Should she tell him where she was going, and why? Whirr poked his head out of her tunic and blinked at her.

Although his fingers were still clenched whitely around his mug, Lazuli gave her a tentative smile. 'I wanted to say ... I would like us to be friends.' Her smile encouraged him and his expression lightened. 'I was angry. I'm sorry.'

Resisting the impulse to grab his hands, yearning for his friendship but not wanting to give any false hope of anything more, she smiled sadly. 'I know. We were both unprepared ... and taken unawares by events.'

Putting the mug down, Lazuli crept his fingers across the table and held her hands in his warm, strong ones. 'I was so afraid when you were taken by that Riverwood man! I couldn't bear it if you were killed.' His lips compressed. 'And I blamed the Traveller.'

Squeezing his fingers, she murmured, 'I understand that. Everand blamed himself too. But it was Malach who did wrong and is to blame. Everand did his best to right it by allowing himself to be taken.'

Lazuli's eyes flickered. 'He did?'

Lamiya nodded. 'He has much more power than Malach, but he allowed Malach to subdue his magic so he could be taken as well to protect me.'

'I didn't understand that.' Lazuli's frown deepened. 'I don't understand anything the Traveller does.'

Giving his fingers another squeeze, she said gently, 'I'm glad you and the others came for us. I'm not sure what would have happened.' She withdrew her hands, thinking she really did owe him more information. 'I'm going on a long hike and I expect to get thoroughly sodden. Do you want to come? I promise to explain more on the way.'

'Are we leaving now?' Lazuli gave her the lopsided grin she adored and light danced in his eyes.

'Yes,' she said, rising. 'You should've brought your cloak!'

'Let me run and borrow one from Lattic.' Lazuli leaped to his feet, then paused in the doorway. 'Don't go without me.' He dashed away.

Doubt poking unwelcome fingers at her, she wiped and packed away the plates and mugs. Was this wise? Could she concentrate with Lazuli there? What if he tried to hug or kiss her? She only just caught the mug as it slipped from her fingers, and Whirr scolded her with shrill peeps.

Too late now: he was coming along.

CHAPTER TWENTY-SIX

Everand nestled closer to Lamiya. Her hair was covering her neck, so he gently prised it away, revelling in the silky strands, the subtle scents of grasses, and tucked it behind her shoulder. His lips tingled in anticipation; he adored her elegant neck. Planting the gentlest of kisses, he worked his way from behind her ear to the point of her shoulder. On impulse, he nibbled at the muscles there. She drew in a breath and arched against him, the invitation to explore her body clear. He moaned, heat throbbing through him and collecting painfully in his groin. Not sure he could contain his desire, he reached his hands around … and met smooth sheet.

Blinking, he fumbled around in the dark. The bed was empty. Where had she gone? His pulsing desire receding, he sat up. The sky outside his window reflected the faintest of silver light, suggesting sun-up was nigh. Blinking harder, he scanned the bed and his room. He was alone, but Lamiya had felt so real. Was she a dream, or something more powerful? Had she been calling for him in her sleep? The concept appealed but was also disconcerting. What sort of unseen power was at play here?

Concluding that no more sleep would be had, he stared at the lightening sky. Hugging his knees to his chest, he turned his mind to planning. In two more sun-ups, he and Agamid, Saiphos and Pelamis would go to Riverwood to capture Malach. How could he warn Malach? He scratched his chin on top of his knees. How could he sneak out and back without triggering the wardspell and without anyone noticing? Mantiss would schedule further meetings of the Inner Council to refine the details, and alarms would ring if he didn't attend and couldn't be found.

First light crawled over the windowsill, fingers of wan light reaching across the floor. Was it cloudy? Probably, since Mizukaze had promised the provinces more rain.

He thought harder. Mage Beetal had snuck out frequently. How? Mage Beetal's rooms had been left untouched after his demise, since no-one wanted to claim the traitor's quarters. Mantiss and Agamid had searched the rooms early on and removed artefacts of power, such as Beetal's scrying globe and the knife he'd used to bind his allies to him with blood. Perhaps they had missed some subtler clues. Another search of Beetal's rooms would be a logical next step, with a focus on any connection to Riverwood and hints of how his mentor had gone there.

He got up, bathed and regarded his collection of robes. His eyes were drawn to his favourite azure robes, but he needed a colour other than his signature one. Tugging the dove-grey robe with the silver trim off the hanger, he dressed quickly, determined to search Beetal's study before any meetings were called.

Exiting his quarters, he climbed the stairwell to the tenth floor. Mage Beetal had enjoyed a commanding view of the other buildings and gardens from his rooms. The only higher floor held the stables where the transport beetles were housed. An eerie sense of déjà vu stalked him as he walked the familiar corridor and stopped outside the ornate mahogany door to his former mentor's quarters. Taking a breath, he held the brass handle firmly, relieved when it acknowledged him and turned in his hand.

As soon as he stepped into Beetal's study he was bombarded by vivid memories, accompanied by the aroma of polished wood and the tangy scent of fermented wine. His mentor used to quaff red wine with obvious pleasure. Everand had tried it once, the bitter taste not to his liking. He stood for a moment in the centre of the silk rug, the pattern a red sky with swirling black planets and silver stars. His austere, wooden, apprentice chair was still there, pushed against a wall.

Half expecting his mentor to appear and pace the rug, as was his wont, he blinked away a vision of himself sitting there while Mage Beetal droned on and on about the stagnation of the Guild, trying to persuade him to agree. Unexpected sadness filled him. His mentor had betrayed the Guild but his intentions, at the outset at least, had been ambitious rather than evil.

Protective walls began to slide up around his emotions and gritting his teeth, he pushed them back down. If he truly loved Lamiya, he must learn to acknowledge and accept his feelings. A feather-light touch patted his elbow and he jumped. In his mind Lamiya smiled, her eyes clear and happy, encouraging him: *Be whole*. A tremble accompanied his slow breath in and he allowed the memories of his apprenticeship to fly at him.

After a while, he felt a smile tug at his lips and realised he'd enjoyed his lessons. Mage Beetal was astute and passionate in his beliefs, and had oozed power. His mentor had been a good teacher, and he had learned much and well.

If only he'd been able to deflect the mage from his ambitious course — instead of floundering, helpless, while his mentor made one poor decision after another until the consequences were too severe to ignore. Anger sparked in his chest. It shouldn't have been up to him, the apprentice, to avert the clever and powerful mage. Could his true master, Mantiss, have acted earlier to prevent the end disaster? He blinked furiously. *Focus. This is why Beetal's son deserves a chance. This is why you are here.*

Still blinking away regret, he approached the expansive desk that remained buried under a scattering of papers, pens and books and even an empty wine goblet, as if his mentor would return imminently. Scrutinising each object, he saw nothing out of the ordinary. Moving behind the desk, he eased open each drawer in turn. The top one held more pens and inks, nestled on a velvet cloth. The second one held sheets of different types of paper, and the third one dirty wine goblets. Sliding the drawer shut, he blew out a breath to dispel the acidic odour.

Next, he scanned the bookcase that lined the wall next to the desk. He could have recited the titles of all the books, in the correct order, because he'd spent so much time in this study. Skimming the spines, he wondered why Hydrelaps hadn't claimed the books for the library. He should suggest it to the librarian.

Halfway along the middle shelf, he paused at the dusty space between the neatly aligned books. What books had sat there? The spines of a red book and a blue book came to mind. *Influencing Compounds* in bold, black, sloping letters ran along the spine of the red book. Pushing down his unease, he focused. The second one? *Summoning Spells*, etched in blocky silver letters on the blue spine.

Had his mentor used these books to train Malach and then left them with his son? His unease magnified. He'd assumed Malach was using some of Mage Beetal's supply of personality-adjuster compound to make the tree-moths, viper, jumping fish and eagles aggressive, but what if the half-mage actually knew how to make it? He'd have an unlimited supply.

Turning, he looked out through the window. The sky was a dull slate grey, the clouds low and bulging. Mages in a variety of coloured robes traversed the paths, but none were hurrying to the Great Hall. Good, no meetings yet. He eyed the door to Mage Beetal's bedroom and reluctantly moved that way.

The bed was made, the dark-red coverlet tucked neatly under the pillows. Everand opened the wardrobe doors, his eyes greeted by various shades of brown robes hanging there with a pair of sandals lined up below each one, typical of his mentor's precision. *Wait.* In the darkest corner, right at the end of the row of sandals, was an incongruous grey, oval stone. Picking it up, he hefted it in his hands. The smooth surface was ingrained with dark-grey flecks and looked like granite. What was it for?

When he probed his senses into the stone, it warmed in his hands and glowed as if lit from within by a crimson hue. Bending his will into it, he sensed a distant corresponding stone also turning crimson. Probing harder, he perceived the stone and wood walls of a cabin around the far stone. Elated, he withdrew his connection and put the stone in his robe pocket. *This* was how Mage Beetal had told Malach and his mother when he was coming! Simple and effective. No doubt about it, his mentor had been deviously clever.

Closing the wardrobe doors, he skimmed over everything else in the bedroom. Nothing leaped out as being out of place or anything other than ordinary. Next, he checked the wash area. Other than a faint coating of dust, the bath was empty and clean, the jars of soaps and oils arranged in precision along the shelf above it.

Going back to the study, he stood behind the desk, gazing vacantly out of the window. So, he now knew how Beetal had communicated with Riverwood, but how had the mage got there? The clouds hung ponderously above the wardspell, their bellies dark and distended with imminent rain. He tapped his fingers on the windowsill. The wardspell would let rain through, but not solid objects. Could Beetal have shape-shifted himself into water and snuck out when it was raining? Even if that were possible, it wasn't likely, because his mentor would have needed to have control over when and how he went.

A transport beetle approached the rooftop landing pad, the orange robes of the rider suggesting it was Pelamis. Leaning on the windowsill, Everand watched the underbelly of the beetle pass above. His breath caught. Could Beetal have gone to

Riverwood on his stag-horn beetle? Yes, because Malach had mentioned the beetle! Was there a gap in the granite wall? His pulse raced. Given that his mentor had gone many times, would the stag-horn remember the path? There was one way to find out.

Everand exited the rooms and pulled the door shut. Taking long strides, he traversed the corridor and climbed the stairs to level eleven. He walked through the double wooden doors, the complex odour of insects mingled with the rich smell of the peaty floor assaulting his nostrils. He paused to gauge the activity.

Arranged in a large circle were forty stalls with a top and bottom door to enter by. There was a large room for all the bridles and reins, the stable cleaning tools and another area where the insects' food was kept. Each stall was big enough for the occupant to move around for basic exercise. The circular area in the middle was covered in peat and was sometimes used to train new beetles in being handled and mounted.

Given the weather, none of the stalls looked empty, all containing beetles snuffling in the peat and clacking their jaws. A bevy of human boys was mucking out stalls, polishing bridles and mixing up tubs of smaller grubs and leaves for the sun-high feed.

As he walked along the front of the stalls towards his own mount's stall, his footsteps became uncertain. What would happen to his orange beetle when he left to live in Riverplain? Could he free it before he left or should he leave it here in case his plan failed and he needed it to escape later? The gigantic beetle might wreak havoc on Lamiya's birds. He'd better leave it here.

Ahead, a beetle with a shiny orange carapace reared at the front of its cage, waving its antennae and chirruping. *His* mount. Was it calling to him? A number of stableboys paused in their chores and watched with interest. Hurrying the last few steps, he put his hand up to the grille and the beetle reached long, narrow antennae through the bars to brush tickling against his fingers. With a finger, he stroked the end of the antenna and the beetle made a soft chirrup. It had never done this before. Why so affectionate now?

'Mage Everand, sir, do you wish me to bridle it?'

Dropping his hand, he turned to regard the lad with curly brown hair, who looked to be about twelve. 'No, thank you. Can you bring me some treats to feed it?'

The boy's mouth dropped open and he twisted his hands. 'Treats?'

Of course, the boy had no idea what he meant because mages did not feed their mounts. 'Just bring me a handful of food.' When the boy scurried away he frowned, worried that his unusual request would be talked about. He slid open the bolts to the upper door and his beetle leaned its head over with another chirrup. Patting its shiny face, he wondered whether it was responding to the inner changes in him. What did it mean? Did it mean anything?

The boy approached to drop a handful of leaves and grubs into his outstretched hand.

Everand held the morsels up to the beetle, feeling its jaws scrape across his palms as it gobbled them up. He patted its face again. Did the stableboys have names for the insects? Turning his back to where the gaggle of boys worked, he placed both palms along his mount's cheeks. *I name you Hover. Now be calm. I must go.* With a wave of its antennae, his mount backed into the stall.

A high-pitched screech sounded behind him, followed by clattering and shouting. Spinning around, Everand saw that three stalls along, a massive black-and-white beetle was ramming itself against the front of its stall. Two boys stood outside the stall yelling at each other. A taller, red-haired youth shoved backwards the boy who'd given him the food.

'It's your turn!' shouted the taller boy.

'Is not!' replied the smaller one, righting himself.

The taller boy threw down a metal-pronged fork. 'Use this and get on with it!'

'No. It's your turn.' The smaller boy kicked the fork.

When the beetle crashed into the front of the stall, both boys leaped away.

Everand closed the gap in three strides. 'What's the problem?'

Both boys paled and bowed with muttered apologies. The enraged beetle crashed into the grille.

'Look at me,' he said. 'You're not in trouble. Tell me what the problem is.'

Surprisingly, it was the smaller boy who spoke. 'Mage Everand, sir, this mount is wild and we don't like going in there.'

His eyebrows lifting, Everand looked at the creature. The massive beetle paced its stall, clacking its jaws and waving its front pair of legs threateningly. Turning back to the boys, he asked, 'Is this Mage Beetal's mount?' When they nodded, he said, 'Bring me the bridle.'

The boys looked at each other without moving.

'It doesn't matter who fetches the bridle because I will be going in there and you need not.' When the smaller boy, who he'd begun to like, ran off towards the tack room, he looked at the other boy. 'I take it this mount hasn't been exercised since Mage Beetal died?'

Mutely, the boy shook his head and flushed.

'Very well, I will take it out.' Realising the situation could be used to his advantage, he eyed the red-haired lad, whose freckles stood out against his pale skin. 'It would be better if you worked together to tend this mount. I'll take it out a few times to calm it down and make it easier to manage.'

'Thank you, Mage Everand.' The boy bowed respectfully.

'Here you are, Mage Everand.' The other boy held out the bridle and reins. Shuffling from foot to foot, the boy said reluctantly, 'Will you need me to bridle it?'

Everand took the reins, fingering the soft, polished leather. 'I can manage. Go back to your chores.' He waited while they walked away, the taller one elbowing the smaller one in the ribs. He almost asked their names, but he'd attracted enough attention already.

When he opened the bolts to the stag-horn's stable, the creature charged at him and he hastily held up a hand with a command spell to stop. The stag-horn slithered in the peat until its face was level with his, and emitted a growl-like sound. A pungent smell of rotted leaves wafted up. He put his hand on the tip of the stag-horn's face. *I will take you out. I am Everand, apprentice to your former master.*

The stag-horn waved its feelers and then lowered its head, ready for the bridle. Moving quickly, he fitted the bridle and tugged the reins to lead it out of the stall, relieved when it followed obediently. Ignoring the astounded looks from the stableboys, he walked the beetle to the sloping ramp that led up onto the roof.

The stag-horn's feet clattering on the ramp behind him, he emerged onto the roof. A light drizzle tickled his scalp and his breath misted in chill air. Wishing he'd brought his cloak, he took the stag-horn to the landing pad, put the reins over its head and jumped up, positioning his legs to leave its air spiracles free to breathe. For a moment he sat adjusting to the feel of the mount, which was longer and wider than his customary beetle. If there was a gap into Riverwood, where would it be? He nudged the beetle's side repeatedly with a heel so that it slowly pirouetted while he surveyed the landscape.

Riverwood was to the north, above the lands where the senior mages had their country estates. Surely, any gap would be that way. But he'd have to fly over the senior mages' estates and might be seen. Checking there were no other beetles flying in, and there was no activity along any of the paths below, he mouthed the spell of invisibility.

The stag-horn fidgeted with all six feet. Did it anticipate a clandestine flight? Loosening his hold on the reins, he projected an image of Riverwood with its tall pine trees and granite boulders. The creature clacked its mandibles, raised its outer wings and rose into the air.

Drizzle sprinkled Everand's face while the stag-horn flew directly north. He let it set the course and it flew higher than the usual flight paths, but far enough below the wardspell not to trigger it. The air was moist and cool, and goosebumps formed along his arms. Thinking of the maps he'd seen, he keenly observed the view. The Guild gardens were already behind him and below stretched fields of crops and a cluster of squat marble houses, where the humans lived. Close enough to walk to the Guild buildings with their produce.

Next came the groves of massive sunflowers. He'd taken Elemar there once, to give her a change from being cooped up in her Guild quarters. Teasing him, she'd run away and hidden in the forest of flowers — until she'd backed into an enormous spider web and he'd had to save her from the advancing poisonous spider. He recalled his fright at almost losing his charge from another world so unexpectedly. His cheeks were growing stiff from the cool breeze, but he managed a smile. There were definitely some similarities between Elemar and Lamiya. *Lamiya.* His heart gave a throb.

Soon, he was passing over Mage Mantiss' country estate. There was the large oval dome of the insect training arena, next to the breeding complex and the fields of tall grass and bushes the beetles liked. Next along was Agamid's estate, with its massive cocoon-shaped translucent domes where the silk moths were bred. Beside these were a couple of small houses for the spinners and weavers, and a cloth storage dome. He liked Agamid's estate. The mage's house was pleasing in design and the gardens were peaceful with their ponds and Bellflower bushes.

His heart panged with the memory of how he'd taken Elemar there, and they had sat on a bench beneath a Bellflower bush while he told her she should move into his quarters so he could protect her from Mage Beetal. It had seemed like a good idea at the time, but look where that action had led him! He'd fallen in love with, and then lost, Elemar. But she had prepared his heart to meet Lamiya. A shiver traced down his back. Was some greater force influencing matters?

The stag-horn banked sharply, scattering his reflections. Everand sat up and focused when his mount flew closer to the granite wall, then progressively dropped height until it was skimming alongside the massive blocks of granite and the ground was rushing by at a dizzying speed. Squinting, he could just ascertain where the bottom edge of the wardspell fed into the top of the wall. There was a subtle blue, red and yellow shimmering to the air where the ward dropped down and mingled with the top row of solid grey boulders. His pulse raced: the shimmering did not extend down into the rocks!

Squinting hard, he tried to see beyond the curved subtle shimmer of the wardspell, but although it looked as if he should be able to see through, the air was distorted and he couldn't tell if Riverwood was on the other side. The stag-horn gave a chirrup and he patted it. Were they nearly there, wherever *there* was?

The stag-horn flew resolutely along the wall for longer than he expected, then it dropped to just above ground level. He eyed the ground whizzing past; no falling off at this pace! Fixing his gaze forward, he scanned for any distinctive landmarks, but the boulders all looked similar, neatly moulded into and on top of each other. The land that fed away from this part of the wall was flat, bare dirt, with sporadic enormous rocks rising away to the west.

With a chirp, his mount flew slower and Everand leaned forward and focused. They were almost at the northern-most end of the wall, a long way from the Guild buildings. Up ahead was a darker rock. Unguided, the beetle landed, walked towards it and stopped.

Everand laughed. Before him was a gap in the rocks. How, by the stars, had his mentor discovered this? He slid off the stag-horn and stepped towards the gap, which transpired to be a low, narrow tunnel, an earthen ramp leading *beneath* the granite wall. By stooping, he was able to walk through. The stag-horn followed closely behind, exuding eagerness.

How wide was the granite wall? After only twenty paces, a blur of white-brown light appeared ahead. Another twenty paces later, he emerged into an open field of tall, waving, gold, green and brown grasses. Large raindrops tumbled from the leaden sky and he was soon soaked. Shielding his eyes with a hand and ignoring the water running over it, he discerned the rows of pine trees on the far side of the grassy expanse. He assumed the raptor cages and the village where the people lived were on the other side of the pine forest. In his mind's eye, he imagined his mentor arriving to greet a young Malach and his mother waiting patiently under the shade of the trees.

Well, well. For all its anxiety at keeping mages in and others out, the Guild had proved most remiss in failing to regularly check its perimeters. Whoever had built the granite wall and generated the wardspell must have been supremely confident in its longevity. His history lessons said the wardspell had been activated after Mage Thrip travelled outside of Axis. *Wait.* The granite wall was already in place then, however, having been built very early on by the first arrivals.

Intrigued, he eyed the impressive, solid boulders, crammed tightly together and stretching to twice his height. This wall looked distinctly like it was designed to keep others — or something — out. What made the first mages think they would need it? The ships, boat warfare and the wall ... all hidden history ... but *somebody* must know the full details. The original history must be recorded somewhere.

'Not this time.' He snagged the reins when the stag-horn moved to pass him to go across the field. Considering his next steps, he stared across the grasses at the darkly shrouded pines, clumped as if sharing secrets in the gloom beneath their boughs. If he activated the summoning stone, would Malach see it and know to come to this place? Would the stone at the Guild end indicate the summons had been received? Tossing the reins from one hand to the other, he reasoned there was only one way to find out. And it would have to be next sun-up.

Tugging the stag-horn after him, he moved back through the tunnel, brushing the jagged roof and sides with his fingers. Had the tunnel been painstakingly crafted over many visits? Could Mage Beetal have used magic this far away from the Guild without being detected? His former mentor was turning out to be full of surprises. But how had he known the effort would be worth it? How had he known what was on the far side?

Everand stopped dead, pushing at the stag-horn when it bumped against his back. Maybe his mentor hadn't known. What if his mentor had tested whether he could create a gap in the wall and happened to find the Riverwood woman while he explored? He rubbed a hand over his face. Had Mage Beetal then developed a taste for freedom and a desire to travel further afield? That made sense, given the pattern he'd observed of his mentor becoming increasingly bold in his decisions and actions. Brief regret rose again. If only he could have deflected Mage Beetal.

The stag-horn bunted him with its head, but his feet still would not move. What would have happened to Malach if Mage Beetal *had* been persuaded to set aside his ambitions? *Think, man, think.* Would Mage Beetal have asked the Guild if his son could be brought in for training? Unlikely, because he'd first have had to confess to his transgressions. Too much of a risk. Mage Beetal would have continued to train Malach in secret.

When the stag-horn butted him again, he walked. Was Mantiss worried that Mage Beetal had committed further treachery that they hadn't uncovered as yet? Was *that* concern what had really underpinned his unusual mission? How could he ascertain how much Mantiss already knew? He must get back, and fast.

Absorbed in his thoughts, his feet and legs felt far away while he traversed the last part of the tunnel. What hadn't he been told, and why not? But he hadn't been entirely honest either and if he failed to report the tunnel under the wall, he would be further deceiving his master *and* leaving the Guild open to risk. What if others, either inside or outside of Axis, found the gap?

His breath misted in the cool air of the tunnel, and he blinked when he emerged back into the light. The stag-horn fidgeted and pulled at the reins in his hand when he turned around to stare at the high wall, his instinct nagging that this was a defensive wall. Who or what had it been built to keep out? Hadn't his history lessons taught that Ossilis was unpopulated when the mages arrived? So why had they needed the wall? A wall that had been maintained for four generations and been strengthened by a wardspell. He was such an idiot. A trusting, compliant idiot. Why hadn't he thought to ask during his lessons?

Mounting the stag-horn, he thought 'home' at it. The beetle set off with a chirrup and he let his mind rove until the Guild buildings came into view. Unease coiled and slithered about in his stomach. He hadn't anticipated so many layers of deception when he'd decided to choose Lamiya over his life at the Guild. Mantiss, who called him 'son', did not deserve to be deceived like this. But what else could he do?

Cheeks stiff with cold, he tilted his face down against the drizzle. Was he the only one doing the deceiving? No, he felt sure of it. Mantiss, at least, knew more than he was saying. There were too many undercurrents in the council meetings, and in this odd mission. And why remove the antiquity section of the library?

He had been trained in stealth by a master strategist and the leader of the Guild. Was he about to test his skills against those of his master?

An icy-cold knot formed in his chest.

Chapter Twenty-Seven

'Sorry.' Lamiya slowed down when she realised Lazuli was jogging to keep pace.

'You seem focused,' observed Lazuli, tugging the cloak tighter around his shoulders. 'Where are we going?'

'Ha! You should have asked that before you agreed to come. We're going to the hills at the far end of the lake.' It was difficult to smother her grin at his look of incredulity.

'We are?' Lazuli strode faster. 'Why?'

'To see if there's a dragon,' she replied snippily, laughing when he stopped in his tracks.

'Are you sure you're the Lamiya I know?' he said around a grimace. 'The one I know is a bird caller. What makes you think there's a dragon in our lake?'

'A hunch.' After a massive shrug she set off again, glad that the brisk pace was at least keeping her warm. The way the water was running off the feathered cloak, she'd be quite chilled otherwise. Lazuli's hood peaked in the middle and water was dripping off the point and onto his nose so that he frequently brushed the moisture away with the back of his hand.

'Alright,' he said slowly, wiping more water from his nose. 'You've a hunch there is a dragon at the far end of the lake and we're going to look for it. Why?'

Twisting to look at him while she walked, she waved a finger. 'Good questions. The answer to both is I'm not sure.'

Lazuli laughed. 'Maybe you are the impetuous Lamiya I know!'

She smiled, enjoying his company for the long walk and finding it helpful having someone to bounce ideas off. Lazuli had a quick mind and knew her well enough to challenge anything she said that didn't ring true. A sideways glance told her he was thinking hard, his forehead pinched and his grey eyes focused inwards. Already, they were beyond the groves of nut trees and were passing through the uncultivated lands.

Flexing her fingers to warm her hands, she wished the incessant niggling in her stomach would go away, wanting to yell to the skies that she *was* hurrying. To distract her mind, she admired the shapes of the leaves. Some looked like large fat hands with fingers spread wide, and others with feathery points reminded her of elegant female hands with slim fingers.

The path grew progressively narrower and less clear, taking them ever closer to the water.

'You have brought food, haven't you?' asked Lazuli. 'I doubt we'll be back by dark-fall.'

For answer, she patted the pouches hanging from her belt. Tilting her face up, she peered out from beneath her hood. The clouds had taken on a mottled look and were higher in the sky, so it would stop raining by the time they reached the far end of the lake. For a while they walked in single file in comfortable silence, and she noticed the trees changed to taller, elegant ones with smooth, creamy trunks and glossy, dark-green leaves. Some had bright-red or pink flowers, standing out in the gloomy atmosphere.

Unable to resist, she plucked a red flower and waved it under her nose. It smelled beautiful, and the petals were soft and velvety. When Lazuli prised it from her fingers and tucked it into her hair, she ducked her head at the wistful look on his face. His cheek was still a mottled green and purple where Everand had hit him.

They stopped twice to scoop water off leaves to wet their mouths and to munch on nuts. To the east, the hills loomed larger, reaching up into the grey sky, and crowds of colourful trees lined the distant lakeshore. The rain eased to drizzle, and with a sigh she wriggled her toes in her sodden sandals, anticipating blisters.

'How will you know where to stop?' asked Lazuli.

'I'm hoping I'll know when I get there.' She shrugged.

'You are changing,' Lazuli said softly, watching her face.

Anxiety stirred in her stomach at his words, followed by a gush of relief. If he understood that she and Everand were being driven by larger forces, he might come to accept the situation. 'I feel different ... that there's a path I must follow ... but I don't know where it leads.'

Lazuli touched her elbow. 'Are you afraid?'

'Sometimes,' she admitted. 'I have to believe the path leads to something good.' Squirming under Lazuli's assessing look, she ploughed on. 'I guessed early on that Everand wasn't who he said he was, and had a purpose for being in Riverfall. I was intrigued, and thought it'd be fun to find out. Then, when I understood what he was trying to do, I wanted to help him.'

Peering into Lazuli's troubled eyes, she murmured, 'Everand helped me to find more power within myself ... but now this ability continues to grow and to drive me, even when he's not here.'

A shudder wracked her and Lazuli grasped both of her hands. Squeezing his warm hands back, she glanced away. It didn't feel right to tell him she might be destined to be the next guide, especially when U-Mali and U-Lumin hadn't spoken of it. She frowned. Was this journey a test? Maybe that was why her instinct was nagging at her so hard — she had to find a dragon to prove herself — without Everand. Her heart skipped a few beats.

'What?' asked Lazuli. 'I can tell you've thought of something important.'

'I think this is a test. And you are to witness it.'

His eyebrows quirked upwards so comically that she giggled. He opened and closed his mouth twice, and she giggled again. 'Yes, you! And you thought you had a choice about whether you came with me!'

'We'd better get on with it then.' Releasing her hands as if he'd been stung, Lazuli took the lead along the dirt track.

Following, Lamiya watched Lazuli's easy lope and the muscles working in his legs. The spirits were devious, drawing him into this. Whatever *this* was. Letting him set the pace, she thought about what she was trying to do. The first step was to see if anything suggested there might be a dragon nearby. If she found a hint, she'd try to call the dragon. Her forehead ached. What if it was massive and powerful like Mizukaze? Or, her mood brightened, what if it was lithe and elegant like Flight?

What was Lazuli's other question? After a few paces it came to her: *Why?* Several paces later she admitted she had no idea. Did they need another dragon? Perhaps the dragon would know. If there was one.

The drizzle dissipated and although the air remained moist and heavy, she drew back her hood, sighing at the tangled curls adorning her hair. The red flower fell out to land in a puddle with a faint splat.

'Wait,' she called to Lazuli, watching the red petals bob on the puddle surface. A powerful, invisible tug rocked her and she remembered that one of the images in her strange vision had been red petals showering over water. *This was a sign.*

She faced the lake. The water stretched away, a moving mass of gleaming dull-grey streaks, and the distant shore was obscured by a mist that shrouded the tops of the trees and left the trunks poking below like legs. East, the hills towered greenly into the grey-purple sky.

Drawing in a breath, she held it, softened her gaze and then released the breath. Her eyes travelled to a natural curve in the shoreline ahead, where the water looked still and deep. Lazuli stood watching her intently.

'There.' She pointed, and after a bisk nod he set off again.

When she neared the pond-like stretch of water, a tingling anticipation grew and an unfamiliar current of energy travelled through her veins. On reaching the curve, she chose what she thought was the centre and stood admiring the way the slopes of the hills reached right down to the water's edge so it looked as if they were dipping their toes in.

On the far shore, the mist had crept lower and only the base of the trees was visible, as if a mystical hazy wall had come down to separate the lake from the rest of the world. Behind her, the smooth, white tree trunks absorbed the muted purple hues of dusk and the glossy green leaves brushed against each other in a subtle murmuring.

This was a place of the spirits and she felt the beats of her heart slowing. She jumped when Lazuli dropped his hand on her shoulder, his presence incongruent.

'I think you should sit under those trees for a while.' Softening her instruction with a smile, she fumbled with the tie-string of one of the pouches and passed it to him. 'You can eat while you wait.' Seeing the 'how long' forming, she added, 'This might take a while. Sit quietly unless I call you?'

About to turn away, she paused when Whirr clambered out of her tunic, blinking drowsily. She'd forgotten he was there! Crooking a finger for Whirr to climb onto, she passed him to Lazuli and watched him run up Lazuli's arm to perch on his shoulder. 'You two wait together.'

Lazuli squeezed her shoulder, mouthed good luck and headed towards a nearby grove of trees. She waited until he'd sat down with his back leaning against a trunk and started to tip nuts out of the pouch, Whirr promptly hopping into his lap in anticipation. Giving a small wave, she spun to face the water.

After a few steps her sandals squelched in damp dirt and she removed them, placing them neatly a little back from the water. She wriggled her wrinkled toes; the dirt felt good beneath her feet, connecting her to the place. Moving forward, she roved her eyes over the water. A single fish jumped, sending ripples her way. The hills softened in the mauve light and shadows slunk down their sides, while a soft breeze eddied across the water and stirred her hair away from her face. The tingling sensation crawled through her veins.

She waded into the water, cold splashing over her feet and etching up her shins. After a couple of paces she stopped, thinking about how she and Everand had called Mizukaze. Remembering that she'd put her hands in the water, she trailed her fingers in, moving her hands to create gentle swirling patterns. Closing her eyes, she imagined Everand standing behind her, his strong hands on her shoulders, his warm breath travelling over the back of her neck. *Call your dragon, Lamiya.* But how? Had he spoken in a dragon tongue? No, he said he'd projected images to the dragon.

She frowned: they had known they were looking for a blue-and-gold dragon in the likeness of the boat Mizuchi, but she had no idea what this dragon might look like. The fluttering red petals came into her mind, the colours vibrant and tinged with golden sunlight. Was the dragon red and gold? Yes, that felt right. And female. She cast her call into her fingertips.

Beautiful dragon of Dragonfoot Lake, I am Lamiya and I would meet you. She projected an image of herself standing there, fingers dipped in the water, and a bubble of water coming to greet her. Thinking of Mizukaze's excitement at having a boat named after him and racing in his honour, a thrill ran through her: her team needed a new boat.

Please show yourself so we can build a boat in your honour. She visualised a boat with an elegant, arched head, vibrant red scales and shapely golden horns, and a red tail coiled high, a golden barb at the tip.

Water lapped around her fingers and she held her breath. Her mind kept trying to rush off to explore ideas, to ask questions, and sternly she brought it back. *I am Lamiya, glide for Riverplain. Please show yourself.* The water lapped strongly around her fingers and she exhaled before wading further in, ignoring Lazuli's exclamation from the shore. Out deeper, a wide band of current moved towards her and the tingling fizzed through her again. With a swallow, she remembered her vision had hinted at a presence larger than Mizukaze.

The water in front of her burbled, and in the fading light she found herself looking into the long, narrow face of a red-scaled dragon. Definitely female because the head was similar in shape to Flight's. The dragon blinked, long golden eyelashes travelling over enormous yellow oval irises.

Greetings, Great Dragon. What shall I call you? Lamiya made her request as humbly and respectfully as possible and told her knees to stop shaking.

Well met, Lamiya of Riverplain. Call me Akachi, appeared in her mind. She could understand it! How? Never mind that, pay attention! The dragon tilted her head. *What have you done with my daughter?*

Lamiya wanted to pull her fingers from the water in case the dragon bit her hands off. Not only was the dragon massive, she seemed annoyed. *Do you mean the dragon that infused our boat?* She projected an image of the boat, with the dragon Flight peeling away from it at the height of the long race in Riverfall and disappearing into Dragonspine River. Water swirled around her knees and waves slapped her when the red dragon rose and towered high above her.

Fighting down fear, she craned her head back to look up at the dragon. Akachi was longer and taller than Mizukaze, but more sinuous. Cascading golden scales glittered down the dragon's chest and fed into blood-red scales for the body and legs. A long, purple tongue flicked out of the dragon's jaw, which contained rows of impressively sharp white fangs.

Where is she? the dragon asked in an imperious, commanding manner.

The question buffeting her, Lamiya bowed. *The dragon we call Flight, the name of our boat, is now in the lake next to Mizuchi Falls. She is with Mizukaze, the dragon that lives there.*

Another dragon? The words roared around in her head. *Is it male?*

Lamiya flinched, then hurriedly straightened her spine. *Yes, Great Akachi. Mizukaze is a male dragon.* She projected an image of the blue-and-gold Mizukaze speeding through the water and rising up in all his magnificence.

Ah. Where is Mizuchi? The red dragon lowered her head, steam puffing from her nostrils.

Her heart hammering most uncomfortably, Lamiya thought hard. Mizukaze said he was the son of Mizuchi, but he didn't say what happened to his mother. *We ... we ... don't know of Mizuchi, but Mizukaze said he is her son.* When the dragon stared, unblinking, she added, *No-one has seen Mizuchi for a very long time. I'm sorry.* She stumbled to a stop. Was Akachi related to Mizuchi?

Akachi sank lower until she appeared to be sitting on her hindquarters, her head only an arm's length away from Lamiya's face. The dragon held her in a steady gaze and Lamiya's vision began to swirl, the hypnotic pull in the dragon's golden eyes difficult to withstand. Blinking, she struggled to hold her position.

So, Mizuchi is gone. Akachi shook her head, droplets of water sliding off the scales. *But my daughter was right. She fixed herself to your boat hoping to find another dragon.*

The large, yellow-textured irises shifted and writhed and Lamiya was spellbound as the dragon brought its face closer. Uncomfortably hot air wafted over her cheeks.

Bring my daughter back! With the other dragon.

'I can try,' stammered Lamiya. Realising she'd spoken rather than projected her reply, she repeated it. *I can try. It is a far journey from here.* She sent an image of the long, meandering river heading north, and an image of Dragon Lake at the foot of the mountains with the glittering Mizuchi Falls tumbling into it. When the dragon just stared, the golden irises growing deeper, she added, *I will try. Soon.*

I bind you to that promise. Akachi's eyelids closed languorously over the hypnotic eyes and Lamiya felt invisible bands release around her arms and legs.

Her heart pounding, she was consumed by the awful sense she'd started this conversation on the back foot and needed to do more to appease the dragon. *Great Akachi, may we of Riverplain honour you by building and racing a new boat in your name?* She showed Akachi her team and Flight finishing the middle race, gliding away from the other boats to win with clear water behind them.

A rumbling came from the dragon. *You may.* She swished her tail, sending waves curving away across the lake. *Lamiya, Glide of Riverplain, build your boat in my honour.* Akachi dipped her head, like a nod, and edged backwards, the powerful eyes holding her once more.

Lamiya, Glide of Riverplain, bring my daughter Hanachi, and Mizukaze, so we can replenish our kind.

The red dragon lowered herself into the water until only her head remained above the surface and flicked her forked tongue. *This is but one of your purposes. Come to me again.* The dragon sank further, water rising up her face and closing over her ears and burnished horns. A band of current moved steadily away.

Lamiya's knees shook and she gulped in a large breath. She had found and called the dragon! She'd spoken with it — all by herself! And Akachi had tasked her to bring the other dragons to Riverplain. Mizukaze and … Hanachi. She now knew the real name of the dragon from her boat. Her knees gave way and she plopped down. Cold water seeped into her trousers and soaked the bottom half of her tunic and her cloak, the feathers floating out behind her.

Numbness stole over her. Akachi had said this was *but one of her purposes*. What *had* she done?

She heard splashing behind her, and Lazuli's strong hands slid under her armpits and hoisted her to her feet. Before she could protest, he lifted her into his arms and waded out of the lake. Whirr flitted above her face, peeping, while Lazuli hurried across the dirt beach to the shelter of the trees. By then she was shivering and her teeth were chattering.

Lazuli lowered her onto a patch of grass, his face obscured in the gloom. 'Here.' He pressed some dried fruits into her hand. 'Eat these.'

Her hand shook so much she dropped the fruit.

With a curse, he fumbled until he found the pieces and then fed one into her mouth. 'Chew.'

Appreciating the sugar and energy flowing into her mouth, she chewed. Lazuli kept popping fruit into her mouth until she stopped shaking, then he shuffled around to sit behind her and wrapped her cloak tightly about her body, followed by his arms and his cloak. Welcome warmth seeped into her back.

'I'd suggest you take your wet clothes off,' he murmured next to her ear. 'But I don't want you to get the wrong idea.'

Her numb lips and cheeks etched into a smile.

'It's dark. I suggest we rest.' His breath huffed over her ear. 'Mighty dragon caller, as I will swear that I witnessed.'

Her head drooped until her chin rested on her chest, but elation warmed her.

Surely, she had passed this test.

Chapter Twenty-Eight

It had stopped raining by the time the stag-horn alighted on the dome pad. Everand slid off and led his mount down the ramp, lost in thought. As he walked the creature to its stall, the same two boys approached.

Handing the reins to the smaller boy, he said, 'You can put him in. He is calm now.' Turning to the other boy, he said, 'Give him a good wipe-down and extra food, please.' When the boy looked at him anxiously, he arched an eyebrow.

'Yes, Mage Everand.' The boy bowed.

'I'll come just after it gets light to take him out again, so feed him early. Two long rides should be enough to restore his training.' Wiping his fingers on his damp robes, he added, 'I'll speak to Mage Mantiss about either reassigning the stag-horn or sending it back to the breeding complex.'

The taller boy gave a shy smile. 'Thank you, Mage Everand.'

Pausing briefly to greet his own beetle, which brushed his fingers with its antennae again, Everand hurried out of the complex and down the stairs.

Back at his quarters, he found a tray of food outside the door. Perhaps Melida was becoming accustomed to his erratic coming and going. Taking the tray inside, he put it on the table and peeled off his damp robe. The material made a loud clunk when it landed on the floor. The stone! Fishing the calling stone out of the robe pocket, he put it on the table beside the tray and stood regarding it, deep in thought.

So, he had the means to warn Malach — he'd activate the stone at first light and hope that Malach would see his call and come to the grassy expanse. His forehead ached. What then? How would warning the half-mage help? He could tell Malach to hide, but the Guild would find him. What if he hid the half-mage somewhere other than Riverwood? Would one of the other provinces be prepared to conceal him? Not Riverfall; it was too close and too obvious.

What about the mysterious ability possessed by the Riverplain guides? Could U-Mali and U-Lumin hide Malach from a Guild mage's power? He rubbed his forehead. But that would make the people of Riverplain complicit and put them in danger. Would any of the provinces even agree to help Malach after his behaviour at the races and his rejection of the offer to trade? If *he* asked, they would do it for him — which would make him responsible for whatever happened as a consequence.

How far was the Guild prepared to go to capture Malach? He tapped his fingers on the table. Ironically, Mage Beetal probably hadn't anticipated the course of events his early actions would precipitate. Everand's mouth twisted at the potential parallel of the actions of both the father and son starting like small ripples and expanding to drawn in so many others.

Tension tugging at his muscles, he ran a bath and soaked in it until the water turned tepid. Sighing, he dried off and donned his azure robe. Then he sat picking at the plate of baked vegetables and wishing Lamiya was sitting at the table opposite him. What would she suggest? He pretended she was sitting there, her beautiful face peering at him. The more he thought of her, the more real the image became.

From her acute perspective, what would she ask him? He swallowed some tea, then sat with his hands in his lap and stilled his mind. Mizu bubbled her fish call and swam a few laps of her tank, the swishing water triggering images: Waterfall. Lakes. Rivers. Dragons.

What are the mages afraid of? Lamiya's essence asked. He absorbed the question — the Guild worried about disruption to their lifestyle, either by outsiders or undesirable actions from those within. They feared anything that challenged the status quo. *Why?* asked his mind Lamiya. Excellent question. The Guild must feel insecure for a reason. Were the answers buried in the library, in the ancient texts?

Now answer what I first asked, pressed Lamiya, her forehead creased in a frown. *What are the mages physically afraid of? What would make them back down?*

His fingers twitched in his lap when the answer hurled into his mind: *dragons.* Mage Beetal had terrified the Guild with his army of the beasts. Mages had been injured. Mages had died. Mage Mantiss had been forced to raise the Staropal and give it to Mage Beetal. The Guild was left in disarray, and the ambitious mage had the all-precious stone, his power magnified a hundred-fold. The ambitious mage had won.

But his mentor had overstepped and used the stone to travel to the world of Chrysalis, where he was overwhelmed by a farseer despite his additional power. In a curious twist of fate, the invaders from Chrysalis were defeated when the farseer that led them was killed by the lead black dragon. In supreme irony, it was his mentor's favourite black dragon that ended up saving the Guild from annihilation.

Tapping his fingers on the table helped bring back the troublesome memories. Once the battle was over, nearly eighty winged dragons remained, lingering masterless and undirected in the gardens and grounds near the Great Hall. The mages were terrified, refusing to come out of their quarters.

It was *his* suggestion that they return the dragons to Elemar's world of Terralis — back to their wild, volcanic world — and the Outer Council of Twenty had jumped at the idea. Now the Guild assumed there were no more dragons in Axis, or anywhere in Ossilis. Problem solved; no more ambitious mage and no more terrifying dragons.

His heartbeats ramming against his breastbone, Everand opened his eyes. None, absolutely none, of his history lessons had referred to dragons in the river in Ossilis! Why not? Did the Guild not know about the river dragons? Were the dragons not there when the mages first arrived? His heart pounded erratically. Axis was a long way from the river — about as far away as possible. Was that a coincidence? A sense of dread oozing into him, he shivered.

When Mantiss and Agamid had asked him to find out about the river provinces, he'd assumed they were referring to the people. What if they also wanted to know whether there were *dragons*? His mouth ran dry and he scraped a hand across his lips. He'd neglected to mention the dragons in his report, and hadn't said the boats were built like dragons. Why *had* he done that? Would Mantiss ask him outright at the next meeting? Laying his trembling hands on the table, he took a breath. Why did he not want to tell the other mages about the dragons? He felt he *couldn't*. The words simply would not phrase themselves.

Mizukaze had come to him and was now his friend. *Wait.* No, both dragons had come to *Lamiya*. Hadn't Mizukaze said something about tricksy people with power were to be avoided? At the time, in the turmoil of the races, he'd thought Mizukaze meant Malach. Had the dragon also met Mage Beetal? A shudder chased down his spine. No, that seemed unlikely because his mentor had easily commanded a hundred of the beasts. If his mentor had met Mizukaze, then surely the river dragon would have been under Beetal's control and trained to also respond to Malach.

Maybe not. He sat straighter, drumming his fingers on the table and making the items on the tray clatter. Even though the beasts were a similar formidable size, Mizukaze had an intelligence and cunning that he hadn't perceived in the winged dragons from Terralis. Mizukaze had magical power — elemental at least — in that he could control the weather. He thought of the strength of the dragon's hypnotic eyes. Mizukaze also had ability in enchantment. The species were different; the river dragons were *far* more dangerous.

How was it possible that the Guild did not know about them? Had he been connected to Lamiya, the mystical bird caller, for a higher reason? A deeper, colder shudder chased across his shoulders. Could he continue to conceal the dragons from Mantiss and the Guild? *I need your eyes on this.* The hues in Mantiss' green eyes had swirled and his master had been so intent when he'd spoken those words at the very start of his mission. Did the *this* mean finding out about any dragons? But why not just say so?

And now he was back, Mantiss hadn't actually asked him whether there were dragons. Was his master afraid of the answer? Or did Mantiss assume that he would immediately report something so momentous? At the next meeting, what if he *did* tell the council? What should he say and how would he describe the river dragons? His thoughts grew fuzzy, his tongue tied itself in knots and his memories of the dragons became blurred and indistinct.

Frowning deeply, he dug his fingernails into his palms to try to bring his focus back. Nothing changed; his mind and tongue still refused to form any coherent sentences, and the more he tried, the more jumbled his thoughts became until such a wave of dizziness swept over him that he had to clutch the edge of the table for balance. Could Mizukaze have cast a spell to stop him from revealing their presence? A dull ache spread across his forehead.

Wait. The dragons had befriended him. They trusted him. And Lamiya. What did that mean? Pulse racing, he felt hope blooming in his chest. Perhaps his wild plan *could* work. Mizukaze and Flight would protect him, if he asked. Would they protect Malach as well if he asked nicely enough? What if Lamiya asked? The notion hovered as a misty thought and then settled, but deep-seated unease squirmed in his chest. Calling on the dragons would be a last resort: he only wanted to leave the Guild, not disrupt it. He tilted his head. There was another uncomfortable parallel here. At the outset, his mentor Mage Beetal had only wanted to change the Guild, not destroy it.

His mind image of Lamiya posed another question: *Is Malach worth it?* Scrubbing his face with his fingers, he cursed. *Lamiya, my love, I don't know.* He took a breath. How would he know? Her essence dissipated with a lingering tendril ... *How can we ever know beforehand?*

His tea sat like a cold pond in the base of his stomach while his thoughts circled in an endless loop, returning always to one fundamental question: does Malach deserve to die? Each time, his heart and mind concurred that Mage Beetal's son did *not* deserve to be summarily obliterated. The half-mage had flaws, no doubt about that, but what if he were trained and mentored? If only the Guild would bring Malach into an apprenticeship and give him a chance.

Buffoons, narrow-minded idiots who can't see past their own noses ... Tempted to use some of the terms his former mentor had applied, his lips twitched. Very well, he would hide Malach and thwart the Inner Council's first attempt. And hope he could come up with a better solution.

For a while he sat watching Mizu swimming laps of her tank and blowing bubbles, the fluid movement of the fish helping to soothe his jangled nerves. If he went at first light, he could take Mizu and release her into Dragon Lake, or the lake by Lamiya's hut. If Malach refused to cooperate, he'd achieve one good thing, regardless.

Rising and going to his bedroom, he opened the wardrobe door and crouched to retrieve the small bowl Mage Beetal had kept the fish in. Returning to the lounge area, he put it on the marble floor next to the tank and just as he straightened up, the summons to a council meeting sounded.

He trotted down the stairs until hurrying footsteps clattering behind him made him pause to look over his shoulder. Saiphos was catching him up, so he waited and they strode along the path to the Great Hall together. 'Do you know what this meeting is about?' Everand asked.

'I think to refine the details of what we will do once the wild half-mage is brought here.' Saiphos' usually calm demeanour looked troubled.

Now or never. 'Are you comfortable with obliterating a person?'

Compressing his lips, Saiphos replied, 'What else would we do?'

'Train him?' Everand suggested softly.

'He is not pure. Would that even work?' Stopping, Saiphos stared at him with wide eyes.

'He's not pure but he has ability, and we lost several mages in the recent battle. Can we afford to waste one?'

Saiphos' eyes widened even further. 'An interesting perspective. Will you propose it?'

'There wouldn't be much support for the idea.' Everand shrugged.

They walked the rest of the way in silence and he hoped Saiphos' concentrated frown meant he was mulling over the idea. At least he'd planted the seed of the concept, not that there was time for it to germinate. He strode up the steps to the hall and quickly crossed the rug to take his seat because everyone else was already there. Were they that keen to capture and obliterate Malach?

The meeting was brisk and decisive, Mage Mantiss setting out the order of events to capture Malach. Agamid rolled out the map again, and they confirmed the plan for Everand to meet Malach at Dragon Lake while the others hid in the forest. They refined the action to agree that Everand would subdue Malach's powers under the pretext that he was training him to conceal them and the others would then pounce and snare Malach in a binding spell. Agamid would communicate back to Mantiss, and the power of the other six from the Inner Council would be deployed to transport them and Malach directly into the Great Hall.

A warded cage would be built to hold the half-mage. The additional ten mages of the Outer Council of Twenty would be present, with three of these, including Hydrelaps, allocated as scribes to record what happened, both in writing and visually in a memory ball. Mage Mantiss would inform Malach of his sentence.

Everand fidgeted, aware of Saiphos casting sideways glances at him. 'Mage Mantiss, may I ask, will we allow Malach to speak for himself?'

Across the table, Tiliqua blinked at him in astonishment. At the end of the table, Pelamis snorted.

Mantiss cleared his throat. 'To what purpose, Everand? You've given us ample evidence that he has illicit power. He is the son of the traitor Mage Beetal, and he tried to use his power for evil to disrupt the other provinces. What could he say that we need to hear?'

Tiliqua, face hard, added, 'Didn't you say he captured you and forced you to train him? Why would you even suggest this?'

All nine mages stared at him. Put like that, there didn't seem much he could say and his resolve wilted. 'It is just that obliteration is so … irreversible. Is there nothing we wish to learn from the half-mage before we execute him?'

The silence was so resounding that Everand lowered his gaze to stare at the dark gleaming wood of the table. Why had he said anything? *Stupid to try*. He couldn't meet anyone's eyes. Especially not those of his master.

Eventually, Agamid said firmly, 'I expect this is harder for you, Everand, because you have met this half-mage, but you need to set that aside. By your own words, you have provided the information the council needed and the decision was unanimous.'

'Thank you, Mage Agamid. Of course, you are right.' He sat looking contrite until the attention of the others shifted away, and the rest of the arrangements were rapidly concluded. His stomach churned, but at least he had tried. Now he knew they wouldn't even listen to any other options. When Mantiss started to wind up the meeting, the others were listening but their gazes kept sliding coldly towards him. *Curse it.*

'… thank you all for your wisdom and attention.' Mantiss rested his arms on the table. 'Agamid and Everand, you are invited to my quarters for the sun-fade meal and further discussion.'

A cold shiver ran a crooked course down Everand's spine, and his heart beat more quickly. Was Mantiss preparing to test his resolve? 'Thank you, Mantiss.'

Everyone rose, and Everand kept his eyes lowered while he tucked his chair in neatly, bowed to the senior mages and turned away. He almost leaped down the external steps and hesitated on the path; it was already nearing sun-fade. Perhaps the greenery and ponds in the gardens would help restore his wildly teetering sense of equilibrium.

Setting off, he strolled along the garden paths, barely seeing the lawns, stone edges, elegant weeping bushes and colourful flowers. His stomach roiled and burned as if he'd swallowed a jar full of acid. Why hadn't he kept his mouth shut? After several laps of the same looped path, he accepted that he'd had to ask to satisfy his own integrity.

There *must* be a reason the mages were so averse to change. Why could there be no magic outside of the Guild? Would the ability that U-Mali and U-Lumin possessed, and Lamiya for that matter, mean the Guild would seek to annihilate them too? Was there any way, any way at all, that he would be able to influence this? He stopped walking. Lamiya would tell him it wasn't his role.

Holding that thought, he sat on an ornate stone bench and stared unseeing into the bed of white and purple flowers. A mantle of melancholy settling over his shoulders, he slumped with his head in his hands. How could he persuade Mantiss and the others to release him from the Guild? Every part of him wanted to be with Lamiya, to crush her in his arms, plant a thousand kisses down her gorgeous neck.

Sitting up, he clenched and unclenched his hands in his lap. He *must* change the Guild, or it would never let him go. Could he plead with Mantiss like a son to a father? The notion did not sit well, but there *must* be a solution. If it wasn't his role to change the Guild, then whose role was it?

Peering into the garden bed for inspiration, he noticed the white flowers were taking on the pink hue of the setting sun.

It was time to go to Mantiss' rooms.

Chapter Twenty-nine

Crunching along the pebble path to Mantiss' quarters, Everand admired the way the setting sun cast a pink and gold aura over the white marble building and softened the sky to hints of mauve. The air nudging past his face had a moist tinge with the promise of a dark-fall dew.

How long had it been since he'd been invited to dine with Mage Mantiss? Before the events with Mage Beetal and the decisive battle, Mantiss had kept their contact to a minimum and they'd met covertly in the library when he had information to report or Mantiss wanted to task him. After the battle, Mantiss had invited him over twice, thrilled with his sleuthing and actions. More recently a distance had developed between them. Was this just because nothing untoward had happened? Until Beram's arrival.

He started up the steps, wondering whether any other factors could be in play. Taking a breath, he rang the bell beside the polished door.

Footsteps sounded inside and the door opened to reveal Tiliqua, curvaceous in a sea-blue dress that accentuated her figure and eyes. Her honey-blonde hair gleamed and tumbled over her shoulders, only the front part braided, and her smile was warm.

'Come in.' Tiliqua held the door open and when he stepped through, she leaned in to kiss him on the cheek. The aroma of violets teased his nose and her lips were cool on his skin.

'Are you well?' Eyeing him critically, she added, 'You look thinner.'

'You look nice.' He brushed her cheek with his lips and stepped away. 'I am possibly thinner. This was a vigorous mission with random meals.'

She closed the door with a laugh and touched his arm. 'You'll enjoy this meal, then. The others are waiting.' The dress swishing pleasantly around her legs, she walked towards the dining area and he took long strides to keep up, given that she was almost as tall as him.

Mantiss and Agamid were seated at the cedar dining table with a glass of wine in their hands. Tiliqua gestured to the seat at the end opposite Mantiss and then settled into the chair facing Agamid. Taking his seat, Everand appreciated the view out the window. Although the quarters were on the ground floor, the vista of the setting sun was spectacular.

A young man scurried in from a side door and filled a glass with wine for him. When the youth left, Everand realised there was an empty chair next to Tiliqua.

Mantiss spoke. 'Elytra apologises for her absence. She is not feeling well.'

'I'm sorry to hear that,' said Everand sincerely. He liked Mantiss' gentle wife.

'It has been a while,' said Mantiss, lifting his glass. 'Before we distracted you with this impromptu mission, how were your research and studies going?'

Taking a sip, Everand let the white wine trickle over his tongue. Not as strong as feeja wine, but crisper. 'Well, I think. I was practising applying the spell of invisibility with a personal shield at the same time.' Agamid raised an eyebrow. 'Both spells require a significant amount of energy and concentration and I was trying to find an efficient approach.' When he paused, Tiliqua gave him an encouraging smile.

'I tried raising the shield first and then adding the invisibility, but the shield wavered when my attention moved to the second spell.' He fiddled with the stem of his wine glass. 'I found if I created the spell of invisibility in a close form, and then generated a tighter shield, it was easier to hold.' He frowned. 'But I doubt that a third spell, such as a defensive strike, could also be used.'

'Are you anticipating trouble?' asked Agamid. 'These are not your average spells.'

Lifting his shoulders in a shrug, Everand replied, 'Not necessarily, but using these spells, and concurrently, seems consistent with my roles for the Guild so far.'

Mantiss' green eyes drilled into him and Tiliqua looked pensive.

'I did have an idea on this mission that might be worth discussion in council.'

'Go on.' Agamid leaned forward, interested.

Looking at Mantiss, Everand said, 'You asked me not to reveal my powers during the mission, but this became increasingly difficult. The work I'd done using invisibility plus another spell, such as enhanced senses, came in useful. But I soon found that using these spells regularly was draining. It made me wonder whether we should practise sustained use of spells and explore ways to restore our power more rapidly.'

Tiliqua smiled widely, showing neat white teeth. 'An interesting point given we always practise spells one at a time.' To Mantiss she said, 'Could I work with Everand on this if the council decides we should proceed?'

With a fond smile, Mantiss said, 'I don't see why not, if the council agrees.' His glance transferred to Everand. 'What do you think? Two of our best minds on this project?'

When he nodded, an almost imperceptible look passed between father and daughter and an uncanny sense of unease wriggled into his mind. What if Mantiss had been training *two* spies all along and Tiliqua was now to spy on him? Picking up his glass, he took several sips, thinking hard. Clearly, Mantiss sanctioned Tiliqua's interest in him and it was flattering to think his master would welcome him as a formal son. Her interest seemed genuine, but perhaps Mantiss had a double motive. Two women arrived with food, and his stomach growled at the plate of steaming vegetables and broiled fish placed in front of him.

The meal passed pleasantly and darkness crept down the windows, cocooning them in the light and warmth inside and concealing the landscape outside. Trying not to imbibe too much wine, he answered their questions as best he could. Tiliqua asked how much energy it had required to use multiple spells, evidently pleased by the opportunity to work on this topic with him.

While the dessert plates were being cleared away, he realised Mantiss hadn't said much for a while. Agamid was explaining how the silk moths were prospering and how Saiphos had helped to create a new colour dye. Letting the words burble over him, Everand surreptitiously observed Mantiss. His master nodded now and then as if he were listening, but his attention looked far away. More silvery greys were forming in Mantiss' hair and beard, and the wrinkle lines around his eyes and mouth were deeper. Dark shadows sat under the green eyes and the bony shoulders were somewhat hunched: his master looked tired.

His gaze was drawn to the tabletop. Was that a faint tremor he detected in the hands that were resting on the table? Was Mantiss unwell? Or had events and the injuries his master sustained battling Mage Beetal taken a greater toll than he'd realised? Concerned, he felt immeasurably sad for his kind and astute master.

Glancing up at him, Mantiss raised a fine silver eyebrow in query and Everand's throat tightened. The opportunity to ask what he so wanted to know had just presented itself. 'Master, when you sent me on this mission, did you suspect someone was using magic outside the Guild?'

Agamid stopped mid-sentence and Tiliqua's gaze sharpened.

'I trained you well.' With a wry smile, Mantiss interlocked his fingers. 'Beram's description of the large, aggressive moths suggested something odd was happening, on top of the sudden complete lack of rain. Everything was too soon after Mage Beetal's disastrous ploy.'

Out of the corner of his eye, Everand observed that Agamid sat quietly poised, his face not reflecting surprise. Tiliqua's eyebrows lifted, her face otherwise neutral. 'I see,' he said, waiting for his master to elaborate.

'I didn't expect a direct link to Mage Beetal. However,' Mantiss leaned forward, his expression serious, 'in many ways this is a welcome finding. The alternatives would be far less palatable.'

'You were worried about another ambitious mage?' Everand asked.

'That's why we sent you.' Mantiss gave a tight nod. 'My boy, who else could we trust?'

Ignoring the rush of warmth at being so highly regarded, Everand looked at the others. 'By "we", you mean you and Agamid?' He leaned back, appreciating the support of the chair. 'Why didn't you tell me?'

Both had the grace to shift uncomfortably on their chairs and Tiliqua narrowed her eyes, displeased by his challenge of her father's judgement.

Clearing his throat, Mantiss said, 'As before, dear boy, I didn't want to influence your findings. Set you looking for things that might not exist.'

Agamid stirred. 'We felt it best not to involve the councils until we knew more.'

'I worked it out,' said Tiliqua, looking smug and then fondly at her father. 'The explanations for why you missed a couple of meetings didn't ring true. You wouldn't simply miss them, so I deduced you were on another mission.' Holding his gaze, she asked pointedly, 'If we obliterate this half-mage, is the risk removed?'

Not liking the direct question, Everand frowned. 'As far as I can see, Malach is the only person with magical power, and he didn't intend any harm to the Guild. He has local ambitions. The river people are intent on farming and fishing and even if they do trade among themselves and hold their boat races, I don't see any risk to us.' He placed his hands flat on the table, breathing out through his nose and trying to convince himself his words were reasonable.

Stroking his beard pensively, Agamid said, 'Maybe, but will the provinces come running to us again the next time something goes wrong? Or if it doesn't rain?'

Everand bit his tongue to refrain from saying rain wouldn't be an issue now they were friends with the dragon. 'Possibly. If something untoward *did* happen again, wouldn't we be better off knowing about it?'

'What are you suggesting?' demanded Tiliqua. 'Will something happen?'

He held his hands up in placation. 'I have been recalled, and Malach will mysteriously disappear. Hopefully, nothing else will happen. All I'm saying is that *if* it did, to the extent the provinces needed us, wouldn't it be better if we knew?'

The silence stretched for so long he sat back and folded his hands in his lap. If there was ever a moment to suggest a shift in Guild views, he had inadvertently just done it.

'I don't see why we'd need to know,' said Mantiss eventually. 'We could strengthen the wardspell so no-one could even get close enough to throw rocks at it.'

Disappointment coursing through him, Everand closed his eyes.

'Are you alright?' asked Agamid.

Opening his eyes, Everand murmured, 'Sorry. I'm still tired from the mission. I need more rest before we go to capture Malach.'

'Of course, my boy, of course.' Mantiss flapped a hand and looked concerned.

'It has grown late while we talked, but we do appreciate your ideas.' Agamid smiled.

Everand didn't suppress his spontaneous yawn. 'Master, thank you for the enjoyable dinner.' To Tiliqua he said, 'I look forward to working with you, assuming the council agrees to the research.' To Agamid he said, 'The new colour sounds intriguing and I'd like to order a robe.'

Everyone stood when he did, and murmured farewells. Tiliqua offered to show him out and he paused at the doorway, uncomfortable at the expectant look in her eyes. Mirroring her initial greeting, he leaned over and brushed his lips across her cheek, taking a step back before she could reach for him. 'See you soon, after this next part of the mission is over.'

He walked down the steps, acutely conscious of her eyes on his back. From the path he gave a cheery wave, waiting while she waved back and then slowly closed the door. Creating a globe of light, he set off. Had he said enough to convince them of his continued loyalty?

Halfway back to his dome, he extinguished the globe and looked up at the inky sky laced with wispy clouds dancing around the half-disc moon. The air drifting past his face and hands was refreshing.

Breathing in deeply, he thought of Mantiss sitting subdued, his posture weak and the tremor in the lean, wrinkled hands. At sixty-eight, Mantiss was the oldest mage. The pebbles crunched crisply under his sandals and his thoughts drifted to the other influential mages. The next senior mages were Agamid and Hydrelaps the librarian, both over fifty. If Mantiss became unable to lead the Guild, Agamid was likely to be the interim Head of the Guild until an election could be held.

His footsteps faltered: Agamid, although a wise, fair and pleasant mage, walked firmly in the shadow of Mantiss and would not be a strong leader. Hydrelaps would be useless. That opened the possibility for leadership to pass to one of the younger mages. His feet stopped and he stared at the moon, shrouded in shreds of cloud. *Two of our best minds on the project.*

A chill ran from the top of his head all the way to his toes. Did his master's expectations exceed those he recognised? Had the mission to the river provinces also been a test of his ability and loyalty? A shiver raced down his spine. They'd admitted they *had* suspected someone was using magic but, this aside, the Guild had *no* interest in the river provinces — and from the discussion just held, they never would. They'd *known* he would volunteer. Was it possible Mantiss and Agamid had let him go as a way of assessing his resourcefulness and suitability to lead should Mantiss fail in the near future? His throat clenched. He couldn't lead the Guild! There must be someone else.

Who were the alternatives? Simoselaps, Pelamis and — Tiliqua. Did she perceive the chance to become the first female Head of the Guild? Or, if not her, then she wanted to be married to, and influence, whoever held the position. Perhaps either option would make Mantiss happy.

A bigger cloud passed before the moon, the path grew grey and shadowy and dank air eased around him, raising goosebumps along his arms. Persuading his feet to resume their trajectory towards his dome, he considered Pelamis and Simoselaps. Had they sensed a weakness developing? Were they jostling, ready to put their case forward? They were becoming bolder in their opinions. If so, the objective to capture Malach had just taken on yet another dimension.

His throat tightened as if an invisible chain had been placed around it.

Chapter Thirty

Mage Mantiss waited until Tiliqua resumed her seat and took a moment to assess her demeanour. The sea-blue dress suited her and highlighted all her womanly aspects. Had this appealed to Everand? Had his spy even noticed? Hard to tell. As always. She held an aura of energy and her cheeks glowed a pale rose; perhaps contained excitement at the joint research project. When Agamid left, he would take the opportunity to gauge her feelings for his spy.

Leaning his elbows on the dining table, he interlocked his fingers. 'What do you both think? Has Everand told us everything?'

Agamid tapped a forefinger on the table, shadows of thoughts chasing across his hazel eyes. 'He is always hard to read, but I can't help feeling that he was withholding something.'

'I have that sense too. But is it something important?' Mantiss' eyes narrowed.

Tapping his finger faster, as if the clacking noise could urge his thoughts along, Agamid said slowly, 'He has always been adept at concealing his feelings, yet I perceive he is not fully comfortable with the plan to capture and obliterate this half-mage.'

'Out of principle, or some misplaced loyalty to his former mentor?'

Withdrawing his hand to his lap, Agamid said, 'Perhaps both. We know that Everand consistently desires to do what is right. He has interacted with this half-mage, possibly sees some potential, and perhaps holds doubts about our collective judgement.'

Mantiss switched his focus to Tiliqua, who was turning her head to look at him or Agamid as they each spoke, a frown marring her perfect features. 'What do you think, my dear?'

'I agree Everand seems imperceptibly unsettled. But his research proposal is well considered and suggests he assumes things will return to normal after the rogue has been dealt with.' Tiliqua shifted in her chair and tilted her head. 'Do you think I should go with the others to help with the capture? I could keep an eye on Everand.'

Mantiss squeezed his interlocked fingers together. The idea had merit but if the event went awry, did he want his daughter in danger? Instinct suggested he'd be unwise to pit Tiliqua against Everand, as talented as she was. 'Thank you, my dear, but it would look strange if we added you to the capture group now.'

Before she could become disappointed, he added, 'I would rather you were here with me and the others because I suspect back here is where things might become difficult. From what Everand said, this half-mage will not surrender easily.'

'Very well.' Her clipped tone hinted at disappointment.

Agamid's lips wrinkled with a suppressed yawn. 'Is there more to discuss? If not, I have a busy schedule ahead at the silk moth complex.'

'Thank you, my friend. Moths aside, we need you well rested for this sortie.'

Rising, Agamid nodded to them both. 'Don't get up. I'll see myself out.'

On hearing the door close, Mantiss asked Tiliqua, 'Tea?'

'That would be nice.' His daughter was preparing to stand but she settled her weight back into the chair, the gleam in her eyes indicating she understood there was more to discuss.

Mantiss pulled closer the lacquered tray with the ornate ceramic teapot that Delma had left ready on one corner of the table. The herbs were already in the base of the teapot, and he picked up the small, matching ceramic jug to tip the water in. His hand shook, and he spilled some over the rim. Relieved that Tiliqua made no comment, he murmured the spell of warming to heat the water, inhaling the subtle aroma of chamomile and lavender that promptly rose above the table.

'Let me.' Tiliqua reached across the table and slid the tray towards her so she could pour the tea. Smoothly, she passed his cup to him. 'Your tremor is growing worse, Father. I worry for you.'

Appreciating the heat from the cup seeping into his fingers, Mantiss blew on his tea. 'It is a minor thing.' He blew on his tea again when her lips compressed, a sign that she disagreed. Time to deflect her focus. 'I want you to work more with Everand. Get closer to him. The research project is an excellent opportunity, although I'm sure working with you wasn't what he anticipated when he mentioned it.' He raised his eyebrows at her. 'You like Everand?'

A faint pink blush stealing up her neck, Tiliqua lowered her eyes. Peering up from beneath thick, curved, golden eyelashes, she said, 'He is powerful, intelligent and … resourceful.' When she looked up, her eyes were dark and unreadable. 'Although, he is an enigma. I thought that when Elemar left he might feel lonely. Instead, he has closed himself off.'

Mantiss admired his daughter's courage in confessing, subtly, her interest and hopes. 'Your assessment is astute, and I share your disappointment. Everand is like a son to me, and I would welcome a partnership between you two. For a brief while, he softened and I detected a warm relationship between us. You are right in that he remains considerate and obliging, but his heart and mind are distant.'

He took a cautious sip of tea and eyed his daughter over the rim of the cup. 'If you can change that, I'd be grateful.'

The pink blush grew bolder, edging up to Tiliqua's jawline, and her throat moved in a swallow. 'I can try, Father.' Her gaze sharpened. 'You will help me?'

'Where I can. I am sure the council will approve this research project, which I imagine you two will do excellent work on, and which will naturally lead to follow-up work.' Around a smile, he concluded, 'Consistency of researchers will be essential.'

Tiliqua drank her tea and put the cup down. 'This will be interesting, if nothing else.' Holding eye contact, she said, 'I like it when you confide in me.' With a rustle of silk, she stood and came around the table to kiss his cheek. 'Sleep well. I'll start work on a formal research proposal first thing.'

Cool air wafting around him with her departure, he listened to her footsteps fading down the hallway. With a wave of a hand, he muted the orb lights and sat with the pale moonlight shining through the window, casting shadows and highlighting random edges. Tea spilled over his fingers when another tremor beset his hand. Irritated, he shakily put the cup down and clasped his hands in the warmth of his lap. Tiliqua would do her best, no doubt about that, and she would perhaps observe aspects of Everand that he was too blind to see after all this time.

Closing his eyes, Mantiss recalled the lanky boy of twelve season-cycles who had stood mute and expressionless while he and Agamid discovered, and then discussed, the body of his father, Mage Tenuis. The boy had been impossible to predict and read back then, so why did he even consider this could be changed now?

A strange, roiling current passed through his chest. *Hope.* He *wanted* Everand to change, wanted him to be a formal son — no, *yearned* for him to be a formal son. He had *used* Everand mercilessly, relying on his skills and loyalty to do the hard things he didn't want to do himself.

And now he was using him again, relying on him to win through and without even knowing the full risks. Trusting, loyal, courageous Everand deserved to be rewarded with a position of authority and a place in his family. If he would accept them.

Mantiss' right hand shook harder and he gripped it with the left one, forcing it to be still. He was becoming sentimental as he aged. Or was this the spreading weakness murmuring its way from his body into his heart and mind?

Another band of current travelled through his chest, leaving an aching tightness. *Fear.* What had Everand omitted in his report? Surely, not a dragon? Surely, his spy would report something so momentous? He clenched his jaw. He would have to ask. Directly. His fault, given that he hadn't tasked his spy to look for any signs of or references to water dragons. *Trust begets trust.* Who had told him that? Too late now. Would his spy withhold information if he felt he'd been misled? Possibly. But for what purpose?

A cloud shrouded the moon's face and the silvery light dimmed, plunging the room into darkness. *How apt.* Everything he'd become, everything he'd achieved, was waning. Fatigue coursed down Mantiss' limbs, leaving them heavy and chilled. His feet felt anchored to the tile floor.

Stirring in his chair, he forced his spine straighter. *No.* All was not yet lost. The rogue half-mage would be dealt with, then Tiliqua would worm her way into Everand's affections. Or at least garner his trust. He just needed to be patient and continue with his strategy. No dragons had been discovered.

A strong and suitable replacement head of the Guild would be found, one who would adhere to the course set by Lapemis.

His legacy would be to leave behind a firm and united Guild.

Chapter Thirty-One

Lamiya rose towards awareness, as if she were underwater and swimming lethargically to the surface. She opened her eyes. It was dark, and there was a steady drip-drip-drip nearby. Disoriented, she blinked until she discerned the dark lake stretching away in front of her and realised the dripping was residual raindrops falling from trees. Her back was snug against a firm, warm chest and someone's strong left arm was wrapped around her, holding her close. Deft fingers were kneading the muscles down the right side of her neck.

The sensation was delicious and she leaned into it, feeling a breath waft past her cheek. The fingers massaged at her tension, following just the right bands of muscle down her neck and into the ridge of her shoulder. How did Everand know which muscles to follow? The fingers drew small circles across the muscles of her shoulder blade, pausing to work at a niggling pressure point. She gasped: not Everand — Lazuli. Only another paddler would know exactly where to massage.

Breathing slowly, she reached her senses into the man behind her. Definitely Lazuli. Her heart beating steadily, she absorbed his broad, muscled chest touching her back, the strong thighs surrounding her hips and legs and the power in his arm that wrapped her close. She became aware that her buttocks were nestled against his crotch, became aware of his manhood subtly touching her.

Squeezing her eyes shut, she chastised herself. How could she have failed to notice the magnificent man he was becoming? Lazuli could choose any Riverplain woman he wanted. He could be a magnificent partner; handsome, strong and funny. How could she have been so blind? Her heart slowed, her sight dimmed and her breath caught. *A vision? Now?* Relaxing into Lazuli's fingers, she let the vision sweep over her.

She stood upon the grassy plain watching a herd of hopeepa. Muscled arms wrapped around her, Lazuli was behind her, holding her tight and planting kisses into her hair. Before them, two small boys bounded through the waving grasses, shrieking and waving their arms at a group of young hopeepa gathered to the side of the herd.

'Oi!' called Lazuli. 'Don't scare them!'

The boys, one with dark-brown curly hair and a younger one with bright golden curls, ignored him and ploughed towards the hopeepa, shrieking in delight. The young animals threw up their heads, twirled their tails in alarm and cantered in wild loops. The two boys hollered and ran behind them while the older hopeepa lifted their heads and watched calmly. Lazuli laughed and swung her around in the air.

The imagery was vivid but the edges were blurred, and wisps of mist were creeping inwards to obscure the scene. Did this mean the vision was a possibility and not a certainty? The idea held an aura of truth. She frowned. If this was the case, then there was another possibility: Everand.

Closing her eyes fully, she slowed her breath, willing the other vision to come. For a moment, she saw nothing but darkness. Fright jolted her. Was Everand dead or to be killed? Telling herself to be patient, she drew a measured breath. The darkness faded to the edges and she gazed upon herself seated in the guide's chair in the Meeting Place.

Her breath caught. In this vision she looked so assured, so graceful, so elegant, dressed in a long pale-blue dress that offset her hair and eyes just so. Her hair was wound in tiny, impossibly neat braids and coiled around her head, with the middle flowing freely in thick waves down her back, reaching to her waist. The turquoise token of the guide hung around her neck, cocooned between her breasts. An unknown supplicant kneeled before her, and her lips moved as she spoke to him.

The vision shifted to show Everand sitting tall in the chair beside her, wearing his azure mage robe. His starlight hair was loose, but the sides at the front were plaited into intricate braids that fell gently down his cheeks. He looked wise, relaxed, calm and happy. She turned to ask him something and the love brimming in his cobalt eyes made her want to cry out in joy. He murmured something, agreeing with her, then turned to speak to a child on the floor on the other side of his chair.

Her heart bounded at the beautiful young girl playing with two carved wooden hopeepa. Silvery-blonde hair with dark-blue tinges fell in waves down the girl's shoulders, and she turned eyes the colour of Everand's towards him, smiling to show neat white teeth in a perfect oval face. Lamiya's heart thudded loudly. Was she their daughter-to-be? Was *this* the future that awaited her? There were no misty edges to this vision, which burned bright and true. The vision vanished and she stared across the black water.

Awareness of Lazuli surrounded her and she clasped his left hand with both of hers, twining her fingers in his. Dear Lazuli. Sorrow rose at what might have been. *Could still be*, deep within prompted. Could U-Mali explain the two visions? She must speak with the guide as soon as possible.

'You awake?' Lazuli murmured.

'Mmn,' she replied, wanting to savour the moment.

'We should start back. We've a long way to go.' He stopped massaging her neck.

She sighed. He was right, and it would be almost light by the time they reached her hut. Her stomach rumbled and she wished she'd brought more food. Lazuli wriggled, preparing to stand up. Legs numb, she waited until he extended a hand to help her up. Lazuli stood close, grasping her elbows, and her heart beat quickly at the tender look in his face. She should tell him she now truly saw him as a man. When she parted her lips to speak, he placed a finger across them.

'Don't. I want to say something.' His grey eyes grew darker in his shadowed face and his finger moved to gently trace her cheek. 'I understand now,' he said in a deep voice. 'I'm glad I came with you and saw you with the dragon. I see you have a path … one that is beyond you and me.'

She opened her mouth and he put his finger on her lips again.

'I love you, and I always will. This is for what might have been.' His face blotted out the scant moonlight and his lips chased over hers, tenderly at first, then growing into a firm kiss. His lips were warm and uniquely him and after a few breaths she kissed him back. With Everand, there was a current that was powerful, undeniable, overwhelming. With Lazuli, their love would have been a slow burn for her, growing deeper over time. The kiss was a bittersweet acknowledgement and a farewell.

Pulling away, he held her, mumbling nonsense into the top of her head. She hugged him fiercely, conveying her regret while doubt warred inside her. There was nothing she could say to ease the moment, so she waited until he was ready.

Lazuli planted a kiss on her head and stepped back, his eyes glittering in the pale light. 'Let's walk?'

'Let me say goodbye to Akachi, in case she's watching us.' Drawing her cloak around her shoulders and stepping to the water's edge, she bowed respectfully and said clearly, 'Great Akachi, I promise to return. We will build a new boat, and I will try to bring Mizukaze and Flight, I mean Hanachi. Until then.' She bowed again, certain that the water in the middle of the lake rippled.

Taking the hand Lazuli extended, she began to walk and after a few steps asked, 'Is Whirr with you?'

'Sleeping.' Lazuli patted his tunic chest.

Smiling, she stepped out briskly.

By the time they reached the groves of nut trees, the clouds were drifting away and wan light shone through the trees, the raindrops glistening in myriad hues and the leaf colours becoming more vibrant. Tilting her face up, she sniffed the crisp air, thinking it might become sunny. A nagging urgency flowed into her, making her skin prickle and the hairs lift across her nape. She shivered: something momentous would happen this sun-up. Would Everand return?

Her spirits lifting, she continued walking. When Lazuli gave her a sideways glance and lengthened his stride, she said, 'Something is going to happen.'

'Something good or something bad?' He raised an eyebrow.

She shrugged. 'I can't tell. But it will be important.'

'Does it involve Everand?' he asked, his forehead bunching into a frown.

'Maybe.' An odd sense of indetermination swirled through her. 'I think …' she hesitated '… I think whatever it is may not be fully determined. I can see no clear path. Perhaps the guides will know.'

His lips pinched together, Lazuli gave her a concerned look.

She strode faster until sweat trickled under her armpits and she had to remove her cloak.

'Your bird pecked me!' Lazuli reached into his tunic and passed Whirr to her.

Cupping the bird in her hand, she laughed while Whirr scolded her. 'He says you were jostling him.'

'I'll do more than that if he pecks me again,' growled Lazuli, but he was smiling.

They marched past the fruit trees and pink-blue light danced across the lake in the subdued sunshine. Glad to see the sun, she hoped the rain had been enough to refresh their crops. She turned to Lazuli. 'Did I mention we need to build a new boat?'

He gave her a wry grin. 'No. Why?'

'I promised Akachi we'd build a new boat in her honour. Besides, now the essence of Flight, who is apparently really named Hanachi, has left our boat I think we need a new one anyway.' When Lazuli quirked an eyebrow, she added, 'As our important right-hand pacer, will you help me present the idea to the team?'

'Of course,' he said simply. 'A red-scaled boat with gold trim and horns? I can back you up on that at least.'

'Excellent. We'd better gather the team.' Her hut came into view ahead, neatly camouflaged in the copse of trees with elegant weeping leaves. 'After we eat.'

CHAPTER THIRTY-TWO

Malach rolled over to lie on his back. Muted light crawled under the door and he couldn't hear any patter of rain. Good, he and Torrap would hunt, and he could spend time training his new birds. Next sun-up, Everand was to return to continue his training. What if the mage failed to keep his promise? If he did come, would he help him call the dragon? Imagine sitting astride the great beast the way Everand had! All that power at his call, just like Mage Beetal with his tales of his mighty black dragon.

A flickering glow pierced the periphery of his vision. On the shelf along the far wall, the calling stone was glowing bright ruby. He bolted upright, his heart beating wildly. Was his father not dead, after all? No, Everand had confirmed his father's demise. Was the stone broken? Scrambling to his feet, he rushed to the shelf and picked the stone up. The oval shape was smooth and warm in his hands and, no matter how many times he blinked, the stone pulsed a deep red.

Was *Everand* calling him? His mouth ran dry. A trap, or was Everand coming earlier than promised? Only one way to find out. Putting the stone down, he dressed and gulped down some water. The stone was still glowing — Everand *must* be coming — but how had he activated the stone? His questions grew while he put strips of dried bunya meat and handfuls of nuts into a bag, fetched his largest hunting knife, slung a cloak over his shoulder, picked up the stone and went outside.

The village was quiet, with only the tops of the trees hinting at light. Should he fetch Torrap? Maybe not. If Everand didn't come and nothing happened, he'd look foolish. Holding the stone, he set off on the narrow trail towards the raptor cages and Hanaki Forest. His birds stirred on their perches when he strode past to enter the twisty, narrow trail he and his mother used to follow. The forest was brooding and shadowy and his footfalls were muted as he padded over the pine needles, the pungent aroma filling his nose and clearing his head. Energised, he hurried on.

By the time he'd wound his way along the twists and turns and reached the far edge of the forest, the expanse of grasses stretched away in hues of greens and browns with a dusting of sunrays. The granite wall towered a solid, dark mass, the edges of the stones glinting hints of pinks and yellows. Just like on the first time he'd stood there with his mother.

Wait! Everand was supposed to be coming from the south, from Riverplain or Riverfall, and had suggested they meet at Dragon Lake! So, why was he standing here waiting for the stag-horn beetle to emerge through the wall? Curse it, he'd come out of habit.

Shifting his weight from foot to foot, he considered. This wasn't the arranged meeting time, but maybe he should wait a bit. He fixed his eyes on the grey rocks. Before long, something moved at the base of the wall and a shape consistent with his father's stag-horn beetle and a rider peeled away from the boulders. The shape, definitely a beetle with a robed rider aboard, was halfway across the grassy expanse already. Whoa! What if it wasn't Everand? What if the slippery mage had betrayed him? Drawing his cloak close about him, he melted into the shadows of the trees.

The enormous black-and-white stag-horn landed in the exact spot his father's beetle used to land on. It even looked like the same beetle, although perhaps the species all looked alike.

The rider threw back his hood to reveal pale hair the colour of starlight, consistent with Everand. The tall, lean frame looked like Everand. But why was he coming from Axis? Malach slid further behind a knotted and twisted tree trunk.

The rider dismounted and peered towards the trees. *Malach? Are you there?* Everand's voice sounded in his mind. *There you are. Are you alone?*

Malach didn't move and slipped his hand towards his knife sheath. Why had Everand changed the arrangements? The tall mage strode towards him, leaving the stag-horn to forage in the grass. Soon, Everand was standing right before him, his angular face serious.

'You are wise to be cautious.' Everand spoke softly. 'I've come to warn you.'

'Why do you come from Axis? I thought you were in Riverplain,' snapped Malach. 'Warn me of what?'

'Four mages will come for you, using your meeting with me as a trap. I've come to give you time to hide.'

In disbelief, he exploded, 'Why would you do that? And you haven't answered why you've come from Axis!'

Rubbing his face with a hand, Everand said, 'I can explain, but we don't have much time. I must hide you and return before I'm missed.'

Why had Everand returned to the Guild? Was he to be part of the trap? Did he intend to separate him from his people so they couldn't defend him? Malach's stomach clenched. 'Why should I trust you?'

'If you don't trust me, your life will be ended.' Everand's eyes darkened and his shoulders lifted in a shrug. 'As I told you before, I am the only ally you have.'

Wanting to believe, Malach stared deep into Everand's eyes, but trust came hard. What would happen to his people if he were killed?

Everand rummaged in his robe pocket and drew out, of all things, a clear globe with a silver-and-red fish swimming in it.

'I think your mother gave this fish to Mage Beetal as a gift. I want to release her into a lake.'

Malach watched the fish swimming in tiny circles. His mother, Chinfe, had caught a fish and presented it to Mage Beetal on one of the mage's final visits. It seemed unaccountably sentimental of Everand to want to release it here. Didn't they have ponds in Axis? 'Yes, she gave him a fish.' He shrugged. 'I fail to see the relevance. You digress, and you haven't given me reason to trust you. Why have you come from Axis? Why did you go back there?'

With a resigned expression, Everand put the globe with the fish back in his pocket. 'The Council of Ten used their power to take me unexpectedly from Riverplain and transport me back to the Guild. I had to report on my mission.' Regret passed over his face. 'Your use of aggressive tree-moths gave you away, and I had to declare your existence. I'm sorry.'

'Wait,' said Malach, thinking of the discussion he'd held with Torrap. 'When you arrived, did you know about me?' This was the crux of it. Was Everand being manipulated as Torrap had suggested?

'No. You have my word on this.' For a heartbeat Everand looked uncomfortable, but then he schooled his features into a bland expression. 'I suspected someone like you existed early on due to the incidents with the tree-moths and the viper, but when I was first sent to Riverfall I thought it was an unusual but relatively simple task.'

Malach stared, heart thudding, wanting more.

'Of course,' continued Everand, 'I recognised your power and your similarity to Mage Beetal immediately. How could I not?'

Irritatingly, he stopped there and Malach blew out a breath. 'I thought you were in a hurry? Spit it out! Did the Guild know about me when they sent you?' He squared his shoulders. 'And why would you help me against the Guild's wishes?'

Drawing up to his full height, with steel glinting in his dark-blue eyes, Everand said sternly, 'My help is not unconditional. The Guild will not sanction a non-pure mage, but it's not your fault you were born as a result of Mage Beetal's misdemeanours. Personally,' he shrugged, 'I don't see why you couldn't be accepted into the Guild and trained.'

His expression hardened. 'But it's not up to me and I am a sole voice. *If* I help you, I want your word that you'll *never* use your powers against the other provinces again. You must help them instead.'

'Help them how?' The question burst from Malach's lips. 'And you still haven't said whether any other mages knew of me.'

'I now know the Head of the Guild suspected there was magic outside the Guild. But I don't know how much else they know, and I want to find out. I can't keep you — or myself, for that matter — safe otherwise. I must be part of the planned trap in order to delay them and give you more time.' Looking frustrated, Everand ran a hand over his bound hair. 'How could you help the other provinces? For a start, your people could rebuild the bridge. Otherwise, just leave them alone. They mean your people no harm.'

Tapping a foot while he considered, Malach found it easier to believe that unlooked-for help would come with conditions. This seemed very rushed and inconsistent with the cunning that Everand usually showed. 'Where do you propose to hide me? What happens after your trap fails?'

'Not in Riverwood, because the other mages will be able to trace the aura of your powers. Riverfall is too close and too obvious, so I was thinking Riverplain.' Everand called to the beetle, which began to move towards them.

Stay with the people with all the little birds and crazy splotched creatures? Malach shuddered. That would not be his choice. His mouth went dry, remembering how fiercely and determinedly the boatwoman's people had rescued her. 'Will they agree?' He took a step back at Everand's penetrating gaze.

'Only if *I* ask it. You haven't endeared yourself to them.' The mage's eyes grew darker. 'Lamiya and some of her people have unusual abilities. They might be able to help conceal you if the Guild looks for you there.'

'A lot of ifs. Why would you do this?' Malach's head swirled in confusion, and his stomach squeezed at his innards. Why would Everand, or *any* of the province people, help him? Was this an elaborate trap?

'Valuable time passes. I do this because you don't deserve to be obliterated without any chance to redeem yourself. And you are the son of my mentor,' Everand murmured, running a hand across his hair. 'I've never contradicted the Guild before and I hope you'll prove your worth, given the chance.' The azure eyes bored into him. 'What do you say? Do I have *your* word?'

Malach wavered, feeling judged and found wanting. Could he tolerate the other provinces and their differences? A sour taste eked into his mouth. Everand was right on one point though; the provinces had invited his people to the races and trade negotiations in good faith. Turning his face aside, he spat out a globule of bile.

Could he lead his people in a different direction? The trade wasn't necessary but the boat races had proved challenging. Could his people be cordial but keep the other provinces away from Riverwood? Away from the lake and the dragons. Would the mages really kill him without trial? His clenched gut told him Everand spoke the truth. His father had shown him how lethal a mage's power was, and Everand said four of them were coming. He wouldn't stand a chance.

In exchange for a peaceful approach, Everand was offering to hide and then train him. He scanned Everand's face. Was this mage an ally? Hard to tell with his flat, unreadable expression.

If Everand intended to return to the Guild, he wouldn't dare cross them. But offering to hide him was not the only digression Everand planned — the apprentice was following in his mentor's footsteps by chasing after a woman. Perhaps they *could* work together.

'Malach, decide!' Everand picked up the reins of the stag-horn and held them out. 'Here. If you have trouble trusting me, you can direct the stag-horn and I'll sit behind you. We'll fly to the end of the grasslands and tether the beetle there. For speed, I'll transport us the rest of the way to Riverplain and take you straight to their leaders.' Doubt flickered across the austere face. 'Let's both hope they agree to help you.'

Rasping a dry tongue over his lips, Malach concluded that his own people wouldn't be able to protect him, and many of them would die trying. For their sake, he should try Everand's bizarre plan. The annoying mage was right in that if *he* asked, the boatwoman's people might agree.

He reached out to take the reins.

Chapter Thirty-three

Lamiya tumbled through the feather screen into her hut, her limbs frozen and her stomach rumbling. Throwing himself down on her cushions, Lazuli lay spread-eagled as if exhausted, bringing a smile to her lips.

'You drive a hard schedule, great glide!' Lazuli declared with a crooked grin. 'No wonder we're the best team.'

'I'll feed you well to compensate.' She wagged a finger at him while Whirr hopped around cheeping, determined to join in.

Turning to her shelves of food, she grabbed an array of sweet cakes, berries and savoury bread. Then she lit the small hearth to boil water and, lost in thought, watched the flames dance merrily beneath the clay pot. So much had happened! An ache to go back to the grove to confer with her parents' spirits infused her whole being. No, she must speak to U-Mali first about the two visions — and about Akachi.

'The vivid pink suits you, but you'll be scalded if you stand there any longer,' warned Lazuli.

Feeling the heat across her cheeks and nose, she looked at the bubbling water. After making mugs of ginger brew for energy, she carried everything to her table. Still mulling over what she needed to do, she devoured everything on her platter. Lazuli also emptied his plate, making her smile again by the way he eyed it as if he might will more food to appear. Relenting, she fetched him another loaf and more berries, laughing when he rigorously defended these from Whirr.

Lamiya? She almost dropped her mug, thinking she'd heard Everand. Curling her fingers around the mug, she took another sip. *Lamiya?* The gingery liquid went down the wrong way and she coughed.

An eyebrow arching, Lazuli peered at her over the rim of his mug.

She lifted a hand. 'Wait. Something's happening.' Easing in a breath, she calmed her mind and Everand's presence drew clearer. *Come to the Meeting Place.* His essence was strong, as if he were nearby. Did he mean now? *Yes, now. Hurry.* Then his presence withdrew.

Carefully, she put down her mug. 'I must go to the Meeting Place.'

Lazuli opened and shut his mouth, then shrugged.

'Come with me,' she said. 'Whatever's happening will be important.'

'Okay.' He gave her a crooked smile, which rapidly faded. 'Is the mage there?'

'I think so.' Standing up, she wiped her sticky palms down her dampish tunic, wondering if she had time to change into fresh clothes. No, Everand had said to hurry. 'Let's go and find out.'

Striding towards the Meeting Place with Lazuli beside her, she became aware of the odour of stale sweat and lake weed wafting up from her clothes and clinging to her nostrils. On her shoulder Whirr shuddered, agreeing that she smelled. Pushing down her embarrassment, she hoped the guides would accommodate her less-than-respectful appearance. Ahead, the roof of the Meeting Place gleamed in the early light and, squinting, she discerned the outlines of people gathered near the guides' chairs. The height of one, a full head above the others, suggested Everand. Her heart skipped with joy.

She hurried up the steps and executed the ritual cleansing of her hands as quickly as could be deemed passable. Slipping off her gritty sandals, she pattered across the rush mats, hoping she wasn't leaving a trail of muddy prints. The guides were seated in their chairs, with two people kneeling on the floor before them. Everand was clad in a long, grey robe that pooled around him concealing his feet. His hair was bound back, as usual. Although he smiled at her over his shoulder, he seemed tense.

Her feet jerked to a halt when she recognised the dark hair and swarthy features of Malach. What, by all the spirits, was *he* doing here? The Riverwood glide gave her an uneasy nod, his arrogance absent. Behind her, Lazuli gasped. Hurriedly gathering her wits, she nodded at Malach and stepped into the space next to Everand to greet the guides.

'U-Mali Guide, I greet you and welcome your wisdom,' she said with a low bow. Twisting, she repeated the greeting to U-Lumin and then knelt beside Everand, her mind churning and her heart racing while Lazuli murmured his greetings and knelt on her other side.

U-Mali leaned forward in her chair, wispy hair straying from her braid, and looked at her with deeper than usual creases traversing her brow. 'Lamiya, dear one.' U-Mali's glance slid to Everand and then back to her. 'Mage Everand has approached us with an unusual request.'

Lamiya's heartbeats pounded against her breastbone. If Everand were asking for something, it would be difficult for them to refuse. She kept her eyes focused on U-Mali.

'Mage Everand has requested that the people of Riverplain conceal Malach of Riverwood for a time.'

Of course! Lamiya felt like slapping her forehead. Everand had said all along that the mages of his Guild would kill Malach if they found out about him. He'd seemed troubled by that, but she hadn't expected him to try to defy the might of the Guild! A cold shudder travelled down her back and she quelled the nagging vision trying to emerge.

Inside her head, she felt U-Mali's light touch. *Thank you; you have confirmed what Mage Everand told us*. The feathery touch lingered, and understanding that the guide intended to communicate with her both openly and secretly, she inclined her head in acknowledgement. Beside her, Everand shuffled on his cushion. Had he sensed the unspoken exchange?

U-Mali glanced at Everand. 'For the benefit of Lamiya and Lazuli, I will summarise what you told us.' Speaking evenly, she said, 'Mage Everand advises that next sun-up four mages from the Guild will go to Riverwood with the intention of capturing Malach of Riverwood and forcibly taking him to Axis, where they will apply their combined power to obliterate him. We understand this to mean the undoing of his entire being.'

Pausing to smooth away the expression of horror from her face, U-Mali said hoarsely, 'Not even his soul will remain. Mage Everand says this is because Malach of Riverwood is not a pure mage, which is not allowed under the Guild rules.'

Lamiya flicked a glance at Malach, who knelt with his head tucked down and shoulders squared. U-Mali fixed an intense gaze upon her and waited. Was the guide seeking her opinion? Bowing, she said, 'Permission to speak?'

Both U-Mali and U-Lumin nodded.

'Everand … Mage Everand … told me this before. I sensed his discomfort at the possibility and I admire his integrity.' Her cheeks grew warm, 'However, this action brings great risk to Riverplain and our people.' Her cheeks grew warmer when U-Mali smiled and conveyed *Well put*.

U-Mali roved her gaze over the four of them before saying to Malach, 'Unlike the mages of Axis, we of Riverplain give you the opportunity to speak for yourself. Malach of Riverwood, tell us why you are here.'

Twisting sideways so she could observe Malach, Lamiya admired U-Mali's cleverness in insisting that he speak for himself so they could measure him as a person. Between her and Malach, Everand sat back on his heels and dropped his eyes, indicating he wouldn't intervene. She noticed a bead of sweat trickling a ragged path down Malach's forehead. How would this ruthless leader of a fierce and proud people convince them they should help him?

Stiffly, Malach said, 'I welcome the chance to speak. I am uncomfortable seeking your help, but I believe Everand when he tells me my life is at risk from the Guild.'

When U-Mali held up a gnarled hand, her fingers crooked like bird claws, Malach faltered to a confused silence. 'Words can conceal true intent. You will allow me to mind-read you, with Lamiya as witness.'

She was to join in the mind-read? Lamiya gulped down her dismay, observing that Malach was already squirming and pushing his hands down hard on his knees, as if trying to stop himself from leaving.

With a stern frown, U-Mali added, 'Failure to agree will result in denial of Mage Everand's request. The people of Riverplain deserve to understand the nature of a fugitive they must conceal at great risk.'

Awe filled Lamiya at the steely strength of this slight and aged guide. 'What would you like me to do?'

U-Mali extended her right hand. 'Come to my side. Take my hand and grasp Malach's left hand, then I'll connect the three of us by taking his right hand. You will observe whatever his mind reveals to me and bear witness.' With a sharp glance at Everand and Lazuli, she said, 'You two wait.'

Moving quietly to Malach's side, Lamiya positioned herself between him and U-Mali's chair. This left her facing Everand and Lazuli, who gave her worried looks. Kneeling, she took U-Mali's leathery and tiny hand as if she were cupping one of her precious birds. After a calming breath, she held her other hand out to Malach, flexing her fingers at him when he hesitated. His powerful fingers grabbed tight, and she suppressed a wince at his nervous energy jangling into her fingers and palm.

'Close your eyes and I will begin,' instructed U-Mali. 'Malach of Riverwood, you will find memories called to reveal themselves. You must not hinder these. You will know when I'm finished.' Gently, she added, 'Lamiya, dear heart, contain your reactions. You are to witness the memories and not influence them.'

Excitement bubbling at the trust U-Mali was placing in her, Lamiya hoped she could comply. Malach's hand felt clammy around hers, and she remembered how shaken Everand had been after U-Mali had read him. *Dear one, you are bouncing around like your birds. Be still,* chided U-Mali. Mortified, she emptied her mind and closed her eyes.

For a few heartbeats only darkness pressed behind her eyelids, then a feathery touch slid into her left hand and a silver beam of essence whispered through her, tinged with wisdom and compassion. Malach's fingers pinched her other hand, and swirling black and red mists poured into her consciousness. Was this the manifestation of Malach's fear, distrust and revulsion at being read? Surprise nudged her when she realised that he resented the touch of women.

The feather-light, tickly touch from U-Mali streamed through her to push at the wall of mists, and she squeezed Malach's hand, aiming to reassure him. His fingernails stopped digging into her palm and the mists faded to roiling greys. Her vision shifted, like a bird in flight watching events unfold from a height.

As if floating on an air current, she gazed upon Malach as a dark-haired toddler with a hunter who seemed to be his father, ruffling his hair and showing him how to lob a stone. The boy was trying hard. The image shifted to the grassy plain between the granite wall of Axis and the cabins where the people of Riverwood lived. She quelled her amazement when a brown-robed mage astride a massive black-and-white beetle emerged from the granite wall. Impressed, she watched the young boy hold his ground when told by his mother that *this* was his father, even when the mage raised a hand crackling with power and threatened to kill him.

Quick images of visits by this bristling and imposing mage showed him coaching Malach in basic spells. The boy's adoration and longing for this occasional father eked through, and she felt a pang of sympathy. Malach's fingers pinched hers during the memory of the hunter-chief challenging the mage, and the swift death of both his parents.

Thrust into an abrupt and early leadership of his people, Malach rapidly grew into a strong man. Silver and blue mists snaked through the memory, reflecting his momentary fear that he could not lead such a fiercely proud and independent people, followed by a cold determination to be a strong and ruthless leader, made more confident by his clandestine powers.

Three seasons passed, and she looked down upon Malach often visiting the edge of the grasses to wait in vain, forlornly scuffing his toes, for the mage to appear. She saw him go to Dragon Lake and try to call the dragon, dropping his arms in frustration when the dragon refused to appear. She held her breath during his final attempt to lure the dragon with tainted offerings. Her mind tried to slide away to remember what Everand had said about this incident, but U-Mali squeezed her fingers in reprimand.

Sadness nudging her, she observed how Malach used a potion the father-mage had left behind to influence various birds and animals. Dismayed, she saw him begin to breed and train the massive tree-moths in the depths of Hanaki Forest. Then came the invitation from Riverfall to be part of the festival and join the trade negotiations. Black and red mists coiled again as Malach failed to disguise his fear and anger at the invitation. Her forehead grew tight. Why such annoyance and distrust?

The rest of the memories she was familiar with, and Malach clutched her hand as if it were a lifeline while U-Mali forced him to reveal his violent efforts to disrupt the races and trade. She marvelled that no hint of emotion or judgement seeped from U-Mali at seeing her and Everand being captured and forced to help Malach.

Finally, they saw Everand arriving on the same stag-horn beetle to warn Malach. They sensed Malach's warring emotions, his reluctant decision to accept help and then his agreement to cooperate with the other provinces. While this image faded, a pale-blue mist hovered and, surprised, she sensed his relief. Then blackness swam behind her eyelids and cool air washed over her hand when U-Mali released it.

With a sigh, Lamiya brought herself back to the present and found Everand and Lazuli watching her with open curiosity. Feeling as if time had slowed, she looked across at Malach, who was still gripping her hand, his dark eyes fixed on her face. Was this an almost apology? She raised an eyebrow and he snatched his hand away. Giving him the tiniest of nods, she moved back to her position beside Everand and faced the guides. U-Mali sat deep in thought, her eyes pinched and unseeing, but U-Lumin gave her a pleased smile.

Everand tapped her shoulder and asked if she was alright. Sounds and awareness trickled in: the dream-catchers tinkling in a breeze, the breathing of the three men, birds calling on the lake below. Crisp air caressed her cheeks in a velvety touch and fluttered strands of her hair.

U-Mali's eyes snapped open and latched onto hers. *Is this half-mage worth the risk to our people?*

Honour and dismay flooded Lamiya. Was this another test of her suitability to become the guide in the future? Uncertainty clouding her thoughts, she swallowed. Her head wanted to shriek, 'No, he isn't!' But something held her back. She glanced at Everand, who waited with impeccable poise and patience, clearly not wishing to influence her.

Sliding a finger over her lips, she conveyed, *I am not sure. However, I trust Everand's perspective and he thinks we should at least try to save Malach of Riverwood.* Tilting her head, she added, *Malach is conflicted. He has done nothing to earn our help, quite the opposite. However, I agree it seems harsh for the mages to obliterate him due to the actions of his true father, who seemed to love his mother. If we give Malach up, are we condoning the Guild's judgement? Would this make us no better than them?*

U-Mali's eyes glinted and the creases around them formed multiple rivulets. *Astute points.* The guide gave Malach an assessing gaze then turned to Everand. 'Mage Everand, I am inclined to grant your request that we the people of Riverplain hide Malach of Riverwood for a time.'

Leaning forward until her face was close to both of them, she said slowly and clearly, 'But know this: we will not risk the lives of our people on Malach's behalf. If it comes to the threat of violence, we will yield Malach to the mages of Axis.' Sitting back, U-Mali composed her hands in her lap.

Lamiya's heart pounded while Everand lowered his forehead to the rush mats, tapping Malach's knee to encourage him to do the same. 'Thank you, U-Mali, Guide of Riverplain. Your people are wise and generous.'

'Perhaps. We have yet to find someone who will agree to conceal our fugitive.' The guide's eyes twinkled.

A short silence ensued.

'I will hide Malach,' croaked Lazuli.

Astonished, Lamiya stared at the pacer. His offer was noble beyond belief, and warmth surged into her heart. How could she be blessed with such loyal friends?

'My hut on the plains is well away from most of our people, and I can bring my hopeepa herds in close to help confound the mages' search,' Lazuli said, his grey eyes holding hers.

Her throat tight, Lamiya patted his hand. He was growing and changing too.

If the guide was surprised, she didn't show it. 'Lazuli, your brave offer is accepted.'

Lamiya's lips twitched at the flush that stained Lazuli's cheeks, and pride roared through her. She fervently hoped Malach appreciated the extent of his reprieve.

His mouth compressed into a hard, thin line, Malach nodded tightly to each of them. Was he unable to form appropriate words, or just unaccustomed to showing gratitude? She looked up into Everand's eyes, which conveyed gratitude, relief — and trepidation.

A shiver trickled down her spine.

May we both not come to rue this decision.

Chapter Thirty-four

While the others prepared to take their leave, Everand sat conscious of U-Mali's gaze hovering on his face in an uncomfortably searching manner, but there was nothing he could say with honesty to allay her concerns. Much rested on the reaction of the Guild mages when they failed to capture Malach. When U-Mali gave a bird-like dip of her head, he realised she understood this. Humbled, he bowed and reversed to the entry, forgetting to retrieve his sandals until he felt the warm steps under his feet.

The others were waiting at the base of the steps, the lake behind them glinting with cascading sparkles of sunlight, surrounded by lush greenery. Observing the group, he descended slowly. Malach stood to one side, rigid bands of muscle standing out on his neck. Lamiya and Lazuli were conferring in low voices with their foreheads almost touching. His heart skipped a few beats. What had passed between them while he was away? A hint of jealousy arose, but Lamiya turned at his approach with a wide smile and warmth in her eyes.

Relieved, Everand went to Lazuli first. 'Thank you for your offer. I hope it won't be for long.'

'We'll see.' Lazuli's grey eyes sharpened. 'Depends on what happens when your mages come.'

'I can't predict what they will do. It's best you take Malach now and that I don't know exactly where you are.' That came out more tersely than he intended.

Lazuli raised an eyebrow and then looked incredulous. 'You fear they'll compel you to reveal what you've done?' Something that might have been admiration flickered in the paddler's eyes. 'We'll go now.' He turned to Malach. 'Come. We have a way to walk.'

When Malach hesitated, looking to him for guidance, Everand said, 'Go with Lazuli. Stay hidden for as long as possible. Dress like these people, act like them and under no circumstances use any of your power.' When Malach gave him an unfathomable look, he quickly added, 'When — if — it is safe, I'll find you. Or Lamiya will. I can't promise you more than that.'

'Understood,' said Malach gruffly, spinning away and striding out to catch up to Lazuli.

Rubbing a hand over the back of his tense neck, Everand watched their receding backs. Malach had a way to go before he endeared himself to anyone.

'What will you do now?' Lamiya peered into his face.

The sun was already above the hills but was still less than halfway to the sun-high position. He should get back to Axis before he was missed, but the way Lamiya's gaze was lingering on his face, her eyes wide and dark ... what she wanted was clear. His body ached for hers. How could he deny her, or himself, any further? And he had the other small but important task to achieve. Rummaging in his pocket, he eased out the globe with Mizu in it and held it in front of him.

'You brought your fish!' exclaimed Lamiya.

'I thought ...' he cleared his throat, 'I thought we could go to your hut and you could help me release Mizu into the lake.'

Lamiya touched a finger to the side of the globe. 'I'd like that. Besides, I have much to tell you.'

'You do? I haven't been gone long!'

Peering coyly from beneath her lustrous eyelashes, she said smugly, 'Perhaps you shouldn't go away again. Prepare to be astounded when you meet my new friend.' With that, she spun around and strode away along the shore, glancing briefly over her shoulder to call, 'Try to keep up.'

Grasping the globe firmly, he took long steps after her, his heart racing. What had she been up to? *This is not sensible! You're supposed to be in a hurry.* Striding faster, he reasoned he could transport himself directly to the stag-horn beetle after … after whatever this rashness led to.

When he caught up, Lamiya gave him a mischievous smile and his curiosity won out. 'Who is your new friend? And I see you and Lazuli have repaired your friendship. You *have* been busy.'

'I now understand more about what might be, and what might have been. If you hadn't arrived, I *would* have partnered with Lazuli.' Her expression serious, she glanced at him. 'But you arrived, and we're caught up in events that we don't yet understand. Lazuli accepts this now.' Twisting her fingers, she murmured, 'He is a good man and like a brother to me. I hope you two can come to be friends.'

Everand tucked the globe back in his pocket and touched her shoulder. 'I'll try. Does this mean he won't punch me again?'

'You should have seen yourself brawling on the beach like that. I didn't realise mages possessed those talents.' Laughing, Lamiya tossed her hair over her shoulder, the mahogany waves rippling and blue threads glistening in the sunlight.

Feeling warmth in his cheeks, he replied, 'They don't. What about your other friend?'

'I might show her to you once we've released your fish.' Snapping her lips closed, she sped up.

Intrigued, he snuck sideways glances at her. She looked stronger, more confident, and U-Mali had called upon her skills as a witness and conferred by mind-speak with her. Were her abilities growing? If only he had more time! There were so many things he wanted to ask her. Surprise dawned when he realised how much he yearned to confide in her, to seek her astute views about the Guild and their actions ... and Mantiss.

Misjudging his step, his foot clunked down and he wobbled. He righted his balance, wincing at the sharp look from Lamiya. Never before had he felt this aching need to discuss what he felt, and what he should do. He squared his shoulders: he had set a course in motion and had best follow it.

On reaching her hut, Lamiya faced him and arched an eyebrow.

'Let's release Mizu first,' he said.

With a coy smile, she took his hand and led him towards the water. He took a deep breath, letting the tranquillity of the lake and surroundings infuse him, then brought the globe out of his pocket. Here was perfect. When Mizu swam in giddy loops and blew a stream of bubbles, sorrow panged in his chest. He would miss her.

'Such a pretty fish should be free. You need to wade into the water.' Lamiya put a hand on his arm, her lips quirking. 'Your robe will get wet. Perhaps you should take it off.'

Everand's heart hammered at the mix of mischief and longing in her eyes. A thrill shuddering through him, he roamed his eyes over her mahogany wavy hair, high cheekbones, elegant, curved neck and lithe, muscled body. She waited for him to decide, the subtle hitch in her shoulders the only sign of tension about his response.

He passed the globe into her hands and undid the sash to his robe, shrugged out of it and put it on the soft dirt. Quickly, he glanced both ways along the shore to confirm they were alone. Blood and heat rushing to his groin, he stood in his under-cloth with the soft breeze flowing over his skin.

Passing the globe back to him, Lamiya slipped her tunic over her head, the defined muscles in her arms and shoulders rippling. Her breasts were wrapped in a cloth that held them firm and disappointingly concealed. He forgot about that when she stepped out of her trousers, revealing long, lithe legs and only a small loincloth covering her hips. Fixed on his face, her eyes grew wider and darker. Moving closer, she clasped her hands over his around the globe, and began to walk into the water.

Keeping his eyes on her face, he gasped at the cold water closing over his ankles and rising up his shins. Trusting her, he waded until cold water eddied around his middle. Goosebumps chased up and down his arms and his desire shrank.

'Is this deep enough?' she asked, seemingly impervious to the temperature of the water.

'I believe so.' With her fingers still clasped over his, he lowered the globe into the water and dissolved it. Mizu leaped between his curved fingers into the lake and swam a circle around them, her fanned tail and fins swishing elegantly. Regret filling him, he told himself the fish was back where she belonged. Mizu approached, her tail shimmering, and gently nibbled at his fingers. With a crooked finger, he stroked the top of the fish's head once in farewell, then Mizu swam away and he watched her gauzy tail until she disappeared into deeper water.

'I like that you did this.' Lamiya put an arm around his waist and leaned against him, her skin cool against his. 'She will find other fish.'

He put an arm around her shoulder, an unexpected lump in his throat. Turning to face her, he put his other arm around her and drew her close. As he hoped, she tilted her face up for a kiss. A deep feeling of rightness settled when his lips merged with hers, so soft, warm and loving. The kiss extended and she pressed her body against him, the touch of her skin electric amid the cold water washing around him.

His breath and heartrate quickening, he pushed his body against hers. The sensation of her skin all along his was too much. Breaking the kiss, he put his arms under her buttocks, scooped her into his arms and waded to the shore. She clung to his neck, wet and slippery, nuzzling at his collarbone. Scanning ahead, he ploughed towards a tree with weeping branches and a splash of green that promised soft grass at its base.

'Nice,' she murmured when he pushed through the trailing branches and lowered her onto the grass. He lay down beside her, the wispy grass tickling his bare skin and the dangling leaves forming a cool green curtain separating them from the rest of the world. She rolled against him and pulled him into another kiss, her tongue exploring his upper lip and sending jolts of pleasure through him. He slipped his tongue into her mouth to explore her bottom lip. When their tongues met in the middle, he thought he would explode from the pressure building inside.

Lamiya arched against him, pushing her breasts forward, and his hands travelled of their own accord down her shoulder to slip inside her chest cloth. Her breasts were round and soft, the nipples hard and erect. When he ran a thumb over one nipple she gasped and pressed harder against him, so he did this again and again, enjoying her moans and the way she yielded to him.

'Take it off,' she whispered hotly into his ear.

He fumbled at the material until it started to unwind. His fingers snagged in it, and Lamiya giggled at his impatience when he tried to shake his hands free. Finally, he tugged the cloth away and dropped it on the grass. Her bare breasts brushed against his chest, the tingling indescribable. Her fingers scrabbled at the edge of his loincloth, trying to tug it down over his hips.

His heartbeat roaring in his ears, he yanked at the cloth, kicking his legs to ease it down and over his feet. Lamiya wriggled beneath him, her silky skin brushing against his groin, and the waves of pleasure grew unbearable. Impatiently, she kicked off her loincloth and, before he could draw breath, she rolled onto her back and pulled him on top of her, the strength in her arms crushing him to her. Arching against him, she hungrily planted her mouth against his, her tongue diving deep.

All thoughts of taking his time to wonderingly explore her body fled. He pushed his throbbing penis against her, the combined heat of their bodies scalding. She opened her legs and his penis slid over moist, hot flesh, sending shudders through him. Caught out by the intensity of her desire, he gasped for air. He had intended to ask before he took her, but she hitched her legs up over his buttocks and thrust her hips at him so that he naturally slid inside her.

Pleasure surrounding and absorbing him, he and Lamiya merged, her essence and the scents of grasses and flowers all around him and roiling inside him. She planted urgent kisses along his neck, driving him wild. He squeezed a hand between their bodies and caressed her breast, tracing circles and marvelling at how wonderful the hard nipple felt against his hand. Lamiya arched and moved beneath him, pushing her hips up to meet his, and he rhythmically withdrew and inserted himself, gasping at the rolling waves of pleasure until she trembled and cried out beneath him. Her inner muscles gripped him so tightly he came unbelievably deep inside her, and still she thrust against him, refusing to release him, her lips and hips demanding that he stay and come again.

Eventually, he broke the kiss for air, sweat running down his neck and back while Lamiya nuzzled his shoulder, holding him fiercely. Easing away to lie beside her, he pulled her close and kissed her hair. His heart pounded in his ears and his muscles felt weak and limpid. Revelling in the moment, he waited for his heart to calm.

Gentle fingers stroked his face and tilted his chin to get his attention. With a shaky smile, he gazed down to see a single tear rolling down her cheek. He brushed it away with a butterfly touch and caressed her cheek with the back of a finger. Nothing he could say felt adequate. Perhaps she felt the same because she cuddled against him, looking into his eyes and tracing circles over his shoulder with soft fingers.

A breeze whispered through the dangling leaves and branches, brushing coolly over his skin in an unwelcome reminder that reality and other events waited. He shivered.

'Do you have to go back?' Lamiya whispered, her grey-blue eyes serious. 'Can't you just stay here?'

Everand grappled with the idea. Could he stay and hide too? What would the council do when it couldn't find him? *But it would. The council took you right from Lamiya's hut before. This is the first place they'd look.* He stroked her cheek. 'There's nothing I desire more, but that would make matters worse.'

Her arms tightened around his back. 'Going back to Axis is such a big risk.' She buried her face into his chest. 'I couldn't bear it if you did not return.'

'Me too,' he murmured, planting kisses all over the top of her head, his mind racing. She was right, he had plotted a dangerous course. But if he didn't return now, Mantiss would order the council to look for both him and Malach, and the people of Riverplain would have no time to prepare. The more time he could buy, the more likely a way forward would materialise. His worry doubled: if Mantiss *was* ailing, how strong would his master's ire be if he rejected the Guild during a time of trouble?

Wriggling until she could look into his face, Lamiya said, 'Talk to me.'

He traced her cheekbone. Could he confide in her? He wanted to. She elbowed him in the ribs. 'Ow! I confess my plan is not fully formed.' He looked into her eyes. 'I'm hoping the council will reconsider when they can't find Malach. I suppose I'm counting on the belief that the mages won't want to disrupt the provinces with any overt actions.' He took a breath. 'But I might be wrong.'

'I see.' Her expression grew distant, and then she focused again. 'Your council who decides these matters, are any of them like you? Can you persuade any to reconsider?'

As usual, she'd cut right to the heart of it. 'I suppose I'm counting heavily on Mage Agamid, who is the second most senior mage, and his former apprentice, Saiphos. They are wise and reasonable.'

Lamiya's eyebrows drew neatly together. 'Only two out of a council of how many? These are not good odds, my mage.' She caressed his cheek, her eyes travelling over his face. 'Something else troubles you.'

His chest fraught with bands of tension, he took a shallow breath. 'You see so much. Most of all, I worry about the reactions of the Head of the Guild, Mage Mantiss.' The pending words spilling around in his mind, he faltered.

'He is important to you?' Lamiya put a hand over his heart. 'I see by the pain in your eyes that he is more than the Head of the Guild.'

Burying his head against her shoulder, he drew in a ragged breath. *You must tell her.*

Holding his face in both hands, Lamiya forced him to look at her. The blue flecks danced and spun in her grey eyes. 'You admire and respect this mage,' she said simply. 'You fear his reaction. You fear disappointment — and rejection.'

She'd put his dilemma far more eloquently than he ever could, and his words tumbled out. 'My parents were both powerful, but they fought. My mother never wanted me and resented my birth.' Bile filled his mouth. 'My name ... comes from her shrieks that she'd be saddled with a brat *for ever and beyond.* They argued about that.'

Pain slicing through him, he forced the next words to come. 'I woke late one sun to find my father dead in his chair, poisoned, and my mother had vanished. Mage Mantiss and Mage Agamid came to the door looking for my father, who was a council member.' A shiver crawled down his spine, turning each bone chill with its passage.

'I let them in and stayed so quiet they forgot I was there while they discussed what had happened. Because of that, Mantiss realised my potential for stealth and took me under his wing. He gave me my own quarters and trained me in secret as a spy.'

'He gave you an identity and a purpose,' murmured Lamiya.

'For most of my life I have reported covertly to Mantiss. I gather information so he can lead the Guild wisely and anticipate and avert trouble.' Everand swallowed. 'I uncovered the plot by the traitor who was Malach's father. Mantiss refers to me as his son.'

Misery rising, he couldn't utter the final part: son and preferred replacement as leader. What if he were wrong and it was mere arrogance that he thought this?

Sitting up, Lamiya hugged her knees to her chest, her brows slanted in a frown. 'But now you don't support his actions. You feel you are betraying Mantiss, after everything he has done.'

Mirroring her posture, Everand nodded.

'I understand now why you must return.' Lamiya blew impatiently at wisps of hair that drifted across her face, then continued slowly, 'You hope your master Mantiss will change his mind and see reason. You feel you must give him that chance. For Malach. For you. For your Guild.' Her look became grim. 'And if he doesn't, you'll act against his wishes because his course is not just — and you will lose your master, your father, your saviour.'

Pain lancing into his fingers, Everand gripped his knees so tightly that his knuckles went white. Her abilities were growing faster than he could possibly imagine.

Struggling with further thoughts, Lamiya rocked herself to and fro. 'You want Mantiss to sanction your departure and, above all, you want him to release you from your vows to him so that you can be with me.' She brushed away a strand of hair with the back of her hand. 'How can I ask that of you?'

The turmoil in her face releasing the stranglehold on his thoughts and muscles, he unclenched his hands to pull her close. 'Lamiya,' he breathed into the top of her head, 'that part is decided. I yearn to be with you, and will come regardless of Mantiss' views. But I fear his retribution — for us, *and* your people.'

Wriggling out of his grasp, Lamiya leaned back so she could look up at him. 'You must change this all-important mage's mind then.' She stretched up to brush his lips with hers. 'You *must* try. I see that. And if your Guild refuses to let you go, then I will stand with you while you challenge them.'

Love overwhelming him, he moulded his mouth over hers and kissed her long and deep, hope exploding in his chest.

CHAPTER THIRTY-FIVE

Lamiya shivered while Everand ran to retrieve their clothes. Running back already dressed, he handed over her tunic and trousers. She tied the chest cloth tightly around her breasts, noting his flicker of disappointment, and hurriedly shrugged into her tunic and trousers.

He crushed her to him in a hug and planted more kisses into her hair, then stepped back. 'I must go.' His face softened. 'I'll count my breaths until I can be with you again.'

A lump swelled in her throat at the fathomless depth in his blue eyes. 'Me too,' she murmured, even as he shimmered and dissolved before her eyes. Left staring at the lake, she felt as if part of her had just peeled away and vanished. Tracing her lips with a finger, she blew him a farewell kiss and pushed away niggling doubts about whether he'd return safely. *He must.*

Faint voices carried across the still expanse of water and on the far shore, outlines of figures moved around the boat dome. Training would distract her from the ache in her soul. Besides, she and Lazuli had to broach the subject of a new boat in Akachi's likeness.

She spun on bare heels and jogged to her hut to change, and it was only when she was brushing through the feather curtain that she realised she'd forgotten to tell Everand about Akachi. Hoping this wouldn't prove to be important, she washed quickly with a sponge and tugged on her training outfit. Whirr was nowhere in sight.

'Yo!' Lapsi called through the doorway just as she reached for her paddle.

'Coming!' She slipped on her sandals and rushed out the door, a knot of disappointment forming when she saw that Lulite wasn't with Lapsi. 'How is Lulite?'

Lapsi tossed his paddle from hand to hand. 'Tired and a bit queasy. She might not feel like training for a while.' He started to walk. 'We need to find another paddler because Levog won't be able to paddle for a while yet. His leg still gives him pain.'

Falling into step with him, Lamiya said, 'We have an unexpected visitor who can paddle. Lazuli will bring him.'

With a surprised glance, Lapsi asked, 'Your mage friend?'

'I'll explain when the whole team is there.'

While Lapsi chatted about races and training, her mind latched onto the dilemma of hiding Malach. The paddlers would recognise him, but should they give him a false name for the rest of her people? Would the guides call a meeting to explain his presence, or would they consider the fewer people who knew about their fugitive the better? She was still undecided about how much to tell the team when they drew near the boatshed. Flight was already out of the shed and nestled on the soft sand. Paddlers milled around the boat, polishing the wooden rim and seats.

'Is Lazuli coming?' Larimar gave her a shy smile, but his forehead was creased with concern.

A ribbon of unease grew in her stomach. Was Malach already being difficult?

Larimar looked past her. 'Oh. Here he comes. With someone.'

Over her shoulder, she saw Lazuli was still two hundred paces away. 'Gather around.' As soon as the paddlers had collected in a gaggle, she said, 'Lulite isn't feeling well, and Levog's leg isn't healed so we're a paddler short. However, we have an unexpected visitor who can paddle.'

Their gazes sharpened.

'Lazuli is bringing him now. It's the glide from Riverwood … we need to make him welcome, whether he deserves it or not.'

Frowns crossed their faces and several eyes slid towards the approaching figures.

'The guides have agreed we will shelter Malach. If the mages of Axis find him, they will kill him because he is only a half-mage.'

When the team frowned and fidgeted, she raised a hand and added, 'I know he wronged us — wronged me — but we must rise above this. The guides have decreed that Malach does not deserve to die simply because he is not a pure mage.'

'How did he get here?' asked Luvu, his eyes narrowed. 'Why here, not Riverfall? It was their idea to hold the festival, and their idea to send for a mage.' The paddlers looked at Luvu, many nodding.

Aware that Lazuli and Malach were near, she swallowed. 'Mage Everand brought him.' Several mouths opened and she rushed on, 'He trusts us to shelter Malach. Riverfall is too close to Riverwood and is the first place the mages of Axis will look.'

Everyone looked at Luvu, who scowled fiercely. 'I don't like this.'

'I know.' She gave a small shrug. 'I need to explain more.'

'You better,' snarled Luvu.

Pushing down her rising panic, she spread her hands in apology. 'Let's train and then discuss everything. Lazuli and I need to tell you about another thing too — a good thing.'

Luvu opened his mouth but closed it again when Lazuli stepped into the circle.

When she saw Malach, Lamiya felt her own mouth open and close. Without his beard, he looked completely different, much younger and less threatening. His hair was cropped shorter and tied behind his nape instead of pulled up in the austere warrior topknot. He looked uncomfortable in Lazuli's spare training outfit, with the tunic pulling across his bulky torso. Impressed, she wondered how Lazuli had persuaded him to remove his beard.

'Sorry I'm late,' said Lazuli with a disarming grin. 'But I bring an extra paddler.'

The responding silence was not encouraging and Lamiya sighed. 'Well team, let's board. Lattic, can you run to the shed to find a paddle for Malach?' Next looking at Luvu, she said, 'Can Malach sit with you at the back? It'd be good to have a strong pair at the back of the boat.'

'If you say so,' said Luvu grudgingly, his face creased in a scowl.

Finding Malach watching her expectantly, she said, 'Our training may differ from yours, but please follow our drills.' She refrained from saying 'my instructions', sensing that as the captain of his own team he'd be reticent about taking orders. Especially from a woman.

To her relief, the team boarded without further comment and paddled smoothly and powerfully. Malach was silent for the entire training session but followed the tips that Luvu occasionally grunted at him. As a pair they worked well, and the boat felt good with two powerful men at the back. At one point a large ripple appeared beside the boat and she wondered if Akachi had swum nearby, but the dragon didn't show herself. She decided against trying to call to the dragon; let the team absorb one thing at a time.

All too soon, she was directing the boat back to shore, where the paddlers disembarked and quickly carried Flight to the dome and used soft cloths to clean her. Malach did his best to pitch in, although he didn't speak and no-one spoke to him. Lamiya chewed her bottom lip. How could she smooth this over? They really needed Malach to blend in, or Everand's plan wouldn't work.

Once the boat was clean, the team sat in a circle in front of it and Lopa and Laza handed around mugs of brew and a basket of dried fruits. Malach ended up sitting beside her, leaving a small gap between them, with Lazuli and Lepid on his other side. Most of the team sat with hunched shoulders and eyes averted. Trying to muster her courage, Lamiya swallowed some brew. She would need Lazuli's support to help ease their displeasure.

An unseen hand squeezed her shoulder, and U-Mali's voice whispered, *Tell them everything. We need their help.* Her frown eased: it felt right to properly include the team. She finished her brew, wiped her hands down her tunic and told them everything as best she knew it. Occasionally, she looked to Malach and asked him to confirm her words. Each time, he nodded stiffly, his dark eyes glinting with unfathomable thoughts.

'So,' said Lepid when she stopped speaking and put her hands in her lap. 'Much depends on what happens when the mages go to Riverwood next sun-up.' His eyebrows furrowed, he glanced at Lazuli. 'How will we know what happens?'

Lamiya answered him. 'I expect Everand will find a way to tell us.' She swallowed. 'To warn us, if necessary.'

'How can we resist powerful mages?' asked Lapsi, wringing his hands.

'U-Mali agreed we'd hide Malach, but also decreed if it comes to the threat of violence, we ...' she felt uncomfortable, 'we will yield him.'

Everyone's eyes slipped to Malach, who sat tautly erect with a flat expression.

'You place a lot of faith in your mage friend,' commented Luvu.

Heat stained her cheeks. 'Everand has proven himself so far. U-Mali made this decision, meaning she believes in his word too.' She pushed back strands of hair that were tickling her ears. 'More than Everand's word, it is the *principle* that

U-Mali has agreed to uphold. If we simply deliver Malach to the mages of Axis then we, as a people, also countenance the taking of his life simply because he isn't a pure mage — something Malach had no control over.'

Encouragingly, several paddlers nodded, so she waved a hand at Malach, inviting him to speak. Surely the man understood how important it was that he at least appear to be grateful?

Malach cleared his throat. 'I am in debt to the people of Riverplain. Your help is … unexpected.' His mouth twisted. 'Everand has persuaded me that Riverwood could cooperate better with our nearby provinces and I regret our former actions. Our ways are different, and we didn't want to join in regular trade.'

Tipping forward, Lepid said sharply, 'Why attack us then? Why not just decline the invitation from Riverfall?'

An excellent point! Lamiya held her breath.

After a tense pause, Malach shrugged. 'We wanted to frighten you and stop the trade discussions. Make you go away and leave us alone so we wouldn't feel obliged to participate.' He compressed his lips into a thin line, his spine taut. 'I see now the other provinces should be able to trade if you want to. Riverwood can choose to be different … and to accept your choices.'

Lamiya felt her eyebrows lift. That must have been difficult for him. A soft breeze murmured inside her and words flowed from her lips. 'We hope Riverwood will join us as true neighbours, when you are ready.' Blinking rapidly, she snapped her mouth shut. Had U-Mali *made* her say that? Lazuli gave her an odd look. The others smiled uncertainly at Malach and she saw some of the tension leave his spine.

'Well, best team in all the provinces,' she said to attract everyone's attention. 'We have another matter to agree, and Lazuli is the best person to explain.'

With much exaggeration and waving of his hands, Lazuli described how she'd called a red dragon named Akachi from their lake. He even adopted different voices to relay the gist of her discussion with the dragon, and the team sat spellbound, awe spreading on their faces. Except Malach, who kept giving her curt sideways glances. When Lazuli concluded his tale, the paddlers enthusiastically agreed to build a boat in Akachi's likeness. Larimar and Lattic clapped their hands and wanted to start straight away.

'Wait!' said Lazuli, laughing. 'We need a design! The boat will need to be elegant.' Here, he looked at Lapsi. 'Could Lulite draw the design?'

'Wonderful idea!' Lamiya gasped at his cleverness in including Lulite.

'I can help,' said Lopa shyly.

'And I'll need to see the design so I can make matching paddles,' Lattic hurried to add.

Lamiya hid her smile; he and Lopa would be a couple by the time the boat was built. Toying with the mug in her hands, she sat back while the team finished their brew and chatted about the new boat. When she looked up, she found Malach scrutinising her.

'How did you call the dragon?' he asked in a low, deep voice. 'Your people don't have power.' He glanced at Lazuli. 'And how did he hear what was said?'

Sensing envy behind his questions, she put her head on one side. Being truthful might help to bridge the gap. 'My family has inherent ability to call birds, and sometimes people, with our minds.' She lifted her shoulders. 'Everand showed me how to call the dragon using images instead of words. The first time, we called the dragon Mizukaze together. I was surprised I called Akachi by myself.'

'You used imagery, like Everand said?' Malach's eyes bored into her.

'Yes, at first. I imagined the dragon coming to greet me. Somehow, I knew she would be red and gold.' She frowned. 'We could understand each other's thoughts, and now that you ask, I'm not sure how that was possible.' She flicked a glance at Lazuli, who was turned away from them, conferring with Lepid. 'Lazuli couldn't hear us, but I told him afterwards. He has exaggerated the story.'

Malach sat back, then immediately sat forward again. 'Why do the dragons follow Everand?'

She understood the unspoken question: why did the dragon Mizukaze respond to Everand and not to him? Nervously, she ran her tongue over her lips. 'When we were in your forest in Riverwood, didn't Everand say your mage father bred and trained dragons? Perhaps Everand learned how to communicate with the beasts from him.'

Stillness surrounded her and a quick peek confirmed the entire team was listening. She must choose her words carefully because Malach had also been shown how but had failed, and personal honour was important to the hunters of Riverwood.

Opening her hands wide, she encompassed the whole team in her words. 'These are good questions. What started as a suggestion the provinces trade together has evolved into larger events that we don't understand. If I remember correctly what Everand said, the dragons your father trained were all removed from Axis and taken to another world.'

She paused when Malach's eyes flickered. 'Yet we have dragons here … in the lakes. Everand said your father's dragons had wings, and the ones here don't.' She looked at Luvu, the oldest paddler. 'We haven't seen dragons for two generations, but our records say that in the past there was a bond between the people of Riverfall and a dragon in the lake by the waterfall. The one they called Mizuchi.'

Luvu added, 'Riverfall has built boats in the likeness of a blue dragon since before our peoples divided. Riverplain kept the tradition going too.' He looked back to her to continue.

Thinking hard, she said, 'The population grew, towns were built and crops flourished and the traditions were forgotten. Except for recently, when it became dry for so long that our crops and lands started to struggle. Atage was trying to revive the tradition of honouring the dragon through the four provinces racing one another. He wanted to persuade the dragon to make it rain again.'

Subtle lines of tension tightening his face, Malach shifted uneasily and, her heart racing, she remembered how U-Mali had coaxed the memory from Malach about putting offerings laced with potion at the lake. It was from *then* that Mizukaze had refused to summon the rain. Curse it, she'd put Malach in a vulnerable position. He winced and shifted his weight, but said nothing.

Sighing, she wasn't sure whether she should feel relief or disappointment that he didn't confess what he'd done. Sitting taller, she thought harder about the order of events. 'Perhaps it was more than any one specific thing. The dragon in the lake, Mizukaze, wasn't the Mizuchi of old. I think something *needed* to happen to reconnect the people and the dragon because although Mizukaze knew how to make it rain, he didn't know anything about the people …' She trailed off at the magnitude of what was evolving.

Everyone's eyes fixed on her. 'Akachi wants me to bring Mizukaze to *our* lake. The red dragon said something about replenishing their kind. Whatever happens with the mages of Axis, a series of changes has been set in motion.'

Her breath caught. What had Akachi said? *Well met, Lamiya of Riverplain* and *Come speak again soon.* What if … what if *she* hadn't called the dragon but the dragon had called *her*? Was the incessant nagging to go east a summons from Akachi? The back of her neck tingled and she felt the blood draining from her face. Feeling faint, she flapped a hand at Lazuli.

After giving her a short, worried frown, Lazuli grinned at the others. 'So, we must build a new boat and make friends with

Akachi. This part is clear.' Smiling broadly, he waved his hands in a flourish. 'We're lucky we have our own dragon caller.'

Murmuring assent, the entire team regarded her with wonder and respect.

Humbled, Lamiya folded her hands in her lap. 'I'll confer with U-Mali and U-Lumin for guidance.' Still feeling shaken, she said, 'The dragons have firm ideas about how they prefer to be approached, so we need to tread carefully. But Lazuli is right: we build a new boat and plan for a festival to outdo the one Riverfall held!'

The team stood up and prepared to go their various ways, and she was left hovering there undecided about what to do next with Malach's cold, dark eyes fixed on her. Unease crawled into her stomach.

First, they had to survive what happened when Everand and the other mages arrived.

CHAPTER THIRTY-SIX

Relieved the return journey had been uneventful, Everand hurried down the ramp. Tired from the long flight, the stag-horn carried its head low and dragged its feet across the floor. The stableboys would get no argument from it for a while. Nodding at the same two boys who approached to take the reins, he rested his hand on the stag-horn's face to thank it before he turned away. He might not see the creature again. After pausing to murmur a farewell to his own transport beetle, he jogged down the stairs to his quarters.

Melida had just arrived at his door and had one hand poised to knock when he strode up behind her. She almost dropped his tray of food in fright, the plates and cutlery clattering as she managed to juggle the tray and give a curtsey.

Reaching past her, he touched the handle and the door swung open. 'You first.'

She scurried into his room, put the tray on the table with a jangle of items, kept her face averted and rushed back out past him. With a wave of his hand, he closed the door. Was he so stern and imposing? He scrubbed a hand over his face. Perhaps Lamiya could explain it.

Heading straight for the bathroom, he discarded the dank grey robe and washed himself, the touch of the cloth on his skin sensuously reminding him of caressing Lamiya and how utterly their bodies — more than that, their souls — had merged. Making love with her had surpassed all expectation.

Away from her he felt like a hollow shell of himself, and his hands shook disconcertingly while he dried his legs. *Collect yourself, or others will notice.* Shrugging into his azure robe, he envisioned his mantle of responsibility and usual self-control settling over him, as snug as the soft silk that moulded to his shoulders.

While he ate his meal, his eyes were drawn to the empty tank in the corner. Mizu was swimming free in a beautiful lake, where she belonged. His heart swelled — would he too soon be roaming free in Riverplain? The food cloyed in his mouth, sticking to his palate with a sour taste, and he pushed the plate away deciding that he might as well enact his plan to go to the library and behave as if he'd been there since breakfast.

He bounded down the curling flights of stairs two at a time and hurried along the paths, his mind running over how the events might unfold at first light. What could go wrong? By the time he reached the steps to the library, he'd conjured an alarmingly long list.

Entering the library, he breathed in the scents of wood polish and paper, feeling his heartrate calm and his mind cool. He would miss this place, having spent so much time here, absorbing so much knowledge — but not enough to understand properly what was going on.

'Everand! Good to see you.' Hydrelaps came across the entry hall, his face creased in a smile. 'I asked Mage Mantiss on your behalf, I hope you don't mind, and he said you are welcome to keep the books on boats and to choose some other texts, if you wish.' The librarian twirled the duster in his hands, propelling fine yellow particles into the air around him.

Feeling guilty that Hydrelaps was unwittingly participating in his subterfuge, Everand said, 'That was kind of you. I will choose a few now, if I may?'

'Of course,' said Hydrelaps. 'I will open the antiquity section for you.'

The librarian set off towards where the older texts were kept and Everand followed slowly, thinking. Hydrelaps would report his choices to Mantiss so if he chose a number of texts, this should add to the impression that he was here to stay. The tension eased from his forehead; he should also enquire about texts that might be relevant to his proposed research project with Tiliqua.

'Do we have any texts on conducting multiple spells at once? Or on how to recover quickly from using power? I might be working on a new research task on these aspects.'

'None spring to mind, although ...' looking over his shoulder while he walked, Hydrelaps said, 'the books on defence might have some relevant material. The shelf is next to the one with the books on boats.'

'Sounds possible. I'll check there.' Now he thought about it, learning additional defensive tactics could prove beneficial. Just in case.

Hydrelaps opened the door to the antiquity area and, as before, bustled about tidying and dusting shelves while Everand went to the shelf with the books on boats. He pulled out the three he'd looked at previously and placed them in a neat pile on the floor before moving to the shelves with books on defence. The titles on the top shelf were recognisable as texts that his tutors had drawn upon for the basic defence spells during his apprenticeship studies, covering bolts of energy, defensive strikes and raising shields.

The titles of a few on the second shelf sounded familiar as additional concepts that Mage Beetal had taught him, such as moving objects with force and weaving binding spells.

He fingered the spine on the silvery-grey book on invisibility, a lump forming in his throat. Mantiss had patiently coached him in advanced and subtle techniques of invisibility and stealth, often in a secluded corner of the library well after the moon had risen. Grief washed through him: Mantiss was going to be so disappointed in his choices.

His knees cracked when he crouched to peer at the books on the lower shelves. Judging by the threadbare spines and tattered edges, these were older texts, the musty odour tickling his nostrils suggesting they were unused. Suppressing a sneeze, he roamed over the titles on the slim spines until a tiny volume, almost hidden between two taller books, made him pause. *Complex Battle Tactics* was etched in a spidery and faint cursive script, barely legible along the narrow spine.

Holding his breath, he eased the book out, alarmed when a few spots of mould dropped off the cover and the pages crackled as if they'd disintegrate upon being turned. Cradling the book across a flat palm, he used his fingertips to pry open the front cover and skimmed the list of contents. The crinkly paper rasped beneath his fingers, as parched as dead brown leaves became when they dropped from the trees in cold-leaf season.

His mouth ran dry and his heart sped up. The contents listed several techniques *not* covered in apprentice training, along with a whole section devoted to deploying spells, concurrently or consecutively, as well as how to disguise intent from a foe. The final section was simply titled 'Recovery of power'. *Exactly* what he needed.

The muscles in his thighs began to burn from holding his crouch too long. Glancing over a shoulder to check Hydrelaps was still busy, he closed the tiny book and selected two random larger volumes to place on either side of it. Awkwardly pulling himself to standing, he turned around, the books in his hands. 'These look interesting. Do you mind if I take them to the sunny reading room?'

'What have you got?' asked Hydrelaps, approaching but then stopping by the small pile of books on the floor. 'You want these three on boats?'

'Yes please, and to look through these to see if I'd like to ask for them as well.'

Hydrelaps squinted at the top book and nodded. 'I'll send some tea up for you. If you want them, I'm happy to ask Mage

Mantiss for you.' Bending over, he scooped up the three books on boats. 'You might as well take these with you.'

Everand managed to hold his books flat enough for Hydrelaps to pile the other three on top, clutching them to his chest for stability and to keep the slim volume concealed. Then he headed for the stairs to the reading rooms. On the third floor, he padded towards the room at the far end — his favourite, because it attracted the most sun and looked out over the gardens and lily pond.

On passing the middle reading room, he noticed the door was pulled almost to and, hovering, he detected voices. Two mages, conferring in suspiciously low voices. Intrigued, he flattened himself against the wall, listening.

'He shows possible vulnerability,' murmured a gruff voice, discernible as that of Pelamis.

'How so?' asked Simoselaps. 'So far, Mantiss continues to place an annoying level of trust in him.'

They were discussing him! Dampening his aura, Everand held his breath.

'Yes, but Mantiss didn't like Everand's suggestion we give this half-mage the right to speak, did he? And why, by the stars, did he suggest that anyway?' said Pelamis.

'True,' responded Simoselaps. 'But the course of action for obliteration is determined, and Everand agreed to go along with it. So where is his vulnerability?'

Straining to hear the next part, Everand visualised the two mages hunching close together to speak in whispers.

'Wait and see,' murmured Pelamis. 'When it comes to the act of obliteration, I suspect Everand will prove reluctant and his weakness will be revealed.' He sounded sure, smug even. 'Then Mantiss might be forced to reconsider where he places his favour.'

'How does that help us?' asked Simoselaps.

'We show ourselves to be strong, committed to upholding the Guild values and ready to back Mantiss all the way on his decisions.'

Everand released a shallow breath. He heard a faint rustling of robes and Pelamis spoke again.

'Our illustrious Head of the Guild is fading, or haven't you noticed? Something is amiss and Agamid increasingly covers for him.'

'Hmm,' responded Simoselaps. 'Now that you mention it, Mantiss rarely goes anywhere without Agamid in tow. But Mantiss isn't that old! Not nearly as old as Lapemis, Carlias or Pygopus before they passed over.'

'True. I wonder whether Mantiss is not properly recovered from the treachery of Mage Beetal. After all, that happened right under his nose and under his leadership, and he sustained significant injuries.'

'But he was healed.' A chair creaked and then creaked again as if Simoselaps had sat back and then immediately sat forward again. 'Do you think he's lost his will, the courage to lead?'

Alarm rattling through him, Everand shifted his weight carefully. He should move on now; the risk of being discovered eavesdropping was greater than the benefit of anything more he might learn. But then Pelamis spoke.

'Possibly. In which case, the discovery of this half-mage and yet further treachery by that obnoxious Mage Beetal creates opportunity. Mantiss relies too heavily on Everand, as well as Agamid, when he needs tough, strong supporters at this time. There is still much not explained about how this half-mage came to be. Everand is strange and annoying, but he isn't stupid. He knows far more than he's revealed, and we should be vigilant for opportunity.'

Robes rustled. 'I'm not sure what kind of opportunity we're looking for,' murmured Simoselaps.

A chair creaked. 'Opportunity to catch him in a lie, or some form of deception.' Pelamis' voice was clearer. 'That, more than anything, would disrupt his favour with Mantiss.'

'I see,' said Simoselaps. 'I wish I was coming with you at first light. What if the opportunity presents while you're in the other place?'

'Me too. Agamid and Saiphos are not robust enough to deal with events if they go awry. Let me think on that.'

Worried the two were concluding their discussion, Everand glided to the end room and slipped inside. Lowering the books to the table, he crept back to the door and pushed it until it was only a hand-width ajar, then he regarded the room. How could he make it look as if he'd been here for ages? He fluffed up the cushions and scattered them across a couple of chairs as if he'd been changing seats, then spread the books on boats across the table, flattening them open at random pages. He took one of the taller defence books and opened this at a page depicting different kinds of bolts of energy.

Finally, he sat in the chair nearest the window and appreciating the warmth from the sunlight streaming in, opened the second tall book on defence tactics and placed the slim volume inside the open pages. For good measure, he read the open pages in the larger book so he could say what it was about if anyone asked.

His heart beating erratically, he eased open the first page of the tattered slim volume. After a while, he realised he'd moved his eyes down the page three times but hadn't registered a single word. His mind kept flitting from snippet to snippet of the two mages' discussion. How and when had Pelamis and Simoselaps noticed a change in Mantiss? Had everyone on the Inner Council noticed, or only these two? If Agamid was covering for Mantiss, as suggested, then he must be aware there was a problem. Tiliqua, as Mantiss' daughter, must also have observed any changes in his master's wellbeing.

Sighing, he put the books down and stood up to look out the window. Nerves fraying and insides jangling, he wrangled with his haphazard stream of thoughts and emotions. Lamiya said he should choose the path and the life *he* wanted, but how could he abandon Mantiss with the others plotting like this? Leaving the Guild he could do, but leaving his master of so long was harder — especially with a fresh internal threat emerging.

Fighting the urge to slam his fist down on the windowsill, he clenched his hand. Every time he thought he had a clear direction, some twist or complication arose. He scrubbed rigorously at his face with both hands. If only Lamiya was here. His arms twitched, aching to hold her close and take solace from her warmth and subtle scents.

A tinkling sound alerted him to someone approaching just before there came a soft knock at the door. Spinning away from the window, he sat in the chair, crossed his legs, snatched up the tall book and called, 'Come!'

When the human girl entered, he peered over the top of the book and nodded politely. She placed a small tray with a pot of tea and sweet cakes on the table, reversed with a curtsey and pulled the door ajar again. The aroma of lavender and black-leaf tea wafted in the air. Swirling unease quelled his appetite for his favourite honey-laced cakes, thoughtfully requested by Hydrelaps. Soothing tea first. He poured a cup and sipped, coaxing his sense of order to return.

One step at a time: the current step was to absorb new spells from the slim volume in case he needed them. The next step was to go with the others to Riverwood at first light. What would transpire would transpire, and new steps would be decided — most likely, he'd flee to Riverplain to hide, like Malach. Or, if a miracle occurred, he'd possibly return to Axis for a more open discussion.

Lost in thought, he chewed on a honey cake then wiped his hands on the cloth provided before picking up the intriguing slim book. By page three he was memorising an intricate spell to juggle invisibility with raising a personal shield, while imparting defensive bolts *and* making translocation jumps so that he could strike from sudden random directions. After reading the spell three times, he lowered the book.

Why was this spell not taught? Because the Guild didn't think they needed it? However, someone, three generations ago, *had* required this level of defensive strategy and had devised and recorded the spell — and everything else in this book. Had the text been written before the granite wall and impenetrable wardspell were created? Perhaps the Guild had felt safe since then and had allowed the old spells to lapse, especially those associated with violence.

He drummed his fingers on the table, ignoring the clattering of the empty pot, cup and plate the vibration caused. These books had been sealed away from general access, and now Mantiss wanted to remove them under the guise of remodelling this area of the library. The more he tried to snag them, the more the niggling tendrils of concern eluded him.

Mantiss' actions would result in containing the mages' powers and spells largely to what was already known and taught. Was this his master's intention? Was this conservatism a natural outcome of the shock of Beetal's treachery and the fact the ambitious mage had secured fellow mage allies at the time? Did Mantiss fear a recurrence now that some of the younger mages were pushing for access to more power?

Or was it because the provinces had initiated contact and Mantiss worried the Guild would somehow become vulnerable? He must be missing something; there had to be more to this.

He sipped at his empty cup before remembering that he'd drained the pot. If Mantiss wanted to curtail the Guild's power, why had he sanctioned his research suggestion about concurrent spells? He gasped. Two birds with one stone. If he *was* being considered as the next Head of the Guild, then he might need these skills, and if he disappointed, then Tiliqua would have the same skills and knowledge. One thing Mantiss had always been good at was strategy. Long-term, covert strategy.

Nervous energy driving his legs, he paced by the window. After several laps he stopped and stared out across the verdant lawns, ornate flower beds and tranquil lily pond with the artistic array of stone benches and weeping-leaf trees. Order and balance — a measured and comfortable existence — Mantiss sought to sustain this.

Leaning on the windowsill, he rested his forehead against the glass. He'd been assuming that if he left this lifestyle, the Guild would continue uninterrupted. That his departure would be a mere ripple in the council, his position soon replaced. Was he arrogant enough to think he made a difference? He'd promised Lamiya he would be with her. *Lamiya. Riverplain and the beautiful lake. Beram, Mookaite, Tengar and all his province friends.* He closed his eyes, the glass pane pressing hard and cold against his forehead, a symbolic barrier to his heart's desires.

Lamiya's gorgeous face filled his mind, her eyes wide with concern, the blue flecks jittering. *Is it your responsibility, my mage? I adore your integrity, your truthfulness, but you are not responsible for everything.* She tossed her head to throw her luscious hair over her shoulder, so real that he moaned. Was he imagining this would be her advice, or was she projecting to him from such a distance?

Sighing, he pushed away from the window. Either way, this was astute advice. With the arrival of first light at the lake in Riverwood he would be responsible for creating an unexpected scenario, but he was *not* accountable for what the others did in response. Although his mind-Lamiya nodded, doubts curdled in his stomach.

Gently picking up the slim volume of battle tactics, he probed it to see if the book was warded against being removed from the library. It wasn't, so he slid it inside his robe and tucked it deep into his loincloth. Gathering up the other five books, he left the room, observing as he passed it that the middle reading room was now silent and empty. Back downstairs, he peeled the books on defence from the top of his pile and handed them to Hydrelaps, confirming he'd like to keep them. The librarian beamed and promised to ask Mantiss.

Outside, the sun was becoming low in the sky, shadows reaching across the lawns and paths, the warmth gently evaporating from the still air. At the bottom of the library steps, he hesitated, chill creeping along his arms. In Riverfall or Riverplain he wouldn't be by himself. There'd always be some activity or gathering, or he would share a meal with Lamiya, or Beram and Mookaite. A lump swelled in his throat. Even after all this time, there was no-one here he could call friend enough to visit for company.

The lump in his throat became painful.

How badly would he need a friend on the lake shore at first light?

CHAPTER THIRTY-SEVEN

Cocooned in darkness and snug in his warm bed, Everand lay recounting the new spells to firmly fix them in his mind. Imminently, events would unfold rapidly and he'd face another life-changing decision. The analytical part of him tried to go over all the possible scenarios and options and he took a deep breath. No point cycling over these again. His mouth twisted; if this mission ran like it had so far, something unanticipated was going to present anyway.

He was as ready as he could be. *That's the spirit*, said his imaginary Lamiya. *You can only do your best.*

More sleep unlikely, he rose and padded into the bathroom. Scrubbed impeccably clean, his skin and face tingling, he donned his azure robe, laced on his best sandals, brushed his hair until it shone and bound it back with a matching azure thong. The summons chime still hadn't sounded. Going to stand by the window, he watched the translucent slip of moon dip below the horizon to be replaced by a narrow, glimmering promise of light.

The chime sounded on his desk, a tinkling knell for whatever was to come. Pivoting in a full circle, he swept his eyes over his rooms in farewell, and marched to the door.

Surprisingly, he didn't come across Saiphos or any others on their way to the Great Hall. Perhaps they hadn't woken as early. The crisp air snatching at his face, and energy gathering in his mind and body, he took the steps into the Great Hall two at a time. He was crossing the silk rug when a row of round orbs flickered into life, bobbing along the wall on the far side of the council table. Warm yellow light cascaded over Agamid and Mantiss, already seated in their customary chairs. Everand ascended the dais and bowed.

Rising, Mantiss came around the edge of the table to clasp his hands. 'Everand, my son.' The green eyes looked deep into his. 'After this, we can hopefully return to routine.'

Everand gripped Mantiss' hands, noting his master's clasp was less firm than in the past. 'Yes, master.' He wanted to thank Mantiss for everything he'd done for him but quelled the emotion, conscious that Agamid sat nearby, watching them.

'Be safe,' said Mantiss, releasing his hands. The words sounded heavy, ominous.

'I'll try, master.' Everand lowered his gaze.

Without speaking, Agamid gave him a respectful nod.

Footsteps sounded on the steps and Saiphos scurried across the rug. 'Am I late?'

'Relax, Saiphos. The others aren't here yet.' Agamid shook his head and sighed.

Everand glanced around the hall and his breath caught. The orb lights played across a shimmering cage against the back wall, tucked between two tall sets of dark mahogany shelves. To Mantiss, he said, 'This is the cage for the half-mage?'

At Mantiss' nod, he walked around the great table and went to the back wall, stopping a pace away from the glinting square. Enhancing his senses, he detected the multiple wards of binding woven into the translucent shield with the residual auras of Menetia, Tiliqua, Neelaps, Caimanops and the stronger orange and beige auras of Pelamis and Simoselaps. The resultant frame was as unyielding as the rocks in the granite wall and he smiled wryly, thinking the neat box was a good analogy for the restrictions on the mages' powers and the containment of their culture.

The cage was twice as wide as a person and stretched an arm's-length higher than his head. He frowned at the red-hued oval disc built into the centre of the roof. Dismayed, he understood this was where the mages would feed in their combined spell of obliteration, from where crackling death would shower down upon Malach. Would the half-mage batter and rage at the invisible shield, or stand resolute in a warrior's death? His tongue pasted to the roof of his mouth.

A light touch passed over his shoulders and he quashed all emotion. Mantiss was subtly reading him. He spun around, his expression bland. 'We feed the spell of obliteration in through the roof?'

Coming to stand beside him, Mantiss murmured, 'It will be quick with ten of us. Hydrelaps has agreed to be the key independent witness.'

Surprised the gentle librarian had agreed, Everand said slowly, 'As librarian and custodian of our history that makes sense.' To his relief his voice didn't waver to betray his turmoil. Mantiss continued to stand by his side. Did his master have something more to say?

Rapid footsteps pounded up the steps and in quick succession the remainder of the Inner Council of Ten entered and hurried to stand behind their chairs at the great table. All were dressed in their signature colours and Everand nodded politely to each, giving Tiliqua a faint smile in response to her assessing look. The tight smile she returned made him wonder if she was worried, wanting him to return safely.

After a short pause, more footsteps sounded and the other ten mages that made up the Outer Council of Twenty entered. With a wave of an arm, Agamid indicated they should gather at the base of the dais. Hydrelaps looked up and gave Mantiss, and then Everand, a brief nod. Everand nodded back, thinking how relieved the librarian would be when his allocated duty as witness did not come to pass. His throat then tightened at the way a few of the mages glanced sideways at Pelamis. So, Pelamis and Simoselaps had already collected colleagues they could influence.

Resting his hands on the back of his chair, Mantiss opened with, 'I formally thank the members of the Inner Council. I also thank the Outer Council of Twenty for bearing witness, and Hydrelaps for being the key witness and for memory-recording this event.' His voice gathered strength. 'This light, we fulfil one of our most difficult Guild obligations, but as a combined council we must honour our governance responsibility. We must strand strong and united. We act on behalf of all the mages and people of Axis. Never forget that.'

Grasping the back of his chair, Agamid tilted forward. 'The lines of magic must remain pure, and we the senior mages applaud your resolve.' His glance flicked to Everand and away.

'For the good of the Guild,' said Pelamis loudly.

'For the integrity of the Guild,' said Simoselaps quickly, the words then echoed by each mage around the table.

Everand's heart began to race.

Mantiss stood taller, although his grimace suggested this took some effort. 'Agamid, compose your team for translocation, if you will.'

'Those going to Riverwood, stand in the centre of the rug,' said Agamid, stepping down from the dais and positioning himself in the middle of the rug.

Following, Everand took his place beside Agamid, and Saiphos came to stand facing him. The other mages fanned out in a wide circle around them, with Pelamis stepping closer to stand facing Agamid.

With a swish of beige robes, Simoselaps stepped into the inner group beside Pelamis, forming an uneven pentagon. Everand opened his mouth to protest, then pressed his lips shut. Saiphos shuffled his feet awkwardly and Agamid's mouth tightened, but he didn't look surprised. When Pelamis smirked at him, calculation in his shrewd brown eyes, Everand returned his best bland look and shrugged.

'Pelamis persuaded me that the greatest risk in this sortie lies in the capture of the half-mage in the distant province. Accordingly, I agreed Simoselaps should go too,' Mantiss said, taking a step forward and passing to Agamid a small orb laced with spidery green veins.

Peering at it, Everand could see a bell inside it. He pushed aside the twinge of annoyance at how useful one of these would have been on his mission. It was harder to set aside the next thought that Mantiss had indeed been deliberately testing him. *Focus! You are in greater danger on this mission.*

'When you're ready to be translocated home, activate this bell,' Mantiss instructed. 'We'll be waiting.'

Once Agamid had carefully tucked the orb into his robe pocket, Mantiss stepped back to the outer ring and turned to his daughter. 'Tiliqua, stand with me to part the wardspell, please. I call upon you all to gather your power for the translocation.'

Everand flexed his fingers, coaxing his power, while Tiliqua moved smoothly to stand beside Mantiss, the similarity in their facial features striking as they concentrated to build their power. After giving him a quick glance, Tiliqua half-closed her eyes and extended her arms. The turquoise of her robes deepened in hue, and her quartz necklace glinted, throbbing with magic. Mantiss stood more hunched than erect, his eyes narrowed and his hands held out not quite straight, while lines of green energy ran up and down his arms.

A thrumming began, drifting upwards into the cavernous roof of the hall. The remainder of the Inner Council stood around them, mouths working while they summoned their power.

Inhaling steadily through his nose, Everand began constructing in his mind a detailed image of the western shore of the high lake, generating the landing spot for the translocation. He visualised the grey water lapping at the pebbly beach, the silvery cascade of the waterfall tumbling into the lake at the base of the darkly rising hills, the gloomy stand of trees at the rear of the beach. Focusing, he chose a spot midway along the beach, a little away from the water's edge. The waterfall thundered, the trees cast shadows behind and to the south the water stretched away over the rocky ledge. Furrowing his brows, he added light and shadows as they would play with the rising of the sun. His chest grew tight with anticipation.

Green and turquoise lights shimmered from Mantiss' and Tiliqua's hands and they held them aloft, their chanting growing louder, gathering depth and energy until the air thickened and the sound was almost tangible enough to touch. Menetia's lilac aura coiled around her, accentuating her planed cheekbones and braided hair, Caimanops shivered a silvery-blue, blending with his robe colours and Neelaps glowed a vivid moss green. Colours of life, thought Everand, not those of impending death.

Crackling light erupted over them and Mantiss spoke sharply, 'The alarm is turned off. Agamid, gather your team. Everand, project the image!'

Everand grabbed hands with Saiphos and Agamid and sent a large orb into the air above them with the vivid and layered image of the lake shore. Words, air and magic bubbling around him, he fought to hold the image steady. Multi-coloured swirls mixed with a wall of shimmering grey and the Great Hall began to dissipate. Cold air pressed around him and his eyes watered, but he knew what to expect. His palm stung from the pinching grip of Agamid, and Saiphos' fear eked into his other hand. There was a hesitation at the coruscating green and turquoise outline of a large, round door, and then they were through the wardspell.

The air warmed and in the wan light he sensed the granite wall receding behind him. They hurtled over the grassy expanse, the murky dark pines and the haunting granite outcrops, and the grey lake zoomed towards them. Instinctively, Everand bent his knees — they were heading in way too fast. 'Brace yourselves!' he yelled.

The pebbles raced towards his feet and he let go of the others' hands to hold his out for balance. The pebbles scrunched, slamming into the soles of his sandals, and he pitched forward, toppling to his knees and just managing to get his hands down in time. Shock waves jarred his legs and arms and his teeth rattled. Saiphos fell heavily on top of his back and it took all his strength, the stones biting into his hands, not to fall onto his face. The taste of iron and an annoying stinging filled his mouth and he sighed; he'd bitten his tongue again.

Saiphos rolled off his back, tangled with Agamid's legs, and the pair went down in a flurry of legs and robes.

Rapidly pushing up to his feet, Everand assessed what was happening. Pelamis and Simoselaps had cleverly faced each other, holding their hands in a square for balance, absorbing the landing well. Simoselaps was pale, but Pelamis was already poised and alertly scanning the area.

Helping Agamid to his feet, Everand asked, 'Are you alright?'

'Are we in the right place?' Agamid nodded tightly, brushing the grime from his purple robes and looking around.

'Yes. This is the meeting place, and behind us are the trees for you to hide in.'

'That was … uncomfortable. Is distant translocation always like this?' asked Agamid, peering at him.

'In my experience, yes.' Tilting his head, Everand couldn't resist making the point. 'It's far worse if the wardspell isn't opened properly.'

Agamid gave him an unfathomable look, unaware he had bits of grit sticking to his trim beard. 'We'd best get into position. How soon will this Malach come?'

Everand looked at the way the sky was lightening at the top of the waterfall, tingeing the water silver where it fell over the rocky ledge. To the east, a yellow-pink aura was emerging behind the dark trees. 'Sun-up is nigh. It'll take a little while for Malach to walk from his village.'

'Good, that gives us time to find a vantage point and prepare the trap.' Agamid turned to the others. 'Follow me.'

Saiphos and Simoselaps moved after Agamid, but Pelamis remained, squinting across the lake. Everand's heart sank.

'Is there something in the lake?' Pelamis asked sharply, still squinting at the deep water.

'Fish.' Everand shrugged.

'Big ripples for a fish,' snapped Pelamis.

Everand shrugged again.

Several strides away, Agamid paused and called over his shoulder, 'Pelamis? Come along! We must prepare.'

Pelamis glared at him and then strode after the others, soon disappearing into the trees and blending with the shadowy trunks. Extending his senses, Everand could detect no sign of the mages' presence. His palms clammy, he paced the pebbly shore as if waiting impatiently. Had Mizukaze surfaced when they arrived? Was that what Pelamis saw? How could he warn and deflect the dragon? He kicked over a few pebbles with his toes, and a smooth, beige pebble caught his eye.

Picking it up, he rubbed it between his fingers, subtly feeding a message into it: *Greetings Great Mizukaze. Stay hidden unless I call you. I may need you soon.*

Facing the water, with a flick of his wrist he hurled the pebble so it skipped across the water, the extra energy taking it a long way before it gave a final plop and sank. For good measure, he skipped another six stones as if passing the time. Blinking rapidly, he hid a smile when the original pebble shot out of the water, spun in the air and dropped back in. The surrounding water rippled and then went still.

After several more laps of the beach, he glanced east. The crown of the sun was a yellow disk above the jagged silhouettes of green-grey trees, and the waterfall had become tumbling ribbons of colour. How long should he pretend to wait for Malach? Until the others questioned him, or should he be the one to say something was wrong? At the end of his next lap, he glanced towards the shadowy trees and shrugged to convey that Malach should have arrived. Nothing moved, so he continued to pace.

Soon, his feet grew sore from the uneven pressure of the pebbles and he sat down to watch the waterfall.

Almost as soon as he'd sat down, Agamid's light touch reached him. *Should Malach be here by now?*

I would have thought so, Everand projected back. *What do you wish to do?*

Do you know where he lives? asked Agamid.

Not his exact cabin, but I know where the village is.

Wait while I confer, Agamid instructed.

Clasping his arms around his knees, Everand stared at the water, willing his heart and breathing to remain calm. If he were in charge, he'd suggest they go to the village. Pebbles crunched behind him. Rising, he turned, seeing no-one, but the scrunching and shifting of pebbles conveyed the path of the invisible approaching mage.

'We are to go to the village.' The voice of Pelamis. 'Make yourself invisible.'

Repressing a jump when Pelamis roughly gripped his elbow, Everand complied. 'Translocate us to a safe spot.'

After briefly considering where would be best, Everand chose the raptor cages, knowing they could slink along the path to the village from there. He felt for and gripped Pelamis' elbow, visualised the flat area in front of the cages and muttered the spell.

When they landed, the raptors screeched and fluttered around their cages, sensing the disturbance of the air. He wished he could see Pelamis' face.

'What are these?' hissed Pelamis close to his ear.

'Hunting birds,' he murmured. 'These people are hunters and warriors. We must be careful because the birds are trained to attack.'

'Noted,' said Pelamis. 'Lead the way.'

When Everand started to walk along the twisty track to the village, Pelamis let go of his elbow but the pull on the back of his robe suggested the mage was holding onto it. Moving fluidly and silently, he was grateful for the pine needles that cushioned their footfalls. Ahead, he heard voices and smelled the smoke from cooking fires. On reaching the outer ring of cabins, he paused.

'They live in these?' Pelamis sounded incredulous. 'How basic. They look cold and draughty.'

'No hot baths,' murmured Everand. 'No meals delivered here.'

'Huh,' said Pelamis. 'How will you know which cabin we should check?'

'Malach is their leader so perhaps there's a sign of a sort.' Everand moved slowly through the outer ring of cabins, which all looked the same. One cabin somehow felt like Malach, but there was no distinguishing feature. If he were the leader, would he live in the inner circle? Or, with his interest in raptors, was it more likely Malach lived in the outer circle?

A man moving briskly came into view and Everand slithered to a halt. *Torrap.* Curse it. The man walked through the second ring and headed directly towards them, taking long, strong strides. Everand slid sideways behind the nearest cabin, feeling the tug on his robe as Pelamis followed.

This is a trusted hunter, he thought at Pelamis. *Let's see if he goes to Malach's cabin.*

Torrap strode past them, wearing his hunting tunic and carrying a bow and quiver of arrows. Did he expect to go hunting with Malach? That didn't make sense, given Malach was supposed to be meeting with him. Torrap stopped at a large stone and wood cabin in the outer row at the apex, closest to the raptor cages. It was the one he'd paused beside.

The hunter banged on the door. 'Malach! Are you there?' At the lack of response, Torrap banged on the door more loudly.

Is it possible we passed the half-mage on his way to the lake? thought Pelamis.

Wait, replied Everand, noticing a second hunter approaching. The swarthy man was one of the paddlers but he couldn't recall his name.

'Is he there?' asked the new arrival on reaching the cabin door.

Torrap shook his head. 'I haven't seen him since we hunted the sun before last.'

'Where can he have gone?' asked the other man.

'Don't know, Mahog. He didn't say anything to me.' Torrap shrugged.

Mahog tapped his knife sheath, the clacking noise rhythmic. 'When was he supposed to meet that mage for training? Is that where he is?'

'You could be right. The meeting is this sun-up.' Torrap's frown cleared but almost immediately he frowned again. 'But that doesn't explain where he was last sun, when we agreed to hunt.'

'Do you think something's wrong? Is it possible the mage came early?' asked Mahog, beginning to half pull out and then sheathe his knife again, the blade rasping.

Torrap shrugged and fingered the feathers of an arrow. 'I never liked the idea. Something seems off.'

Feeling Pelamis' hot breath near his ear, Everand tensed. Mahog's blade continued to rasp gratingly in and out of the sheath.

'Where were they to meet?' Mahog grunted eventually.

'At the lake,' said Torrap, now fiddling with his bowstring. 'You think we should go there?'

'Can't hurt,' said Mahog gruffly. 'If they're not there, we can hunt on the way back.'

The two turned and headed along the track towards the raptor cages. 'What should we do if they're there?' Torrap's question drifted back through the tree trunks, but Mahog's mumbled reply was lost in the dank air.

Cooler air washed over Everand's neck when Pelamis stepped back. 'Are they all like that?'

'From this province, yes.'

'Primitive.' Pelamis' voice shook, as if he had shuddered.

Peeling away from the cabin wall, Everand asked, 'Shall we go back to the others?'

After a short silence Pelamis said, 'Let's check this man's cabin first. See if we can collect any evidence to support his connection to Mage Beetal.'

Everand swallowed the implied insult that his report was inaccurate. No point goading Pelamis. He crept towards Malach's cabin, his unease growing to queasy anxiety. Pelamis was cunning and intent on following his own agenda. His skin started to crawl, his instinct shrieking that something momentous was about to unfold.

The cabin door swung open at his push and Everand stepped inside, wrinkling his nose at the acrid odour of charred meat and unwashed hide clothes. Pelamis shoved against him, roughly brushed past and then clumped around the cabin. Random objects lifted and lowered as Pelamis picked them up and replaced them. Everand's heart beat quickly and his mind raced: what could Pelamis discover and what would he do with it?

His heart jolted when Pelamis abruptly became visible and faced him.

'Make yourself visible.'

'Why?' countered Everand. 'What if another hunter comes?'

'Make yourself visible,' insisted Pelamis, flexing his fingers and flinging a spell to seal the door closed. 'I want to see what you are doing.'

Dissolving his spell of invisibility, he gave Pelamis a blank look.

'What made you conclude this half-mage is related to Mage Beetal? Where is your evidence?'

'You want to take evidence back with us?' said Everand, thinking furiously and choosing information the council already knew. 'I found traces of a personality-altering compound in a viper, just like the compound Mage Beetal devised to make his dragons aggressive.' He looked past Pelamis to a rough-hewn wooden shelf adjacent to a similar one with cooking utensils. 'Try those jars. See if we can find it.'

Watching Pelamis examine the row of jars, Everand hovered awkwardly until a taller jar with a dark stain caught his eye. He pointed to it, saying, 'Try that one. I'm pretty sure it contains the potion that quelled my powers.'

Pelamis picked up the earthen jar, tentatively turned it around and sniffed at it. 'You are correct. We'll take this jar.' His nose wrinkling with distaste, he thrust it at Everand to hold.

Taking the jar, Everand checked to see if the lid was firmly pushed in, then hesitated. What if he threw the contents over Pelamis? He shook the jar, the faint slop suggesting there wasn't much left. Using a thumb, he eased the lid looser. 'Try the next jar,' he suggested. 'The one with the crimson stain around the rim.'

While Pelamis inspected and sniffed that jar, Everand swept his gaze around the cabin. The bed was a pile of dried and stretched animal hides on the floor in one corner, the odour of hide mingling with rank sweat. Above the bed was a set of short shelves with folded tunics made from a mixture of cloth and skins, and from nearby hooks hung sturdy leather belts and an array of pouches.

Beside the bed was a carved wooden box. Would any books on magic be in there? Above the box was another rough shelf, with several knives in sheaths. His gaze travelled the length of the shelf and rested on the smooth grey stone at the end: Malach's communication stone. In plain sight.

'What's that?' Pelamis thrust the second jar of potion at him. 'Hold this while I see what it is.'

Curse it. His hands now inconveniently full, Everand juggled the two jars. Horror rising, he watched Pelamis pick up the stone and heft it in his hands. Flicking his glance down, he noted which jar was in which hand: Pelamis required subduing, not more aggression.

Around a sardonic smile, Pelamis said, 'Well, well. This appears to be a communication stone.' Power crackled from his fingers to merge into the stone, while he stood with his eyes fixed upon Everand. 'I detect a faint and cold aura of Mage Beetal. This must be how they connected. How devious. There was a matching stone in Beetal's study?' Frowning, Pelamis bent his concentration deeper into the stone.

Slowly reaching a hand behind his back, Everand dropped the jar with the personality-adjuster compound onto the hide bed. The dull thud did not attract Pelamis' attention. He prised off the lid to the jar with quelling potion and waited.

Grinning smugly, Pelamis looked up. 'Well, well, even more interesting. *You* communicated with this Malach only two suns ago, and now he is missing.' Narrowing his eyes, Pelamis flexed his fingers. 'I wonder what Mage Mantiss will make of *this* revelation?'

Everand tossed the meagre supply of the quelling potion at Pelamis and prepared to translocate. Strands of grey light wove throughout the cabin, but through them he saw Pelamis swing the stone up to deflect most of the liquid and then fling the stone at him. He ducked. The stone sailed over his head and he sped up the translocation, the pebbled path in front of the

Meeting Place by the lake in Riverplain fixed in his mind. The stone and wood of the cabin walls blurred into a spinning mass of grey, black and brown and his body grew light.

Just as the cabin walls vanished, he felt Pelamis clench both hands onto his robe and the material pulled sharply, the robe now weighing heavily across his shoulders. Curse it all! Pelamis was translocating with him!

Rapidly, he adjusted his destination image to the western shore of the lake, where the others would be waiting.

First, he'd have to dislodge Pelamis.

CHAPTER THIRTY-EIGHT

Mid-translocation, Everand compartmentalised his mind just like the slim book of defence spells had coached. Raising a block over the front of his mind so that his thoughts and intentions couldn't be read, he made himself invisible again and concurrently drew deep into his source of power. The tiny book had revealed much about how to draw a further quantum of power from the allocation he had been born with. Conjuring in one section of his mind an image of the Staropal, he visualised the colourful star expanding his original pool of power until even his toes tingled with magical energy.

Another part of his mind registered the dense treetops hurtling below, punctuated by sporadic outcrops of rocks. He sailed over the top of the ridge and the pebbly shore rushed at him. Air passed his ears in a deafening roar and he blinked away tears from the cold. His cheeks felt numb.

Calculating his landing, he shot over the edge of the lake and swung about violently, chopping roughly at Pelamis' hands. The mage let go and dropped into the water with a shriek. Slowing his momentum, Everand made a stumbling, running landing on the shore and came to a stop, his chest heaving. Immediately, he drew power, absorbing it and storing it, until he felt he'd explode with suppressed energy.

Clutching his sodden robe hem at knee height, Pelamis splashed angrily out of the water. 'Show yourself, traitor!' Looking towards the trees he shouted, 'Agamid! We've been betrayed!'

Everand made himself still, and Pelamis' furious mind search swept right over him, unable to detect the gauze-thin intricate ward. He almost smiled, but the others came running out of the trees.

Simoselaps reached Pelamis first, brown hair flopping in an unruly manner. 'What are you saying? What happened?'

When Agamid and Saiphos came to a puffing stop, Pelamis said flatly, 'The half-mage is gone. Everand warned him.'

'What?' said Agamid. 'How? Why?'

'A communication stone. The same stone that traitor Beetal must have used. Everand used it two suns ago, and two hunters said Malach has been missing since.'

'You spoke to hunters?' Agamid asked, eyebrows raised.

'Of course not,' snapped Pelamis, as if Agamid was an idiot. 'They came looking for the half-mage and we heard them.' Pelamis looked around, waving his arms jerkily. 'We must find Everand. He's here somewhere. He's a traitor, just like his former mentor.'

Slowly enough not to disturb the air, Everand levitated and glided closer. How could he communicate with Agamid without being attacked by Pelamis?

'I don't understand,' said Saiphos, staring wide-eyed at Agamid. 'What would Everand gain by doing this?'

'Who knows why Everand does anything!' Pelamis shook his head and jerked his arms around again. 'Can't you see? He set us up! He told us the half-mage would be here, and then he warned him.'

Gliding past Pelamis, Everand edged closer to Agamid and hovered where he could see everyone clearly. Face flushed a deep red, Pelamis was gesturing impatiently.

'We must alert Mage Mantiss,' said Simoselaps sombrely, sliding to stand beside Pelamis. 'The full council agreed a course of action and Everand has thwarted that. Who knows what he'll do next?'

'He can't be trusted,' insisted Pelamis, almost spitting the words. 'He is a traitor.'

'We must warn Mage Mantiss,' repeated Simoselaps, his goatee beard jutting out.

Everand glided closer, wishing Agamid would say something rather than just let Pelamis rant. Saiphos was no use at all, with his face creased in dismay and wringing his hands, looking to Agamid for guidance.

Appearing to be deep in thought, Agamid stroked his trim beard with one hand while Pelamis and Simoselaps kept insisting they had been set up and must act accordingly. Abruptly, Agamid raised the other hand. 'Quiet! Let me think.' *Finally.*

'There's nothing to think about!' shouted Pelamis, stepping closer and waving his hands wildly. 'Everand is a traitor, plain and simple. Why else would he warn this half-mage and then hide from us now?'

Heat infusing his neck and cheeks, Everand felt like giving Agamid a shove. *Come on, senior mage, stand up for me!* So much for hoping Agamid and Saiphos would be reasonable. They were even more spineless than he suspected.

'He's a traitor,' repeated Simoselaps, nodding vigorously.

'Give me the recall orb,' said Pelamis sharply. 'If you won't warn Mantiss and the rest of the council, then I will.'

'For the good of the Guild. We agreed.' Simoselaps stepped forward too, glaring at Agamid.

Everand's heart thudded against his breastbone. He should leave them to it and translocate to Riverplain! Why didn't they just go? He'd expected a tad more from Agamid. Disappointment filling him, he clenched his jaw. Would Pelamis go so far as to attack Agamid? The feral expression on the young mage's face suggested he might. What if he made himself visible? Pelamis would undoubtedly divert to attack him instead.

Lips stretched in a snarl, Pelamis advanced on Agamid, hand out, and spat, 'Give me the orb. *Now*. Or are you in league with Everand?'

The air zinged and Simoselaps screamed then stared at the arrow shaft protruding from his arm. Blood flowed into his beige robes, discolouring the sleeve. Mouth open, he gaped at Pelamis.

Torrap and Mahog! The forgotten hunters had arrived! Another arrow zinged right at them, and Pelamis disintegrated it with a casual wave of a hand. Horrified, Everand watched Mahog, stupidly brave, run out of the trees brandishing his knife. Pelamis' crackling red bolt took the hunter in the chest and Mahog fell, smoke rising from his smouldering tunic and charred body.

'Primitive *and* stupid,' muttered Pelamis. 'Where's the other one?' He scanned the trees.

Mind-tracing where Torrap was hiding, Everand sent a stun spell, mind-watching the hunter keel over unconscious behind a thick tree trunk. That should confound Pelamis. Next, skip-locating to stand right behind Agamid, he placed his hands on the mage's shoulders, ignoring the immediately tensed muscles and gasped gulp. Urgently, he said, 'I won't hurt you. Take the others and leave before more hunters arrive.'

'What are you doing?' hissed Agamid.

'I *couldn't* obliterate anyone. Tell Mantiss I'm sorry.'

'Why don't you tell him yourself?' Agamid made a shushing motion at Saiphos, who was watching him intently.

'I'm not coming with you. Go! Before Pelamis does anything else rash.'

Twisting his head, Pelamis stared at Agamid, his eyes narrowing. 'Is Everand there?' He hurled a stun bolt, accurately pitched at just over Agamid's shoulder.

Deflecting the bolt wide so it didn't bounce off his shield and hit Agamid or Saiphos, Everand made himself visible and stepped away from Agamid.

Saiphos jumped. 'Everand! What *are* you doing?'

'Explain yourself!' Agamid spun around and spread his hands.

Doubting Pelamis would give him time to explain, Everand took a step back, eyeing the orange-robed mage with distaste.

Pelamis flexed his fingers, drawing power, and snapped at Simoselaps, 'Stop whining and help me!'

'My arm!' moaned Simoselaps, his hands clenched over the wound, vainly trying to stem the blood.

'Saiphos,' said Everand, exasperated. 'Help Simoselaps. Dissolve the arrow and seal the wound. Quickly!' He ducked the bolt that Pelamis sent and skip-located twice so the following bolts hit thin air and dissipated harmlessly upon landing on pebbles. Despairing, he shouted at Agamid, 'Gather them and go!'

Time lumbered while Saiphos moved towards Simoselaps, who stood with a pale face and teeth gritted, and Agamid fumbled in his pocket for the recall globe.

Everand backed to the lake until he felt water lapping at his heels, all the while Pelamis advancing on him, hurling stun bolts from alternate hands. These disintegrated upon hitting his protective shield and he yelled, 'Pelamis! I'm no threat to the Guild. Go, make your report!'

'You're a traitor *and* a threat!' growled Pelamis, increasing the flurry of bolts. 'Come and answer for your actions. Show Mantiss the traitor you are! Or are you too much of a coward?'

Feeling Pelamis' contempt washing over him, Everand deflected a swarm of bolts and ground his teeth. What, by the stars, was Agamid doing? Did he intend to let Pelamis injure or capture him? He rapidly refocused when Pelamis changed his bolts to lethally sharp barbs and sent a hundred all at once. The barbs tinkled upon striking his strengthened shield and he swallowed. The tips were sharp: Pelamis intended no mercy. Where had he learned that trick?

Not daring to look away to see what Agamid was doing, his jaw throbbing with tension, he thought that if Agamid didn't take control soon, he'd have to attack Pelamis and then he would indeed be a traitor. Reluctantly, he started to form a spell that would implode the air around Pelamis until he was crushed and couldn't breathe.

A deafening roar shook the air behind him and a wave slapped the back of his knees. Regaining his balance, he flinched when an almighty ball of flame flew over his head and enveloped the space where Pelamis stood. He felt the blood drain from his face but when the flame subsided, he saw Pelamis standing encased in a protective shield, his mouth open and eyes wide. Shouting warnings, Simoselaps and Saiphos ran behind Agamid, who was clutching the green-tinged orb in both hands, too petrified to act.

'Wait, Mizukaze!' Everand raised his arms wide, air buffeting his back as the dragon reared up with a roar as loud as overhead thunder. He smiled. Mizukaze must look awesome, blue scales glistening, gold horns glinting and powerful forelegs armed with cruel talons. Not to mention the hypnotic, dazzling, golden eyes.

Another wave slapped the back of his knees, and everyone's eyes slid to the side of him when Flight reared up, her roar not as deep. Elation coursed through his veins — the dragons *had* come to protect him!

'See?' Pelamis screeched at Agamid. 'He is *just* like Mage Beetal. He even has dragons! He *must* be destroyed!'

Slowly, Agamid turned to look at Everand, deep sorrow etched over his face, mingled with disappointment — and fear.

'Agamid, *go*. Before everything becomes irrecoverable.' Everand flapped his hands in a shooing motion.

'He tricks you!' snarled Pelamis. 'We must take him!'

'No!' Everand shouted back. 'I mean the Guild no harm. *Please* leave. I am staying here.'

Pelamis glared at him but stayed behind his shield.

'Are you sure?' called Agamid.

'I'm sure,' said Everand firmly. 'I beg you to tell Mantiss how sorry I am.'

The dragons waited, poised behind him, their forked tongues flicking in anticipation. The air thrummed thick with possibility, and the waterfall cascaded in a continual background thunder.

'You failed to mention the dragons in your report.' Agamid gave him a steely look. 'Mantiss will be deeply disappointed.'

Sadness whipped through Everand's chest and he gasped in a breath, dispersing the emotion. He must not show weakness now. 'Words cannot describe my sorrow, or the depth of my apology. Mantiss is like a father to me. Take care of him, won't you?'

Movement caught the edge of his vision and he flung out a spell to bind Pelamis where he stood.

Finally, Agamid said heavily, 'I am sorry too. I don't pretend to understand what you are doing, but we will go now.' His hands tightened around the orb and the green veins flared vividly. 'Gather close,' he directed at the others.

Relief coursed through him when Saiphos threw him a sad, wistful glance and hurried to grab hold of Agamid's robe. Simoselaps scowled, but he also grabbed a handful of Agamid's robe. Pelamis' mouth tightened in a grimace and he raised both hands, hurling a massive fire-strike and death bolt concurrently.

Swift as an arrow, Everand skip-located upwards and backwards in a somersaulting arc, landing on Mizukaze's back and raising a wall so the two strikes, which unerringly followed him, bounced off and dropped into the lake. The water sizzled and steam rose. The dragon's ribs heaved as Mizukaze drew in air and prepared to envelop Pelamis in fire. Flight sent a bolt of lightning to the ground just in front of Pelamis.

Undeterred, the mage raised his hands to strike again while the space around Agamid and the other two shimmered with the initiation of the recall.

Swim away now! Take me to Riverplain, Everand commanded. Mizukaze roared and spat flame, which mingled with the ball of flames from Flight to create an intense, crackling bolt of searing fire. Pelamis gave an enormous leap sideways and then scurried to Agamid.

Leave these. We must go, Everand reinforced his command.

If you insist, grumbled Mizukaze, but he obeyed, turning around and swimming toward deeper water. Flight followed, with her mouth open in what looked like a dragon grin.

Valued friend, thank you, sent Everand. A last glance over his shoulder confirmed that the four mages had almost dissipated. He herded his thoughts away from the reaction of Mantiss and the others when they arrived back in the Great Hall empty-handed — and without him. *Try not to drown me on the way,* he said to Mizukaze. *Please take me to Lamiya and her people.*

Flight bobbed up alongside, her head drawing level. *We go to my lake?* She fluttered long eyelashes at him, her golden irises shifting.

We go to your lake, confirmed Everand.

Mother will be delighted! Flight gave a series of humping skips through the water.

Everand almost choked. *Mother?* There was *another* dragon? That explained Lamiya's mischievous grin when she'd announced she had a new friend to show him. She'd found the other dragon, by herself? He shook his head. He didn't mind this kind of surprise on his wayward mission. The Pelamis kind of surprise, less so.

The sun spread fingers of warmth across his back while Mizukaze considerately swam just below the surface, leaving him above water from the waist up. Water coursed over his legs at incredible speed, and in no time the two dragons had picked their way down the rocky ledge and plunged into Dragonspine River at the bottom. The sun had barely moved higher when they reached the unnatural pool of murky water, jammed with debris and rubble from the destroyed bridge. Everand tucked his legs higher to avoid the flotsam and Mizukaze slowed down and began to nose at the debris, pushing some aside.

Good idea. Let's move some of the rocks and the trunks in the middle so the water can flow better, suggested Everand.

The dragons used their forelegs and chests to nudge the worst of the rubble from the middle while he helped with pushing and lifting spells. The new spells he'd learned were amazing, and he marvelled at the never-ending source of power he was able to conjure. Soon, they had created a narrow but deep channel and a strong wash stormed through the middle. Mizukaze flowed through the gap, riding the current.

In quick succession, the waterwheels and fields of wheat and marching rows of cotton bushes flashed past. A lump formed in Everand's throat when the pink walls of Zuqart loomed just ahead. Should he stop at the town and tell Atage and the others what had transpired? Or was it better if they didn't know? What if the Guild sent mages to question them? He concluded it was better not to stop.

The dragons were closing on the southern wall and gate when he saw the boat with the familiar outline of Tengar standing at the back, the team's paddles splashing in perfect time. Giddy happiness surged through him and Mizukaze veered closer to the tail of the boat, his body buzzing with excitement.

'Race you to the ramp!' he shouted when Mizukaze drew level with Tengar, laughing freely at the way Tengar twisted around so suddenly he nearly fell off the boat. Paddles clashed and clanked when the paddlers turned to look and the boat wavered. 'Nice timing!' Everand said, still laughing.

'What are you doing?' shouted Beram from the back row.

Go closer, Everand asked Mizukaze. *Then we race*, he added quickly when the spines on the dragon's back began to bristle.

'We're going to Riverplain. Can you and Mookaite come? This sun, if possible.' When Beram looked amazed, he said, 'I'll explain when you get there. It's important.'

'Okay.' Beram nodded and smiled.

'Me too,' said Tengar sternly. 'If it's important.'

Pleased, Everand nodded. The man's sound thinking and leadership could be useful. 'Now we race!'

Tengar leaned forward and yelled, 'Yosh! Go!' And the boat surged forward.

Diving beneath the boat, Flight sprang up on the other side, splashing her tail playfully. Everand gripped tightly when Mizukaze levelled out and raced the boat, the team paddling faster and faster, massive bubbles of white surging back from their paddles. When he saw Ejad in the second row, thrusting his paddle in determinedly, his troubles slipped away. He *did* have friends. He'd done it. He'd survived the mages' trap.

The boat ramp flashed by, the team stopped paddling and the boat slowed.

Sitting up, he waved a cheerful farewell and the two dragons swam onwards downriver.

To Lamiya. His heart danced.

CHAPTER THIRTY-NINE

Mantiss roamed his gaze around the Great Hall. Time seemed to have slowed, with the waiting mages standing in small groups or sitting in chairs at the back of the hall looking bored. The initial buzz of excited conversation when the party of five dissipated had faltered to an uneasy silence.

Tiliqua met and held his gaze, her jutted chin reflecting faint hurt that he'd added Simoselaps to the party at the last moment when he'd told her she couldn't go because it would look odd. He moved towards the dais, intending to take his seat at the mahogany table and indicating with a tilt of his head for her to follow.

Once she was seated, he murmured, 'I had to send Simoselaps. He and Pelamis cornered me. I'd far rather you were here with me in case–' Distracted by the unexpected chill crawling across his nape and the overwhelming feeling that something was going wrong, he glanced quickly at the communication orb, which remained lifeless on the table before him.

Also peering at the vacant orb, Tiliqua murmured, 'What can be taking them so long? Do you think the half-mage hasn't showed up? Or that he somehow sensed the subterfuge?'

'Everand seemed confident the rogue was keen to be trained, and how could one half-mage with limited training outwit five trained mages?' Stroking his wispy beard, Mantiss wished his fingers felt stronger and less apt to shake.

'And you trust Everand.' Tiliqua's mouth twisted in a wry grimace. 'I wish you'd confided in me earlier. I wish I had a better read on him.'

With each one of her words, his sense of imminent disaster grew stronger and his heart skittered for a few beats. If his trust was misplaced ... *anything* could happen. Agamid! What if something happened to his friend? *Curse it.* He should never have allowed Pelamis to outwit him like that. If Everand was not doing what he said he would, Saiphos would be of little help against Pelamis and Simoselaps working together and Agamid would be left to fend for himself.

His hand started to shake and he hurriedly put it in his lap out of sight. Fixing his gaze on the opalescent, lifeless, communication orb in the centre of the table, he willed it to glow green. *Come on, Agamid. Tell me you're ready to be brought home.*

Her hair plaited and coiled austerely, Menetia folded elegantly into her chair two down from Tiliqua and looked down her nose at him. 'They are taking a long time.'

With a rustling and swishing of robes, the other mages approached to stand in a colourful cluster around the table. Hydrelaps cast the orb an anxious glance, clutching his notepad and pen to his chest.

A tinge of green pulsed in the orb. Mantiss sat up straighter and blinked. By the others' sharpening of attention, he knew he hadn't imagined it. The orb flickered again, a vein of green running up one side. 'Take your positions,' he croaked. 'Get ready,' he said more firmly.

All around, mages moved swiftly into position. Five moved to stand in a curve on the far side of the cage. Hydrelaps and the two other witnesses stepped to their place on the near side of the cage, between it and the mahogany table. Wishing his legs would not wobble so, Mantiss pushed up to his feet and made his way back to the open space before the dais, choosing to stand at the very centre of the silk rug. Tiliqua and the other three members of the Inner Council moved smoothly to stand with him, ready to part the wardspell again.

Lifting his hands and staring at his empty fingers, Mantiss drew in a sharp breath. He'd left the communication orb on the table. Tiliqua patted his elbow and went to the dais to fetch it. He kept his hands held out ready, and she gently placed the orb on his palms with a nod, as if that had been the plan all along.

Immediately, the orb crackled with veins of green, like ivy shooting up a wall, and warmth spread over his palms. Placing the orb on the floor by his feet, he straightened up and raised his arms. 'Part the wardspell. They are ready.'

The remaining mages of the Inner Council raised their arms and in unison chanted the spell to open a slice in the wardspell. Tiliqua coiled her energy into his, binding and strengthening it, disguising his weakness. *Focus!* Mantiss turned his will to the rift and the sense of the others returning, searching for the signature energies of Agamid and Everand. What would the rogue feel like? *Pay attention.* His hands wobbled. The energy signatures felt … disrupted. The mages' energies writhed and jarred, a mish-mash of purple, crimson, orange and brown, like dyes dropped into a puddle.

He heard shouting. Or was he imagining this? His heart raced and a wall of heat rushed down his body. Something was terribly wrong! Agamid's purple energy was agitated, buzzing; the orange of Pelamis burned bright and hot; Simoselaps' brown energy was limpid; and Saiphos seemed frozen. Where was Everand's azure energy? Where was the rogue?

'Where's Everand?' gasped Tiliqua.

The wall of heat rushed back up Mantiss' body, flooding his brain and smothering the air in his mind. Everand *was* missing! The roiling ball of mage energies shot through the rift and dashed towards him, spiked with words. Agamid and Pelamis were arguing.

'Traitor!'

'Wait!'

'Betrayed us!'

'Wait! I command you.'

'Close the rift!' Tiliqua's voice, close to his ear.

Mantiss wavered, and his energy was wrenched away by Tiliqua taking control and guiding the other mages to close and seal the rift. The air right in front of him bucked and distorted, then Agamid, Saiphos, Pelamis and Simoselaps landed on the rug with a thud. Simoselaps sank to his knees, his robe stained with blood. *Blood?* Frozen, Mantiss could only gape when Agamid yanked Saiphos to one side and held up a hand to ward Pelamis away.

Swelled with fury, his puce face outshining his orange robe, Pelamis shook a fist at Agamid. Then he spun on a heel, wagged a finger at Mantiss and spat, 'Your precious favourite is a traitor! He betrayed you! Betrayed *all* of us. The trap was set for *us*!'

'How dare you!' said Tiliqua coldly, stepping forward. 'Compose yourself and address Mage Mantiss properly.'

Pelamis sneered at her. 'Mantiss is a failure. The rogue is on the loose and Everand …' he spluttered '… Everand has run away with his tame dragons! *Just* like his mentor.'

Dragons! He said dragons. Mantiss felt two mighty hands clench around his heart, squeezing the life from it. *Everand. My boy. What have you done?* Pain lanced across his chest, sharp and searing like a knife wound, and his mind filled with red and black broiling clouds. Dizzy, he put a hand to his heart, trying to press the excruciating pain away.

Dimly, he felt Tiliqua's fingers grab his elbow. Shouts pierced the space around him. Tiliqua's pale face and wide blue eyes swam in his vision. Then blackness descended.

☪

Something cold and damp crossed his forehead. Brief flashes of light showed through his eyelashes. Flames roared across Mantiss' chest and when he drew in a shallow breath, his ribs exploded with fingers of pain.

'Father. Are you with us?'

A familiar voice. He couldn't quite place it. Female. Not Everand. *Everand.* His heart pulsated with sorrow. *Everand was gone.* With *dragons*. His spy had let him down. After all this time. His heart gave a massive, deadly, warning throb followed by stabbing pain. As the Guild leader, he had failed — utterly and abysmally.

Squeezing his eyelids closed, he reached out to recall the darkness, glad when his heartbeat tottered unsteadily, ready to embrace oblivion. Better to let his soul go than be accused and forever branded the Head of the Guild who had undone everything Lapemis had created.

Warm fingers encased his hand. 'Father. Wake up.' The woman, more insistent.

'Mantiss. Wake. Your Guild needs you.' A gentle male voice, teasing his mind with recognition.

Hot tears splashed onto his cheeks and a hand caressed his face. 'Mantiss. Don't leave me. Please.'

Recognition jolted into him. *Elytra*! Begging him. He forced his fuzzy eyelids to part. Blurred colours merged and shifted, like a vivid dream passing, gradually forming into the faces of Elytra, crying, Tiliqua, pale and grim, and Agamid, fear etched in his expression. Grabbing his hand, Elytra held it against her cool cheek.

With a wan smile, Agamid said, 'Your time is not up yet, my friend. Wake up, we have much to do.'

Mantiss groaned. By the way the faces were hovering over him, he must be lying down. He groped around by his side. Crisp sheets. He was home, in bed. Much to do? Very well. He tried to put weight onto one elbow to push up, and his whole arm shook like a tree branch in a storm.

'Wait,' commanded Tiliqua. 'We'll sit you up.'

Weakness flooding his limbs, he let the others prop him up against two pillows. His chest hurt horribly and his mouth felt like someone had stuffed a handful of grit into it. His tongue and lips were as stiff as a board and simply refused to form the words to ask what had happened.

'Neelaps said your heart stopped. Must have been the shock of everything.' Agamid patted his shoulder. 'He and Hydrelaps worked together to restart it. No, don't speak. We'll tell you everything.'

Mantiss sank back into the pillows, feeling as if his heart had been wrung dry, the heartbeats weak and thready. His mind whirled with fuzzy images of the Great Hall, a rift, chaos erupting. Pelamis shouting at him. The heartbeats paused and jolted. He struggled to breathe with his chest compressed as if someone was leaning on it.

'Enough,' said Tiliqua. 'Father needs tea and food first.'

'Let him rest this sun,' said Elytra, still clutching his hand. 'I know matters are urgent, but he can't lead the Guild if he dies.'

Agamid lifted a hand to stroke his beard. 'True. I will propose an urgent council meeting for next sun and delay the others until then. I'll come back later.' Patting Mantiss' shoulder again, he said gently, 'Rest up, my friend.'

Flapping a hand on the bed cover in farewell, Mantiss watched Elytra take Agamid's elbow to see him out. Tilting his face to the side, he waited while Tiliqua fetched a chair and pulled it close to the bed, her intent expression suggesting she had news.

Leaning in close, eyes dark and expression stiff, Tiliqua spoke in low, fast words. 'You must know that Pelamis is rallying mages to him and will make a bid to depose you.' She sniffed. 'By his actions, Everand has given Pelamis … opportunity. Apparently, the rogue mage was nowhere in sight.

Pelamis claims Everand warned the rogue, and there is no evidence to suggest otherwise.'

Biting at her lower lip, she said more slowly, 'I am sorry, Father. Your trust was misplaced.'

Closing his eyes, Mantiss sank deeper into the pillows, wishing he could merely melt away into their downy embrace. Another ambitious mage already. *Twice* during his time as the head? Surely, Everand had not meant for this to happen. Something else was going on. But his spy had not confided in or consulted him. His heart gave a twinge, followed by another. *Focus.* Everand would not attack the Guild. But what about the dragons he'd found?

Forcing his eyes open, Mantiss dragged his tongue across his lips. 'There …' The effort weighed him down, pinning him to the bed and pillow. 'Bigger risk.'

'What?' Tiliqua leaned in so her ear was close to his mouth, her hair tickling his chin. 'I can't hear you. What risk?'

Mantiss grappled with his wooden tongue, which refused to comply. He was sworn to secrecy. But *everything* was at stake and *someone* else must understand. Everand didn't know what he was doing. 'Dragon.' The word floated out with his breath.

Her nose almost touching his, Tiliqua turned to look at him. 'The dragons went back to Terralis.' Her mint-scented breath flowed warmly over his face.

Blackness started to creep in at the edges of his vision and his heartbeats skittered and skipped. He was going to faint. *Not yet.* Forcing his tongue to lift from the base of his mouth, he croaked, 'Red water dragon … *Here.*'

Tiliqua sat back, her mouth forming an O of surprise. She turned her head. 'Your tea is coming.' Turning back, she gave a quick, subtle nod. 'I'll tell Agamid.'

The tea could wait. Exhaustion crashing over him, Mantiss allowed the wave of darkness to sweep him away.

Like discarded flotsam.

Chapter Forty

The sun grew higher and warmer as the riverbanks sped by. On the Riverwood side, the wild grasses waved in a breeze, the trees lining the ridge like silent sentinels. Everand flexed his fingers. What would the proud hunters do when Torrap staggered back to tell them about the mages by the lake, and with Malach still missing? Had Torrap overheard Pelamis' accusations that he had hidden Malach?

On the Riverplain side, grassy plains stretched away, dotted with clumps of colourful hopeepa. Not far inside the border to the province, he saw a couple of thatched huts close together and a dense herd of purple-splotched animals gathered around the huts and wooden yards. Lazuli was right; this was a good spot to hide Malach, well away from the rest of the people.

Soon, the river narrowed, and he saw the oblong thatched roof of the Meeting Place and the lake stretching away like a shimmering blue silk scarf on the far side. Flight nudged ahead of Mizukaze, her tail thrashing to exhort the larger dragon to speed up. Presumably, as the home dragon, she would show Mizukaze the way.

Shortly after, the dragons veered into the tributary that fed into the lake and when they swam under the small, raised bridge, shouts rang out from people along the shore. His heart thudded loudly: where was Lamiya?

The dragons swam into the top end of the lake and he squinted across at the boatshed, seeing outlines of people moving along the shore. *Try that beach, where the boat dome is*, he suggested to Mizukaze, but Flight was already racing ahead, her tail slashing gleefully through the water and sending up spurts of spray. The boat was on the beach, training recently finished.

Multiple faces turned his way and, with a cry, Lamiya dropped her glide oar and waded into the water, her arms reaching out to him.

His vision blurring with tears, he slipped off Mizukaze's back, gasped at the cold water snatching at his legs and chest and ploughed his way into Lamiya's arms. He clamped his arms around her, loving the way she buried her face in his damp chest and gripped him so tightly he could barely breathe. A rousing cheer went up from the shore and he smiled weakly at the gathered paddlers.

Mizukaze and Flight swam loops, splashing the paddlers with spray from their tails. Dodging the exuberant dragons, the paddlers cheered and laughed. A deep, throbbing roar sounded from the middle of the lake.

Lifting his chin from Lamiya's head, Everand stared at the fast-approaching blur of water and red-gold dragon. 'Your new friend?'

'Akachi,' said Lamiya, her smile fading. 'We need to talk about the dragons. Akachi wanted me to bring the other dragons, but you've saved me the journey. As thoughtful as ever, my mage.' She tilted her face up and he kissed her hard. His soul sighed and his lips and body melded with hers.

Waves slapped them as the three dragons gambolled in circles, then Mizukaze thrashed his tail and they were both showered in cold water. With a choked gasp, Everand broke the kiss and tugged Lamiya toward the shore. When they staggered out of the water, clothes sodden, hair plastered to their heads and necks, the paddlers clapped.

Pleased but embarrassed, he eyed the group, his gaze stopping at the aloof paddler hovering to one side. Without his beard, Malach blended in well. His pleasure ebbed at the prospect of telling the guides what had happened — and revealing the death of Mahog.

Lamiya's arm tightened around his waist. 'We need to meet with U-Mali and U-Lumin.' Her gaze became distant. 'They're going to the Meeting Place now. They want Malach and Lazuli to come too.'

'The guides communicate with you directly?' Everand peered down, his heart still leaping at the sight of her.

'We have much to talk about,' she murmured. A frown chased across her face. 'I hope we can keep up. Everything is happening so fast.' Then she beamed. 'But we are together!'

Disconcerted by her rapid change of emotions, he hugged her. 'We'd better go then.' He looked up into Malach's hard stare, the man's eyes burning with questions. 'You and Lazuli need to come with us to see the guides.'

Hearing his name, Lazuli broke off from chatting. 'Now?'

Everand nodded.

'Come, my mage, and explain yourself,' Lamiya said, tucking her arm through his.

They set off, with Lazuli and Malach following. Everyone was asking him to explain himself, but could he find adequate words?

'Don't worry!' yelled Lepid from behind them. 'We can put the boat away!'

Lazuli waved over his shoulder at his brother without looking back.

The Meeting Place soon loomed close above them and Everand's mind churned with questions, mainly about the dragons. As Lamiya said, events were moving quickly. Now three dragons were involved, and the Guild knew they existed. Pelamis' words still stung: *He is a traitor, just like Mage Beetal. He even has dragons!* What would Mantiss and the council think of him? His heart grew heavy in his chest.

Beside him, Lamiya walked with a focused expression, withholding her questions and waiting to hear it all when he told U-Mali and U-Lumin. Every now and then she looked at him thoughtfully. He tried to raise a smile, but worry and sorrow were getting the upper hand.

Working saliva into his mouth, he removed his sandals and washed his hands at the purifying bowls. In silence, Lamiya, Lazuli and Malach purified themselves and then followed him to tread across the rush mats and bow deeply to the two guides. The wind chimes hung silent in the still and expectant air, and Everand hovered unsure whether to sit or wait to be asked.

'Welcome again, Mage Everand. Be seated.' U-Mali's face creased into deep rivulets and she waved a hand at the cushion on the floor in front of her.

Conscious he was damp and smelled of river water, he eased onto the cushion, choosing to sit cross-legged and spread the azure robe ends neatly over his legs and feet. Wisps of hair tickled his cheeks and he brushed them back; his thong was loose and his hair untidy. His discomfort amusing her, Lamiya's lips twitched as she sat beside him. Lazuli chose the furthest cushion, leaving Malach to fold tensely down on the other side of Lamiya.

U-Lumin clapped his hands, the sound sharp in the stillness, and a woman carrying a tray of mugs and a pot entered from a well-hidden door in the wall along the far short side. She walked smoothly across the mats, bowed to the guides and proceeded to pour a mug of what smelled like herbal tea with hints of parsley and mint. She handed a mug to each of them with a nod and a shy smile at Lamiya.

Everand sipped at the brew and felt his mind clearing and his mouth refreshing, ready to speak.

Wizened hands curled around her mug, U-Mali sipped from it and peered at each of them with bright, shrewd eyes.

Fixing her bird-like gaze on him, she asked, 'Mage Everand, what happened?'

Out of the corner of his eye, he noticed that Malach's hand shook slightly when he put his mug down, and Lamiya was sitting tall with her full attention on him. Quickly, he recounted his actions and spoke of the translocation of five, not four, mages to the western shore of Dragon Lake. He took a deep breath before telling them about the discovery of the communication stone in Malach's cabin and of Pelamis' rapid deduction that he had betrayed the Guild.

When he paused for breath, Lamiya put a reassuring warm hand on his knee. Throughout, Malach sat rigid, not looking at anyone and breathing heavily through his nose.

Looking steadily at Malach, Everand relayed the events leading to Mahog's death. 'I'm sorry, but I saved Torrap. He can tell your people what happened, although he didn't see me because I was invisible, and your people still won't know where you are.'

His knees creaking, U-Lumin leaned forward. 'That could be important if the mages return to Riverwood.' The old guide sat back, his chair and knees creaking, and a heavy silence pooled over the group.

Rapidly, Everand completed his tale of how the dragons had protected him, the mages had finally left and he had hastened to Riverplain. 'Beram, Mookaite and Tengar from Riverfall will arrive soon, probably before dark-fall. I think we will be glad of their help.'

Dark eyes glittering, U-Mali rubbed at her chin, her fingers rasping over her leathery skin. Lamiya squeezed his knee to tell him he'd done well, and he put his hand over hers and interlaced their fingers, feeling her love seep into him. U-Mali's eyes twinkled.

Fidgeting, Malach and Lazuli failed to conceal their impatience about what the forward plan would be. Although

Malach kept giving him sideways glances, Everand waited for the guides to speak. This was their land, their people.

Finally, U-Mali lowered her hand and leaned forward to peer keenly into their faces. 'This Mage Pelamis represents additional risk?' U-Mali's eyes drilled into him. 'What do you think your Guild will do?'

The key question. 'I believe the Guild will send mages for me and Malach. Guild Law is crystal clear about forbidding the use of power outside the Guild, and the councils will not be able to ignore this.' He tilted his head. 'But the councils will have to be convened and they will take some time to decide. We have until next sun, possibly longer, depending on how divided views are.'

'What will they aim to achieve?' rasped U-Lumin, his eyes intent.

Meeting the old man's look squarely, Everand said, 'They will still aim to obliterate Malach — probably here and instantly. Me?' He shrugged, his mouth running as dry as gritty sand. 'Me, I am not so sure. If Mage Mantiss retains his position as Head of the Guild, they'll try to capture me or persuade me to return.' Drawing a breath, he concluded with, 'If Pelamis and Simoselaps argue their way, they could decide to obliterate me too.'

Lamiya's fingers pinched his painfully and he winced.

The guides sat back, faces twisted with worry and expressions distant. Straightening his fatigued back with effort, Everand squared his tight shoulders. 'If I may? We have some advantages.' He disentangled his fingers from Lamiya's so he could use his hands to count. 'One, there are two of us with power.' He glanced at Malach, who twisted his body to focus on him, his dark eyes gathering light. 'With two of us we can mount a greater defence and develop a strategy.'

'And secondly,' said Lamiya, her eyes shining, 'we have the dragons!'

'Exactly. And we have our own dragon caller. While I work with Malach, Lamiya can be working with the dragons.' He smiled fondly at her.

'What about us?' said Lazuli, bouncing on his cushion. 'What can we do?'

U-Mali raised a hand. 'We agreed to avoid violence.'

'Yes, U-Mali Guide.' Dipping his head in deference, Everand said, 'Our plans will be formed to avoid violence. If needs be, although it would break my heart, I will yield and return to Axis.' He gave Lamiya a forlorn look, averting his eyes quickly at the distress rising in her face. 'But we need to be prepared if the mages come with anger and bitter intent.'

Everand folded his hands in his lap, noticing that his crossed legs were growing numb. The air wafted around him and the others sat poised like stone statues waiting for the guides' decree. By the way U-Mali and U-Lumin were sitting erect, hands clasped in their laps and eyes closed, he assumed they were conferring with their spirits, or whatever the source of their uncanny abilities was.

Somewhere on the lake a bird hooted mournfully. Lamiya's energy quivered next to him, and he thought about her eagerness to work with the dragons. This boded well because he sensed the dragons were far more important than he'd first thought. Everyone needed to learn where they had come from, and how the great creatures expected to interact with the people. Atage had set in motion an impressive sequence of events with his simple idea to introduce inter-province boat races and trade.

A bud of hope blossomed in his chest. Things had gone wrong, but so far they had mainly worked out for the better. Perhaps the outcome would turn out alright.

As if waking from a dream, U-Mali stirred and reached over to hold U-Lumin's hand, then spoke in a clear and firm voice. 'Mage Everand, Lamiya, Lazuli and Malach, we call upon you to devise plans to protect yourselves and the people of Riverplain. You have this sun to prepare. When the sun next rises, we will gather all of the people of Riverplain to hear your proposals.'

'Prepare and choose wisely,' added U-Lumin. 'We and our people rely upon you. Never before has Riverplain faced such a challenge.'

Everand bowed so low stray hairs fell forward and tickled his cheeks. 'Thank you, Guides of Riverplain. We will do our best.'

'Go now,' said U-Mali, and to Lamiya she added with a smile, 'Yes, Lamiya, he may. Spirits forbid we should try to separate you two at this time.'

Eyes bright with amusement, U-Lumin gave a short laugh.

Heart thumping, Everand sat up quickly. Did that exchange mean what he thought? He could stay with Lamiya in her hut? The coy smile on her lips and rosy tinge to her cheeks suggested it did.

Then they were all bowing and standing up to leave.

At the bottom of the steps, the four of them gathered to decide who would do what next. A wave of dizziness washed over Everand — this was exactly where and how they'd stood only the previous sun, which seemed such a long, long time ago. Would each sun-up bring such life-defining events? A shiver crossed his nape.

'Well,' said Lamiya brightly, holding her arms out, 'we've much to do, and I'd like to be in fresh clothes.' She faced him. 'The parcel of clothes Beram gave you is still in my hut. I suggest we go refresh and eat.' To Lazuli, she said, 'You should tell the paddlers about the meeting next sun and get everyone to spread the word, ahead of the guides' call to gather.'

When Lazuli nodded, she kept going. 'Speaking of Beram, if he and others are coming, we need a hut for them to stay in. Maybe he and Mookaite can stay with me, and Tengar could stay with Lattic.'

'Yes, great glide,' said Lazuli around a teasing grin before turning to Malach. 'You'll get used to her; she is quite the captain.'

Malach grunted and said to Everand, 'When do we start working on our defensive preparations?'

'After we eat and refresh. You and Lazuli talk first, then come to Lamiya's hut at …' Everand looked at the sun, now approaching maximum height '… when the sun is halfway to setting. That still gives us plenty of light.'

A bounce in their strides, Malach and Lazuli walked briskly away.

Stealing her fingers into his, Lamiya tugged him towards the track that led to her hut. 'Let's talk, my mage,' she murmured, 'before others arrive and our chance is lost.'

Acutely aware of time leaping and skipping around them, Everand slipped his hand out of hers, put both hands around her waist and skip-located them to the grass in front of her hut.

'I like this trick!' she exclaimed, throwing her arms around him and stretching up to kiss him.

With his lips sealed over hers, he reached under her buttocks, lifted her into his arms and staggered through the feather curtain into her hut. Lamiya squirmed out of his grasp and when he reached for her, she backed away and bent over to pick up a wooden tub, which she thrust into his outstretched hands.

'Fill this with water and heat it,' she said breathlessly, her eyes dancing with desire. 'Let's wash each other.'

Heat flowed down him and gathered in his groin. He ran outside and screeched to a stop. Did she mean river water? How would that make them cleaner? When he stuck his head back through the curtain she was waiting, laughing. 'From the barrel of rainwater at the side of the hut.'

He hurried, sending strength into his arms to carry the full tub and simultaneously magically warming the water so it steamed gently by the time he pushed back through the curtain.

Concentrating on not spilling any, he lowered the tub to the floor next to the low table and cushions.

'Clever mage, didn't spill a drop,' Lamiya said archly, moving to stand in front of him and pulling at the sash to his robe. Her eyes grew darker and wider when the silk cloth released and the front of his robe fell open.

His legs trembling, he breathed shallowly while she slid the robe from his shoulders and let it slither sensuously down his back to pool on the floor behind him. Her fingers shook while she tugged at his loincloth, and her chest rose and fell in shallow gasps when she peeled the cloth away.

'Sit,' she said huskily, pointing to the cushion. 'Facing the door.'

With shaking legs, he sat, closed his eyes and held his breath. Water swirled and rippled, and then a feather-soft cloth sponged the back of his neck. Shivers of delight ran down his spine as Lamiya dabbed at his skin, washing away grime and sweat and sending love through her fingers where they brushed him.

When she planted a kiss on the back of his neck, he groaned. How much longer? At this rate he wouldn't be able to wash her in exchange. Her fingers fumbled at the thong in his hair, and his shoulders and cheeks tingled when his hair fell forward, the odour of river oozing around his face.

Lamiya then sat in front of him and passed over the warm, moist cloth. He rested it on his leg while he removed her tunic, unwound the cloth around her breasts and tugged her loincloth over her hips and awkwardly down her legs. His manhood pulsing hot and hard, he dipped the cloth into the tub, then trailed it over her shoulders and breasts. Her lips parted and she wriggled on her cushion. He trickled water over her nipples, deliberately allowing his fingers to feather the erect tips.

She grabbed his hand. 'Enough, my mage.' She kissed him and, somehow, they managed to tumble down onto the cushions, where she squirmed underneath him.

Pausing long enough to look into her eyes, to revel in her beauty and tenderly caress her cheek with the back of a finger, he whispered, 'My caller of birds and dragons. My reason for being.'

Her eyes growing moist, she tightened her arms across the back of his neck. 'I so like those words, my mage,' she whispered hotly into his ear, '*my* reason for being.' Then she rasped her tongue over his ear and down his neck and his restraint fled.

He'd thought nothing would be able to compare with the first time they'd made love but, as before, her beauty and presence filled and surrounded him, her desire just as ardent. Abandoning his body and soul to her, he clung to her and filled her until they both lay spent, muscles languid, sinking heavily into the downy cushions. He stroked tendrils of hair away from her face.

Snuggling closer, she kissed his throat and then his jawline. 'Never leave me again, my mage.'

'Not if I can help it,' he murmured, planting butterfly kisses along each eyebrow. The tranquillity of her hut enveloped him. It was unusually quiet. He leaned up on an elbow. 'Amazing we weren't interrupted. Where is your bird?'

Lamiya laughed. 'It's growing season. I expect Whirr is surrounded by eager females.' Her face more intent, she said, 'I have high hopes for the intelligence and plumage of his offspring.' A mysterious, distant expression crossed her face.

'What?' he asked, tracing zig-zag lines down her cheeks.

Looking him in the eye, she arched an eyebrow and said, 'Same for ours.'

His saliva went down the wrong way with his gulp and he sat up, spluttering. Lamiya giggled while he recovered his breath and wiped a tear from smarting eyes. Closing his eyes, he pushed away his immediate dark thoughts about the reaction of the Guild to any non-pure offspring, no matter how intelligent or attractive.

Sitting up, Lamiya hugged her knees, her grey-blue eyes steady. 'I know. Our daughter will be a half-mage, just like Malach. We must protect her.' She chewed at her lower lip. 'I wasn't sure whether I should tell you.'

Our daughter? 'You foresee this?' he croaked.

'She will be beautiful, with your star-spun hair and deep azure eyes. You will adore her, and she, you.' She rested a hand on his knee. 'You *must* change your Guild's views, and I will stand right beside you, my mage.'

Words failing him, he tried to imagine a young girl with a combination of their looks and his heart swelled so much it hurt. Could this really be? Hope thudding harder, he focused on her face. 'In your vision, how old is this daughter?'

'About six.' Mischief danced on her radiant face. 'I'm the Riverplain Guide and you are my consort, sitting quietly beside me and minding our child.'

The air flowed heavily around him while he grappled with the concepts. 'So, if you foresee true, we'll at least live long enough to see this.' Energy tingled down his arms and legs. 'That bodes well, doesn't it?'

'It bodes well.' Lamiya rested both hands on his knees, a frown marring her brow. 'But visions can change, alternatives can arise.' She paused, a shiver passing down her spine. 'I saw an alternative, but this vision burned brighter.'

Looking deeply into her eyes, he tried to read what he saw there and found a morass of swirling emotions. '*You* will be the next guide of Riverplain?' At her nod, he gripped both of her hands. 'How do you know?'

'The spirits of my parents told me, and the way U-Mali confides in me confirms it.' She shrugged minutely. 'I feel I'm being trained to be ready.'

Sensing her unspoken doubt, he squeezed her fingers. 'You will be amazing. No, you *are* amazing.' His heart lifted and his lips curved into a smile. 'This is wonderful. We *both* have ability. You're right, there's so much we need to talk about.' Leaning forward, he chased his lips lovingly over hers. 'I'm glad you told me.'

Lamiya pushed her hands firmly into his and sat back. 'I yearn for the fulfilment of this vision, but we'll have to work for it.' She chewed her lower lip. 'There's more. This sense of being pushed and pulled by unseen forces … it could be the dragons.'

'What?' Cold air ran across his nape.

'When I take you to meet Akachi, you'll understand.' A frown pinched her forehead. 'Akachi is bigger, older … somehow more important.'

'So, this mission has gained yet another layer. I wish I knew how many more are to come …' Everand stopped when another wave of déjà vu tumbled over him. As well as gaining unanticipated layers, the cursed mission had gone into a loop!

'Why so sad, my mage? The vision is bright and strong.' Although Lamiya smiled, her eyes looked troubled.

'It's just …' Everand pushed loose hair back from his cheek, '… we've been in this exact situation before! At the feast after the races, I was deliriously happy but at the same time dreading the mages' retribution for my decision to stay in Riverplain with you. Now, six suns later, we're back at the *same* point, full of joy but also dreading the arrival and retribution of the Guild. Except this time, Malach is waiting with us.'

Lamiya tilted her head, the light casting pretty glints in her hair. 'I see. So, we have old *and* new layers. But, my love, even though we're being guided by unseen forces, we're still together. And it wouldn't be an adventure if we knew what to expect.' The blue flecks in her eyes danced amid the grey irises.

'True.' Love for her indomitable spirit spreading through his entire body, he lifted his chin. 'Perhaps we should get dressed before we continue our adventure.'

Laughing, Lamiya tossed her head, her mahogany hair rippling. 'Practical as well as powerful. You're such a catch!'

Everand stood, tugged her to her feet and kissed the top of her head. 'Very funny. Others will arrive soon and this meandering mission will continue.' He kissed her hair again. 'We have much to do before the sun next rises.'

'Together,' said Lamiya, standing on tiptoe to brush his lips with hers. 'That's the part I like best.'

ABOUT THE AUTHOR

Kaaren lives on the South Coast of New South Wales in Eurobodalla Shire, a place of many beautiful waters entirely suitable for kayaking and dragon boat paddling. An avid lover of stories, as a child she was often sprung reading under the sheets by torchlight long after 'lights out'. One of her most vivid childhood memories is of sitting in the sun-filled, wood-panelled library at high school while her English teacher read aloud *The Hobbit*. From then on, she wanted to write fantasy.

The Mage and the Bird Caller is her third fantasy with romance series. As well as being an author she is a professional freelance editor, and a volunteer judge for several of the Romance Writers Australia competitions. Her short story 'The Bridge' was published in the Sweet Treats anthology in 2022. Her story 'Lollipops up!' is to be published in the 2023 anthology. When she isn't writing, she is editing fiction — or paddling.

Fascinated by the history and mythology of oriental culture, Kaaren has a B.A in Asian Studies, specialising in East Asian Civilisations with Honours in Japanese language. Kaaren was immediately intrigued by the origins of dragon boating in Chinese mythology, and hooked by the camaraderie and mental and physical discipline of the sport. She soon discovered that as a breast cancer survivor, she could also be a 'pink' paddler and joined Dragons Abreast Australia.

The time created by the Covid lockdowns, combined with her new passion for paddling, led to this fantasy trilogy containing romantic elements, enchanting river dragons and several teams of dragon boat paddlers …

Dragons Abreast Australia

Many tears are shed over a breast cancer diagnosis. The disease robs us of many things — our energy, our appearance, our confidence. Once a survivor has had surgery and other treatments, we need hope and connection with those who understand and others who have this lived experience. We need to be physically active; to tread a new life by learning something new; to attain peace through mindfulness. And we can give advice and support to help other survivors. Then the tears will be of happiness, while we power down many rivers and waterways of the world.

Founded in 1998 on the principles of participation, awareness and inclusiveness, Dragons Abreast Australia is a national charity with groups spread across the country. We are a network of paddling groups comprising breast cancer survivors of various ages from a great variety of backgrounds, athletic abilities and interests. High on our list of priorities is having fun and travelling across the rivers, lakes and harbours of the world to help us restore ourselves.

Being able to paddle and socialise in the company of others who have travelled the same path helps to restore the confidence, spark and sense of adventure we need to permit a full and active life after treatment.

We invite you to join us in the boat at www.dragonsabreast.com.au

Many regattas hold designated 'pink' races, where paddlers combine to form 'pink' teams and meet new people. There are numerous Dragons Abreast Clubs around Australia. To find a club near you, go to https://dragonsabreast.com.au/location/

The author participated in 'pink' races at the Masters Games in Adelaide in 2019, and had an absolute ball! After major surgery on her spine in 2021, Kaaren is thrilled to be back in a dragon boat and once again able to participate in 'pink' regattas. She is delighted to donate some of the proceeds from book sales to support DAA.

About the McGrath Foundation

The McGrath Foundation's mission is to ensure that no one goes through breast cancer without the care of a breast care nurse.

We raise funds to support people with breast cancer by providing specialist McGrath Breast Care Nurses where they are most needed across Australia.

The McGrath Foundation currently funds 185 nurses who provide essential physical and emotional support *for free* to anyone experiencing breast cancer and their families from diagnosis and throughout their treatment.

Breast cancer is the most commonly diagnosed cancer in Australia, the risk of diagnosis for women in Australia in their lifetime is 1 in 7. As the rate of diagnoses increases, so too does the need for more McGrath Breast Care Nurses.

Funding is needed to meet our goal of 250 McGrath Breast Care Nurses by 2025.

To find out more and ensure that no one misses out on care go to:
www.mcgrathfoundation.com.au

As a survivor who has benefitted from the advice and compassion of a breast care nurse, the author is also pleased to be able to offer the McGrath Foundation some of the proceeds from book sales.

How to find out more about dragon boat paddling in Australia

The Dragon Boat Festival, also known as the Double Fifth Festival, is one of the oldest festivals in China with a history of 2,500 years, and is now celebrated throughout the world.

Revered as the controller of water, the water dragon is a symbol of divine power and energy and is one of the most important creatures in Chinese mythology. In ancient times, fishermen would pray for abundant rain for their harvests. From the second century onwards, the festival also became associated with the commemoration of the poet Qu Yuan, a well-loved poet and patriot of the Chu dynasty.

The first modern dragon boat races were held in Hong Kong in 1976, and following their success other nations began to hold races. The International Dragon Boat Federation (IDBF) was founded in 1991 and by 2021 had a membership of 87 countries. The IDBF principles are intended to maintain the Chinese traditions and culture of the sport.

For more information visit www.dragonboat.sport

The first Australian involvement occurred in 1980 when the Penang Tourist Development Corporation invited the WA Surf Life Saving Association to send a team to the Penang Festival. The next year WA and NSW sent teams to what was then considered the unofficial world championships on Hong Kong Harbour. As interest grew, state dragon boat bodies sprang into being, and in 1997 voted to start a national body, the Australian Dragon Boat Federation. More information can be found at www.ausdbf.com.au/about-us/

There are numerous dragon boat clubs around Australia, and paddlers join for fitness, fun and camaraderie as well as competitions. Visit the Australian Dragon Boat Federation website and follow the link to your state Dragon Boat Federation, which will have details about the clubs in your states and the calendar of regattas and other events. Paddles up! Give it a go.

Undercover Mage

Book One of The Mage and the Bird Caller

A simple mission ... with twists and meanders that capture his heart and divert his destiny.

A grumpy river dragon withholds rain. Their crops wilting in unrelenting sunlight, the provinces plan a festival of dragon boat races to appease the dragon. But someone doesn't agree ... As the incidents of sabotage mount, Riverfall sends a desperate messenger to the aloof Mages' Guild hidden behind its deadly warded wall.

Mage Everand, a spy, is astounded when his master sends him to Riverfall to find out what is going on. The catch? *'Under no circumstances, none whatsoever, must you reveal your powers.'* The undercover mission unfolds with layer upon layer of intrigue, until Everand starts to question everything he believes. The alluring boatwoman, Lamiya, insists on helping him, making it increasingly difficult to conceal his purpose — and retain control of his heart. Everand faces an irate dragon, a rogue half-mage and, worst of all, a legacy of treachery and secrets underpinning the foundation of his beloved Guild.

Can he save the provinces and make things right without sacrificing his soul and sense of self?

Eminent Mage — coming mid-2023

Fugitives in Riverplain, Everand and the rogue Malach prepare to face the ire of the Mages' Guild. Lamiya and her people stand ready to protect them. Much depends on the politics of the Guild and whether Everand's master, Mage Mantiss, retains his position as Head of the Guild or is overthrown by the ambitious and ruthless Mage Pelamis. Conflicted, Everand fears he has betrayed Mantiss, but he must stand firm to uphold justice for Malach as well as protect the river provinces and Lamiya, the woman he has come to respect and love.

On top of this threat, the dragon Akachi sets Everand a nigh-impossible task — one that would right past wrongs but unravel the very foundations of the Mages' Guild. Everand struggles to chart a course through conflicting, turbulent waters. Can the rogue Malach be trusted as an ally? Lamiya, rapidly increasing in power and authority, devises her own plans to protect the mage she loves as the way forward becomes increasingly fraught and unpredictable.

The future of the dragons, the Mages' Guild, the river provinces — the entire population of Ossilis — is at stake, with only the mage and the bird caller to save them.

What readers are saying

Kaaren has created an exquisite impression of a time when river dragons were respected to keep a balance in the environment. Racing dragon boats honoured the dragons, and paddlers felt 'the essence of the dragon' infusing their boats. This is an inspiring story for all current and any would-be paddlers!
Marian Matti, sweep, Nature Coast Dragon Boat Club, Moruya

I really enjoyed this story. I highly recommend it to anyone who loves epic tales full of mystery and intrigue, with a touch of romance. This story has all that, and a whole lot more. Read it now. You won't regret it.
Wendie Daniels, Romantic Suspense author and finalist in Romance Writers of Australia's Sapphire Award

A delightful and beautifully written novel that will appeal to a wide range of readers, whether fantasy fiction aficionados or not. A stunning and believable world of river boat racing, provincial heroes, mages – self-serving and altruistic – and majestic dragons. Everyone loves a good romance, and Undercover Mage does not disappoint as Everand and Lamiya battle against the odds, and their mutual attraction. I want more! Thank goodness the author is writing a trilogy.
Gail Tagarro, Accredited Editor,
The Book Writing Coach at editors4you.com.au

Finally, someone has written a fantasy tale with a female dragon boat sweep/coach as the lead! And a dragon boat festival as the culmination of the first book in what will be a trilogy. Do read it. I loved it.

Even if fantasy is not your genre you will enjoy this book – with its stunning romance between the undercover mage spy and our feisty sweep heroine as well as four fiercely competitive dragon boat teams and some real river dragons. The novel captures the competition and the camaraderie of a great regatta.
Susan Chalmers Pitt, sweep and coach,
Dragons Abreast Canberra

I just love the world Sutcliffe has created, and the complexity of the characters. The possibility of redemption for the rogue half-mage makes the story totally absorbing.

Garry Thorpe, fantasy reader